INSIDE OUT

Also by Elise Title

INSIDE OUT

ELISE TITLE

ST. MARTIN'S MINOTAUR
NEW YORK

www.minotaurbooks.com

Library of Congress Cataloging-in-Publication Data

Title, Elise.
    Inside out / Elise Title.—1st ed.
        p. cm.
    ISBN 0-312-28582-5
    1. Women correctional personnel—Fiction.   2. Halfway houses—Fiction.
3. Prison wardens—Fiction.   4. Massachusetts—Fiction.   5. Transsexuals—
Fiction.   6. Ex-convicts—Fiction.   I. Title.

PS3570.I77I577   2003
813'.54—dc21

                                                            2002191952

First Edition: August 2003

10 9 8 7 6 5 4 3 2 1

To Jeff, for freeing my imagination

acknowledgments

Heartfelt thanks to all of the people in the Massachusetts Department of Corrections who gave their time and support. Again, I want to thank Bill and Marilyn Dawber, who not only offered me help and guidance during the writing of this series, but during the many years we all worked together in the prison system.

I am lucky to have Helen Rees as my literary agent. My gratitude for her constancy can never be fully expressed. My editor, Kelley Ragland, once again was a great partner and advisor in this project. I also appreciate the efforts of her excellent assistant, Benjamin Sevier.

Very special thanks to my daughter, Rebecca Blake Title, for her expert proofreading of the manuscript and her fine editorial comments, and to my son, David Title, for his efforts to bring this series to television. I am truly blessed to have such a loving, supportive family.

As ye sow so shall ye reap . . .

INSIDE OUT

prologue

DETECTIVE MITCHELL OATES, a burly African American, was standing a few feet from an open doorway to one of those *Architectural Digest*–style bedrooms in a posh town house in Boston's historic Beacon Hill. He stepped aside to give his partner, Leo Coscarelli, a better view of the body. The two detectives had been teamed up for close to three years now. Oates, at thirty-one, was the younger by two years, but you wouldn't know it to look at them. Coscarelli had the guileless face and lean, wiry body of a post-adolescent. Coscarelli's boyish looks, surprisingly, had turned out to be his biggest asset as a homicide detective. Many suspects over the past seven years had made the mistake of thinking the lieutenant was wet behind the ears, and therefore a pushover. What often happened was, they'd let their guard down, get sloppy, and find out the hard way that it was never smart to judge a book by its cover.

Oates had been at the crime scene for about fifteen minutes. Coscarelli had just arrived. Like his partner, Coscarelli was supposed to be off-duty that day, but given the high-profile victim, he and Oates had been handpicked by the Homicide chief to take charge of the case.

When the call came in at 10:05 A.M. to hightail it over to the Slater home, Coscarelli was still in bed. But he wasn't sleeping. And he wasn't alone. He was having sex with Suzanne Holden, an ex-druggie and -prostitute he was endeavoring to "rehabilitate." In hindsight, he wished the call had come in a few minutes earlier. Then it could have been one of those "saved by the bell" situations—the situation being one he definitely should not have been in in the first place. But "saving bells" rarely went off in real life.

Coscarelli peered down at the bare-chested body of the criminal defense attorney—revered or reviled, depending on whether you were the defendant or the plaintiff.

"You knew him, right?" Oates muttered.

"Who in Homicide doesn't know Matthew Slater?" Coscarelli answered, noting, with a modicum of envy, that for a guy in his late forties, Slater was enviably buff. Not that all those workouts at the gym were going to do the poor bastard much good now—unless you counted looking pumped in your casket.

Coscarelli looked over his shoulder at Oates. "So, what's the story?"

"Call came in at nine-oh-five A.M. A local unit got here at nine-twenty A.M. with a couple of paramedics. Slater was pronounced dead by one of the EMT boys. Coroner and CSI team are on the way."

"Media got here quick enough."

Coscarelli squatted down, took in the dead attorney's facial bruising, including what looked to be a badly broken nose. But he doubted it was the punch, or more likely, punches, that killed Matthew Slater. "Gotta wait for the ME, but my money's on manual strangulation." Not touching the corpse, he pointed to the darker bruise marks around the lawyer's neck. "Who found him?"

"Joyce Halber . . . Slater's secretary. She got worried because the boss didn't show up at the office for an important breakfast meeting scheduled for eight A.M. and she couldn't reach him on his cell phone. So she drove over. Got here at approximately eight forty-five A.M. When he didn't answer her rings or knocks, she let herself in. Oh—she had a key to the house. Said Slater had given it to her when she first started working for him three years ago. Anyway, like I said . . . she came over here, unlocked the door—"

"She said it was locked?" Coscarelli interrupted.

Oates flipped open a notebook and retrieved a handwritten report from the cop who'd arrived on the scene first. "Yep."

Oates continued, referring to the report. "She looked downstairs first, then figured he must have overslept—she said that he took sleeping pills on occasion. So she went upstairs and found him right where he is now. She swears she didn't touch him or anything else in the room."

Coscarelli nodded. "I'd say by the looks of our corpse and the smell, our killer struck a good two, three days ago. Nobody missed Slater before this morning?"

Oates shrugged. "It was the weekend. According to what the secretary told the uniform, the Slaters have a place out on Martha's Vineyard. The wife spends the summer there, and Slater flies out most weekends. Halber assumed he was there. Just before I talked to the secretary on the phone, I heard from the sheriff on the Vineyard. He'd just come back from informing the wife."

"How'd he get word so quickly?"

"Halber."

"Efficient secretary." Coscarelli paused briefly. "So, how'd the wife take it?"

"Sheriff said she didn't break down or nothing. His interpretation, she was probably in shock." Oates cocked a thick eyebrow. "Could be shock, I guess. Anyway, she told the sheriff her husband phoned her Friday afternoon saying he was staying in the city to work on a brief. She didn't try reaching him and wasn't surprised that he never contacted her over the weekend. It's supposedly the way he is when he's deep into a case."

Coscarelli rose to his feet. "Secretary tell you what case he was working on?"

Oates gave his partner a crafty smile. "According to Halber, our boy was in between cases at the moment."

THURSDAY, 8:33 P.M.
NOVEMBER 24

"You ready for her, Lieutenant?"

Coscarelli lifted his eyes from the typed statement to the dark-skinned, heavyset cop standing at the door. He caught the uniform's slight inflection on the "her," but he let it pass. He might as well get used to it. Chances were high this was going to be the hottest copy since O.J., a shoo-in for Court TV if it went to trial. Exploitation in the name of edification. A surefire spectator sport. And a profitable one. For everyone but the defendant.

"We got her fingerprinted and booked. Her one call was to her lawyer." The cop smiled slyly. "You'd never guess, to look at her. Just thought I'd let you know."

Coscarelli glared at the uniform, who motioned behind him with his hand, then stepped aside.

Lynn Ingram appeared in his doorway as Coscarelli was slipping her statement into the murder book. He gave an involuntary start when he saw her. Hector Rodriquez was right. No way he'd have guessed. And it wasn't even that she was all dolled up in some ultrafeminine dress, or sported high-heeled shoes, big hair, or went over the top on the makeup. Anything but. To the naked eye, Coscarelli could discern no cosmetics save for a touch of gloss that accentuated full, sensual lips and a whisper of blush accentuating the high cheekbones of a fashion model. If she'd undergone rhinoplasty, her plastic surgeon had to have been top-caliber because her straight, slightly elongated nose perfectly suited her face. That face was both striking, and unnervingly delicate, framed by ash-blonde hair that fell softly to her shoulders, straight, silky, tastefully styled. Even her outfit was decidedly understated, expensively tailored. Slim black suede jeans and an off-white cashmere blazer worn open over a teal-blue, fitted T-shirt that was a pretty good match to her eyes.

There was no getting around it. The tall, slender but nicely endowed twenty-eight-year-old certainly did look the epitome of femininity. With the exception of her hands. Even with the expertly manicured nails and the slender, shapely fingers, there was no question that Lynn Ingram's hands were large. Still, plenty of tall women had large hands. And Coscarelli judged Ingram's height to be close to six feet.

Coscarelli couldn't help wondering what it would have been like if he'd met Lynn Ingram under *normal* circumstances. Would he ever have surmised the truth? No, he was sure he wouldn't have—as sure as he was that he would have most definitely found himself attracted to her. But then, it wouldn't be the first time he'd been attracted to an "inappropriate" woman. Ingram's presence reminded him of the morning he'd been called to the Slater murder scene. A morning when he'd let his attraction to another inappropriate woman—namely a young and beautiful ex–drug addict/prostitute—get seriously out of hand. Since then he'd been working hard to get his errant libido back in check. Lynn Ingram wasn't helping his progress.

He caught a faint smile on Ingram's face, like she had a good idea of his reaction to her. That shook him a little. She shook him. More than a little.

Fighting the urge to clear his throat, he said, "You don't have to say anything, or even be in here, until your lawyer arrives."

"You mean I can wait in a cell. No thanks." There was a hint of huskiness in her tone, but it was more sexy than it was masculine. He was impressed that she seemed not to be making an attempt to artificially raise the pitch of her voice.

"I'm going to turn on a tape recorder."

She nodded.

He hit the RECORD button on the compact machine on his desk, his eyes fixed on her face as he stated for the record, "This is Lieutenant Leo Coscarelli with Lynn Ingram. The date is Thursday, November twenty-fourth. The time is—" He took a quick glance at his watch. "Eight thirty-eight P.M."

"Do I sit down?" she asked.

He gestured to a straight-backed wooden chair on the other side of his desk.

She gave his nondescript cubicle of an office a quick glance, then considered him for a few moments before crossing to the chair. Was she checking him out as a cop, thinking that he looked way too young for Homicide? Or was she merely checking him out as a man? Or both? No way to read this one. But he couldn't pull his eyes off her.

She crossed the small space, moving with a dancer's grace, lowering her long, slender body into the proffered chair.

"I imagine you thought I'd look more like a drag queen."

Coscarelli wasn't walking into that one. "Look, Ms. Ingram, I'm sure your lawyer advised you not to say anything until—"

"*Dr.* Ingram."

Coscarelli's eyebrows shot up. He hadn't picked up that tidbit in her statement. "Medical doctor?"

"We don't all earn our keep as drag queens, Detective. I'm a clinical psychologist with a specialty in pain management. I work with Dr. Harrison Bell, an anesthesiologist, at the Boston Harbor Community Pain Clinic. I've been there since I got my Ph.D. from Boston University two years ago." She crossed one long leg over the other, looking surprisingly contained for someone who'd just walked in off the street and voluntarily confessed to a murder she'd committed over three months ago. Maybe she was putting it on. Passing, not only as a woman, but as one who was re- markably self-possessed given the situation. Coscarelli had to ad- mit that Ingram's talent for "passing" was highly successful, if he was any judge. Then again, if what she said in her statement was true, Lynn Ingram had gone a major step past merely *passing*.

"That's how I met Matt," she went on evenly. Coscarelli was certain that Ingram was going against the direct advice of her attorney. Still, that was her choice, the proof that he had in no way coerced her recorded on tape. "He had chronic joint pain in his right knee due to an old college soccer injury. He started coming in for treatment in May after being referred to the clinic by one of his law partners—"

"And that partner would be?"

"Aaron Hirsh."

"He's the attorney you indicated in your statement would be representing you."

"That's right, Detective. I phoned him a short while ago. Needless to say, he was most unhappy that I'd already given a statement." She shrugged. Even this gesture had a distinctly natural feminine quality. "Aaron's flying in from La Guardia Airport. He keeps an apartment in Manhattan because his firm also has offices there. Actually, he and Matt shared the apartment. They were friends as well as law partners."

"And yet you chose Hirsh?"

"He's the best. And he's my friend as well."

Coscarelli gave her a closer look.

She smiled, revealing even, pearl-white teeth. "Just a friend, Detective."

"Why did you make a statement before Hirsh got here?" Coscarelli asked.

"To be honest, I didn't know I was going to do it. I was having dinner with a friend just down the street. Putting it lightly, I haven't had much of an appetite for the past three months, and my friend expressed concern. I told him it was nothing. But, quite obviously, that was a lie. I've been in a state of torment since that awful night. I selected the restaurant, by the way. I'm sure Freud would make something of the fact that it's one block away from police headquarters. And the wise doctor would be right. I even parked my car directly across the street from this building. I left the restaurant, started for my car and . . . found myself walking in here instead. I shouldn't have acted so precipitously. Meaning I should have waited and come in with Aaron. But the damage is already done. I made a statement. I stand by that statement. When Aaron gets here, that will still be my statement."

"Why turn yourself in now?"

Her gaze fixed on his. "Conscience." He saw a sadness brim up in her deep-blue eyes, but he didn't trust it.

Ingram drew her eyes away, focusing on the poor excuse for a Christmas cactus sitting on top of his file cabinet. The plant hadn't bloomed this past Christmas, or the two before that. Coscarelli wasn't sure why he kept it around. Maybe he was waiting for a miracle.

"On the Monday after . . . it happened, I was scheduled for surgery. I flew up to Montreal Sunday night, and I was at the hospital for ten days. Then I stayed at a nearby hotel a couple more weeks for outpatient checkups and to . . . get physically and psychologically settled."

"Slater's death must have complicated that."

She winced. "I didn't know Matt was dead. My actions that evening were a matter of self-defense, pure and simple."

Coscarelli found it interesting that Ingram referred to her lethal assault on Slater as "actions." As for the "pure and simple"—he was pretty sure the psychologist was smart enough to know that when it came to the murder of a Brahmin lawyer, there wasn't one single aspect of this crime that was either pure or simple.

"Matt was still alive when I ran out of the house. At least, I thought he was."

"You're a doctor. You didn't check?"

"I'm not a medical doctor. And I was frightened. I ran. I'm not proud of myself. But as I said, I didn't know Matt had . . . died. There was nothing in the news that whole weekend before I flew to Montreal, and if it made news up in Canada at some point later on, I never saw or heard about it while I was in the hospital or afterward—while I was recuperating up there. I assumed Matt was okay. I knew he wasn't about to press charges for my attack on him. If anything, I was sure he was afraid I would be the one pressing charges against him. He beat me up quite severely. You can confirm that with Dr. Claude Brunaud."

"And Brunaud would be—?"

"The Canadian plastic surgeon who did my vaginoplasty." Her eyes held his.

Coscarelli had all he could do to keep himself from physically squirming, but he sure as hell was squirming on the inside. Ingram smiled, and he was certain it was at his expense.

But the smile wilted quickly. "That recuperative period—it should have been the happiest time of my life. I was finally whole. Right. Truly me. You can't know how long I'd dreamed, prayed—"

The smile died altogether. "But I was never more depressed. Oh, my shrink at the hospital said depression wasn't uncommon in my situation. He likened it to a new mother's postpartum blues. But that wasn't it. You see, I'd envisioned a life with Matt. A normal, happy, loving, lasting relationship. I thought he'd be there for me."

"Yeah, hard to envision living happily ever after with a dead man."

If he expected to shake her up, rile her, he wasn't having any luck. Ingram's expression was, if anything, sadder. "I didn't murder Matt. He attacked me. We struggled. I had no choice but to protect myself. Save myself. It was self-defense."

Coscarelli made no response, noting that as the silence lasted, Ingram shifted slightly in her seat. And, as he'd anticipated—or at least hoped—started talking again, a bit faster this time. A hint of agitation. So, she wasn't as cool and composed as she'd tried to make him believe.

"The truth was too much for Matt. He told me very bluntly that he'd rather see me dead than risk its coming out. He said he would not be a national laughingstock. Interesting, don't you think, Lieutenant Coscarelli, that he wasn't particularly concerned about being seen as a man cheating on his wife?—just about being seen as a *deviant*. I truly believed Matt would have killed me if I hadn't . . . stopped him. He . . . attacked me. Viciously. As if . . . I would ever tell anyone." She shook her head. "Matt couldn't understand that I was devastated."

"How's that?"

"I loved him." Her lips quivered slightly, and, for a moment or two, Coscarelli thought her well-constructed facade was going to crack. But then she pulled herself together with a resolute sigh. "It's all in my statement, Detective. I don't know why I'm rehashing it. I'll only have to do it all again when Aaron gets here."

Coscarelli tipped his chair back. "What should we talk about while we're waiting?"

She waited several beats. "Don't tell me you aren't curious." Her eyes locked with his. "Or do you know other postoperative M-to-Fs?"

"M-to-Fs?" But then he got it. "Male-to-female."

"We don't all look like this. I'm one of the lucky ones.

Growing up, I was often taken for a girl. Especially before I shot up to nearly six feet when I was about sixteen. I was blessed—or cursed, if you were to ask my father—with a pretty face. I've needed only the most minor facial reconstructive surgery and, naturally, some electrolysis. Even there, it wasn't a long or elaborate process, as I'm very fair. I couldn't have grown more than the most scraggly of beards even if I'd wanted to. And that was before I began hormone treatment. I'm the envy of most of my transsexual friends."

"And Slater didn't know or guess before that night?"

"Would you have guessed, Detective?" Ingram eyed him defiantly. "Did you ever see the film *The Crying Game*? Well, that Friday night was *The Crying Game Redux*." There was a false ring of flippancy in her voice. "In the movie, the hero falls in lust with this exquisite woman at a bar, she takes him back to her apartment for a night of sexual bliss, and he freaks when he discovers she's got one little added appendage he hadn't counted on. Even so, he ultimately ends up falling in love with her."

"In your case life didn't imitate art, I assume."

"Matt was horrified. Then he got angry. Very angry."

"You might have warned him beforehand."

She gave him a pained look. "You can't imagine the number of times I've cursed myself for being so . . . blind. So . . . trusting. So damn stupid."

Coscarelli tried to imagine himself in Slater's place. How would he have reacted? He'd have been good and shaken, certainly. But would he have struck out at her? At *him*? Easy to *say* he'd have kept his cool.

Ingram leaned forward in her seat. "I don't expect you to understand this, Lieutenant, but in my heart and soul, in the very fiber of my being, I was a woman before the operation. I've always been a woman locked in the wrong body. I fell in love with Matt almost from our first encounter, but I took it very slow. It wasn't until I truly believed he was feeling something deeper than just lust for me, that I risked it. I deluded myself into believing he would understand. Not that he wouldn't be taken aback at first, but that he could get beyond it."

"You could have waited until after the surgery. Aren't I right in thinking he wouldn't have even known?"

A faint flush colored Lynn Ingram's cheeks. "Thanks to Dr. Brunaud, when I am fully healed, I will have perfect female genitalia. Indistinguishable from that of a genetic female. The good doctor even assures me that I should, in time, be able to achieve orgasm." Her tone was purely clinical.

"You still didn't answer my question." Coscarelli didn't get easily distracted.

"I wanted Matt to know," she said, a touch of fire in her voice now. "I'd spent too much of my life living—no, *suffering*—a lie. I thought I owed it to Matt for him to know the truth. To *see* the truth. I realized, too late, it was crazy, but at the time I thought it would help him be more accepting in the end. I thought he might even . . . come up to Canada with me. Hold my hand, so to speak. I knew Matt was married, but he told me he was going to leave his wife. He swore his marriage had gone sour long before we met. That I wasn't responsible for breaking them up. He told me . . . he loved me. He told me he believed we had a future. I believed him." Her lips quivered in earnest now, tears finally arriving. "I was a fool."

One is not born but made a woman.

—SIMONE DE BEAUVOIR

one

*I was the victim, not Matt. He attacked me. I was only
defending myself.*

LYNN INGRAM
(EXCERPT FROM TRIAL TRANSCRIPT)

HORIZON HOUSE PRERELEASE CENTER—INTAKE MEETING
BOSTON
MONDAY, SEPTEMBER 10, 2001

"I DON'T LIKE it. Ingram was trouble behind the wall and she's
gonna be even more trouble here." Gordon Hutchins, the head
CO, a stocky man fighting an ever-growing paunch, gray hair
shorn military-short, caught the superintendent's disapproving
expression. She watched him pull back, not because he was afraid
of her, but because he knew that open combat just made her
more obstinate. At thirty-two, Natalie Price might be twenty-

seven years younger than Hutch, and he might have a good thirty years on her in the system, but Price was from the new school—which included all the right credentials, even a Ph.D. in criminal justice—and as superintendent at Horizon House, she was the one who got to make the final decision.

"Ingram didn't cause the trouble, Hutch," Price said succinctly, to bring the message home. "And she meets all of the center's qualifications. So, let's just move on."

Jack Dwyer, Price's dark-haired, dark-eyed deputy superintendent, who most closely resembled a slightly over-the-hill street tough, wasn't ready to "just move on." Like Hutch, he was both older than Price—nearing forty and not enjoying it—and also had been in the system longer than she had. Unlike Hutch, he happened to enjoy butting heads with her. He'd have enjoyed doing more than that with her, but their relationship outside of work, convoluted from the get-go, had gotten especially twisted over the past year. He'd been making a concerted effort to un-snarl the tangles, but somehow, the more he tried, the more knotted they got. Jack Dwyer was not typically a patient man. On the other hand, he was used to getting his way. But then, so was Natalie Price. They just wanted different things.

"Whether she caused the trouble or not," Jack said, zeroing in on Nat, "Ingram did need to be placed under protective custody after several assaults and at least one rape. And even though she refused to identify any of her assailants, it didn't win her any fans among the other female inmates or the male and female staff."

"Maybe she kept mum because they weren't really *rapes*," Hutch muttered. "Maybe she was looking for some action."

"Maybe she was scared of getting whacked for ratting any of them out," Sharon Johnson said heatedly. Although you wouldn't guess it to look at this elegant, full-bodied, cocoa-skinned woman in her crisp russet Donna Karan suit, the thirty-eight-year-old job-placement counselor knew what she was talking about, having done three tough years at CCI Grafton.

Sharon was one of two ex-con staff members employed at Horizon House. The other, Akeem Ahmal, was the center's cook, or "chef" as he preferred to be called. Nat had had to fight tooth and nail to secure those appointments, these two people being the only ex-cons employed by the Corrections Department within the confines of a prison facility.

And make no mistake, Horizon House, a tidy, renovated Victorian building that in its first incarnation at the turn of the last century served as a proper hotel for young women, might lack concrete perimeter walls and armed guard towers, and it might be located smack-dab in the middle of downtown Boston so the inmates who qualified for a placement there might get a taste of the "real world," but there was absolutely no question that this six-story brick edifice was a prison, albeit the only corrections facility that housed male and female inmates in the same building. While the men and women had secured quarters on separate floors, and unsupervised fraternization was strictly forbidden, all of the rehab programs—alcohol or drug treatment, anger management, parenting skills, whatever—were now intentionally coed. It had taken all of Nat Price's considerable persuasive powers to convince the commissioner and the governor that the potential benefits of this reality-based approach far exceeded the potential pitfalls, never anticipating the whopping pitfall on the table today.

"Who's Ingram into, anyway? Men? Women? Both?" Hutch addressed the question to the group.

Sharon glared at him. "What difference does her sexual preference make?"

Hutch raised both palms in her direction. His style of apology. Although Nat had known for some time, Sharon had just recently come out of the closet to the rest of her colleagues. A couple of weeks ago, she even brought Raylene Ford, her partner of several years, to a staff picnic. The two women met up when they were incarcerated at CCI Grafton over eight years ago. They were friends inside and became lovers after they were both released. Nat first met Ray during a crisis last year at Horizon House. It was during that chaotic time that Nat also got to know her employment counselor a lot better.

"Look, Sharon, I don't mean any disrespect," Hutch verbalized his apology. "But I think we have a right to know who Ingram might target. Let's face it, we can keep our boys and girls segregated except for supervised programs, but we all know, 'Where there's a will there's a way—'"

"Let's stick to the point here, folks," Nat interrupted, wanting to guard against turning this intake meeting into a gossip session about which inmate had tried to hit on or somehow succeeded in scoring with which other inmate. Sure, it happened, but not that often; the risks—a one-way ticket back to the joint—far outweighed the benefits for most of the cons. This facility was a bridge for inmates between a walled prison and the street, placement running from six to nine months, max. Some of the inmates engaged in catch-as-catch-can flirting, but since they were doing "short time"—meaning they'd be hitting the street soon enough—for the most part they kept their ardor in check.

"The point, as I see it," Jack said, "is that Ingram had to serve all but four months of her three years isolated from the general population. Even given that it was no fault of her own, she needed protection. No way are we equipped to provide that kind of security here and we all know it. For her own best interests, as well as ours, I think she should finish up her six months right where she is now."

Dr. Ross Varda cleared his throat, glancing across the brown Formica conference table at Nat Price. She gave the slightly overbearing, tall, young Freud look-alike a nod, relieved to let the visiting psychiatrist have the floor. Adjusting his wire-rimmed glasses, then smoothing down his neatly trimmed beard, the thirty-four-year-old shrink took in each of them in a clockwise turn—Nat, then Dwyer, Hutch, and Sharon Johnson, then back to Nat again—as he spoke in flat, measured tones. "I have been meeting with Lynn twice a month throughout the duration of her incarceration at CCI Grafton. I believe this move is in Lynn's best interest. With Superintendent Price's approval, I will be continuing psychiatric sessions with my patient here at Horizon House, as well as overseeing her medications."

"Meds. So she *is* nuts," Hutch said. "I mean, no big surprise there. Any guy who'd go and have his—"

"Lynn Ingram is legally and physiologically a female," Dr. Varda cut in sharply, his voice no longer flat nor his words measured. "And she is not 'nuts'. I did put her on an antidepressant shortly after she was placed in isolation at Grafton—who wouldn't suffer depression being stuck in that kind of a setting never mind the horrific assaults that required her placement in protective custody in the first place. However, with the prospect of being transferred to a prerelease facility, Lynn's depression lifted substantially, and I approved her discontinuing the Zoloft. She is now only on a maintenance dosage of hormone replacement therapy."

Jack gave the psychiatrist a curious look. "How'd she get the okay on the hormones?" A good question. Certainly inmates suffering diabetes received insulin; those suffering HIV or AIDS got whatever drug therapy was required. In short, the Department of Corrections had to, by law, provide life-supportive medical treatment to all men and women under its charge. It could easily be argued that hormonal treatment for a transsexual was not a medical health imperative. But Nat imagined that without the hormones, the threat to her mental health would be another matter altogether.

"She was forbidden her hormones at first," Varda said, an edge of irritation in his voice. "However, with my help, her lawyer appealed and got the decision reversed by an appellate judge."

Hutch snickered. "Otherwise what? Cinderella would have turned back into Cinder*fella*? Only without a dick?"

"That's enough, Hutch," Nat snapped. Although she was plenty angry at her CO for these crude, not to mention biased, remarks, she was pretty sure none of them, except perhaps Dr. Varda, was immune to disquieting feelings about a person who had undergone sex-reassignment surgery. It was just a matter of how they each processed those feelings. Nat had encountered a fair number of both male and female cross-dressing inmates in her eight years with Corrections, but none of those she'd encountered had undergone an actual sex-change operation. Still, what experience had taught her was, in general, when all you saw was a stereotype, you saw nothing. And you missed everything.

The psychiatrist was frowning at Hutch. "It's precisely that kind of ignorant thinking that will provoke problems for Lynn here at Horizon House. I'm very sad to learn I was misled into thinking that this facility was both progressive and inclusive."

Admittedly, the psychiatrist was not getting the best picture of her progressive staff, but whenever any of Nat's people were attacked by outsiders she got very testy.

"You don't have to concern yourself about Gordon Hutchins causing any problems if Ingram's transferred," she told Varda crisply. "He's the best chief corrections officer I've ever had the good fortune to come across. I'm exceedingly lucky to have him."

Varda parted his thin lips, mostly hidden by the sandy-colored full beard–and–mustache combo (a compensation for his prematurely thinning reddish hair?), but then pressed his lips together, clearly—and wisely—thinking better of arguing with her.

Hutch, never one to appreciate a woman fighting his battles— even a woman he liked and begrudgingly admired—nailed the shrink with a smirk. "You call all your patients by their first names? Or just the pretty ones?" Hutch needled, then caught Nat's *cool it* gaze in his direction. He heaved a sigh. "Sorry, Doc." He didn't say it like he meant it. He didn't even try.

Red blotches decorated Varda's cheeks, or what could be seen of them above the beard. Nat wasn't sure if the psychiatrist was angry or embarrassed. He wouldn't be the first shrink to get overly and inappropriately involved with an attractive patient. From what Nat had seen of Lynn Ingram on Court TV and in the tabloids four years back, the transsexual was more than attractive. She was stunning.

"Can I raise a point here?" Jack wasn't really asking permission. "We can all vouch for Hutch, no question about it," he added, eyeballing Varda, "and for the rest of our staff. The inmates, though, that's another question. Some of them could be a problem. And we don't need problems." He leaned back in his chair. "Which is precisely why I say we pass."

"And I say that if we start eliminating inmates who qualify

for the program based on our inability to provide a safe environment for them, we might as well close up shop and go home." Nat's tone was emphatic.

Jack shifted focus to the psychiatrist. "I'm curious about something, Doc. Has Ingram ever accepted the manslaughter charge the jury handed down?" Jack posed the question with a deadpan delivery that only made Varda shift some more in his chair.

"Lynn—Dr. Ingram"—Varda spoke through pinched lips, more red blotches on his cheeks (a wry smile on Hutch's lips)— "has been consistent in holding to her original statement of self-defense. Nonetheless, there is no question she feels deep remorse for having been the cause, unintended though it was, of Matthew Slater's death."

Sharon Johnson, her expression openly showing her growing irritation and frustration with the way the proceedings were going, noisily removed a sheet of paper from the thick file in front of her. "I have a letter here from Dr. Harrison Bell at the Boston Harbor Community Pain Clinic, where Dr. Ingram previously worked, requesting that she be allowed to do her work-release program at his facility."

"She can't treat patients anymore." Hutch was quick to correct the employment counselor. "She lost her license to practice psychology when she was convicted of second-degree manslaughter."

"Dr. Bell understands that Ingram is no longer licensed as a clinical psychologist," Sharon said impatiently, then glanced down at the letter. "He indicates, however, that she can still work in a lay capacity as his assistant. I don't see any reason why this wouldn't be an ideal placement—"

Hutch eyed Nat. "Look, I hear what you've been saying, Nat,

and . . . okay—in general I'm with you one hundred percent." A snicker from Sharon produced an honest smile on the CO's face. "Okay, maybe seventy-five percent. I don't wanna be the bad guy here, but I also remember that not too long ago, we came damn close to being forced to close up shop thanks to another inmate fiasco. Are we really ready to dive back into that fray again?" Although the question was addressed to the group, Nat knew that Hutch's words were meant expressly for her.

No one spoke, but Nat had no doubt everyone around the table was vividly recalling that all-too-recent debacle. Less than a year had gone by since Dean Thomas Walsh, an inmate at the center who was finishing up a sentence for rape, escaped after being accused of murdering a beautiful young English professor who'd become his writing mentor. The professor, Maggie Austin, also happened to be Natalie Price's closest friend. And Jack Dwyer's lover.

Hutch was right. It was truly a miracle that their then–one-year-old prerelease facility had withstood the maelstrom of public outrage resulting from the Walsh debacle. Nat was still suffering the effects of that catastrophe. She'd lost her best friend, and her job had been put in jeopardy, not to mention her life. She'd also come dangerously close to getting romantically involved with her deputy, and—maybe worse—fallen for the detective in charge of the Walsh case. Leo Coscarelli. The same guy who'd been the lead detective in the Matthew Slater murder investigation.

Dr. Varda broke the long silence: "I should mention that one of the current residents at Horizon House shared a cell with Ms. Ingram before she was placed in protective custody. They became friends. Lynn feels she'll be a good ally here. Her name's Suzanne Holden."

As if there weren't enough complications. Suzanne Holden also happened to be the mother of Leo Coscarelli's child.

two

IS SHE OR IS SHE NOT . . . *A SHE? And a Murderess to Boot? Jury's Still Out.*

(TABLOID HEADLINE DURING INGRAM MURDER TRIAL)

THE INTAKE CONFERENCE was over a few minutes before noon with Lynn Ingram's transfer to Horizon House still up in the air. Nat announced to the team that she'd decided to go to CCI Grafton that afternoon and have a one-on-one meeting with Ingram before making her final decision.

Everyone cleared out of Nat's office except her deputy. Jack remained seated at the round conference table as Nat purposefully walked diagonally across the large oak-paneled room over to her desk near the bay window that looked out on Providence Street. She was acutely conscious of the pulse of stop-and-go traffic outside.

"If you're hanging around to continue your argument with me about Ingram, forget it, Jack," she said, studiously avoiding eye contact. "I've got a budget meeting first thing tomorrow that I've got to get ready for, not to mention a half-dozen exit reports to go over, a review-board hearing—"

Jack rose from the table and crossed over to her desk, perching himself on one corner of it while she busily riffled through a sheaf of papers that made up the semiannual budget report. The lists of numbers were a blur.

"You're wearing that NO TRESPASSING sign around your neck again."

"Don't start with me, Jack."

"I started with you way before now."

She glanced up at him. He was smiling. Not one of his seemingly chiseled "sneering" smiles that were usually laced either with sarcasm or derision, and which Nat had learned to handle with aplomb over time. This was one of his rarer smiles, one that had a touch of tenderness in it. Jack always threw her off when he came across as endearing. Until she rushed back in and reminded herself of his two disastrous marriages, his secret love affair with her best friend, and his on-again, off-again bouts with the bottle.

Nat focused on the budget report, pretending intense concentration.

Jack cupped a hand under her chin, forcing her head up. "Let's go get some lunch."

She brusquely shoved his hand away. "No," she said firmly. What gave her the edge in her battle not to fall prey to her juvenile sexual attraction to Jack was her not-so-secret weapon: Leo Coscarelli. Now, Leo didn't have the obvious charisma of Jack Dwyer, but what he lacked in overt allure he made up for one-hundredfold in genuineness. In his own inimitable way Leo was as sexy, tough, and tender as Jack. And Leo had it all without the drinking problem, and without any previous marriages, disastrous or otherwise. Which wasn't to say Leo had no baggage of his own. He did—the heaviest "carry-on bag" being inmate number 479984, Suzanne Holden . . . and their four-year-old son, Jacob.

Nat didn't want to get hurt—again. The ink on her divorce papers was still wet. No matter how hard she tried to analyze the disintegration of her marriage to Ethan Price, the word *failure* glared like a 300-watt bulb in front of her eyes. Nat did not take well to failing. Or to having rugs pulled out from under her. You would think that with all the radically shifting rugs of her dysfunctional childhood, she would have learned by experience, if nothing else, how to handle failure better in adulthood. You'd be wrong.

"Come on, Nat. Even a busy super's gotta eat," Jack coaxed, his voice piercing her meandering thoughts. She glanced up, catching his smug look. *Smug* was better. Safer. *Smug* reminded her of Ethan. Ethan reminded her of why she had gone through with the divorce even when her errant husband was having second thoughts . . .

"We owe it to ourselves to try again, Nat. We had eight good years—"

"Good for you, maybe."

"I made a mistake. A big mistake."

"So did I, Ethan."

"I brought a sandwich," Nat told Jack brusquely, turning her attention back to the budget report, not adding that she'd brought an extra sandwich in case a certain little boy who was presently out in the visiting room decided to pop into her office.

Complicated as her relationship was with Leo Coscarelli, there was nothing complicated about Nat's feelings for his four-year-old son, Jakey. She adored the child.

"You look pale, Nat. And too thin. I really think you should let me take you out for a nice, hearty lunch," he pressed.

Nat was not about to argue with him about her appearance. At five foot seven she should probably have weighed a good twenty more pounds than the hundred and eighteen her scale had been reading for months now. She'd tried to put on some weight, to no avail. Even went to her doctor for a checkup a few weeks ago. He said it was stress. Nat had said, *"So what else is new?"*

Jack snatched at an errant corkscrew strand of her impossibly unruly auburn hair that had escaped its French knot. Nat shoved the strand back into the knot. Jack cocked his head, checking her out.

"You're still beautiful."

She gave him a wry look. "I can't still be something I never was, Jack." Nat wasn't being coy or digging for more compliments. She'd always been realistic about her looks. In her self-analysis, she came off as merely attractive. She had olive skin that rarely broke out, hazel eyes, slender nose, lips that were neither too thin nor full enough for the current vogue. Her curly auburn hair was her most striking feature, and her most irritating. It kept fighting her. The "her" that wanted to present a crisp, professional, no-nonsense image. The kind of image appropriate to her position. That was why she always wore her hair pulled back into a French knot when she was at work. That was also why she wore almost no makeup, low-heeled pumps, and tailored suits—gray, black, blue—the skirts always hitting below her kneecap.

Jack was not swayed from his determinedly seductive mode.

"You're always so hard on yourself, Nat. You need to lighten up a little. Smile more. You've got a knockout smile. It makes the corners of your eyes crinkle—"

"Those crinkles are age lines. I'm edging onto thirty-three, and on days like today, I feel and probably look about one hundred. So cut the bullshit, Jack. I'm not in the mood—"

"For trouble?"

"Exactly," she said.

"So then tell me why you're asking for it, Nat."

She looked up at him. The charm was gone. So was the smugness. Back to business. Nat should have known he was simply looking for an "in" to continue the argument he'd left off during the Ingram intake meeting.

"I'm doing my job, Jack." She reached into her tote bag for her sandwich, slowly unwrapping the turkey and cheddar on rye. There was a gnawing sensation in her stomach. But it wasn't the result of hunger. It was good old stress.

"Did Suzanne Holden ever mention Lynn Ingram to you?" he asked, watching her careful ministrations.

"No. But I'll talk to her. And to Ingram."

"Coscarelli handled Ingram's case, you know."

"I know." She crumpled the plastic wrap into a ball, and with a flick of her wrist, tossed it in the direction of her trash can. It missed. They both ignored it.

"You gonna talk to him?"

"Leo and I talk all the time."

"He's out in the visiting room right now. Along with his mother and his kid. Suzanne told me he's been visiting more frequently. On Sunday, he and the kid showed up without Grandma. First time she didn't come along as chaperone. And he stayed for the full two hours. Suzanne told me on Monday, he's been pushing even harder for her to tell the boy she's his mommy."

Nat pushed her sandwich aside, her appetite fully gone. "Is there a point to this, Jack?"

"The point is, I don't want you to get hurt again," he said softly.

"Let's not do this, Jack."

He leaned closer. Close enough for Nat to smell his coffee breath. Better than those days when he reeked of whiskey and mouth freshener. He'd been on the wagon for close to a year. A big plus in Nat's book. Especially since her dad had been an alcoholic who'd served time—once for driving to endanger while under the influence, and a second time for parole violations. Following his second release, after grappling with the pressure to stay sober, work a menial job, make up for lost time with his daughters, and cope with his manic-depressive wife, he blew it. One day, he disappeared, drank himself into a five-day-long stupor, then sobered up enough to hang himself. Nat was seventeen.

"Give me a chance here, Nat. Just crack the door open this much." He measured an inch with his thumb and index finger.

Nat saw the loneliness reflected in Jack's eyes. For the past year, there hadn't been any woman in his life for more than a night or two. After her friend Maggie's death, intense feelings of grief and betrayal had brought Nat and Jack into each other's arms for a very brief time. Nat had come to her senses before it had gotten out of hand, but Jack wouldn't let it go. She saw his persistence as one part bruised ego, and, more significantly, her deputy's way of fending off the pain of losing Maggie.

When Jack got no response from Nat, he reluctantly got to his feet and headed over to the door. "I still think you're making a mistake about Ingram."

As always, a last-word kind of guy.

three

The sentence is an outrage. I don't care what sex that pervert thinks he is, or what he says, he killed my husband in cold blood. And he should have been put away for life.

Jennifer Slater
(post-trial statement to the press)

NAT WAS STANDING by her window watching Anna Coscarelli and her grandson, Jakey, his little hand clasped in hers, exit the center.

"Got a sec?" a voice asked behind her.

Instead of turning to her visitor, Nat watched the pair as they stepped into a waiting taxi. It was a warm, breezy summer day, the first in nearly a week of almost constant rain and grayness. The kind of day meant to be spent out of doors. Out of offices.

"I hear you and Jakey visited Suzanne on your own this weekend." Nat could feel a scratchiness in her throat as she spoke.

"My mother had a stomach bug," Leo Coscarelli said, walking over to her.

"How is she now?"

He was at her side. "What's wrong, Natalie?" Everyone but Leo called her "Nat." She usually liked that he used her full given name. Right now it irritated her. But then, she'd been feeling irritated before Leo's arrival.

"Do you remember Lynn Ingram?"

"She's not someone you'd forget," he said without guile.

"No, I suppose not," Nat said.

"She coming up for work-release transfer?"

Nat nodded. "What do you think?"

Leo leaned against the wall beside the window, hands jammed into the pockets of his blue sports jacket. Nat noticed that he looked thinner, his face drawn. Stress? Brought on by the job— by her—by Suzanne—any combination thereof? *Welcome to the club.*

"What do I think?" he echoed. "I think it could be dicey."

"Did you agree with the guilty verdict?"

"She confessed."

"To self-defense."

He shrugged. "The jury thought otherwise."

"I followed some of the trial."

"Who didn't?"

"Her doctor confirmed that she had suffered a great deal of bruising, which supported her story that Matthew Slater viciously attacked her."

"And the jury believed that she acquired those bruises as a consequence of Slater trying to defend himself against her attack on him."

"What did you believe, Leo?"

"I don't see the point of the question. She was tried by a jury of her peers—"

" 'Peers'? How many transsexuals were on her jury?"

Leo exhaled slowly. A few seconds passed. "I liked her. She was nothing like the stereotype. No affectations. No sign of vanity. No hint of any confusion on her part about who she was—not just in terms of gender, but who she was as a person. Do you want to know what I came away from the whole ugly business feeling the most? Sad. Was she guilty of murder? I honestly don't know."

"Did you know Ingram and Suzanne were cellmates at Grafton?"

Nat saw by his expression that this was news to him. And the news wasn't sitting well.

"Apparently they were friends," Nat added. "I'm going out to Grafton to talk to Lynn Ingram. Before I do, I think I should have a few words with Suzanne about her."

Leo, usually so good at maintaining his poker face, was having a rough time of it today. "It's been—what?—three years?"

"You think Ingram's any less memorable to Suzanne than she is to you?" Nat countered.

"She's having a rough time of it, Natalie."

"I assume you mean Suzanne."

"I doubt she needs any more headaches."

"And by 'headaches,' I assume you mean Lynn Ingram."

"Suzanne's only got a few more months to go before she's out of here."

Nat could feel the tension radiating through her body. *Then what?* Suzanne Holden's exit interviews wouldn't begin until four weeks before her release date. Nat did know from Sharon Johnson that the owner of the boutique where Suzanne had been placed for work-release had offered her a full-time position once she was free. But Suzanne had not, as yet, accepted the offer. Nat felt guilty for hoping Suzanne wouldn't take the job. That she wouldn't stay around the Boston area. Around Leo. She was from the central part of the state. There were plenty of job opportunities there—

"Has Suzanne told you what her plans are once she's out?" Nat tried for a professional tone that fell dismally flat.

Leo let what they both knew was a loaded question hover in the air, which only served to accelerate the rate and flow of Nat's anxiety. Leo had told her long ago the drama of errors that led up to his getting Suzanne pregnant, which in turn led up to his son's birth. Suzanne, who'd served time for prostitution and drug possession, had met Leo shortly after a mandatory stint in a drug treatment center. Actually, Leo's mother, a volunteer at the treatment center, had brought them together. Anna Coscarelli, who'd lost her only daughter to a drug overdose, had taken to mothering Suzanne. She even cajoled her into enrolling in some college classes when she got out of rehab. Which was where Leo came into the picture. Anna talked her son into tutoring Suzanne. He was attracted to her. He admitted that openly. But he never intended for anything to happen.

His libido ultimately won out over his intentions. Only one time, according to Leo, after which he felt guilty as hell. Then he found out Suzanne was pregnant. And that she was planning to abort the pregnancy. Leo talked her out of an abortion only by agreeing to raise the child on his own. Suzanne was adamant about wanting nothing to do with Jacob Coscarelli. Right after she was released from the maternity ward, she handed the newborn over to Leo and disappeared, determined never to see the child again.

Who knew if Suzanne might have relented over time? Who

knew if she and Leo might have worked out their relationship if she'd stayed off drugs, as she'd assiduously and faithfully done throughout her whole pregnancy? She didn't stay off drugs once she ran off. And while under the influence of crack, she got into a row with her dealer/lover who wanted her to go back to working the streets to pay off her mounting drug debts. She claimed he pulled a knife on her. They struggled. And the knife ended up in the guy's gut. No one on the jury mourned the death of the drug dealer, nor did they feel much pity for a longtime drug user and hooker. Any more than Ingram's jury had felt much pity for a transsexual.

While serving time for first-degree manslaughter at CCI Grafton, Suzanne consented to visits from her son and his grandmother, on the condition that Jakey not know she was his mother. He was simply told that Suzanne was "a special friend of the family." Early on, Leo had visited as well, but Suzanne had asked him to stop coming, because having a cop as a visitor wasn't winning her any favors among her peers or "the screws." Since she'd been at Horizon House, the pressure had lifted and Leo reentered her life. What it meant to him or to Suzanne was not something Nat had been able to figure out. Maybe neither of them had, either. Still, no question that, as Jakey's parents, there was a bond between Suzanne and Leo, whether they liked it or not—whether Nat liked it or not.

"Is Suzanne any closer to telling Jakey the truth?" Nat asked, not even bothering to keep the strain out of her voice.

Leo shook his head, clearly not happy about it. "Since he started nursery school, Jakey's been asking a lot of 'Mommy' questions. The other morning at breakfast, he asked his grandmother if he could call her Mommy instead of Grandma. Then he could have a daddy and a mommy."

There was such a note of sorrow in Leo's voice that Nat felt ashamed of her own selfish concerns. She placed a hand on his sleeve. "Would it help if I talked to Suzanne?"

Leo's eyes locked with hers. "She knows about the two of us."

Nat pulled her hand away as if it had been burned. "What? You told her? You told Suzanne we were . . ." For a moment she was so frazzled, she was at a loss what to call them.

"I didn't go into detail. But I felt she had a right to know we're involved."

"My private life is not the business of any inmate in this institution," Nat said hotly.

"My private life is the business of my child's mother. I'm sorry that impinges on your need for privacy, Natalie." Leo paused, his expression softening. "Anyway, I think Suzanne would have figured it out whether I said something or not. Jakey told her a while back that you're his secret mommy."

Nat stared at Leo, dazed. Speechless. Her anger punctured, seeping out of her.

"You wanted to see me, Superintendent?"

There was a marked edge of nervousness in Suzanne Holden's voice, much like that of a child being called to the principal's office and not knowing what she'd done wrong.

"Sit down, Suzanne." Nat gestured toward one of the tweed-upholstered armchairs across from her desk.

Suzanne hesitated, looking around the office as if it held some clue as to why the superintendent had ordered her there. In those same moments, Nat took the opportunity to observe the inmate more closely. The stylish, soft-rose–colored dress she was wearing most likely had been purchased with an employee discount at the boutique. The jersey material followed the svelte lines of her petite body while managing not to cling provocatively. Which, ironically, made her look even sexier.

"Please." Nat's hand was still gesturing toward the chair.

Despite her attempt to sound unthreatening, Nat knew Suzanne heard it as an order. And hearing it as such, she obeyed. It was the same with most inmates, and Nat usually made a concerted effort to say something to ease the tension they were feeling. But she couldn't find the words now. Probably because she was at least as tense as Suzanne. The fact that Leo hadn't told Suzanne any of the details of his personal relationship with Nat in no way assuaged Nat's upset or discomfort. Sometimes, saying a little was worse than saying a lot. It left so much open to the imagination. Did Suzanne imagine Leo and Nat were more deeply involved than they were in reality? Did she assume they were living together—perhaps contemplating marriage? And if she owned any of these thoughts, was she jealous—angry—resentful? Could Suzanne possibly feel as awkward as Nat was feeling?

"Have I busted some rule I don't know about?" Suzanne avoided meeting Nat's gaze—or was Nat the one avoiding meeting the inmate's?

Agitation more than anything else made Nat leap abruptly to the point: "Do you remember a former cellmate of yours at Grafton—Lynn Ingram?"

Suzanne's first reaction was confusion. Clearly, this was not the direction she thought this meeting would take. Her relief was palpable. She almost smiled.

"Lynn? Yeah, sure. Sure, I remember her," Suzanne said. "She was great." She stopped.

Nat watched the inmate's features slowly darken. "It was horrible, what they did to her." She muttered this under her breath, but Nat caught her words.

Nat presumed Suzanne was referring to the attacks and not to her cellmate's having been put into protective custody. "Was it other inmates—officers—both?"

She spied a flicker of alarm on Suzanne's face and then, in the proverbial wink of an eye, blankness. "Huh?"

Nat had seen that look on many inmates' faces. It was invariably contrived, a deliberate battening down of the hatches. The message was clear: *Don't go there.*

"Lynn Ingram may be transferring to Horizon House. I haven't made my decision yet. Is there some information you have that could affect the decision I make?"

Suzanne's reply came after a lengthy pause. "No."

"Would she be in any physical or psychological danger that you know of?" Nat persisted. Both her body language and her brittle responses suggested to Nat that Suzanne knew more than she was saying; they also suggested her fear. Ratting out another inmate, male or female, put any inmate in serious jeopardy. Ratting out an officer could put an inmate in hell.

"Nothing you tell me will leave this room, Suzanne. I promise you—"

"I have nothing to tell you." For a moment the look on the inmate's face was imploring. Then she just shut down again, her expression blank.

Nat had witnessed this kind of closing-off from many inmates. Sometimes she could break through the barriers they erected. But it took time. It took figuring out a strategy that would work. Even when Nat succeeded, it never came easy. And because of all the complications implicit in Nat's dealings with Suzanne, finding a way through this inmate's defenses was going to be especially tough.

Suzanne was on her feet. "Can I be excused?"

Nat nodded wearily. But when the inmate got to the door, Nat said, "This isn't going away, Suzanne." Although her statement was intentionally vague, she could see from the inmate's parting look that the message, with all its ambiguities, had hit home.

four

A miscarriage of justice has taken place here today. If my client was not a transgendered person, she never would have been found guilty.

ATTORNEY AARON HIRSH
(POST-TRIAL STATEMENT TO THE PRESS)

IF THE ELECTRIFIED razor wire ringing the stone walls of CCI Grafton didn't exist, nor the iron entry gates monitored by two uniformed and armed corrections officers, the institution might have been taken for a somewhat run-down college campus.

Past the gates, Nat drove into a large parking lot where staff and visitor spaces were clearly demarcated. Nat opted for one of the visitor's spots.

As she made her way past the lot, she came to a central green, the facility's buildings forming a U around it. Two inmates were mowing the grass. A couple of others were tending to the weeds around the mums and marigolds rimming the concrete paths that crisscrossed the green.

There were a smattering of inmates sitting together on benches, most of them smoking—there was now a "No Smoking" mandate in all public buildings in the Commonwealth. The bench scene looked like a smoke break at any workplace, as, unlike men's prisons, the women were permitted to wear street clothes, with the exception of miniskirts, cutoffs, midriff-length tops, stretch pants, or shoes with heels over one inch. It was another matter for the women placed in isolation. They were issued state uniforms—orange jumpsuits, black oxford shoes. This was to make them instantly identifiable.

Nat took the path that ran straight across the green and led to a central three-story brick structure of pseudo-Baroque design. This building contained the administrative offices, visiting room, dining hall, medical infirmary, and a small mental health unit. An L-shaped addition added to the right of the building housed the educational and vocational area. A good decade before Nat's time, inmates could actually attain college degrees while incarcerated. Because of endless budget cuts and the strong pro-punishment political climate, however, the educational offerings were meager today—mostly classes focused on helping inmates who never graduated high school get their GED certificates. There were a few outdated computers in a small lab, but class instruction was minimal at best. The main vocational training–cum–work program in the institution—beyond lawn/garden care and housekeeping/janitorial maintenance—was flag making, primarily the cutting and machine-stitching of the American flag and state flags.

A half-dozen low-slung one-story concrete buildings that reminded Nat of bunkers surrounded the main building: three on the right, three on the left. These were the dormitories housing the female inmates. There were no bars on the windows, and there were no traditional cells. But the front doors of the units were locked after nine P.M., and female and male correctional officers, always in pairs, were stationed within the dorms around the clock.

Behind the administration building was one additional dormitory, not only separate from the others but enclosed within its own electrified chain-link fence. This was the isolation unit, "the IU" in prison lingo. While there were no bars on these windows, either, there was wire mesh embedded between the double-glass panes. Whereas women doubled or tripled up in the other units, here every woman was confined to her own locked room. And there was no mingling with any of the inmates in the institution at large.

Women who couldn't function within the general population were placed in UI. They might be so hard to control that they were forced to spend their entire sentence in isolation; they might be remanded there on a time-limited basis because of severe infractions of the prison rules; or, like Lynn Ingram, placed in isolation to protect them from the other inmates. Whatever the reason, they took all their meals alone in their rooms, exercised alone for only one hour a day, and, when granted visiting privileges, had to use one of four segregated and closely supervised one-on-one spaces located within the unit.

There was no question this was a grim way to have to do time. It was one thing when you brought it on yourself and were placed there for incorrigibility or an infraction of the rules. It was another, when you were put in isolation through no fault of your own. Nat knew, going into Grafton, that she was already feeling sorry for Lynn Ingram and would have to guard against letting her emotions get the upper hand.

Nat had a brief and disappointingly uninformative talk with Joan Moore, the recently appointed superintendent at Grafton, who had nothing of substance to offer beyond what Nat had already read in Ingram's file. Moore then cleared out, allowing Nat the use of her large, airy, cherry-paneled office for her meeting with Lynn Ingram. Ingram arrived dressed in the mandatory sexless orange jumpsuit, accompanied by an IU officer.

Nat noticed a faint lowering of the inmate's shoulders as the door shut. Still, Ingram looked far from relaxed, staring down at the floor, avoiding eye contact. This didn't surprise Nat. Inmates soon learned it could be dangerous to look a superior in the eye. It was often read as insolence, seen as a challenge. Even among themselves, men and women who were incarcerated, quickly discovered who it was safe to eyeball and who it wasn't.

The officer lackadaisically tucked the cuffs into his back pocket and waited for Nat's verbal dismissal before he shuffled out of the room.

Even though this was the first time Nat had seen the inmate in person she was not thrown off-guard by Ingram's beauty. Neither the garish orange uniform, nor the blonde hair, which she was wearing pulled severely back off her face in a coiled bun, detracted from her genuine aura of femininity.

"Are you here to bring me good news or bad?" Ingram asked with a frankness that Nat hadn't expected.

"I haven't made my decision yet."

Ingram glanced up at Nat for an instant then dropped her gaze. "What do I have to do to convince you to approve my transfer?"

"Sit down. How about some coffee? It's fresh. Milk? Sugar?"

Nat was already at the Mr. Coffee, setting up two mugs. Busy work. Busy mouth.

"I'm too nervous to drink anything," Ingram confided. "But I will sit down."

Nat noticed, as Ingram perched more than sat in one of the super's comfortable maroon leather armchairs, that her hands remained clasped together—as if her wrists were cuffed.

"You meet all of the requirements for transfer, Ms. Ingram," Nat told her, carefully removing the coffee carafe from the stand.

" 'But'?"

Having no real interest in the coffee, Nat replaced the carafe and crossed the office, taking a matching chair across from the inmate. "I'm concerned about providing for your safety."

Instead of jumping right in and trying to disabuse Nat of her worries, Lynn nodded solemnly. "That's understandable. I'm a liability. There's no getting around that."

Nat could see immediately why Leo liked Lynn Ingram. Nat found herself quickly feeling the same way. Lynn was direct without being confrontational, courteous without being ingratiating. She didn't wear her vulnerability on her sleeve, but she didn't seem intent on fiercely hiding it behind a *Nothing can get to me* exterior like many inmates did. *Like so many people do.*

"What I need to decide is, how much of a liability. I'm hoping you can help me make that decision."

"How can I do that?" she asked without hesitation.

Nat reached into her attaché case and retrieved a small sheaf of papers she'd brought with her. "This is a list of all of the staff and inmates presently at Horizon House." She held the pages out, but Lynn Ingram made no effort to take them.

"I'm not asking you to name names, Ms. Ingram. I just want

you to go through the list, then simply tell me if you feel you would be . . . comfortable among us."

Still, Ingram's hands remained firmly clasped together.

Nat leaned forward. "It's a matter of record that you were assaulted on more than one occasion while you were in the general population." She saw Ingram stiffen, but the inmate remained mute. "You were raped, Lynn. At least once . . . more—"

"Please stop," Lynn implored. "I just want to forget."

"You, of all people, know that's not possible."

"Because I'm a transsexual?" There was a note of defensiveness in the inmate's voice.

"Because you're a trained psychologist," Nat said softly.

Ingram flushed. "Sorry. I'm oversensitive about gender issues."

"I don't blame you," Nat said. "You were run through the mill because of it during your trial. And I'm sure it's been a major issue here in prison."

Lynn looked down at the floor. "Yes."

"Will you look at this list, Lynn? I know you've maintained throughout that you never saw any of your assailants here at Grafton, and I understand very well why you've taken that stance—"

"Meaning you don't believe me."

"Meaning," Nat said, "that I know the terrible risks involved if you ever named names. And I'm not asking you to do that. But if there's anyone at Horizon House from Grafton who might pose a serious threat—"

Ingram looked up, her lovely blue eyes meeting Nat's. "If you okay my transfer, I'm not only going to be inside your institution, Superintendent. I'll be on work-release, which means I'll be out in 'civilization' as we affectionately call it here. Are there people outside who might want to harm me? People at Horizon House? People in here? Of course there are. Who they are . . . How many—?"

Lynn shrugged. A shrug of resignation. Acceptance. "To certain people I will always be a freak. Worse, a freak who made a conscious choice to become one. That makes me deserving of their ridicule, their disgust, their revulsion, even their assaults. And then there are those people who, whether repulsed or not, are sexually drawn to the taboo I seem to represent to them. But the truth is, under no circumstances will I ever truly be a woman to them."

As she maintained eye contact, her beautiful face was a study in earnestness. "But I am a woman."

"A woman at risk," Nat was compelled to add. A whisper of a smile flitted across Lynn's lips. It took Nat a few moments to realize Lynn's smile was most likely a result of Nat's affirming that she'd identified Ingram as female. It was true. Now that Nat had met the infamous transsexual, she found herself remarkably *un*conflicted about Lynn Ingram's gender. Not that it would make her decision any easier.

"Being at risk, Superintendent Price, is something I've had to make my peace with, something I will always have to live with, no matter where I finish up my sentence. I will do everything in my power to avoid the risks, but I can't promise you, no matter who's on that list, that I will be safe. I can only tell you that if I have to spend the next six months in a solitary cell twenty-three hours a day, seven days a week, I think I truly will go mad. I suppose you're thinking, 'What's another six months to someone who's already done twenty-nine months, three weeks, and two days in protective custody—?'" She paused, smiled fully, winsomely. "But who's counting?"

five

Dr. Ingram never behaved in an improper manner at the clinic. Not with Matthew Slater. Not with any of her patients. Nor with any members of our staff.

DR. HARRISON BELL
(EXCERPT FROM INGRAM TRIAL TRANSCRIPT)

"SUPERINTENDENT PRICE?"

"Yes."

"This is Dr. Harrison Bell. I'm the—"

"I know who you are, Doctor." Nat picked up the catch in the anesthesiologist's voice. *Oh, God, something is wrong,* she was already thinking—fearing. "Is it Lynn?"

"She was . . . attacked. She's in the hospital. I don't . . . I don't know if she's going to . . . make it. Christ, it's all my fault. We were about to leave the clinic to get some lunch, but I had to finish up a report on a patient, so Lynn went on ahead to get a table—at this little Greek place she always eats in. Then, just as I was halfway out the door, my wife called and was all upset about our son Josh. The boy got into a fight at school. Boys do. He only got a day's suspension, but my wife has this tendency to blow things out of proportion."

"What happened?" Nat had let the doctor prattle on this long because she was feeling too short of breath to break in. And even as she asked, she was thinking, *Five weeks.* Five weeks almost to the day since Lynn Ingram's transfer to Horizon House. Five gloriously uneventful weeks. Nat was starting to actually think her fears for the inmate's safety were, while certainly not unfounded, greatly exaggerated. So much for that pathetically naive assessment.

"I couldn't have been more than fifteen minutes behind her. The thing is, there's this shortcut in back of the pain clinic. Kind of an alleyway, really. Cuts out a block. And what with the rain . . . I almost . . . didn't see her. I was dodging puddles, looking straight down. God only knows what it was that drew my eye over to the Dumpster."

He stopped. Nat could hear a muffled cry. She waited silently for him to continue, her hand white-knuckling the phone.

"I saw her hand. Just her fingers, really. Like she was trying to pull herself out. If the Dumpster hadn't been full, she'd never have . . . I'd never have known she was in there. Christ, she was bleeding everywhere. All . . . cut up. Her chest, her face . . . even . . . I can't believe anyone could do such a . . . monstrous thing. A maniac . . . It had to be—"

"What hospital?"

Nat's office door opened. Jack popped his head in. He heard her last question. Opening the door fully, he immediately stepped inside, his hand gripping the doorknob—waiting, lines of concern creasing his naturally furrowed brow.

"Boston General."

"And the police?"

"There are two detectives here. I would have called you sooner, but there were all these questions—"

"I'll be right over." Nat hung up the phone and jumped from her chair. But a sudden rush of dizziness slammed her back down. Jack rushed to her side. Nat could feel his anxiety overriding hers, enough so that she could tell him what had happened. Which amounted to very little information.

"I'll go," he said.

But Nat was back on her feet. Not exactly steady, but less wobbly. "You can drive."

By the time she got into Jack's car, anger mixed with guilt had supplanted her panic.

Lynn Ingram was still in the operating room when they got up to the ICU. She'd been under for a little more than ninety minutes, and there was no indication of how much longer it would be. All they knew was that her status was still listed as critical. "They" included Dr. Harrison Bell, Leo Coscarelli, his partner Mitchell Oates, Jack Dwyer, and Nat. They'd been granted use of the doctors' lounge just inside the ICU. After quick introductions, they all fell into a holding pattern.

Of the five of them, Harrison Bell was the only one seated and the one visibly having the toughest time. Nat had met the anesthesiologist on a couple of occasions prior to this afternoon, recalling him as a pleasant-looking, tidy man in his early forties. Now Bell's face was puffy, the tip of his nose red, his dark brown hair tousled, his gray slacks dirt-smudged, his pale blue shirt and gray sports jacket rumpled and spattered with blood. Lynn Ingram's blood.

Oates leaned closer to Coscarelli, said something out of Nat's earshot, then exited the lounge.

Leo walked over to Bell, dropped down onto the orange molded plastic seat beside the doctor. "We may have some more questions for you later."

Bell nodded grimly. "You've got my home number as well as my office. Anything I can do."

"You staying here for a while?" Leo asked him.

"Yes," Bell said without hesitation. "I've had my nurse cancel all of my afternoon appointments. Claire's very upset about Lynn. Everyone at the clinic is horrified. Lynn was very well liked."

Leo rested a hand on the doctor's shoulder. "Don't count her out yet."

Tears clouded Bell's eyes. He hung his head.

Jack Dwyer and Nat were watching this interchange with interest. Then Jack caught Nat's eye. Nat knew how her astute deputy's mind worked. He was thinking that the good doctor's use of the past tense—"*Lynn* was *well liked*"—might have been a slip of the tongue. The same thought had crossed Nat's mind. No doubt Leo's as well. And if it was a slip, it could have been wishful thinking. Because if she pulled through, Lynn Ingram might well be able to identify her attacker.

Nat followed Leo as he headed out of the lounge, noticing before she exited that Jack had taken the chair just vacated by Leo.

Leo gave the nod to a uniformed cop stationed in the hallway. He had ordered a round-the-clock watch on Lynn. They were all worried that her assailant might make an attempt to finish off what he'd started.

"Well?" Nat asked Leo as soon as they passed the cop. He motioned for her to follow him out the electronic swinging doors that separated the ICU wing from the rest of the seventh floor. Once they got beyond those doors, Leo stopped, looked around. The area was empty. Then he looked at Nat, but he was still not saying anything.

Nat felt his stare as a silent accusation. She'd asked for this. She was the one who'd adamantly dismissed everyone's—including Leo's—arguments about the dangers of approving Lynn Ingram's transfer to Horizon House

"I know you're beating yourself up, Natalie," Leo said finally, putting his hand gently on her arm. "Don't. This didn't happen to her at Horizon House. It happened on the street. And even if you hadn't okayed her transfer and she'd remained at Grafton, what happened to her today could just as well have happened five months from now. After her release from Grafton."

The physical contact, more than Leo's words, soothed her a little. "Do you have any leads?"

"We don't have much yet. No weapon so far. Our best guess, given the nature of the wounds, is some kind of hunting knife. We've got a couple of our people canvassing the neighborhood. Oates is going back to the pain clinic to get statements from staff and get names of patients who were there at the time. CSI is going over the alley and that Dumpster with a fine-toothed comb. It doesn't help that Bell disrupted the crime scene when he moved Ingram. But if he hadn't, we'd most likely be dealing with a homicide right now."

Nat swallowed hard. "We still may."

"I want to talk to Ingram's shrink. I'm hoping she told him something that will provide us with a lead."

"I doubt you'll get anything out of him," she said. "He's a by-the-books psychiatrist. Which means he'll uphold confidentiality to the bitter end." She shivered as she said this, realizing how close Lynn Ingram *was* to the bitter end.

"We'll get a court order, if it comes to that," Leo said. He put his arm around her. "I'll be coming over later."

"I'll probably get home late."

"I meant to Horizon House."

"Oh." Nat nodded. "You need to talk to Suzanne."

He removed his arm, put his hands in the pockets of his blue jacket.

"They've been rooming together at the center. They've reestablished their friendship." He hesitated. "I think Suzanne's going to take this hard."

Nat said nothing, inwardly hating herself for the flash of jealousy she felt over his wanting to be there to comfort his child's mother. As soon as Suzanne entered Horizon House, Nat should have cooled things with Leo. She knew damn well it could become an untenable situation. Nat was competing with one of her charges for the affections of a man who had been sexually and emotionally intimate with both of them. Maybe now was the time to step out of the competition. Maybe Leo would be relieved if she did.

"She may know something, Natalie."

"What?" Nat was already feeling the ache of separation. Was it only after deciding to break it off that she could allow herself to admit just how much Leo Coscarelli had come to mean to her?

"I think we should talk to her together." He cocked his head, observing Nat closely. He had this knack for reading people. Her especially. "Lynn may have shared some information with Suzanne that could help us. At least give us some direction. Right now, we've got zip to go on." He checked his watch. "Suzanne's due back from work around six, right?"

"Yeah." Meanwhile, Nat's mind was busy backpedaling. *Never make personal decisions in the heat of a crisis,* she was thinking. And this certainly qualified as a crisis. Okay, so she was giving herself a temporary reprieve.

six

Fifty-two percent of male-to-female transsexuals admit to having been victims of violent crime—this is in the community at large. These are vulnerable people even without the stresses of transition and the isolation of prison life.

GENDER IDENTITY STUDY

JACK DWYER WAS alone in the ICU lounge, still seated in the same molded chair, when Nat returned.

"Any update on Lynn?"

He shook his head.

"Where's Bell?" she asked.

"Men's room. Been there awhile. Bad case of the runs."

"That can happen when you're upset."

"Or when you're scared shitless."

She sat down beside Jack. "Did you learn anything useful from him?"

Jack scowled, his hard-edged features sharpening. "Something about that doc." He glanced over at the doorway to make sure Bell wasn't on his way back in. "I think he had the hots for Ingram. Maybe going back a long time. Like when she was first working for him. He visited her at Grafton. They wrote back and forth. I'd like to get a gander at some of his letters."

"He was on the phone with his wife while she was being attacked."

"So he says."

"It's easily verified."

"She wouldn't be the first wife to verify a husband's lie."

"Even if her husband was cheating on her?"

He eyed Nat in a disquieting way. A silent reminder that she had willingly lied for her husband during the Walsh investigation, even when Ethan had already left her for another woman. Even though her lie could have affected the outcome of a murder case. *What we won't do for love.* Or was it, *What we won't do to delude ourselves?*

"We can't dismiss the attacks on Lynn at Grafton," Nat said, eager to change the focus of the discussion. "There could be a connection. A corrections officer who had today off, or called in sick, or quit the job. An inmate who's out on parole."

"Possible," Jack admitted begrudgingly.

They both looked up nervously as a middle-aged woman in a white lab coat entered the lounge. She gave them both a formal nod. "I'm Dr. Ellen Madison. Ms. Ingram is out of surgery."

"Will she pull through?" Nat asked anxiously.

"She's suffered multiple knife wounds and a massive loss of blood. The next forty-eight hours will be crucial. If she does make it, she's going to need extensive reconstructive surgery." The doctor hesitated. "To her face, her breasts, and her pubic region. I'm not a detective, but I would say that these areas appear to have been the assailant's deliberate targets. There were some other superficial cuts to the patient's extremities, but I believe those were acquired in her attempts to stave off the attack."

"All frontal cuts. So she must have seen her assailant," Nat said.

"It would seem that way."

"Do you know that she's a transsexual?" Jack asked.

Madison nodded. "Dr. Bell informed us when she was brought in."

"Is she conscious?" Nat asked. "Can I talk to her?"

"No, to both," the doctor said firmly.

"When—?"

"Not for another twenty-four hours, at the very earliest. I'm sure you realize that the psychological ramifications resulting from her facial and bodily disfigurement are likely to be quite severe. Is Ms. Ingram currently under any psychiatric care?"

"Yes. She's being treated by Dr. Ross Varda. He's with the Department of Corrections—"

"I strongly suggest he be present if and when you are able to speak with Ms. Ingram."

The "if" rang in Nat's head. *A death knell.*

"You've already heard?" Leo watched Suzanne closely.

She nodded. "One of the salesgirls caught it on the news on her way home. She drove back to the store to . . . tell me." She brushed her hair from her face. Nat could detect the tremor in her hand. "Is she going to make it?"

"It's touch and go," Nat said.

"Sit down, Suzanne." Leo made the request.

Nat was already seated behind her desk. Leo, who was standing, waited for Suzanne to take a seat across from Nat, then he took occupancy of the chair beside her.

"What can you tell us that might help us find out who did this to Lynn?" Leo asked. His tone was gentle.

"How do you know it wasn't some random act? Some lunatic who spotted a . . . a beautiful woman he'd never seen before, and . . ." Suzanne looked down at the floor.

"We're not ruling out any possibilities," Leo said.

"Lynn likes you, Suzanne," Nat broke in. "I presume you like her."

Suzanne's head popped up. "I like her well enough. But I can't help you. She didn't say anything to me."

"Nothing?" Nat gave the word a distinctly sardonic note.

Suzanne turned to Leo. "You know what I mean."

"How did Lynn seem to you these past few days?" he asked.

Suzanne shrugged. "Fine. She was . . . happy. She loved her job. She loved being out of that . . . that cage. She never griped about any of the rules here. Most of us count the days until we're on the street . . . full-time, but Lynn just kind of took each day as a blessing." Her hand went up to her face. Her fingers pressed into her eyes in an attempt to stem the tears threatening to spill out.

It was clear to Nat that Suzanne Holden cared more about Lynn Ingram than she was saying.

"Did Lynn ever talk about her boss, Harrison Bell?" Leo asked.

Suzanne seemed surprised by the question. "Bell? She says he's brilliant. You don't think . . . ?" The tip of her tongue darted nervously over her bottom lip.

"Lynn was horribly disfigured. Even if she pulls through, it's going to be a nightmare for her," Nat said, ignoring Leo's scowl at her bluntness.

Suzanne shut her eyes. And then, as if the images playing in her mind proved too disturbing, she opened them quickly.

"I don't know who did it," she said hoarsely. "I swear I don't."

Nat could see beads of sweat forming above Suzanne's lip line. She also saw Leo place a comforting hand on the inmate's shoulder. Nat tried not to let this get to her. But, of course, it did.

"I need a cigarette," Suzanne said with an addict's note of desperation in her voice. She gave Leo a pleading look.

"Go outside and have your smoke," Nat said. There was no smoking in the building, but there was a porch in front of the building where inmates and staff could light up.

Leo was not happy with Nat. He wasn't ready to dismiss Suzanne. But Suzanne was more than ready. She was on her feet and making a beeline for the door practically before the words were out of Nat's mouth.

As soon as the door closed behind Suzanne, Leo was on Nat's case. "Why the hell did you do that, Natalie? She was just starting to—"

"Starting to come unglued," she finished for him. There was a bite in her voice, matching the bite in Leo's.

"She knows something," he said, his scowl etched across his brow.

"Of course she does. She knows plenty. She's also scared."

"She knows me well enough to know I'd never put her at risk."

"How well is that?"

Leo didn't look so much angry as disappointed.

"Maybe you shouldn't be working this case, Leo. There's a real conflict of interest here."

"There's a conflict all right," he said tightly. "But it isn't mine."

He rose slowly to his feet. "I'm going outside and talk to Suzanne some more. This *is* my case, Natalie. If you can't handle that—" He stopped, his expression softening. "Sorry. I know you're upset."

"We're both upset," Nat said.

He touched her cheek. She placed her hand over his. "How about after I finish up with Suzanne, we go grab some Chinese and have it over at your place?" Leo suggested. "Sound good?"

Nat hesitated, dropping her hand from his. Since Suzanne's transfer to Horizon House, and the Coscarelli family's biweekly visits, Nat felt a growing strain when she and Leo were together. "Why don't we see how . . . ?"

Leo drew her to him, silencing the rest of her words with a brief but potent kiss. "Do I have to arm-wrestle you next?" he teased.

Nat smiled. "No. I give."

"Good." His gaze lingered on her, his expression turning serious. "I want this to work, Natalie. We have something here. I don't want to let it slip through our fingers."

"Neither do I," Nat said. But she also knew that wanting something not to happen didn't mean it wouldn't.

Jack was on his way into Nat's office as Leo was exiting. The two men merely nodded in passing, neither a fan of the other. Leo deliberately left the door open as he exited. Jack deliberately shut it.

Nat merely shook her head.

"You catch the latest news flash?" Jack asked.

"What?" she asked, suddenly anxious.

"Heard it on the radio driving back here. Some reporter got to Jennifer Slater."

For a moment Nat drew a blank. Then it came to her: Matthew Slater's widow. How could she forget? During Lynn Ingram's trial, Jennifer Slater had made headlines in the tabloids and was on TV almost daily. Nat remembered the widow as a striking, rather than beautiful, woman in her late thirties. A tall, elegant brunette with catlike eyes who oozed fine breeding and wealth. Matthew Slater, a working-class boy from South Boston, had married well.

At no time during those stressful days following Matthew Slater's murder and, almost seven months later, during Ingram's five-week-long trial, had Nat ever observed Jennifer Slater lose her poise. Of course Nat had no idea what took place when the cameras weren't around. Not that Jennifer Slater volunteered much in the way of interviews. On the few occasions when she did make a statement, she vehemently maintained the position that her husband had been not only a victim of cold-blooded murder, but of a perverse and unwanted seduction.

"What did Jennifer Slater have to say in the interview?"

"Basically that Ingram asked for it."

"*Asked* for it? Asked to be mutilated? Nearly killed?"

"I don't think there's any love lost between those two women," Jack said facetiously.

Nat sighed. "I have to say I felt sorry for Jennifer Slater during the trial. Bad enough when a victim gets dragged through the mud, but when members of the victim's family get dragged along as well, it's horribly unfair."

"I imagine it doesn't do a hell of a lot for any woman's self-image to discover that her husband's having an affair, not to mention with a transsexual. I'm sure Jennifer Slater took it especially hard. According to the reporter's run-in before the Slater news bite, the widow's become something of a recluse since her husband's death. Spends most of her time at the family compound in Martha's Vineyard. Apparently her social life's pretty much nil. She's still involved in charity work, but when an appearance at a fund-raiser or banquet is required, she usually sends her kid brother."

Nat recalled the brother, Rodney Bartlett, a tall, thin-to-the-point-of-gaunt young man who had been Jennifer Slater's constant companion throughout the trial. Bartlett was always trying to run interference for his sister with the media. But, as Nat recalled, he rarely succeeded. Nat never saw him without a scowl on his face. A scowl that deepened when the verdict was handed down. Both he and his sister made it clear they would have been happy with nothing less than the death penalty for Lynn Ingram. Certainly a second-degree manslaughter conviction was a far cry from what they considered justice.

"Sounds like Jennifer Slater's still very bitter," Nat remarked thoughtfully.

Nat was on the phone to the hospital when Sharon Johnson rapped on her door and popped her head in. Nat motioned for her to step into the office.

"Thank you, Doctor. Yes, give me an update anytime. Day or night." The receiver felt oddly weighty as Nat set it back in its cradle.

"How is she doing?"

"Still unconscious. Still listed as critical."

"You look lousy," Sharon said, but there was a note of clear affection in her voice.

"I feel worse," Nat confided. A big admission for her. And one that she probably wouldn't have made to anyone else on her staff. As a superintendent who was both female and not yet thirty-five, she felt compelled to present herself as a person in control of her emotions when she was at work. Away from work, too; only it wasn't so easy in either case.

"I'm just about to leave for the day," Sharon said. "How about coming back to my place? Raylene's making her signature frittata for dinner. And she's just finished this incredible painting, a self-portrait, that she'd love to show you."

"How about a rain check? I already made plans for tonight."

"With Leo?" Sharon asked, a half-smile on her full lips. "I saw him outside on the front porch having a powwow with Suzanne."

"I asked him to remove himself from the case."

Sharon gave a little laugh. "Let me guess what his answer was."

Nat rolled her eyes.

"He's not going to get much out of Suzanne," Sharon said.

"He thinks he can."

"Which is what's eating at you."

Nat gave her employment counselor an angry look. "If Suzanne can tell us anything that will give us even a miniscule clue—"

"That's not what I meant." Sharon cut her off. "You got this love triangle thing going, Nat, and it's ripping you apart."

"It's not easy," Nat admitted.

"When is it ever?"

"Did anyone ever tell you, you should be a shrink?"

"Speaking of shrinks, have you heard from Dr. Varda?"

"He's at the hospital. I spoke to him briefly before talking to the surgeon. He's pretty shaken up."

"I hope you mean Varda," Sharon teased. "We don't want a shaky surgeon."

Nat managed a weak smile.

"Did Varda say anything? About who might have attacked Lynn?"

"Anything Lynn might have said to him was told under doctor-patient confidentiality." Nat understood Varda's position. Even respected it. But still, she found it excruciatingly frustrating. Varda might very well know the identity of the assailant. Or he might, at least, be able to make a solid educated guess. It would give them a lead. Someplace to begin looking.

"And I gather you haven't found anything in Lynn's room that might give you a clue." Sharon asked.

"Hutch did the search himself. Nothing."

"No . . . scribblings? A diary, maybe?"

"No. Why?"

"Just that a couple of times I saw Lynn writing stuff."

"In a diary?"

"No. It was on loose sheets of paper. She told me they were letters."

"That makes sense," Nat said. "Doesn't it?"

"I suppose. But I never spotted any envelopes. And one time I saw her slipping a piece of paper she'd been writing on into a kind of a loose-leaf binder. She caught me observing her, and she got all flustered. Told me she'd run out of stamps. I don't know. There was something . . . furtive . . . about her behavior."

"If they were letters," Nat mused, "who was she writing to? When she was at Grafton, the only person she maintained any regular correspondence with was Harrison Bell. And she wouldn't need to write to him now. She's with him at work every day."

Nat checked in with Hutch on her way out. Although he was officially off-duty, her head CO had opted to hang around for part of the night shift because of the undercurrent of tension in the house—a direct result of the assault on Lynn Ingram. There was the feeling among the inmates that it could have been any of them. It was the rare con who could say he or she had no enemies on the outside. Nat certainly had never come across one.

Hutch had been in charge of the search of Lynn's and Suzanne's room. Nat asked him if a loose-leaf notebook had turned up in the search.

"Nope. Just a Bible and a card. There was an inscription inside the Bible: 'To Lynn, May God's blessing be with you always, Father Joe.' "

"And the card?" Nat asked.

"It was a birthday card. I checked her record. Ingram turned thirty-one on June seventeenth. So she must have got the card while she was still in IU at Grafton. I thought it was interesting she took it with her when she came over here."

"And it's from . . . ?" Nat asked impatiently.

"From the doc."

"Harrison Bell?"

Hutch shook his head. "The shrink. Varda." He smiled wryly. "Interesting, huh?"

"How did he sign it?"

A shadow of disappointment fell across Hutch's broad face. Nat knew her CO didn't think much of the psychiatrist. Especially after that testy intake meeting on Ingram. "Nothing very juicy," he admitted. "Just, 'Best wishes, Dr. Ross Varda.' "

"I'd like to see the card. Did you confiscate it?"

Hutch looked over her shoulder toward the front door, where Leo was waiting for her. "Your detective's got it. And the Bible."

No big surprise. "Does he have anything else?"

"There wasn't anything else to turn over." A little catch in Hutch's voice put Nat on instant alert.

"So, what didn't you show to him?"

He shifted his weight from one foot to the other. "Nothing connected to Ingram." His gaze again drifted down the hall toward Leo.

"Let's not play twenty questions, Hutch," Nat said testily.

"There were some letters. Belonging to Suzanne Holden. From . . ."

"From Leo," Nat finished for him. Not that Leo had ever told her he wrote to Suzanne.

Hutch nodded.

"You read them?" Nat's voice sounded raspy to her own ears. Her throat had gone dry.

Hutch was again looking over her shoulder. Nat glanced back to see Leo heading toward them.

"I didn't read them, Nat," Hutch said quickly.

But he'd obviously seen enough to know who had signed the letters. How many were there? How had Leo signed them? *Best wishes*? Nat doubted that. *Love*? She hoped not.

"I just got beeped," Leo said, approaching them. "My partner. There was a bit of a ruckus over at the hospital. Seems Lynn's mother showed up, demanding to see her *son*."

seven

I think a lot about my folks in here. Especially that awful day when I finally got up the courage to tell them. My father raged and called me a pervert. But my mother broke down and sobbed, "I've lost my boy."

L. I.

WHEN LEO AND Nat arrived at the ICU, Ross Varda was conferring with Ruth Everett in the doctors' lounge. Mitchell Oates, Leo's partner, was waiting for them in the ICU waiting room.

"She goes by the name Everett?" Leo asked.

Oates nodded.

"And Mr. Everett?" Nat asked.

"She came alone. Didn't say anything about the husband."

Leo glanced across the hall at the closed door to the doctors' lounge. "What else?"

"Like I told you on the phone, the mom was on the verge of

hysteria, and the psychiatrist pretty much took charge. Got her calmed down some."

"He knows her?" Nat asked.

"I don't think they ever met before, but he knew her name. Knew who she was right off. I'm guessing Ingram must have talked about the mom in their therapy sessions."

Leo scowled. "You working on that court order?"

"Yeah," Oates said. "I told Varda we're gonna subpoena his records. He gave me a song and dance about being between a rock and a hard place, blah, blah, blah. I told him if he felt that way now, how was he gonna feel if his patient kicked the bucket? Shrinks," Oates muttered, like it was a curse word.

Ruth Everett's hands were clutched around a Styrofoam cup of coffee. When Nat and Leo walked into the lounge, she sprang out of her seat, the coffee spilling over the rim. She looked anxiously in their direction, and Nat realized she was expecting them to be bearing news about her daughter. Or as Ruth saw it, her son.

Leo introduced himself and before he could turn to introduce Nat, Ross Varda made the introduction. Ruth Everett only now became aware of the spilled coffee. Varda gently took the cup from her hand and set it down on a nearby Formica counter.

"Then you don't have any word about Larry?" Ruth Everett's lips quivered. "I . . . I mean . . . Lynn." She said the name like she was speaking a foreign language.

What struck Nat about Ruth Everett first and foremost was that she was an older but no less beautiful version of Lynn Ingram. Even now, under obvious distress, her generous lips pursed, her complexion drained of color, a drawn look around her blue eyes—a shade of blue almost identical to Lynn's—her beauty showed through. Certainly there were differences. Although the mother was a bit shorter, closer to five foot ten, a bit more slender, and her blonde hair longer than Lynn's by several inches and threaded with random gray, there'd be no missing the blood relationship between the two.

Leo glanced over at the psychiatrist. "Would you mind waiting out in the visitors' lounge, Doctor?"

They all knew it wasn't really a question. Nat could see Varda wasn't pleased with the dismissal. He was even more distressed when Ruth looked nervously up at him. She clearly wasn't pleased either. He patted her shoulder reassuringly.

"We'll talk again later," he told her.

Ruth Everett did not look comforted. "I . . . I can't stay . . . very long." Anxiety was etched in each word.

"There'll be other times," Varda told her with the soothing confidence of an experienced psychiatrist.

"Will . . . there be?" Ruth clutched her hands together.

After Varda reluctantly made his exit, Ruth sank back down into her seat.

Leo pulled over a chair and sat down next to Ruth. Nat took a seat across from her. "How long has it been since you've seen Lynn?" Leo asked.

"I . . . I can't get used to that. Calling him . . . Lynn. I named him Lawrence. After my father. Peter, that's my husband, he never really liked the name Lawrence. He thought it wasn't very. . . ." She shut her eyes for a moment, shaking her head slowly. ". . . very masculine." She opened her eyes and smiled ruefully at no one in particular. "That's a good one, isn't it?"

She flushed, looking anxiously at each of them in turn. "There was nothing *sissy* about Larry. I swear there wasn't. You see these . . . these people on those disgusting tabloid shows, and they're always talking about how they played with dolls as children, dressed up in their mother's clothes, hid in the closet and slathered on makeup—" Ruth's mouth set into a grim line. "Larry wasn't like that. He was never like that. If he had been, his father would have killed him."

Tears spilled over and rolled, unheeded, down Ruth Everett's cheeks. Nat dug into her purse for a tissue, got up and brought it over to her. Ruth took it automatically, but merely crumpled it in her hand.

"If he knew I was here, he'd probably kill me." As soon as the words were out, her eyes darted anxiously over to Leo. "I don't mean that literally. Peter's bark is worse than his bite." She tried for another smile but it fell flat.

"How long has it been since you've seen Lynn?" Nat repeated the question Leo had asked earlier.

Ruth hesitated, eyes downcast. "Ten years. It was the summer right before he started his doctoral program in psychology at Boston University. The summer he left his wife."

Nat did a classic double-take. *Wife? Lynn was married?* How come there was no mention of this bombshell in the court or prison records?

She shot a look over at Leo. He was looking as taken aback as she was.

"How long was Lynn married?" Nat asked Ruth.

Lynn's mother was nonplussed. "No. No, you see, it was when he was still Larry. It was only for a few months. I never even met her."

"What was her name?"

Ruth shrugged, looking uneasy. "What does it matter? It was ages ago."

"Just routine," Leo persisted.

"Bethany."

"Last name."

"I think . . . Graham."

"How did they meet?"

"I don't know. A party. She was someone's cousin or friend or something from out of town. I never really got the story straight. It all happened so fast. One day they're dating, the next thing I know they eloped."

"Bethany attended school?"

"No, she worked in some restaurant."

"What did she look like?"

"I never met her."

"Never? That sounds hard to believe," Leo said.

Ruth was getting increasingly agitated. "Well, once, but just for a minute. She was on her way out. To work."

"Your husband must have been pleased," Nat said.

"Pleased?"

"That Larry married."

"Oh. Oh yes. He was. I admit Peter worried about Larry. There'd been some kind of an incident right after high school." She shifted uncomfortably in her chair. "I don't really know what happened. I was away visiting my mother that weekend. When I got home it was obvious Larry and Peter had had a falling-out. Neither of them would tell me why. But then the two of them finally talked and after that, it seemed . . . okay. But there was still some tension between them that lingered."

Nat felt a wave of pity for Ruth, but an even sharper pang of pity for Lynn. How hard must it have been to live a lie? To go so far as to get married? Clearly hard enough so that Lynn finally gave up the pretense.

"Did Larry tell you why he and Bethany broke up?" Leo asked.

"Yes. He told us that he finally confessed to her that he was . . . a transsexual."

"How did your husband take the news?"

"He was upset." There was a quiver in Ruth's voice.

"And what did Peter do?"

Ruth compressed her lips.

"Did it get physical, Ruth?" Nat pressed.

"No."

Nat didn't believe her. She doubted Leo did, either.

"What happened after Larry's revelation?" Leo asked.

"Larry left. And we moved from Dedham soon after . . . that. First to Worcester, then four years ago to Westfield."

"And that was your last contact with your son?"

Ruth bit down on her trembling lip. "Yes. I didn't want it that way, but Peter . . . he said he would leave me if I even so much as gave Larry our new address. As far as he was concerned, our . . . son was . . . dead. Peter even had our name changed so Larry couldn't find us."

Nat tried to keep it from showing, but she was aghast at this mother's willingness to cut off her son so willingly—her flesh and blood—because of her husband's threat. If it were her, Nat thought, she wouldn't have waited for that unfeeling bastard to leave her, she would have left him.

"Are you married, Superintendent Price?" Ruth was looking directly at Nat.

She felt her cheeks redden. "I . . . was."

"The simple truth is I didn't want to be left alone."

"What became of Bethany?" Leo asked.

"I don't know," Ruth said.

"You never saw or heard from her again? You don't know where she went? You have no idea—"

"No," Ruth snapped. "I don't even know why I mentioned it."

Nat believed she never meant to mention the marriage. It had just slipped out.

Mitchell Oates entered the lounge, his expression grim. Ruth gripped the arms of her chair.

"What happened?" Leo asked his partner.

"Brain hemorrhage. She's being rushed back into surgery."

Ruth began to moan. "My baby. My poor baby."

eight

Because much of the patient's post-operative time has been spent going through a traumatic trial for murder and then being in prison, she has had little opportunity as a woman to experience sexual relations.

Dr. Ross Varda
(EXCERPT FROM PRISON ENTRY PSYCHOLOGICAL REPORT)

THE INSTANT NAT'S dog Hannah smelled the lo mein and ginger chicken with string beans, she was all over Leo. It was a toss-up who spoiled Hannah more, Nat or Leo. Either way, Hannah was definitely going to be sharing the Chinese.

"First you need to go out," Nat said, ruffling the dog's shaggy coat, then pulling her off Leo.

The phone rang as Nat was putting the leash on Hannah. She tensed, immediately thinking it was the hospital, fearing the worst. Although Lynn had made it through the second surgery, her condition remained critical. And she was still unconscious.

Nat gave Leo the nod and he hurried into the living room and picked up the phone.

"It's Coscarelli. Yeah, go ahead."

Something was wrong. She could hear it in Leo's voice. "What happened?" she asked the instant he hung up, trying to swallow down the lump of panic in her throat.

"It's Ross Varda. He's in the emergency room at Boston General. Someone mugged him on his way home."

It took Nat a couple of seconds to absorb this unexpected and disquieting news. "How . . . bad?"

"A good-size goose egg on his skull and a few cuts. Not too deep. They'll probably release him tonight."

"Cuts? Leo—"

"I know."

"Did he see who it was? Did he say anything?"

"No. Oates is there now. Varda told him he was attacked from behind; it was dark, he blacked out. Look, I'm going to head over to the hospital. Sit tight. I'll call as soon as I know anything."

Nat was not about to hang around waiting to hear from Leo. After he left, she took Hannah for a quick trip outside to do her business, then drove over to Boston General.

She made it to the hospital lobby just in time to see Leo and a shaken Ross Varda stepping out of one of the elevators. Varda's complexion was almost as white as the bandage over his right eyebrow. There was a dazed look in his eyes. While he might not have been severely injured physically by the mugging, it didn't require a shrink to see that, mentally, he was seriously unnerved.

Leo caught sight of Nat first. He wasn't particularly surprised to see her.

She started toward them. It wasn't until she was less than a couple of yards away that Varda actually spotted her approaching.

"There hasn't been a further update on Lynn?" he asked anxiously.

"No," Nat reassured him immediately. "I came down to see if you were okay."

He forced a poor excuse for a smile. "I'm fine. Just a bit . . ." He shook his head, a description of his state seeming to elude the doctor.

"Why don't I give you a lift home?" Nat offered.

Leo looked even less happy. Nat was sure he'd been hoping to capitalize on the psychiatrist's current wobbly state of mind to try to pump him for some information about Ingram.

Varda, however, instantly jumped at Nat's offer. Probably because he didn't anticipate that she, too, planned to pump him, especially as this mugging struck Nat, not surprisingly, as no mere coincidence.

She voiced her theory aloud to Varda once they were settled in her car and heading over to his apartment across town in Boston's upscale South End.

Out of the corner of her eye, Nat caught Varda's hand moving to his bandaged wound. "I've considered that possibility. That Lynn's assailant sees me as a threat."

"Would he be right?"

"Even if I could break confidentiality, which I can't, there's no way I can know for certain who jumped out of that alleyway. It would be pure supposition."

"Which means you have a good idea."

"I didn't say that."

"He might come after you again, Ross."

"Do you think I'm not worried about that? I'm embarrassed to admit that I'm terrified."

"There's no reason to be ashamed of being afraid," Nat assured him. "Given what's happened, I'm sure that, as a psychiatrist, you know that fear's a healthy response."

He gave a self-deprecating laugh. "I wet my pants. When I was attacked."

"Which is also a very common response."

"Oh, yes, I know. It's one thing to know the theory, another to—" He pressed his hands to his face.

They drove in silence for a few minutes.

"Are you in a great deal of pain?" she asked sympathetically.

"No. I wish I was. It would be a welcome distraction."

Varda gave her directions and Nat turned onto St. Botolph Street, pulling into a parking spot not far from his building. Varda reached for the door handle, but then just left his hand resting on it. Nat thought at first he wanted to tell her something. But then it hit her. He must be scared to go up to his apartment. Scared that maybe his assailant was up there lying in wait for him.

"Would it be okay," Nat asked, "if I used your bathroom? I kind of rushed out of my place when I heard you were injured and I haven't had a chance to—"

"No problem."

She could hear the relief in the psychiatrist's voice. And maybe just a hint of gratitude.

Varda's apartment was on the third floor. There was an elevator, but Varda headed directly for the stairs. He led the way up to his door. Nat heard his harsh gasp, but he was blocking her view. He stepped aside so she could see the door was ajar.

"I am fanatic when it comes to making sure my door is locked whenever I leave my apartment," he told her in a raspy voice. "Someone's broken in."

"That someone," Nat said in a whisper as she tugged him back toward the stairs, "might still be there."

Varda's color went from white to ash-gray as her words sank in.

Nat didn't think he actually took a breath until they hit the street, running. Then again, neither did she.

"Nothing's missing?" Leo pressed. Nat had phoned him as soon as she and Varda had gotten out of the psychiatrist's building.

Varda shook his head numbly as he looked around at the chaos that was once his pristine living room. Books had been ruthlessly shoved off bookcases, several of them ripped and shredded; the large-screen television set was smashed on the floor in front of the fireplace, where it was joined by a stomped-on pair of high-end Bose mini speakers. The bedroom was equally in disarray, all the clothes pulled from the closet and bureau drawers. The bed also had been pulled apart.

The bathroom was the worst. Not so much because it, too, had been ransacked, but because of the red lipstick message scrawled across the medicine chest mirror: KEEP YOUR MOUTH SHUT OR YOU'LL BE WORSE OFF THAN LYNN. No question now of the link between the break-in, the mugging, and the violent assault on Lynn.

"Any idea what the intruder was looking for?" Leo persisted.

"No."

"How about Lynn Ingram's therapy file?"

"It's locked in a cabinet in my office at CCI Grafton."

"We're getting a court order for that file, Doc. I don't need to warn you that it would be a felony for you to destroy or in any way alter those records, seeing as how they're the subject of a police investigation."

"I'm fully aware of that, Detective. And I assure you, police investigation or not, I would never alter or destroy a patient's records."

"Do you know who did this?" Leo asked the psychiatrist bluntly.

Varda was equally blunt. "No."

"Okay, play it that way. It's your neck."

Varda blinked rapidly, shaken by Leo's blunt remark. But he said nothing.

"I don't think it's a good idea to stay here tonight. Anyone you can stay with?" Leo asked.

Nat was about to offer her place, but Varda said he could stay with his sister. He quickly packed a few things and then Leo and Nat escorted him outside and over to his car.

"You sure you feel well enough to drive?" Nat asked as Varda got behind the wheel.

"Yes, I'm okay. Really," the psychiatrist assured her.

Leo turned to Nat after Varda drove off. "And where do I stay tonight?"

"I'm beat, Leo. How about if I reheat the Chinese tomorrow night?"

His eyes lingered on her face for several moments. "It's never as good reheated, Natalie. But I guess it's better than not having it at all."

nine

I was treated like such a circus freak during my trial that I actually felt a weird relief when I was finally put away. How pathetically dumb I was. Being ridiculed and mobbed by the media was nothing compared to the constant abuse and worse I'm suffering now. The nightmare is only just beginning.

L. I.

IT WAS WELL past midnight when Nat finally got home. As she opened her front door, she automatically braced herself, but Hannah didn't rush to greet her in her typical speed-demon fashion, invariably careening into Nat because her paws had no gripping power on the polished hardwood floor.

"Hannah? Here, girl."

Not a bark. Not a whimper.

"Hannah?" An edge of anxiety crept into Nat's voice. Something was definitely wrong. Could Hannah have gotten sick? She'd seemed perfectly fine a couple of hours ago before Nat had left to rush out to the hospital.

It was the absolute silence that alarmed Nat the most. Goose bumps prickled her arms as she tried to rein in her escalating panic.

She remained at the open door, cautiously sliding her hand against the wall for the light switch. She flicked it on, but the hallway remained dark. Maybe if she hadn't just come from Ross Varda's ransacked apartment, she wouldn't immediately have thought the worst. But the break-in, the mugging, the warning scrawled on his mirror, were all playing havoc with her mind.

And now Hannah wasn't responding to her arrival, and the lights didn't work. Had someone broken in here as well? Pulled the fuses? Deliberately intending to keep her in the dark?

At least the light from the hall corridor outside her apartment provided enough of a glow for her to see that the foyer appeared undisturbed. But the light didn't carry into her living room. It could be a shambles. Or, even as she stood there at the door, it could be in the process of being torn apart. The assailant could be in her apartment right at that moment. Holding his or her breath much as she was holding hers.

Nat knew the wise move—the only rational move—was to turn on her heels and beat it the hell out of there, just as Varda and she had done at his place a short while ago.

But Varda didn't own a dearly loved dog who might at that very instant be lying somewhere in her apartment, maybe injured but still clinging desperately to life. How would she live with herself if she abandoned Hannah when a little gumption on her part could have saved her pet?

"Hannah?" she called out again, this time taking a couple of wary steps inside the apartment, still leaving her front door wide open so she could make a fast getaway if she had to. Hopefully she wouldn't have to. Hopefully, if she did have to run, she wouldn't be impeded in her escape.

"Hannah? Here, girl. Where are you, girl?"

Nat listened acutely for the faintest whimper. Naturally, she was also listening for any other sounds. Like footsteps, creaks, an intruder's hushed breathing. If someone was lying in wait for her, he or she had certainly received warning that she was there. She knew it was completely foolhearty to imagine her presence might scare an intruder off, but she couldn't help hoping it might.

She took a couple more steps inside. "Hannah?" If her dog was dead Nat was seriously going to lose it. She was already biting back tears. She loved that dog. Unequivocally. Unconditionally.

She moved cautiously toward her living room. Unfortunately, there were no overhead fixtures in there. In order to discover whether all of the lights were not in working order, she would need to make her way almost halfway into the room to a lamp sitting on an end table next to her couch. At least, it had been there when she'd left that morning. She flashed back on the chaos of what had once been Varda's assuredly tidy, orderly living room.

She took small steps, fearing that she might trip over something. Worse, over someone. Someone like Hannah. *If you harmed Hannah, you shit, I'll make you so sorry—*

But her path was clear. Nothing on her floor that shouldn't be there. The brass lamp with the Tiffany-esque glass shade was right where it was supposed to be. Words couldn't express the relief Nat felt when she pulled the metal chain and the light actually went on.

She silently said a prayer of thanks to Thomas Alva Edison and his brilliant invention.

Her living room appeared untouched. Her morning mug of coffee was still on her coffee table.

Not a chance in a million that Hannah was so dead to the world that she wouldn't respond. Unless . . . Unless she literally was dead to the world.

Nat started frantically racing around her apartment hunting for Hannah, mindless of potential danger rather than fearless of it. Like a wild woman, she was throwing open drawers and closets, crawling under beds, chairs, sofas. She had to find her dog. Dead or alive, she had to find her.

Hannah was a full-grown, sixty-pound golden retriever. If she was in that apartment, there was no place she could be hiding that Nat wouldn't unearth her.

It was only as she approached the closed door to her bathroom that Nat hesitated. Was she, like Varda, going to find a warning scribbled on her mirror? Was Lynn's assailant afraid she'd worm his identity out of Varda? Or figure it out for herself?

Had he left her a scrawled message—or something worse? Gruesome images of Hannah lying sprawled on her tile floor, cut up, dead, or dying, raced across Nat's mind.

As she cupped the doorknob, she could feel a violent tremor shooting from her palm right up her arm. She forced herself to turn the knob and crack the bathroom door open, but she was having trouble opening it wide enough to see what was inside. For several moments, she clutched the knob as though it were her lifeline, and stood there listening.

Silence except for the escalating beating of her heart.

She braced herself—like that was really possible—and flung open the door. The only object on her tile floor was the mint-green bath towel she'd used that morning. Her gaze shifted to her closed floral shower curtain.

Cursing every horror film she'd ever seen where the heroine yanks open her shower curtain either to come face-to-face with a gruesome body or an equally gruesome killer, Nat did precisely that. Other than a faint ring around her tub, there was nothing to be seen. There was only one other conceivable place in there where Hannah might be. Even though her wicker hamper didn't feel heavy enough to be concealing a fifty-pound dog, Nat toppled it and emptied her dirty laundry out on the floor just to make sure.

Ten minutes later, she was standing in the middle of her kitchen, cupboard doors yawning open, having yanked out all her pots and pans from the shelves in the unlikely chance Hannah had somehow managed to wedge herself deep into the back of the pantry—or someone had managed to put her there.

No sign of her. Absolutely no sign. Nor had Nat discovered the slightest indication of a struggle having gone on anywhere in the apartment.

Tears stung her eyes as Nat thought about what a trusting soul Hannah was. How she loved people. Kids especially, but women, men, too. Give her a smile, a vigorous pat and she was your friend. Give her a treat and she'd go anywhere with you.

That was the only conclusion Nat could draw. The intruder had managed to get into her apartment and steal off with Hannah. Her dog had been kidnapped.

But how had the intruder gained entry into her apartment? Nat had checked all the doors and windows by that time. No sign of forced entry. And the only people with keys to her apartment were Leo and her sister. Leo used his key occasionally. Rachel, never.

Nat remained standing there, trying to make sense of things, when she heard scratching sounds. Then a short spate of barks.

Heedless of possible danger, she went racing out of the kitchen and down the hall toward her entry foyer. "Hannah? Hannah, girl?"

There was only silence now. Emptiness. It was like she'd dreamed the barks.

A few feet from her front door, she stopped short. The door was shut.

Nat knew—she was positive—she'd left it wide open. She'd even glanced at the open door several times as she was running from room to room hunting for her dog.

Someone had been here. Moments ago. Someone had been there with Hannah. Nat was certain of it. But why had the dog-napper come back? To get her? But then, why disappear again? It made no sense.

Nat darted the few feet separating her from the door and yanked it open just in time to see the elevator doors sliding shut at the end of the hall. She raced to the windows of her living room that looked down on the street, hoping to get a glimpse of her dog and the dognapper—at the very least, enough of a description of the bastard to give the cops a lead.

Endless minutes passed as she stood at her open window with her gaze fixed on the street. No one exited. Not man nor beast.

Had the elevator gotten stuck? Could the kidnapper have taken Hannah up to the roof?

On the vague chance that they might still use the main entrance, Nat remained stubbornly at her post for a good five minutes longer. Still no sign of anyone going or coming.

Maybe she had imagined it. Maybe she was losing her mind.

The rush of adrenaline that had kept her going up to that moment, deserted her. She felt drained dry. She couldn't even work up the energy to cry. Numb with despair, she sank to the floor beside her window and leaned against the wall.

That was where she was when her front door burst open a good ten minutes later. Before Nat could even gather the strength to react, she saw Leo and two uniformed cops, all three with weapons drawn, charge into the living room.

"What—?" This didn't make any sense at all. Why was Leo here? How had he known something was wrong?

Leo made a beeline for Nat, the uniforms cautiously scanning the space, guns at the ready.

He knelt beside her, grasping hold of her trembling hands, concern and anxiety sweeping across his features. "Jesus, Natalie, are you okay? Are you hurt? Talk to me. What happened?"

"I . . . It's . . . It's Hannah, Leo. Hannah's . . ." And that's as far as she could go. Her bottom lip was quivering, and she knew if she went on, she'd break down completely. She was fighting it desperately. Bad enough to feel so vulnerable. Worse to show it.

"Is she all right?" an anxious and familiar voice called out. A voice accompanied by a series of low whimpers.

Not waiting for a response, Rachel rushed in, doing her best to restrain the large dog struggling to break free from her firm hold of the leash.

"Hannah. Oh, Hannah," Nat cried out.

And then the dog was running to her, careening into her, lapping her, barking, and Nat was holding Hannah so tight it was a wonder the dog could breathe, much less continue to bark joyfully. "Hannah." Nat cried her name again as she buried her face in Hannah's luxuriant golden hair. There might have been a happier moment in her life, but if there was, Nat couldn't remember it.

. . .

"Oh, Nat, I am so, so sorry."

It was nearly one in the morning. Leo and the two uniforms had gone. Hannah had settled herself comfortably on the sofa beside Nat, her head resting contentedly in her lap. Rachel was fussing with the tea she had insisted on making for them, which Nat didn't want.

"I didn't think," Rachel went on as she spooned a heaping teaspoon of honey into each of the mugs. "I must have gotten here no more than ten minutes before you arrived. I heard Hannah barking frantically inside the apartment. I thought you wouldn't mind if I let myself in." She looked over at Nat for reassurance that her assumption was true.

Nat managed a weak smile.

"And then Hannah wouldn't settle down. She kept huddling by the door. I realize now she was probably just waiting for you to come home, but I thought she needed to go out. So I took her for a walk. And then when we got back . . . well, I saw the door wide open, and I knew I certainly hadn't left it that way . . . I was particularly careful to lock it, as a matter of fact . . ."

As Nat listened to Rachel she could almost laugh, it was all making such ridiculous sense.

"So, I panicked. I thought someone had . . . broken in . . . Then I heard noises and was certain the intruder was still in here." Rachel shivered visibly. "Really, Nat, I just wish you'd find yourself a nice, safe career that didn't put you in the middle of packs of hardened criminals."

An old refrain of her sister's. One that she'd sung even more often since the Walsh incident.

Rachel was stirring the honey vigorously into the tea. "So I called the police. Told them it was an emergency involving Superintendent Natalie Price and to get ahold of Leo Coscarelli on the double. I waited down in the lobby for them."

Which explained why Nat never saw Hannah and her "kidnapper" exiting the building. Well, at least that meant she hadn't been hallucinating.

"Leo wasted no time getting here." Rachel handed her a mug. Nat took it only because her sister seemed so desperate to do something for her.

"He looked relieved but a bit disappointed when he left," Rachel said. "I hope it wasn't because of me."

"I don't follow," Nat said.

"Leo. Wanting to spend the night. Not staying because of me."

"It . . . It wasn't because of you, Rachel."

"Oh." There was the faintest hint of a question in her words.

"It's complicated. Because of the investigation into the assault on one of my residents—"

"Lynn Ingram. The transsexual who was . . . cut up?"

Nat nodded. "Jakey's mom is . . . Lynn's roommate." Rachel had met Leo's little boy a few months back, at the Children's Museum. She was there with her three kids and their nanny. Leo and Nat were there with Jakey. They ended up spending the afternoon together. It was nice. It felt like they were all . . . family. Thinking back on that day now, Nat felt this awful wrenching in her gut.

"Jakey's mom is . . . serving time?"

Nat saw the look of shock and reproach on her sister's face. Shock, no doubt, because Jakey's mom was a convict. Reproach directed at Nat for never having shared that startling fact.

Nat felt a pang of guilt, but she was too drained to let it get to her. Besides, now that her panic had been put to rest, her focus shifted to the reason why her sister had showed up at her apartment tonight in the first place.

Nat saw Rachel stiffen as she put that question to her, but Rachel didn't respond. Instead, she sipped her now-tepid tea.

"Are the children okay?" Nat asked, although she couldn't imagine Rachel wouldn't have said something by now if one of them was ill or if something bad had happened to any of them.

If Nat hadn't been through so much trauma that night, she'd have guessed immediately what it must be.

"Rachel, what is it? What happened?"

"He left me."

Nat had to constrain herself from adding, *Again.*

She wished Rachel would sound angry instead of disconsolate. Nat only hoped the bastard would stay away this time. Good riddance to bad rubbish.

"He says he still loves me, but that it's . . . it's all too much for him."

"What exactly does he mean by 'all'?"

Rachel fought back tears. "He didn't say. I didn't ask. What does it matter? He doesn't want to be married anymore. He wants his freedom. He wants—" She compressed her lips. "I suppose there's another woman."

Nat more than supposed it.

"I just had to . . . get out of the house. I needed time to . . . I don't know. I just . . ."

"It's fine, Rach. I'm glad you came here."

"I told Anya I was going to spend the night with you. I know I have to explain to the children, but I'm just not . . . ready yet. And I didn't think I could face them in the morning without . . . cracking up. That would be so awful for them."

"You made a good decision, Rach." Nat patted her sister's shoulder.

Rachel's eyes brimmed with tears, but she managed a weak smile. "You've been through it, too, tonight. I'm sorry about Hannah, Nat. I should have thought—"

"Forget it. I'm glad you're here. I could use the company."

Nat nudged her sister gently toward her. It didn't take much coaxing before they were hugging.

After a few moments, Rachel still in her embrace, said, "Oh, I almost forgot. There was an envelope on your floor just inside the front door. I put it in the bowl on your hall table."

It was only after Nat had made sure that Rachel was sound asleep in her guest room that she ventured back into the foyer. The plain white envelope was, as Rachel had said, in her shallow blue-and-white Delft pottery bowl on her entry table, resting on top of the mail.

The envelope was blank.

Nat could feel her pulse racing, her throat clogging up. Even the air in the apartment felt different. Thicker. Colder. How could such a nondescript item hold so much terror?

A part of Nat wanted to snatch it up, rip it open, and get it over with. Whatever "it" was.

Another part of her wanted to forget it existed. Oh, for her sister's talent at denial!

But in the end she could neither push it from her memory nor open it on the spot. The "special delivery" would have to be treated as potential evidence. The police would need to examine the envelope and whatever was contained inside. Nat's guess was they wouldn't find incriminating fingerprints. Even the least savvy of criminals knew to wear gloves. But they weren't always smart enough to remember not to lick the envelope closed. Saliva might tag a person through DNA testing.

Nat went into the kitchen to get a plastic bag and a pair of tongs, checking the clock on the stove. It was nearly two in the morning. She wasn't going to call Leo at that hour. The poor guy had looked emotionally and physically spent when he'd left her apartment. He needed some sleep.

So did Nat.

ten

Don't I have the right to give, to love, to be loved in return? If only I could make people understand that my desires aren't perverse, but natural longings.

L. I.

IT WAS A few minutes before eight in the morning when Rachel, wearing one of Nat's white cotton nightgowns, groggily entered the kitchen.

"You're dressed already," Rachel said, a touch of disappointment in her voice.

"Yes, and just about to leave, I'm afraid." Nat was at the sink, taking a last swallow of coffee and then quickly rinsing the cup under the faucet.

"You have to be at the center so early?"

"Well . . . I want to stop at the hospital first. To check on Lynn Ingram." Nat was also meeting Leo there. She'd called him a few minutes ago and told him about the envelope. He was ready to drive right over to her apartment, but Nat was determined to keep her sister in the dark about what might well turn out to be a warning similar to the one left on Dr. Varda's medicine cabinet. Rachel had enough to worry about without Nat adding further to her troubles.

"Would you like me to go with you?" Rachel asked.

"Go with me?"

"To the hospital?"

"Oh, no. No. Thanks, Rach. But look, stay here, have some breakfast, shower, relax. And I'll tell you what. I'll try to clear up my schedule so we can have lunch together. I'll call you later. What do you say?"

"Sure. All right." But she didn't sound very enthusiastic.

"Rach. It's going to be okay," Nat said softly.

She nodded. But Nat knew Rachel didn't believe that for a second. Who could blame her? Nat certainly couldn't. She'd been through it herself. When Ethan had walked out on her, she'd thought she'd never get over the pain, the anger, the shame, the terrible feeling of having failed to hold on to her man. It had happened over a year ago, and even now Nat couldn't really say it was okay. Just that it was more okay than it had been twelve months ago.

Certainly, twelve months ago, Nat wouldn't have imagined she'd ever let herself risk getting so emotionally involved with another man.

And look where that involvement had gotten her.

"You'd make a good surgeon," Nat said as she watched Leo meticulously extract the folded sheet of paper from the plain white envelope using a pair of eyebrow tweezers.

"It's the rubber gloves," he said, trying to inject a lightness into his tone. He didn't succeed.

They were alone in the doctors' lounge just outside the ICU. Leo had locked the door so they wouldn't be disturbed. After putting the now-empty envelope in an evidence bag, he unfolded the sheet of white business-size paper. Nat was standing right beside him, already picturing in her mind the words of warning.

A gasp escaped her lips as she saw the open sheet of paper. There were no words written on it. Instead, Nat was viewing something far worse. A crude ink drawing of a woman's face. Only, where the eyes should have been, there were empty sockets colored in with red ink. A half-dozen red lines had been slashed across the nose. And the mouth—the mouth was yawning open. And the tongue—what was left of it—was indicated by a very jagged red line.

"It looks like something a demented child might draw," Nat said once she'd gotten over the initial shock and horror of it.

Leo looked over at her. "You okay?"

"Fine," she lied, glad she was wearing a long-sleeved blouse so Leo wouldn't spot the goose bumps decorating her arms.

Leo eyeballed her. "Will it do any good for me to tell you to back off?"

"Come on," Nat said. "Let's go check on Lynn."

Leo grabbed her by the shoulders. "At least be careful, Natalie. Don't go off on your own, half-cocked. Can you promise me that much?"

"I promise."

Leo didn't look convinced. Smart man.

. . .

Lynn's status remained critical and she was still unconscious, but the surgeon felt it was a good sign that there had been no further deterioration since the second surgery. Leo took off, anxious to get Nat's missive to the lab for analysis, but the truth was neither of them was holding out much hope that they'd get a lead from it. Nat was about to head off as well when she spotted a familiar face over at the ICU nurse's station. She walked over.

"Hi. Do you remember me?"

The pretty young Asian nurse looked up from a medical report she was reading and gave Nat a distracted look. But within seconds recognition dawned.

"Superintendent Price."

The last time Nat had seen Carrie Li was over a year ago when the nurse was working in the emergency room. She'd had the misfortune to be the nurse who'd tended to Dean Thomas Walsh after he'd slashed his wrists at Horizon House. Carrie had walked into his cubicle to administer a hypodermic injection for pain and ended up being grabbed by the inmate and taken as his hostage. It was only after Nat had managed to convince Walsh she was a much better hostage than the terrified young nurse, that he had made the exchange.

Nat could see from Carrie Li's expression that her sense of gratitude remained as fresh now as it had been on that fateful day.

After a brief bit of chitchat, Nat asked the nurse if she was due for a coffee break anytime soon. Carrie checked the large clock on the wall behind the station.

"I can meet you down in the cafeteria in fifteen minutes."

. . .

Carrie cupped her slender hands around her mug of tea. "I took a call at a little past eight this morning. At first he wouldn't identify himself. When I told him we could only give a status report on the patient to immediate family, he said he was the patient's father." Carrie looked across at her. "That's how he put it. 'The patient's father.' Not 'Lynn,' not 'my daughter.' 'The patient.'"

Nat wasn't surprised at Peter Everett's choice of words, but she was surprised he'd called. Of course, she had no way of knowing if it was actually him. Although, again, his choice of words tended to lend credibility. Nat wondered if Leo had already been in contact with Lynn's father.

"I don't think he's ever adjusted to having a transsexual child," Nat commented. *Talk about an understatement.*

"I don't imagine it would be an easy thing to accept."

"No," Nat agreed. "Not easy." She paused for a moment and then asked, "How did he sound on the phone?"

Carrie took a small sip of her tea. "Uncomfortable, first and foremost. But I sensed concern."

"And when you told him she was still listed as critical?"

"He muttered a formal 'thank you' and abruptly hung up."

"Have there been any other calls?"

Carrie seemed suddenly distracted, her gaze drifting away from Nat.

"What is it?" Nat asked.

"There was this woman over at one of the tables near the door . . . she looked familiar."

Even as Nat turned to see who it was, Carrie said, "She left. I could sense her watching us. As soon as I caught her eye, she popped up and took off."

Nat spotted a cup of coffee and an untouched muffin at an

empty table. "What did she look like?" she asked.

"Tall, thin, blonde hair down to her shoulders, very pretty. Maybe late twenties, or at least she looked it from here. Definitely patrician."

Nat scowled. The first woman who came to mind was Jennifer Slater. But Slater was closer to fifty than thirty. Still, a good face-lift . . . Nat wished she'd caught a glimpse of her. "If you spot her again—"

"I'll let you know," Carrie said. "And I'll try to find out who she is. I know I've seen her somewhere before. Maybe it'll come to me." She shrugged. "Anyway, as to phone calls, I haven't personally taken any others besides Lynn's dad, but I did check the Ingram call-in sheet before I came down." Carrie pulled out a slip of paper from the hip pocket of her crisp white uniform. "Last night at eleven fifty-two, Dr. Harrison Bell called. He called again at a little past seven A.M. Dr. Ross Varda called at eight this morning. Lynn's mother called right after the psychiatrist. Oh, and a priest called at nine-twenty A.M. . . . a Father Joe. There were also two unidentified calls noted—one at ten-fifty last night, another at shortly past nine A.M."

She looked up from the paper. "I was at the nurse's station when that last call came in. Janice Bailey, the head nurse on duty, took it. Janice said it was a woman caller but she wouldn't identify herself. When Janice told her she couldn't give out any information, the woman hung up. She must have been angry, because Janice said she slammed the phone down hard."

Nat's eyes strayed to the empty table where a cafeteria worker was gathering up the muffin and coffee. "How about any visitors?"

"None so far. But it's early. And only family are being allowed in."

. . .

Nat was walking up the concrete walk to Horizon House later that morning when someone came up behind her and put a hand on her shoulder.

She nearly jumped out of her skin. Then she spun around, stepped back, and shot her fists up, all in defensive mode.

The young man—tall, husky, dark-haired, handsome enough to be a movie actor—looked almost as alarmed as she must have looked.

"Superintendent Price? I'm Bill Walker of WBBS's evening news. I'm terribly sorry if I—"

Nat dropped her arms to her side, but she was feeling no less defensive. The media. Why were they always around when things were going to shit—they were swarming all over her during the Walsh incident—but never when there was good news to share? For months Nat had been trying to get people from the media to run a story on Horizon House that focused on its positive goals and achievements. Every other day, it seemed, stories were popping up on the front pages about prison riots, rape behind the walls, the escalating recidivism rate, the need for stricter sentencing, a call for more high-security prisons. Nat wanted people out in the community to read about programs that focused on rehabilitation, programs that gave inmates concrete skills as well as counseling so they could return to the community as law-abiding, tax-contributing citizens. The problem was there weren't enough programs inside the walls, and fewer outside them, that emphasized rehabilitation. Those kinds of programs took money and support, both of which were sorely lacking.

But good news didn't seem to be much of a draw for the

media. It didn't sell papers or make for high television and radio ratings.

"I'd like to talk to you about Lynn Ingram, Superintendent."

"I'm not giving out any statements, Mr. Walker." Nat abruptly turned away from him and continued walking up the path.

"I'm the reporter who interviewed Jennifer Slater yesterday. Matthew Slater's widow."

She stopped and turned back around.

He smiled faintly. "And I've got an interview with Mrs. Slater's brother, Rodney Bartlett, that's going to air at eleven this morning. I brought the tape along if you want a sneak preview."

"Come inside."

"... *that Matt told Jen there was this freak who was stalking him—*"

"*Is that the actual word Matthew Slater used, Mr. Bartlett?*"

"*Stalking? Absolutely.*"

"*No. I meant—'freak.' *"

There was a brief hesitation. Nat glanced over at the reporter, who had just gone up a notch in her estimation of him as an interviewer.

"*What else would he call . . . her? 'Him'? 'It'?*"

"*But I thought Matthew Slater didn't know Lynn Ingram was a transsexual.*"

"*Because that's what she said at her trial? Matt knew, all right. And that's why he stopped going to that pain clinic. Once he found out, he wanted absolutely nothing more to do with the freak.*"

"But before your brother-in-law found out, he did see her outside of the pain clinic."

"Matt and my sister had a very solid marriage, Mr. Walker. It was built on devotion and trust."

"You didn't answer my question, Mr. Bartlett."

"If they were seen together, I can assure you it was completely innocent."

Walker paused the tape. "If you recall, at Ingram's trial, several witnesses gave testimony about seeing Ingram and Slater together in public places—a romantic restaurant on Charles Street, a bar near the clinic, and the Slater maid gave a statement about Ingram coming to his home on several occasions for 'pain treatments.' "

Having recently gone over the trial notes, Nat remembered the maid's statement in particular—the most meaningful part of which was that Jennifer Slater was never at home during these "professional" home visits.

Walker resumed the tape.

"Your sister believes Lynn Ingram got what was coming to her. I'm speaking about the recent attack, not her manslaughter conviction."

A harsh laugh. *"Manslaugher. I guarantee you, if Ingram was your typical grotesque-looking transsexual, he'd have got what he deserved. He should have been charged with and sentenced for first-degree murder. My sister got no justice. She was destroyed by this monstrosity."*

"Destroyed?"

"Do you have any idea of the humiliation she suffered? Friends—let's say people she thought were friends—dropped her like she had leprosy. Just when she needed all the support and comfort she could get. Jen was abandoned. Even members of our own family avoided her."

"But you stood by her through thick and thin."

"You're damn straight I did. If I hadn't, she probably wouldn't be here today."

"Are you saying she might have killed herself?"

There was a longer pause. Nat was listening intently.

"I don't want to betray my sister's trust."

Walker hit the OFF button. "That's pretty much it. He danced around all the rest of my questions. But I did some digging. Actually, I haven't been to bed yet." He stretched languidly.

"And what have you found out?"

Walker tapped his fingers on the top of the mini–tape recorder. "Now we're at the moment of truth, Superintendent." He slowly lifted his eyes to her face.

"The cops can track down whatever you've unearthed, Mr. Walker."

"Yes, they can. I guess it depends on how patient you are, Superintendent."

Nat felt disquietingly transparent—the reporter had so easily spotted that patience was not one of her virtues.

"All right, I'll make a brief statement," she conceded, knowing that Leo was going to have her head for agreeing to this. He was rightfully big on keeping the media at bay during an investigation. The waters got muddied enough without leaks, misinformation, and biased slants.

"That'll be fine. For now," Walker added pointedly.

Nat let it slide, figuring she'd deal with later, later.

Walker popped in a new cassette tape and hit RECORD.

Nat not only made her statement about Lynn Ingram, model inmate, she also tried to make the most of it by publicizing the many benefits of prerelease programs such as Horizon House. When she went into overdrive about the need for funding, et cetera, Walker stopped the tape.

"I think we can skip the sermon."

She arched an eyebrow. "For now, anyway."

This garnered a smile from the reporter.

"So what did you dig up, Mr. Walker?"

"Bill. Every time you say Mr. Walker, I feel like my father. And believe me, I'd just as soon not feel like him."

"Okay, Bill. So what did you dig up?"

"Jennifer Slater spent three weeks in a private hospital–cum–sanatorium in March of ninety-eight. That was less than a month after the trial."

"And it didn't hit the papers?"

"She entered under an assumed name. And the place is pricey and private with a capital *P*. Fortunately, I have a few friends in powerful positions who I can lean on."

"So, she was in this sanatorium. And?"

"She swallowed a bottle of sleeping pills. According to my sources it was more than merely a cry for help. She was trying to kill herself. And not for the first time."

"She attempted suicide before her husband's murder?"

"Around four years ago, Slater's devoted hubby had a brief fling with one of the associates in his office. A pretty young tax lawyer by the name of Amanda Bergman. A couple of months into it, Amanda walked into Slater's office and handed in her resignation. She was not only leaving the firm, she was leaving the city. Pronto. A friend of Amanda's claims Amanda had been getting anonymous threatening calls. Then her tires got slashed. The final straw was when her apartment was broken into and ransacked."

Nat felt a chill streak down her spine.

"Amanda freaked and took off for the West Coast."

"And this friend thinks Jennifer Slater was behind all this?"

"This friend witnessed a very emotionally charged scene be-tween Jennifer and Matthew the day before Amanda handed in her resignation. Which was also the afternoon before the break-in. Amanda's name was bandied about during this heated scene."

"When was the suicide attempt?"

"Ten days later. As I understand it, Matthew Slater was in a bad way after Amanda fled the coop, and he started spending his nights at a hotel near his office. Until, according to one of my confidential sources, the missus swallowed several dozen Valium. If you check out the incident in the papers, what you'll read is that Jennifer Slater was admitted to Boston General for food poi-soning and was released two days later. That was also the day Hubby returned home."

"Sounds like Mrs. Slater suffered from some serious emo-tional problems." The question was, was she suffering still? Had she gotten worse?

And had she been hanging around Boston General that morn-ing?

eleven

Before I was put in protective custody there was a young woman two rooms down. She committed suicide. Cut her wrists with a knife she stole from the dining hall. Rumor was, she'd filed a complaint about sexual harassment a few weeks before that.

L. I.

"SICK?"

"My period," Suzanne muttered. "Bad cramps."

Suzanne Holden was lying under a blanket on her twin-size bed in the two-bed room she had been sharing with Lynn. Nat couldn't help but feel an ache in her chest as she glanced over at Lynn's crisply made-up bed. On the wall over her bed was a framed Picasso print, an abstract of a woman.

By contrast, Suzanne had a wide array of children's drawings Scotch-taped on her wall. They were all by the same young artist, Jacob Coscarelli. Seeing these drawings garnered an altogether different but equally distressing ache.

Nat tried to push her pain aside and concentrate on Suzanne's, although she was far from convinced the inmate's pain was legitimate.

"You've never needed to take time off from work before because of your period, Suzanne. Are you sure there isn't something else bothering you?"

Nat saw a flash of anger shadow Suzanne's face, but it disappeared quickly. "I have cramps," she answered flatly. "Do you give all your inmates the third degree if they get sick?"

"I'm not giving you the third degree, Suzanne. I'm trying to . . ." Nat stopped. She wanted Suzanne to talk about Lynn's journal. She wanted the inmate to confide in her. But why should she? Not only was Nat the "authority," she was Suzanne's son's father's lover. Nat was probably the last person she'd open up to.

Suzanne was not waiting for Nat to finish her sentence. She had closed her eyes, and Nat knew she was hoping she would leave without another word. A strong part of Nat wanted to do just that. She was unnerved in there, surrounded by all of Jakey's drawings. Oh, she had many of his drawings as well, plastered all over her refrigerator, held up by little magnets. But it wasn't the same. They were not *her* child's drawings. *Stop,* Nat told herself. *Stick to the reason you came up here.*

"Did Lynn ever talk to you about what she was writing in her journal, Suzanne?"

Suzanne's eyes stayed resolutely closed, but Nat could see her body stiffen under the thin cover.

"No," she mumbled. Only after she uttered the response did she realize Nat had tricked her. Her eyes sprang open, and Nat could see fear there. "I don't know anything about a journal," the inmate said, too late.

Nat wasn't listening. She was busy thinking about what else Suzanne knew. And what it would take to get her to share it. Fear was a great silencer. There was no question that Suzanne Holden was very frightened.

It was close to noon when Leo phoned Nat.

"Nothing on the envelope. It's one of those self-stick kinds. The ink used in the drawing is being analyzed. We're not holding out much hope. Most likely one of those dollar-a-dozen pens you can get in a million stores. We're also getting one of our shrinks to look at the drawing. See if he can come up with some kind of profile. It's a long shot, but we can't leave any stone unturned. What's happening at your end?"

Nat filled Leo in on her meeting with Bill Walker, summarizing the tape he'd played for her. Leo listened intently, saying little.

"I'd certainly like to know where both Jennifer Slater and her brother Rodney were when Lynn was attacked," Nat said.

"Yeah," Leo grunted.

Nat knew Leo well enough to know he wasn't discounting what she'd been saying, but she also knew something else was on his mind. And it was troubling him. He didn't keep her guessing very long.

"When were you going to tell me about Suzanne?"

"How did you know she . . . ?" But Nat knew the answer before she finished the question. "You went over to the boutique to see her."

She could hear Leo's weighty sigh. "It wasn't a social call, Natalie."

"I didn't say it was. She says she's got cramps, but I suppose her boss already told you that." Now Nat was the one feeling disgruntled. "What was this, Leo? A test? You already knew she was here. And, as a matter of fact, I was about to tell you. I just thought my information about Slater and her brother took precedence." Her tone was deliberately cool.

"Have you talked to her?"

"Briefly," Nat said. She felt suddenly very adolescent, ashamed of herself. "Leo, Suzanne knows Lynn kept a journal." The coolness was gone from her voice.

"I'll talk to her," he said.

"When?"

"Probably not until late this afternoon. I want to drop by Rodney Bartlett's office and have a little chat with him, then I'm heading out to Westfield to have a chat with Lynn's father."

"Mind if I tag along?"

There was a brief pause. "I'll pick you up in fifteen minutes."

"You were planning to question Rodney Bartlett before I told you about that tape, weren't you?"

Leo smiled at Nat. "He's been on my list from day one. That tape only puts him up a few notches."

"What about his sister? Did you hear what she told Bill Walker the other day?"

Leo nodded. "Jennifer Slater's got an alibi for yesterday. She was at home in Martha's Vineyard. She's got a housekeeper, a gardener, and her stockbroker to back her up."

"Stockbroker?"

"Gerald Gleason of B. F. Martin was having lunch with her that day. Arrived on the noon ferry. Didn't leave the Vineyard until four o'clock."

They pulled up in front of a beautifully maintained nineteenth-century three-story brownstone on Marlborough Street in Boston's posh Back Bay district. Most of the buildings on the street were of similar design and upkeep, the majority of them private residences. There were, however, a smattering of offices discreetly tucked in.

As they approached the intricately carved front door of number 1604, Nat saw a discreet brass placard to the right that read, BARTLETT FOUNDATION. Leo tried the door. It was locked. He pressed a buzzer on the left.

"What do you know about this foundation?" Nat asked, certain Leo had already done his homework.

"Lots of bucks that get spread around mostly to arts and health-care groups. The original dough was made by Lionel Bartlett, Rodney and Jennifer's great-grandfather. Oil and steel. Subsequent generations invested wisely. Rodney seems to be keeping up the family standards. He—"

Leo stopped abruptly as the door opened. Nat was expecting to see a secretary or maybe a security officer. Instead, she immediately recognized Rodney Bartlett himself. He hadn't changed much in the three years since she'd seen him on television during Lynn's trial. If anything, he was a bit thinner. And there were a few threads of gray in his dark hair that he wore combed straight back from his aquiline face. He was dressed in a navy-blue suit that could never have fit so perfectly if it hadn't been custom-made for him. But, what the hell, he could afford it.

Rodney eyed Nat and Leo like he recognized them as well. Which Nat found both surprising and a bit jarring.

"Won't you come in?" He spoke with an impeccable Boston Brahmin accent. You'd almost think you were listening to JFK.

Rodney stepped aside and they entered a large, sunlit room

fitted with beautiful antique Victorian pieces and an exquisite Oriental rug. The room would have been taken for an elegant front parlor save for the prim middle-aged secretary sitting behind a large cherrywood desk in the far corner of the room, busily working at her computer. She didn't so much as glance their way as they entered.

"If you'll follow me to my office." Rodney was already leading the way down a wide hallway lined with lithographs. Nat recognized a Miró, a Picasso, and a Chagall. She doubted they were prints. No wonder Rodney kept his front door locked.

Rodney Bartlett's office was surprisingly spare. No signed lithographs on the walls in here. No pricey Oriental rug on the parquet wood floor. No antiques. No drapery on the window, just practical mini blinds pulled halfway up the window. A window that didn't offer much in the way of sunlight, as it faced onto a narrow alleyway across from which was another brownstone building.

Rodney settled himself in a swivel chair behind a simple oak desk, and Nat and Leo took the only other two seats in the office, metal chairs upholstered in a sturdy gray tweed fabric that you'd find in any office supply store in town. Doubtful that Rodney entertained any of his high-roller friends or colleagues in here.

"I suppose you've come to ask me about Lynn Ingram." Rodney folded his hands on the desk. Nat noticed that his nails were expertly manicured.

"You know who we are, then," Leo said.

He smiled faintly. "I'm a subscriber to both of the Boston papers. I've seen your pictures on the front page more than once."

"Your picture's been in the paper more than once as well," Nat said.

Rodney's smile deepened, revealing perfect, shiny white teeth. He was not an unattractive man, although his features were too sharp-edged and austere for her taste. "Yes, but usually in the 'Style' section."

"You made it to the front page a few years ago," Leo said in that intentionally offhanded way of his that anyone with a modicum of intelligence knew was deliberate. Bartlett was more than reasonably intelligent.

His smile vanished in a flash. "I can save you a lot of time and bother, Detective. I was at a funeral service yesterday." He picked up a pen and scribbled something on a piece of white linen embossed Foundation stationery. He rose, walked briskly around the desk, and handed it to Leo. "This is the address of the funeral home and the name of the funeral director."

"Whose funeral?" Leo asked.

"The father of a friend of mine. Joseph Ferris. His son Jeff and I were roommates at Brown. Now, if you don't mind, I have a very busy day ahead of me." He was walking to the door and had it open for them before he finished his sentence.

On their way out, Nat paused and looked up at Rodney. "By the way, how's your sister feeling?"

He smiled again, but this time it was a smile tinged with malice. "She'd be feeling a lot better if that freak had kicked the bucket." Gone was Rodney Bartlett's Brahmin accent.

It was close to two P.M. when they hit the turnpike and headed out for Westfield. Nat asked Leo why they were meeting Lynn's father at home rather than at work.

"Let's say he wasn't too thrilled about talking with me at all," Leo said. "He was extremely upset at the thought of a detective showing up at his office. Afraid I'd blow his cover, I suppose." Leo smiled.

"Have you heard from Dr. Varda?" Nat asked.

"No." Leo shot her a quick glance. "Should I have?"

She shrugged. "Did your boys pick up any leads as to who broke into his apartment?"

"No."

"I certainly wouldn't put it past our friend Rodney." She was also thinking about that vile drawing left for her. "We should have asked him where he was—"

"We're not finished with Rodney Bartlett by a long shot. But sometimes it's wise not to show your whole hand all at once. Better to leave a suspect stewing for a while."

"So Rodney is still a suspect? Even if his alibi proves to be airtight?"

"Even alibis that seem to be airtight might have microscopic puncture holes in them. You just have to look real close."

Oates was already on the job. Before they got onto the turnpike, Leo had gotten his partner on his cell phone, passing on the name of the funeral director. Oates was going to have a talk with him before the day was out.

Leo sighed. "My problem in this case isn't not having any suspects. It's having too many of them. As much as I like Lynn Ingram, she's acquired quite a few enemies over the years."

"Speaking of which, what about Bethany Graham?"

Leo scowled. "The ex-wife? What makes you think she's one of Lynn's enemies?"

"I'm not sure she is. But then again, I'm not sure she isn't," Nat said, remembering the woman in the hospital cafeteria who'd taken off in such a hurry. "We don't know how she feels toward the person who was once her ex-husband and is now her ex-wife.

She might not want to risk that information coming to light. You know, old skeletons in the closet."

Leo smiled.

"What's so amusing?" she asked, knowing she sounded a bit defensive.

"You're very smart, Natalie."

"But sometimes too smart for my own good?"

"Maybe not this time."

"Meaning?"

"You know a Boston politician by the name of Daniel Milburne?"

"The rabid pro–capital punishment councilman with the very deep pockets? What's he got to do with Bethany Graham?"

"Only that she might be married to him."

"What? Oh my god, Leo. Talk about not wanting to unearth old skeletons. A creep like Milburne would go to just about any length—"

"Hold on. It's not a sure thing. All we know so far is that the wife's name is Beth. And that according to the marriage certificate her maiden name was Colman."

"Beth Colman," she repeated. "And what makes you think she's really Bethany Graham?"

"On the Ingram-Graham marriage certificate, she was listed as Beth Graham Colman."

Nat's mind shot into overdrive. If Beth Milburne and Bethany Graham were indeed one and the same, then the question was, Did Milburne know his wife was once married to a transsexual? A transsexual who was now also a convicted felon? Nat could just see the headlines if that information ever surfaced. Milburne would be a laughingstock—and he could kiss his promising career good-bye. It was promising, despite her personal opinion of the man's politics. Unfortunately, he had a lot of supporters in the city. And there was talk of him running for mayor in the next election. If word got out about his wife's ex-husband, Milburne might have to kiss the election good-bye.

"What else do you know about Beth Graham Colman? Where does she come from? Where'd she go to school? Where'd she go after the breakup?"

"We're checking into all those things."

She scowled. "With Milburne's dough, he could buy his wife a tidy little past."

"Or we could be talking coincidence here, Natalie. She may be exactly who she claims to be and have no connection whatsoever to the Bethany Graham who was briefly married to Larry Ingram."

"Yeah, I know. But if they are one and the same, you can bet Milburne wouldn't want it coming to light. My guess is he'd go pretty far to keep it quiet."

Leo heaved a sigh. "Just what we need. Another suspect."

"And we can't discount the possibility that whoever raped or tried to rape Lynn when she was at Grafton wanted to finish her off before she got up the courage to rat the rapist out," Nat reflected. "Have you gotten any leads in that arena?"

Leo shook his head. "I spoke to one of the priests on the phone who holds services at CCI Grafton. He said Lynn wasn't a practicing Catholic but that she had met with him and one of the other priests who volunteered at the prison a few times. He implied that it was more a matter of getting out of her cell than really wanting pastoral counseling."

"Did she go to confession?" Nat asked.

"Not that he said. Of course, if she did confess anything to a priest, he wouldn't be able to repeat it."

"Yeah, I know."

"I also spoke to the super, but she's new and wants nothing more than to deflect police focus away from her institution. But I did check Lynn's visitation record and turns out Harrison Bell visited Lynn frequently while she was there. And they wrote each other."

"I know. Jack already told me. And Bell was real eager to have Lynn back at the clinic," Nat added. "Jack thinks that Bell should top our suspect list. He's convinced Bell had the hots for Lynn. Maybe she rejected him and he flipped. Or maybe he rejected her, then panicked that she'd blackmail him or go tell his wife. Who knows?"

Leo shrugged. "It's possible. Anything's possible. Like I said, that's the problem. The suspect list keeps growing."

"I could certainly see Daniel Milburne as prime suspect," Nat said. "He's such an egotistical cutthroat bastard. I wouldn't put it past him to do anything he felt necessary to clear his path to becoming mayor. And I'm sure his political aspirations go much higher than that."

"Look, I'm certainly not a fan of Milburne's politics. But even if we are on the right track here about his wife, it doesn't mean Milburne even knows. I doubt her brief marriage to Larry–aka–Lynn Ingram is something Bethany would want to broadcast."

"Broadcasting and telling your husband aren't the same thing. And if Milburne does know, like I said, he's the kind of sleaze who'd resort to any means—"

"It would be a damn risky move for someone as easily identifiable as the councilman to attack a woman in broad daylight—"

"It was raining. It was a deserted alleyway. Besides, he wouldn't have to even do it himself. He could have hired a hit man. He's rich enough, well connected, and ruthless enough—"

"For that matter, so is Rodney Bartlett."

"True," she conceded. "But I still think—"

Leo was shaking his head. "The hit-man theory doesn't sit well with me. The attack was too violent. Not a hit man's m.o. Hit men like to be tidy and quick. A shot to the head. A knife to the jugular. Leave the body and scram. That's not what we have here. I see the violent and deliberately gruesome attack on Lynn as a hate crime."

"Or a love crime," she said.

There were a number of upscale developments in the exclusive town of Westfield, many of them given elegant names like Mystic Crossing, Hickory Hills, or, in the case of Lynn Ingram's parents, Laurel Lanes.

The homes in this development sat on three-acre wooded lots. Because it was the start of fall foliage season, some of the trees had already begun to turn. Touches of gold, red, amber, and burnt-umber leaves gave the properties an even more lush appearance. Though this development of large, colonial-style homes was far from the most exclusive in the town, it certainly would be considered a very good address for a successful, professional family.

Nat glanced over at Leo as he wound his way slowly through the development looking for number 18. "These spreads have to be half a million and up," Nat commented. "I could see the CEO of a computer software company living here. But an employee?"

"Maybe there's some family money."

"Maybe."

It was close to one P.M. when Leo pulled into the driveway beside a silver BMW parked in front of one of the bays of a three-car garage. The Everett-aka-Ingram home was an oversized reproduction Federal colonial, white clapboards trimmed with moss-green and a barn-red front door. The grounds, while not extravagant, were perfectly manicured. A large maple tree sat in the center of the lawn.

Nat felt a flash of unease as she got out of Leo's car. She realized she was already inclined toward disliking Lynn's father. Maybe *dislike* was putting it too mildly. She tried to tell herself to keep an open mind as they headed up the blue stone walk. She wondered if Leo was telling himself the same thing. Had he, too, already passed judgement on Peter Everett?

A middle-aged man opened the front door just as they were approaching it. He was tall, lean, with thinning gray hair that was cut close to his scalp. He was wearing black-rimmed glasses, but removed them and tucked them into the breast pocket of his overly starched white shirt, which already held a black plastic pencil case and several writing implements. He stuck his hands into the pockets of his chino slacks. He was dressed like your typical enigeer. Unless some rich relative had died and left him a bundle, it was a real stretch to believe Peter Ingram could have afforded this spread on his salary.

One thing Nat noticed immediately about Ingram was that, unlike his wife, he didn't bear any physical resemblance to Lynn. She imagined that was one consolation for him. Okay, so she was having trouble keeping an open mind.

"Mr. Everett?" Leo inquired, his voice showing no sign of any kind of judgement at all. Nat, however, felt an instant flurry of irritation that Leo addressed Ingram by his alias.

Lynn's father made no response, merely opened the door wider. Before Nat and Leo stepped over the threshold, Leo identified the two of them. If Peter Ingram was puzzled or annoyed that Nat was there, he gave no sign of it. He was pretty much giving no sign of anything.

They entered a broad hallway with a black granite floor, walls painted a pale green, and a wide, curved staircase fitted with an Oriental runner. To their left was a graciously proportioned dining room which, while meticulously decorated in reproduction period furnishings, had an unused look. To their right, through a broad archway, was the living room. Federal-style sofas faced each other on either side of a large brick fireplace. Two Chesterfield chairs upholstered in a dark green damask faced the hearth. Again, everything looked perfect but unlived-in. A showplace.

Nat tended to pick up vibes very quickly when she entered someone's home. For all the money and taste lavished on the Everett home, the vibes here were chilly. She doubted much laughter was heard in this house. She doubted much of anything was heard.

"Is your wife in?" Leo asked as the three of them remained standing in the foyer. Peter Ingram made no move to invite them into either the dining room or living room.

Ingram shook his head, stood there for several more moments, then abruptly turned and walked into the living room. He headed straight for one of the Chesterfield chairs. Leo and Nat sat down on the sofa to Ingram's right. Despite the large windows at either end of the room, there was a gloominess to the space, mostly due to the heavy drapery. But Nat also felt the gloom was enhanced by the lack of emotional warmth that was so apparent. She glanced at the beautifully carved oak mantel. There were no family photos, only a pair of brass candlesticks, evenly spaced on opposite ends, the candles in them never having been lit.

Peter Ingram sat erect, his hands folded on his lap. He was waiting.

Nat found herself increasingly irritated by Ingram's silent treatment. Her first instinct was to read it as hostility, but then she tried to open her mind to the possibility that he was frightened, upset, and possibly even grief-stricken. After all, his daughter was, at this very moment, fighting for her life in a hospital in Boston.

His *daughter*. How easy for Nat to think of Lynn that way. Lynn wasn't her flesh and blood. Lynn hadn't started out life as Nat's *son*.

"You have a lovely home," Nat said lightly. "Did your wife do the decorating herself?"

"She had some help."

"I'd love to know the name of her decorator."

"I have no idea." Ingram put his glasses back on—more, it seemed to Nat, to give him something to do than anything else.

"My sister looked out in Westfield a few years ago," Nat continued. "She toured a house in this development, but it was a bit too pricey even though her husband does very well in banking." Leo glanced at her, knowing she was lying through her teeth.

Ingram didn't know it, though, and Nat could see that her comment made him uneasy. "I . . . was fortunate . . . to come into a bit of money," he muttered.

"Oh, that was fortunate," she said.

"Look," Ingram said gruffly, "you haven't driven all the way out here to pay a social call. Can we just get to it?"

"Fine," Leo responded pleasantly, pulling out a pad and flipping it open, then removing a ballpoint pen. "Would you tell me your whereabouts yesterday?"

If Ingram was taken aback by just how quickly Leo got to the point, he gave no indication. Indeed, he met Leo's gaze head-on and responded without even a moment's hesitation. "I was at work until five. I got home at five forty-five, and that's where I was until I got up for work this morning at seven A.M. You could ask me about any weekday and I'd have the same answer. I lead a very uneventful life." Ingram's voice was tight, mechanical, unmodulated.

"I believe your work requires doing some on-site computer troubleshooting. Did you visit any sites yesterday?" Leo was glancing down at a page in his notebook. Nat wasn't sure whether it contained some information about an on-site visit or whether it was a bluff. If it was a bluff, she could see from the way the muscles in Ingram's jaw tightened that he was succeeding.

Ingram lost his rigid control. "Yes, Thursdays I occasionally do on-site . . ." His prominent Adam's apple bobbed as he swallowed hard. "I did make a brief visit to Dekko Computers. It's in Wayland."

"What time was that?" Leo asked.

"I got there before one and left after two."

"How much before one P.M.?"

A thin bead of sweat broke out across Ingram's broad forehead. He clenched his hands together. "I don't know exactly. Twelve-forty, twelve forty-five. Look, I never wanted anything bad to happen to . . . him. I don't suppose you can understand what it's like. Losing a child. We were close, Larry and I. I mean . . . when he was little. You probably think we weren't

because of . . . but we were. I used to take him fishing and camp-
ing. Just the two of us. Did his mother tell you that?"

Nat gave Leo a quick look. Ingram noticed. "Yes, Ruth told
me she went to the hospital. She thought I'd go ballistic." He
sounded suddenly sad, drained. "I'm not a monster. He's our
child. Ruth is his mother. I wasn't mad she went to the hospital.
I understand my wife a hell of a lot better than she understands
me."

"She understands that you disowned your child," Nat
snapped, ignoring Leo's peeved look in her direction for piping
up. But she couldn't help it. Her blood was starting to boil listening to this man talk as if he was the good guy here.

"I gave my son a choice," he answered stiffly.

"A choice? To live a lie in order to be accepted by her father,
versus—"

"Do you have any children, Superintendent?"

"The point is, *you* have one," she shot back. "And you cast
him out of your life without so much—"

Ingram popped out of his chair, again cutting her off. "I was
not going to let him humiliate us. I should have thrown him out
the first time I—" He stopped abruptly. "What does it matter
now?"

"You mean right after Larry graduated high school?" She was
not about to let him off the hook.

Ingram flushed. "Larry told you?"

She didn't respond. Neither did Leo.

Ingram sat back down, clasped his hands together. "He
thought we were gone for the weekend. But Ruthie and I had an
argument. We were at her mother's. Her mother always took her
daughter's side. Never did like me. I stormed out. Drove home."

Ingram unclasped his hands, putting them up to his face.

"Larry was . . . in our bed. With . . . a man. They were . . . I think . . . I could have . . . gotten past that part . . . Not right away, but . . . I mean you think having a kid who's . . . gay is probably as bad as it can get, but—"

"Worse than leukemia? a brain tumor? muscular—?"

Leo glared at Nat for breaking in again.

Ingram was glaring, too. "Larry leaped out of bed when he saw me. He was wearing a wig and makeup. And he was . . . he was dressed in a pair of his mother's bra and panties. *His mother's.*"

He stared starkly at them. "You don't have the faintest idea what that did to me. I thanked God Ruthie wasn't with me that night. I never told her. I . . . never—" He shook his head, the glare replaced by agony.

"What did you do?" Leo asked quietly.

Ingram's eyes filled with tears. "I . . . ran. I ran out of the house. I got to the street and . . . I threw up. I threw my guts up. And then I got in my car and drove. I don't know where I went or, even worse, how I got there. I think a part of me wanted to drive right into a tree. Anything . . . Anything to eradicate that . . . sight. It was obscene."

"But your wife said you made up?"

"Larry promised—never again."

"He even got married," Nat said.

Ingram stiffened. "That didn't last long."

"What became of Bethany?" Nat asked.

Ingram was staring down at the floor again. "I heard she died several years ago."

Nat and Leo shared a look. "Who told you?" Leo asked.

"I don't remember now. Maybe I read it in the paper."

"Your wife never mentioned that Bethany was dead," Nat said.

"I don't remember if I even told my wife. It didn't seem to have any bearing on us."

"Did your son know?"

"Yes. I believe so."

"You believe so?"

"I did think Larry should know. Okay? So I asked my priest to write to him at . . . at the prison."

"So she died during the time of Lynn's incarceration," Nat commented, deliberately referring to his child by her name.

Ingram merely nodded.

"How?" she asked.

"Car accident," Ingram muttered, still looking down.

"Where did it happen?"

"Somewhere in France. I don't know the details."

"And you read about it in a local paper?"

"No. I remember now. It wasn't in the paper. Someone . . . a friend of Larry's from Harvard . . . I bumped into him a few years ago. And . . . he'd known Bethany and he happened to mention it in passing."

"What was this friend's name?" Leo asked.

"I don't remember. And I don't understand why all this interest in Larry's ex-wife," Ingram snapped. "Their whole marriage was a sham. It lasted all of a couple of months. And that was ten years ago."

"Routine," Leo said offhandedly. "What did she look like? Bethany? Describe her for us," he went on, pen poised, maintaining a perfectly calm demeanor.

Ingram's demeanor was anything but calm. "Describe her? For God's sake, why? She's dead. What could it matter—"

"Tall? Short? Blonde? Brunette? Thin—?"

"Average. Just . . . average. Brown hair, I think. Not heavy. Not thin. There was nothing . . . distinctive about her."

Nat was certain Ingram was lying through his teeth about Bethany. Which also made her even more certain that Lynn's ex-wife was very likely the current wife of Daniel Milburne.

"Perhaps your wife will be able to be more specific," Nat said.

"Leave my wife alone. She's nearly at the point of collapse as it is. If you continue to pursue us, I'll press charges of police harassment," Ingram warned.

"You're free to do that, Mr. Ingram," Leo said blandly. And Nat wanted to hug him on the spot for not referring to Lynn's father as "Mr. Everett." "But there's been a serious murder attempt on your daughter—"

Again Ingram flinched. Again Nat wanted to hug Leo.

"And I intend to pursue this investigation until I track down the bastard who did it."

Ingram retreated from his threatening stance. "Please. Please," he repeated. Now there was a note of pleading in his voice. "I don't know if this is something either of you can understand, but I find it extremely painful having these old wounds reopened. It's taken me a long time to . . . heal."

"It's going to take Lynn an even longer time," Nat said. "And I'm not just talking about the horrendous physical wounds."

twelve

I didn't only lie to her, I lied to myself. I honestly thought we could make our marriage work. Talk about self-deception. I hope she will some day find it in her heart to forgive me.

L. I.

"YOU THINK HE was telling the truth?" Nat asked Leo as they headed back to Boston.

"About where he was yesterday?" Leo shrugged. "We need to nail down the time he got to Dekko. But even if he got there at twelve-forty, it leaves open a small window of opportunity."

"And that bit about Bethany having died? Awfully convenient. And awfully vague. Wouldn't you say?"

"Yeah," Leo agreed.

"And I'd still love to know where the Ingrams got the money to buy a home that had to cost at least half a million bucks. A sum like that would be a drop in the bucket for someone as wealthy as Milburne."

"Even if it was hush money, it's still a big jump from paying someone off to keep quiet about a marriage, to attempting a murder."

"Milburne had to be in a panic that Lynn would see a picture of Bethany in the paper or on TV. Politicians and their wives are always being photographed."

"Maybe the wife got a complete makeover. I saw a few photos of her. She's anything but average. She's a real knockout."

"But Lynn was married to her. She might still recognize her, makeover or not. Plus we only have Peter Ingram's word that Bethany was 'average.' And his word isn't exactly trustworthy. And if Lynn saw the photo and recognized Bethany, it makes sense she'd start wondering why she was informed of Bethany's demise. Maybe Lynn contacted her ex. And Beth told Milburne. And—"

Leo was scowling.

"What?"

"Don't go jumping to conclusions, Natalie. But there was a photo of Beth Milburne at a charity ball that she attended on Wednesday night. It made the Thursday morning paper."

"Tall? Blonde? Hair down to here?" Nat pointed to her shoulders. "Patrician-looking?"

Leo was nodding.

So was Nat. Now she knew why the woman in the cafeteria had looked familiar to Carrie Li. The nurse must have seen Beth Milburne's picture at the charity ball as well.

"You going to fill me in?" Leo asked knowingly.

Nat told him about the woman who'd fled the cafeteria that morning.

As they approached the city, Nat called the hospital for a status report on Lynn. It was over twenty-four hours since the attack. But there was still no change in her condition. Which meant she was still unconscious, still hanging by a thread.

"Has anyone else called or shown up at ICU?" Nat asked the head nurse, already having learned that Carrie Li was unavailable. Nat and Leo would have to wait to talk to her about Beth Milburne.

"Dr. Bell came by a short while ago. He was rather upset when I told him Ms. Ingram couldn't have any visitors. It was a bit awkward for me. Dr. Bell does have staff privileges at the hospital and, as he pointed out, he wasn't technically a *visitor*. I told him to talk to the officer posted by Ms. Ingram's door since the 'No Visitor' mandate was a police order."

"And did he?"

"No. He just left. But he wasn't looking very happy."

Nat related this information to Leo. He listened, not looking too happy himself.

"You think it's time to have a little chat with Bell?" Nat asked.

Leo glanced at the car clock. It was just after four. They were approaching one of the refurbished turnpike rest stops with a spanking new McDonald's less than ten miles from the city.

"Let's make a pit stop." He pulled off the exit. "I suppose you want to come along for the chat with Dr. Bell."

"I suppose I'd better. Otherwise, how could you be sure I wasn't off sleuthing on my own?"

. . .

There was a family photo on Bell's desk. He saw Nat eyeing it and smiled. "That was taken this summer down at the Cape. We've got a little cottage in Truro. Carol and the children used to stay all summer when the kids were little. I'd come down on weekends and for most of August. This past summer it was only Daphne, my baby."

Nat glanced at the pretty blond-haired girl swept up in Daddy's arms in the photo. She looked to be around four or five. Her chubby arms were circling her dad's neck and she was smiling brightly. The only one in the family who was smiling.

"We're lucky if we manage a couple of weekends there with the boys. Billy goes to baseball camp and Josh spends half the summer at hockey camp and the other half at basketball camp. Two regular jocks, my boys," he added proudly, a smile on his face now. "Not that Daphne's a slouch. You should see that little one kick a soccer ball. But then, with two big, athletic brothers to teach her—"

"Which boy got in trouble at school yesterday?" Nat asked.

Harrison's smile faded. "That would be the oldest. Josh." He pointed to the taller and heavier-set boy in the photo. "He's fourteen. Teenagers. Hey, they have to rebel. It's healthy. That's what I keep trying to explain to my wife."

Nat's gaze fell on the tall, athletic blonde standing in front of her husband and daughter in the photo, her arms draped affectionately around the two boys who flanked either side of her. Josh was already as tall as his mother.

Carol Bell looked healthy, vigorous, strong. She was pleasant-looking, although Nat certainly wouldn't describe her as pretty. Still, it did flash through her mind that Carrie Li might describe her that way. Was it possible she was on the wrong track believing the woman in the hospital cafeteria was Bethany? Could it have been Carol Bell?

In the photo, Harrison's wife was wearing black spandex biker shorts and a T-shirt, and Nat imagined she was either a biking enthusiast or a runner. While she looked to be trying to smile in the photo, she didn't quite manage it. Her eyes were narrowed to a squint. Maybe it was the sun. Although no one else was squinting. Whatever the reason, her expression made her look considerably older than her late twenties. But how old did she look when she wasn't squinting?

"Billy's eleven," Bell was saying. "Wants to be a pitcher for the Red Sox when he grows up. I always kid him and say he'd better hurry and get there so we can finally win a World Series." He chuckled but it sounded forced.

"Does your wife work?" Leo asked.

Bell looked surprised by the question. "Carol? God, no. She's a diehard stay-at-home mom. Her children are *not* going to be latchkey kids. She's there to watch over them every minute."

Nat picked up a slight edge in his voice.

"You think she's an overprotective mother?" she asked.

Bell appeared insulted. "Absolutely not. Carol's a wonderful mother. I think it's great that she's home with the children. Of course, the boys are old enough to manage a bit more on their own. But Daphne's another matter. She's still a baby." The smile returned. "She hates when I call her 'my baby,' but I guess she always will be my baby."

"I understand you went over to the hospital to see Lynn this morning," Leo said.

Bell looked a bit jarred by the sudden shift of topic. "And was turned away. Can I ask why?"

"Someone tried to kill Lynn Ingram yesterday," Leo said dryly. As if Bell needed reminding. "He or she didn't succeed. We don't want to give her assailant a second chance."

The doctor's mouth opened but he seemed at a loss for a response. "You can't think that I . . . You suspect me?" he finally muttered, his tone etched with disbelief. "You do realize that Lynn wouldn't be alive right now if I hadn't found her and had her rushed to the hospital."

Of course, they did realize that, if he had assaulted Lynn, why didn't he just leave her to die? Did he get cold feet? Have a change of heart?

"Were you alone when you found Lynn?" Leo asked benignly.

"Yes," he said without hesitation. But then he paused. "Well, one of the clerks at the clinic was coming back from lunch, and I did call out to her as she came into the alleyway from the other end. I shouted for her to call nine-one-one."

Nat glanced over at Leo a bit put-out that he hadn't told her about the clerk. It went a long way toward explaining Bell's rescue actions.

"How close are you and Lynn?" Leo asked.

Bell frowned. "We're colleagues. We admire each other's skills and abilities."

Nat sighed, intentionally loudly.

"And we're friends. But if you're suggesting—"

"You wrote to Lynn while she was in prison. And you visited quite often."

"Like I said. We're friends." His tone left no question as to his annoyance with her comment.

Ignoring the doctor's mounting irritation, she asked, "How did your wife feel about your friendship with Lynn?"

That question really put her on Bell's shit list. "Carol didn't think anything of it," he said tightly. But he was clearly rattled.

"She knew you were writing Lynn? Visiting her in prison?"

"My wife has nothing to do with any of this. And I don't see any purpose to these questions, Ms. Price."

"Does that mean she didn't know?" Leo asked. Nat was glad to see Leo picking up the ball. She was pretty sure that he, too, was thinking the mystery woman at the hospital could have been Bell's wife.

Bell relented, realizing it was two against one. "I didn't make a point of telling her each time I visited, if that's what you mean."

"Did your wife ever meet Lynn before she went to prison?"

Bell was working hard to appear nonchalant as Leo continued firing questions. He wasn't succeeding. "Yes. A couple of times. When Carol dropped by the office."

"Did she know Lynn was a transsexual?"

"What difference would it make to Carol?"

"If a beautiful young woman worked with my husband, I might feel a flurry of jealousy," Nat commented. "If I knew she was a transsexual, it might remove that flurry."

"Carol wasn't jealous. She had no reason to be jealous. But . . . she did know about Lynn. I mentioned it to her shortly after Lynn started working here." He cleared his throat. "Is there anything else? I have a very busy schedule."

"Did you know that Lynn was personally involved with Matthew Slater at the time she was treating him?" Leo asked.

Bell pulled out a pack of breath mints from the breast pocket of his pale gray shirt, peeled one off the roll, and popped it into his mouth. As an afterthought he held out the pack to them. Neither Leo or Nat responded. He tucked the roll back in his pocket.

"Yes. I knew. Lynn told me."

"What was your reaction?" Nat asked.

"I . . . wasn't happy about it. It's never a good idea for a physician to get romantically involved with a patient."

"Is that what you told her?"

"She already knew that. But she believed she was in love with him. And," Bell quickly added, "that Slater was in love with her."

"But you didn't believe either was true," Nat said.

Bell folded his hands one over the other on his desk. "Lynn was rather innocent when it came to men." After a brief pause he tacked on, "I imagine she still is."

"Did she tell you what happened that night?" Leo asked.

"No."

"When you heard about Slater's murder, did you think it was Lynn?"

"No. No, it never entered my mind." The doctor's voice had gone up a full octave.

He saw Nat looking dubious.

"I never thought Lynn'd be in Slater's bedroom before—" He hesitated.

"Before her surgery?" she suggested.

He nodded, then slowly shook his head. "It was a foolish thing for her to do. If only she'd waited."

"You knew she was having the operation."

"Yes. I fully supported her decision. I was one of her references. It isn't easy to qualify as a candidate for sex-reassignment surgery. I mean, by a reputable surgeon. For a price, it's always possible to find unscrupulous doctors who will operate, no questions asked. But Lynn was smart enough to know that would have been risky physically as well as psychologically."

"Who was the other reference?" Leo asked.

"Claire Fisher, my head nurse."

Nat saw Leo jot down the nurse's name.

"Did Lynn tell you she was a transsexual before or after she started working at the clinic?"

"When I first interviewed Lynn for the position, she was completely frank with me," Bell said. "I admired her for that. It took guts. She could have easily passed, and I'd never have been any the wiser, I assure you."

"What was your reaction?"

"Surprise," he answered Nat without hesitation. "But I wasn't put off, if that's what you're thinking. And, as you know, I hired her."

"You say Lynn was completely frank with you. Did she tell you about her past? Her family? Other people she was close to?" Leo asked.

"She told me she was estranged from her parents."

"Did she ever mention trying to play it straight? Say, back in high school or college? Dating women—"

"Lynn is not a lesbian. She sees herself as heterosexual. A heterosexual woman. I have always seen her that way as well. Prior to her sex-change operation as well as after her surgery. I wish she'd been up front with Matthew Slater. Then she'd have seen from the get-go that he wasn't the man she thought he was."

"Most men aren't," Nat said. Leo gave her a sideways look. She ignored it. She was thinking about why Bell wished Lynn had been honest with Slater. Was it because he was jealous of the lawyer? Did he want Lynn for himself?

"Has Lynn mentioned anyone—man or woman—in the past five weeks that she's had any involvement with?" Leo asked.

"No. No one. As far as I know."

Bell's intercom buzzer went off. He wasted no time responding to it. "Yes, Mona?"

"Your three-o'clock is here, Dr. Bell."

"Thanks, Mona." Bell rose. "I'm afraid I really can't spare any more time right now."

"Just one more question, Doctor," Nat said as Bell was already heading toward the door.

"Yes?"

"What's your opinion about two colleagues getting romantically involved?"

Bell cast Nat a dark look. "I don't approve of that, either," he said tightly, yanking open the door. Nat was sure he'd have liked nothing better than to boot her out bodily, but he managed to control himself.

thirteen

Sex-reassignment surgery doesn't bring nirvana. The therapist's job is to help his transsexual patients understand that their pasts cannot be rewritten.

DR. ROBERT SCHWARTZ
(EXCERPT FROM *Journal of Sexology*)

"WHAT DO YOU think?" Nat asked Leo as they settled down with their mugs of coffee at a small table in the hospital coffee shop. Claire Fisher had agreed to meet them down here when she finished work at five. It was now a quarter to five.

"I think they were close. How close? I'm not sure yet."

"I wonder how close Carol thinks they were. That business about not telling his wife every time he visited Lynn, says to me he thought Carol might not be too pleased."

Leo's cell phone rang. He checked the number on the screen before he clicked on.

"Yeah, Mitch. What's up?" He listened for a minute. "Yeah, okay. I'm on my way."

"What?"

"The funeral director confirmed Rodney Bartlett's alibi. But Oates got the list of attendees who were at the funeral and started contacting them. One of them was sitting right behind Bartlett at the funeral, and she seems to recollect him leaving before the service ended. But she wasn't willing to swear to it. And can't pin down a time. Oates and I are going to divvy up the list and see if we can come up with anyone else who saw Bartlett make an early exit. Because the thing is—" He paused for effect. "Oates clocked the time from the funeral home to the crime scene. Drove it at noon. Took him just under fourteen minutes."

"So if Rodney did slip out of the funeral service, he could have easily—"

"He could even have made it back before the service was over."

"Wouldn't it be nice if you could get a search warrant for his home and office and discover the knife," Nat said wistfully.

"Something tells me that knife is probably on the bottom of the bay. Whoever did the cutting was too smart to hold on to the weapon."

"Rodney could easily have tossed it in the harbor on his way back from the clinic," Nat pointed out.

"Bell could have tossed it, too." Leo hesitated. "You want to put our talk with Claire Fisher on hold or—?"

Nat smiled. "It'll be okay, Leo. Actually, Claire might be more open without a police detective around."

He took a quick gulp of his coffee, eyeing her over the rim. "Okay, so I'll see you later."

"Right. The reheated Chinese."

Leo looked uncomfortable. "Yeah, that, too. But I meant over at the center."

"Oh . . . right. Suzanne?"

"Yeah," Leo said, not quite meeting Nat's eyes.

Claire Fisher took Leo's vacated chair, setting a steaming-hot cup of tea and a corn muffin on the table. Bell's head nurse was a trim brunette in her early thirties. Her hair was cut stylishly short. She was quite pretty, but not the least bit flashy. She was wearing a crisp white lab coat over taupe slacks. She looked efficient. And friendly.

"How's Lynn doing?" she asked right off the bat.

"Not great."

Claire Fisher shook her head. "It's so awful. I still can't really take it in."

"Were you here yesterday?"

"No. I was home sick. A migraine. I don't get them very often, but when I do, it's pure agony." She focused her attention on her cup of tea, removing the tea bag and setting it on the edge of her paper plate, pushing aside her muffin as some of the liquid oozed out.

"How long have you worked for Harrison Bell?"

"Nine years. Almost ten. I started here right out of nursing school."

"He must be a great boss."

A faint flush crept up her neck. "He does very important work. Chronic pain is a terrible thing. So many doctors just throw pills at you and basically tell you there's nothing to be done for it. You just have to live with it. But they don't give you any help in learning how to live with it. Here, we work on a mind-body approach. Everything from physical therapy to hypnosis to imaging and psychological counseling. We don't help everyone, but we help a lot of people."

"Matthew Slater? Did you help him?"

Claire looked rattled. "Oh," she muttered.

"Lynn confided in you, didn't she?" Nat made the question sound like she already knew the answer.

"She did tell me she was seeing Matthew, but that's only because she believed I suspected something was going on between them." She took a careful sip of her tea.

"Was she right?"

"I did think he made more appointments with her than were necessary. For his physical condition."

"Claire, do you have any idea who attacked Lynn yesterday?" Nat asked bluntly.

"No. No, I can't imagine anyone being that vicious. I guess you see people like that all the time, given your work, but I don't know a soul who would do something so monstrous. And to Lynn, of all people. She's such a good person." A flush made its way up to her cheeks. "Oh, I know that must sound strange for me to say. Considering what happened to Matthew Slater. But I never, ever doubted that it was self-defense."

"How come?"

"Because I know Lynn. And . . . And I knew Slater."

Nat arched a brow.

Claire looked uncomfortable. "He hit on me a couple of times during our physical therapy sessions."

"Did you tell Lynn?"

She shook her head. "Lynn was so desperate to be normal. I mean, she wanted to have a man in her life, have the house with a picket fence, adopt a couple of kids. I felt for her. Hey, I want that stuff, too. But I would never have nominated Matt Slater for that role."

"For starters, he was already married," Nat commented in a deliberately light woman-to-woman mode.

"Yes." Again she devoted her attention to her cup of tea. Something told Nat that Claire was able to identify so strongly with Lynn because the nurse was also coping with her own desperate attraction to a married man. In Claire's case, Nat's money was on Claire's boss, Dr. Harrison Bell. Were Claire's feelings reciprocated? Or were Bell's attentions focused elsewhere? Like on Lynn Ingram? If that was the case, how would that affect Claire's feelings about her friend and colleague Lynn?

How convenient that Claire had an alibi at the ready for yesterday. But not much of one. Unless she had someone who could corroborate her claim. Nat decided to leave that line of questioning to Leo.

"But then, men and women get divorced and remarried all the time," she said instead.

"Yes, that's true." Claire was now examining her tea-stained and as-yet-untouched muffin.

"How would you describe Lynn's relationship with Harrison Bell?"

"What do you mean? They're colleagues. They have great respect for each other. Dr. Bell's been there for Lynn throughout her whole ordeal. I think he felt partly responsible."

"How's that?"

Claire compressed her lips as if she hadn't meant to let that comment slip out. "He referred Matthew Slater to Lynn for treatment. It's ridiculous for him to have felt in any way responsible.

Why wouldn't he have referred him? Slater was a patient just like hundreds of other patients—"

"Maybe he felt responsible for not stepping in when Lynn and Slater became romantically involved."

"I don't even know that he knew they were involved."

"Really?"

Claire's agitation was mounting. "Well, he probably suspected."

"Is it possible he was jealous?"

"What? What are you implying here?" Claire's anxiety was now laced with indignation. "Dr. Bell is a happily married man. Lynn was a colleague and, yes, I suppose, a friend. But that's all it was. And is."

Nat could see a wall drop down in front of Claire Fisher's face. The nurse checked her watch. "My break's up. I have to get back to work."

Nat's inmate clerk was filing reports in her outer office. He gave her a quick glance when she walked in, then returned to his task.

"I saw Detective Coscarelli's car parked outside. Is he in my office?" She gestured toward her closed door.

"He's . . . upstairs," Paul mumbled, avoiding eye contact.

They both knew outsiders, even cops, were supposed to restrict their contact with inmates to the main floor. That meant the visitors' room, the dining room, Nat's office, or one of the small private cubicles down the hall that were primarily used by inmates and their attorneys. To Nat's knowledge, Leo had never met with Suzanne in her room. Maybe they were upstairs in one of the inmate lounges.

There were seven bedrooms on the two women's floors. Two

triples, three doubles, two singles. Allowing for a max of fourteen female inmates. The female inmate count, at the moment, was twelve. Not counting Lynn Ingram. Two more female inmates were due by the end of the week. Giving them a full count. Again, omitting Lynn. When she returned—*if* she returned—Nat would have to figure out a way to squeeze her back in. That was the least of her problems now.

Suzanne and Lynn had the double at the end of the hall on the third floor, across from a small lounge which consisted of a couple of worn but serviceable couches, a TV, a small fridge, microwave, and a pantry. Nat was more than a little dismayed to see that the space was empty.

The door to Suzanne's room was closed shut. Nat hesitated outside the door, thinking, *Do I knock? Do I barge right in?*

A wave of anger swept over her. She was the superintendent of this institution. She was not an intruder. She was not the one breaking the rules. She was not the one behaving inappropriately. Why, in God's name, should she warn them of her arrival?

She didn't exactly barge into the room, but neither did she knock first. She merely opened the door and stepped inside.

Suzanne and Leo were sitting on Suzanne's bed. His arms were wrapped around her, and she was crying softly into his chest. Neither of them appeared to be aware of Nat's arrival.

Nat's first instinct was to make a hasty exit. Because, damn it, she did feel like an intruder. And that was not the only thing she was feeling. Add anger, despair, jealousy, betrayal, abandonment. Predictable emotions, the whole lot of them. And all too damn familiar. Only now they were even more intense.

It was not only that Leo was embracing the beautiful young mother of his child. It was also the look on his face. His eyes were closed and his expression—at least, Nat's interpretation of his expression—was one of pained longing. In all the time she'd known Leo, Nat had never seen that mix of anguish and desire on his face.

As if finally sensing her presence, Leo's eyes opened and he gazed straight at Nat. He didn't look particularly surprised. Worse, he didn't look particularly abashed. Nor did he make any attempt to break away from the embrace.

As for Suzanne, either she was still oblivious to Nat's presence, or she simply didn't care. Her crying, more a mewing sound now, continued unabated.

Without a word, Nat exited the room, leaving the door open. Her one concession to her anger.

"The hospital called," Paul LaMotte informed Nat as soon as she reentered the office.

Moments ago, she had been lost in self-pity. Instantly her full attention was on Lynn Ingram.

Anticipating her question, Paul said, "The doc didn't tell me anything."

Nat was acutely aware of the tremor shooting down her spinal column.

"I'll get her on the phone for you," her clerk said.

She nodded and headed into her office, shutting the door behind her.

The instant the button on her phone went yellow, she snatched up the receiver.

"Dr. Madison?"

"She's regained consciousness, Superintendent."

Nat sank back against her chair. "Thank God," she murmured.

There was a brief pause before Ellen Madison continued. "Lynn's not out of the woods yet. Not by a long shot, I'm afraid."

"What do you mean?"

"There's no guarantee she won't slip back into a comatose state. If she remains stabilized over the next forty-eight hours, the picture will be a lot brighter. Of course, Lynn will still face continuing risks after that, given the number of reconstructive surgical procedures she's going to need. But that's down the road. We need to take it a day at a time. Today is a lot better than yesterday."

"Is she . . . aware of what happened to her?"

"I've given her a very sketchy overview. I doubt she's taken it all in. Which is just as well. As superficial as I deliberately was, it's still an awful lot to absorb at once. We're dealing here with psychological trauma added to an already severe physical trauma. She'll have plenty enough of that to cope with when she becomes aware of the devastating results of her injuries."

"Has she said anything about the attack?"

"Lynn says she has no memory of the attack. Which is quite common in these kinds of trauma situations."

"But the memory loss is temporary, right?"

Nat's door opened. Leo walked in. Even as she tried to continue focusing solely on the doctor's answer, she could feel her heart slam against her chest.

"It can be temporary," Dr. Madison was saying. "But there's no guarantee. And even if it is temporary, there's no way to gauge how long it might take for her to remember. It could be days, weeks, months, even years."

"I see," Nat muttered, watching Leo close the door behind him.

"Don't forget, also, Lynn's on heavy-duty pain medication," Madison added. "It'll be several days before we have a clearer picture of her mental state."

"Can I come over and see her?"

"I'd rather you waited until tomorrow."

"First thing in the morning?"

"Check in with me first."

The surgeon's tone immediately brought back the doctor's warning that Lynn could slip back into unconsciousness again.

"Has anyone else called about Lynn's current status?"

"Harrison Bell called just before I phoned you."

"You spoke to him personally?"

"Yes." There was a brief pause. "Shouldn't I have?" Dr. Madison asked cautiously.

"Did he ask to see her?"

"No. He already knows she's not being allowed any visitors."

"Anyone else?"

"Her mother, who did ask if she could come in. I told her she'd have to contact the detective in charge of the investigation."

Nat was glad that Ruth Ingram had called and that she wanted to see her child. Would she tell her husband? Nat hoped not. After their little visit, Peter Ingram was going to be even more determined to see to it that his wife distanced herself from Lynn. Nat was also sure he'd be warning his wife, in no uncertain terms, not to cooperate with the police. Nat decided to phone her the next day when her husband was at work and see how far she could get with her.

"I almost forgot," Dr. Madison said. "I also had a brief word with a priest who told me he'd counseled Lynn while she was in prison."

"He phoned you?"

"No. Actually, he was at the hospital paying a call on one of his parishioners. He mentioned that he'd counseled Lynn a few times while she was in prison and asked how she was doing."

"What did you say?" Nat wasn't thrilled with word spreading that Lynn had regained consciousness, as it might panic her assailant.

The physician must have picked up on the note of concern in Nat's voice, because she quickly assured her she'd only told the priest Lynn's condition was stable. "I did contact Dr. Varda's service, though, and left a message for him," Madison said. "I thought it was important to alert him. Lynn may want to speak to him once awareness of her condition begins to sink in."

"Right. Absolutely." Nat wondered, however, how keen Varda would be to continue treating his patient after his own attack, the break-in at his apartment, and most especially that warning. Everyone, even shrinks—not to mention prison superintendents—had their limits. "Has he called back yet?"

"No. I only left the message for him twenty minutes ago. His service says he usually checks in around six P.M."

When she hung up, Nat relayed her conversation with the doctor to Leo. Her tone was flat, unemotional, perfunctory. What she wanted to do was throw something at him. Who was she kidding? If she wanted to throw anything at him, it was herself. She wanted to rush into his arms and have him hold her with the same aching desire he'd felt when he held Suzanne.

"Natalie—"

Nat cut him off. She wasn't ready to hear apologies. Or worse, to hear something that wasn't an apology. "What about the mourners?" She was already beginning to mourn the loss of what she'd thought was a great relationship

"Mourners?" Leo looked puzzled.

"The funeral Rodney Bartlett attended," she said by way of enlightenment. "You were going to talk to—"

"Oh, right. Nothing solid yet. But we have a couple of people who don't remember seeing Bartlett at the end of the funeral. And one who—" He stopped. "Are we going to talk about this, Natalie?"

"Your leads?"

He scowled. "Come on. You know I know you better than that."

"And you know Suzanne even better than you know me," she blurted, instantly regretting her remark. She was trying not to hit below the belt. Very unbecoming for a prison superintendent. Very demeaning for a woman who thought she'd possibly found the right man.

"Let's go back to your place, heat up that Chinese, and talk."

"I have other plans," she said tightly.

"Bullshit." He sank down into a chair across from her desk. His arms dropped straight down over the sides of the chair.

Nat's heart was thumping too hard, anger having rapidly given way to panic. *Damn it, Leo. Just dump me and get it over with. For your sake as much as mine.*

"I know how you're feeling," he said quietly. "No, that's wrong. I know what I'd be feeling in your shoes."

Nat wasn't even sure these comments were a prelude to talking about Suzanne. She wasn't sure of anything at the moment.

"And what's that?" She heard the scratchiness in her voice, her throat having gone almost completely dry.

He stared at her unflinchingly. "Lots of things. But mostly . . . scared."

As soon as he said it, she realized that was precisely what she was feeling most of all. The realization instantly brought tears to her eyes. But she rapidly blinked them away.

Now she was the one who wanted to pull back, to put off the inevitable. "I don't think I can handle this now, Leo."

"You think I'm having an easy time of it?" he shot back. "I'm not going to tell you she means nothing to me, Natalie."

"I'm not asking you to tell me that." Really, now she was thinking she didn't want him to tell her anything. Because once he did, she was going to have to deal with it. And her plate was already on the verge of overflowing.

"She's alone. She's scared. She's letting herself trust me. Just a little. But for Suzanne, even a little is saying something."

Nat could cope with his listening to what Suzanne was feeling. Her problem was figuring out how to survive what Leo was feeling.

She got up, too fidgety to sit but not sure what to do once she was on her feet. For a woman who prided herself on being focused, organized, in control, she was slipping badly. "I knew this was a bad idea," she muttered.

"What's a bad idea?" Leo stood up as well.

"When Lynn was attacked, I told you we should cool it. You talked me out of it then. Don't waste your breath trying to do it again."

Leo sighed. She couldn't tell if it was an expression of frustration, disappointment, relief. Probably a combination of all three.

He held her gaze for a few beats. She didn't look away even though she wanted to.

"And from now on, Leo, when you want to talk with an inmate at this institution—any inmate—you're to see them here on the main floor."

Again he made no response.

She reached for her bag. She didn't know where she was going except that she was getting out of there. She skirted around her desk and headed for the door. Leo didn't budge.

"I need an update on your talk with the head nurse at Bell's place, Natalie."

"Tomorrow."

"Jack. What are you doing here?" Nat stepped away from her front door and her deputy walked into her apartment. It was after nine P.M.

"Well, let's see. You breezed into the center at nine-thirty this morning, left at ten-fifteen, dropped back in after seven this evening, and were gone again less than an hour later. We didn't even get a moment to touch base." He headed into her living room without waiting for an invitation.

Nat followed him. "You read the note I left for you about Lynn Ingram?"

"Yeah, I read your note. You might have dropped by my office to tell me in person that she regained consciousness."

"I . . . uh . . . had some things to do."

"You're a lousy liar, Nat. I know about Leo's little tête-à-tête with Suzanne. She told me."

"Did she?" She tried to sound nonchalant, but Jack was right. She was a lousy liar. She dropped into her club chair.

"Want a drink?" Jack asked.

"Yes."

He knew where she kept her booze. And he knew that scotch straight up was her drink of choice when she was in need of a drink.

It was Jack's pick as well. When he was in need of a drink.

He brought her the scotch. A Perrier for himself. Well, at least one of them would stay sober tonight.

Jack made himself comfortable on the couch. "You want to talk about it?"

"No." She punctuated her answer with several throat-burning swallows of scotch.

"How about something to eat?"

"No."

"Wanna take a drive? Catch a flick? Play some miniature golf? Sink into depression?"

"No, no, no. Yes."

"Love. Ain't it a bitch?"

She finished off the drink. "Go home, Jack. I'm going to be lousy company tonight."

He rose to his feet. Even though she had pretty much ordered him to leave, she felt an immediate pang of disappointment. As much as one part of her felt like spending her evening wallowing in self-pity, another part of her didn't want to be alone. Maybe it was just that she couldn't handle any more feelings of abandonment for one day.

"Well, you may not be hungry," Jack said, "but I am. What have you got in your fridge?"

Nat knew he must have seen the flash of relief on her face, but for once she didn't care that she was so transparent. And at least he had the good sense not to rub it in.

After a few minutes she followed him into the kitchen, partly to get a refill. Jack had the bottle of scotch on the counter. At the ready. He was at the stove scrambling up some eggs.

"You had some Chinese food in the fridge, but it didn't seem like the right food for the way you're feeling."

If you only knew, Nat thought.

She poured herself another stiff drink. "You look so domestic."

Jack glanced over his shoulder. "You sound surprised."

She leaned against the counter, watching him sprinkle Parmesan cheese over the cooking eggs. "You never impressed me as a man who knew his way around a kitchen."

"There are a lot of things you don't know about me, Nat."

She took another long swallow of scotch, hoping to dispel her premonition that something was about to shift in her relationship with Jack Dwyer. Whether she liked it or not.

No, that wasn't it. Given her current state of mind, not to mention the current state of her relationship—or lack thereof—with Leo Coscarelli, Nat was afraid she might like it, at least like feeling wanted. At the same time, she knew it would not be a wise move. For either of them.

Jack took two plates out of the cupboard. "Maybe you'll change your mind," he said.

"No thanks."

Ignoring her, he divided the scrambled eggs between them.

The gesture made her angry. She snatched up one of the plates and dumped the contents into the trash. "I said no thanks." She slammed the plate on the counter with so much force, it shattered.

Jack came over to her.

"Go home. Please, Jack. Just . . . go home."

He pulled her into his arms. Even as she was hating herself for being so weak, she folded herself into his embrace. "Damn you, Jack," she muttered, as an image flashed before her eyes of the two of them embracing soon after Maggie's murder. An embrace born out of a desperate need on both their parts to be comforted. Only, that need changed. Or maybe it merely expanded. But that time, Nat came to her senses before she made a mistake she felt certain she would come to regret.

Tonight her mind seemed less in control than it had been then. She blamed it on the two strong drinks. But even as she did, she knew it was a lie. A cop-out. A need to displace the blame so she wouldn't feel guilty and ashamed of herself. Like she was really going to avoid those feelings.

Much to her chagrin, it was Jack who drew back this time. He held her at arm's length.

He was still smiling. But now his smile was tinged merely with sympathy. "You're going to be okay, Nat."

"I said almost those same words to my sister this morning." *My sister. Oh, God, I totally forgot . . . Lunch. I was supposed to have lunch with her today. And I didn't even remember to call and explain why I couldn't meet her.* Now Nat was really feeling guilty.

"Nat? What's wrong?"

She was pushing Jack out of the way as she made a beeline for the phone. Guilt vied with worry as she punched in Rachel's number. One ring. Two rings. Three.

"Hello?"

"Rach. Oh Rach, I'm so sorry."

"Nat? Is that you?" Her sister's voice sounded weirdly chipper.

"I missed our lunch. The thing is, I had this day of nonstop interviews, one of them out in Westfield and then . . . Anyway, our lunch date completely skipped my mind. Are you okay, Rach? Did you tell the kids?"

"I'm in the middle of dinner, Nat."

"Please don't be angry, Rach."

"Don't be silly, Nat. Listen, Gary and the kids are starving. I've really got to go."

"Gary? Did you say . . . ? He's back?"

"Be right off, darling," Nat heard her sister cheerily calling out to the prodigal husband. "Gotta go, Nat. Speak to you soon. Take care."

"Yeah. Right." Nat stared at the phone for a moment before she hung up.

"Everything okay with your sister?" Jack asked solicitously.

"She thinks so," Nat muttered, determined to have a serious talk with her sister ASAP.

Jack walked over to her. Took hold of her hand. Pressed it against his chest.

She tried to swallow down the lump that had suddenly lodged itself in her throat. She'd never been good at dealing with the bestowal of tenderness. She was certain that lack came from rarely having experienced tenderness as a child. Her mother was too emotionally disturbed, her father usually too drunk.

Jack leaned in, kissed her lightly on the forehead. Had he pulled her into his arms and ravaged her lips, she'd have felt less vulnerable. Less weepy.

She turned away, determined not to let him see how much he was getting to her. "Your eggs are getting cold."

"I'll nuke 'em. And then I'll eat and you'll get me up to speed on what's happening with the investigation. And then I'll give you a quick update on the House."

She nodded gratefully. Yes. Talk about the investigation. A respite. Keep the conversation off her and Leo. Off her and Jack.

. . .

It was well past midnight and Nat was exhausted. But she couldn't sleep. Her mind was working overtime. Lynn's assailant, the panic over her dog, Jack, Leo, even Rachel. Nat couldn't believe her sister had taken Gary back so readily. Nat certainly wouldn't have. But then, Nat did not have an easy time denying or forgiving. Maybe that's why she was alone at that very minute.

When her phone rang Nat answered on the first ring.

"Good. You're awake."

"Leo—"

"I'm coming up."

"Where are you?" Nat realized she'd given herself away there. If there was going to be a moratorium she should have said a quick, firm no.

Her buzzer went off, startling her.

"Buzz me in."

"Leo—"

"I'm lousy at this, Natalie." His voice was etched with both longing and weariness.

"Me too," she admitted, and buzzed him in, telling herself she'd no doubt regret it tomorrow.

But tomorrow felt like a long time away.

She waited at the door for him. When he got there, he enclosed her in his arms and she held on tightly. "Let's not talk. Not tonight." Her voice was a muffled whisper against his neck.

"Sounds like a plan," Leo said, relief flooding his face.

They headed straight to her bedroom.

fourteen

Thirty-six states, the District of Columbia, and the federal government have laws specifically prohibiting sexual relations between staff and inmates. A number of the laws prohibit staff-inmate sexual contact regardless of inmate consent, recognizing that such sexual relations cannot be truly consensual because of the power that staff have over inmates.

AMNESTY INTERNATIONAL

AFTER GETTING THE okay from Dr. Madison the next morning to visit with Lynn for a few minutes, Nat called the center and told her clerk she'd be in around ten-thirty. It was now a few minutes before nine. Leo had left at a little past seven A.M. She was still half asleep, but she'd offered to get up and make him some breakfast. He kissed her lightly on the lips and told her he'd have a bite at home. Nat knew he liked to spend some time with Jakey before his mother drove the boy to nursery school.

It wasn't until after Leo left that Nat felt any twinge of regret. Nothing had changed after all. They hadn't talked about Suzanne, but they were going to have to. At some point. However, given all her other worries, Nat was happy to relegate that discussion to the back burner for the time being.

When Nat arrived at the ICU, she was surprised but pleased to see that Ross Varda was already there, sitting at Lynn's bedside. She hesitated at the door, thinking Lynn might want to speak privately with her psychiatrist, but Dr. Varda motioned for Nat to come over.

Nat tried to prepare herself for her first look at Lynn since her attack, but there was really no way to prepare for such a thing. All she could do was hope that she could keep her expression from giving away her feelings of shock and horror at the butchery that had been done to Lynn.

Not that Nat could see any of the actual disfigurement. A specially rigged blanket was draped over Lynn's body so that she was covered without suffering the pressure from the weight of the material. So much of her face was swathed in bandages that the only areas visible were her eyes and her mouth. In a way, all those dressings—not to mention the disturbing array of tubes she was hooked up to and the massive amount of machinery bleeping, blinking, and humming in the background—only served to bring home more powerfully the extent and severity of the assault.

As Nat approached the bed, Lynn's eyes were closed. Nat felt a rush of alarm that she had already slipped back into a comatose state.

Varda got to his feet. "She's asleep," he said by way of assurance.

"Have you spoken with her at all?" Nat asked in a whisper as he offered her the chair. She waved off the invitation to sit.

"For a couple of minutes. She's heavily medicated, but she did recognize me."

"That's a very good sign, right?"

"Yes. Yes, it is."

"And did she say anything about—?"

"No. She's only vaguely aware of where she is, and even vaguer about why."

"Dr. Madison said that's to be expected. Such severe trauma often produces temporary memory loss."

"It isn't always temporary," Varda said.

Lynn's eyes fluttered open, and Varda and Nat instantly stopped their conversation. Nat felt a wrenching sensation in her gut as she saw that Lynn's eyes were so severely bloodshot, there was no sign of whiteness around the sharply dilated pupils.

"Hi, Lynn," Nat said softly, hearing the quiver in her voice and hoping Lynn didn't.

Nat quickly saw it was needless to worry. Even though Nat was standing less than a foot away from Varda, Lynn's eyes remained fixed on her psychiatrist. It appeared not only that she hadn't heard Nat's greeting, but also that Lynn was oblivious to her presence.

"Natalie Price has come to see you, Lynn."

"Who?" she asked in a weak whisper.

"The superintendent of Horizon House," Varda said gently.

Lynn blinked several times, still not pulling her gaze off his. "What's . . . happening?"

"You remember, Lynn. You're in the hospital. You were injured. You're being looked after."

For an instant, Nat thought she detected some sign of cognition in Lynn's eyes. But the brief awareness quickly gave way to a drugged blankness.

Varda looked over at Nat. "It will be like this for a while." He returned his gaze to Lynn. "I'll come back to see you again later. You rest now." He gave Nat a reassuring smile, then took a light hold of her arm, meaning to escort her out.

"I'll stay for a few more minutes," she told him.

Nat could see by his disapproving look that he didn't think her continued presence was in the best interest of his patient, but since Varda knew she had Dr. Madison's permission to visit, he didn't argue.

He exited the room, but Nat could see through the glass wall that he had chosen to wait for her in the corridor.

"How do you feel, Lynn?" Nat sat in the chair Varda had vacated for her.

Slowly, Lynn's eyes shifted in Nat's direction. The blank look remained.

"Do you know who I am, Lynn?"

"Who . . . ?"

"I'm Natalie. Natalie Price—"

"Who . . . did . . . this?"

Having expected almost complete unawareness, her question took Nat by surprise. "I don't know, Lynn. But I'm going to find out. I promise you that." She was shaken by the depth of ferocity in her voice.

Lynn, however, displayed no reaction at all. Her gaze drifted off. A few moments later, her eyes fluttered closed. Nat remained for a bit longer, trying to gain some small measure of comfort from the sound of Lynn's breathing.

When she did leave the room, Ross Varda was still out in the corridor and he was not alone. Dr. Harrison Bell was beside him. They were engaged in a conversation in which neither man looked happy.

The police guard outside Lynn's door was also standing. He was not looking too happy himself.

"I just want to see Lynn for a minute," Bell said to Nat the instant she stepped into the hall.

"Detective Coscarelli has already told you—"

"I know what he told me," Bell snapped, garnering a sharp look of disapproval from the nurse at the ICU monitoring station a few yards away.

Varda was watching Nat anxiously. "Did she say anything more?" he interrupted.

Nat shook her head.

Bell was still on his tear. "Let the cop here come in with me. Hell," he said, his voice sounding strained as he fought to keep it under control, "you can all come in there with me. I just want Lynn to know I'm here. That I haven't abandoned her. That . . . That if she needs me—" He broke off abruptly. Turned away. Stood still for a few moments, then, cursing under his breath, stormed off.

Nat caught Varda's eye. She was pretty sure he was thinking the same thing she was thinking: that Bell's anguished outcry was not merely that of a boss or even a good friend. Nat was also thinking that, given the fact that Dr. Varda was Lynn's therapist, he may have had even more reason to be thinking what she was thinking.

"I need a cup of coffee," Nat said. "How about you?"

"I'm off caffeine at the moment. Bit of trouble sleeping," Varda said dryly. "And I never could see the point of coffee without the caffeine. But I'll keep you company."

When Nat entered the cafeteria, she reflexively looked around to see if there was a pretty blonde lurking about. Yesterday, Leo's partner had shown Carrie Li the photo of Beth Milburne from the charity ball, but in that photo Beth's hair was in an upsweep and she was dressed in a sequin-studded gown. Carrie couldn't make a positive ID.

Oates had also showed the nurse a photo of Harrison Bell's wife. Again, Carrie couldn't say positively, but she was pretty certain Carol Bell wasn't the woman she'd seen.

"I was worried you might want to pull out of the case," Nat said to Varda once they were settled at a small table in the hospital cafeteria.

"Lynn isn't a 'case'," he chastised. "She's my patient. And I have an obligation to continue treating her as long as she wants me to."

"Even after what happened to you?"

"There's no question I was badly shaken. And frightened. I admit I'm . . . still frightened. But I can't let my fear overtake my responsibilities."

Nat found herself admiring Varda even as she found his pompous tone a bit trying. She hesitated and then told him about the drawing that was slipped under her door. Varda seemed more alarmed by the warning she'd received than he was by his own predicament. He bombarded her with questions: When did it arrive? What exactly *was* the drawing? How big was it? Was there any writing?

Nat tried to answer in as much detail as she could. "I'm sure Leo will let you see it," she said finally. "He's having one of his profilers have a go at it, but your input may be very helpful."

"Have the police made any progress at all?" he asked, sounding clearly agitated.

Nat experienced a flash of anger. "They might make more progress if you'd cooperate."

He eyed her sympathetically. "A detective by the name of

Oates showed up at my apartment this morning with a court order for Lynn's records. He drove me out to my office at Grafton so I could turn them over to him. I will tell you, I felt nothing so much as relief when I gave them up. I hope to God it provides them with some leads. If I knew who it was, I do believe I'd go after the sick bastard myself. There's nothing worse than feeling like a sitting duck."

"Tell me about it," she muttered acerbically.

Ruth Ingram picked up the phone after the third ring. As soon as Nat said her name, there was a cold silence.

"I saw Lynn this morning," Nat said, pretending not to notice the chill traveling through the line. "I wasn't sure if you knew she'd regained consciousness," she lied.

"I knew," Ruth said hoarsely. "I can't talk. I have to—"

"I suppose your husband told you—"

"Please, I just can't . . . I've got nothing more to say."

"Wait. Don't hang up, Ruth. Just give me a minute. It's important. And I know it's important to you, too. I also know you're between a rock and a hard place. Just tell me one thing."

"If it's about Bethany—I didn't know she'd died."

"But you know now." Nat's tone was sardonic.

"Yes. Peter told me. As he told you, he didn't think it was relevant at the time. And I completely agree. I hardly knew the girl. Not that it isn't a tragedy. It's always sad when a life is taken so young."

Nat decided she wasn't going to get more now on the topic of Bethany, so she switched gears. "You have a beautiful home, by the way. I was telling your husband that my sister—"

"We're very fortunate. Peter made some very good investments."

"You are fortunate. I didn't do too badly in the market for a while, but unfortunately for me, I didn't have a large-enough sum of money to invest in the first place. My father always used to say, 'It takes money to make money.' " Actually, in his sober moments, Nat's father did, on occasion, say just that.

"Look, if you're implying—" Ruth stopped abruptly. "I really don't have time to spend on the phone with you, Superintendent." Her tone was now sharp, but Nat detected an undercurrent of anxiety.

"What did you think I was implying, Ruth?"

"Look, Peter has never discussed money with me. He's very old-fashioned that way. Now, I really have to hang up."

"Just one more quick question: Do you know Daniel Milburne, Ruth? Does your husband know him?"

"No," she said harshly, quickly. Too quickly. "Please don't call again."

The phone went dead. Nat held on to the receiver absently, thinking how interesting it was that Ruth Ingram, who hadn't lived in the Boston area for ten years, would respond to that question with such an assured no, rather than ask, *Who the hell is Daniel Milburne?*

Interesting how one little no could speak volumes.

She dropped the receiver back in the cradle, her gaze lowering to a clipping she'd cut out of that morning's *Herald*. An announcement of a charity luncheon at the Boston Harborside Hotel that afternoon. One of the organizers of the luncheon was Beth Milburne.

Nat had never crashed a charity luncheon before, but there was always a first time.

. . .

"What are you doing here on a Saturday?"

Nat looked up from the clipping, flustered to see Leo standing in the doorway of her office. She immediately slipped a case file over the newspaper clipping. Leo might not be too happy to discover her luncheon plans.

"Catching up on paperwork. What are you doing here?" She hoped he wasn't going to ask her to lunch, seeing as how she had another pressing luncheon engagement.

Instead of answering her question, Leo asked, "How'd it go at the hospital?"

"Okay—fine. Well, Lynn was only awake for a few moments. Varda was there." She searched his face, looking for any signs of regret on his part.

Leo stepped inside and shut the door. Nat quickly gave him a rundown of her brief visit with Lynn and her equally brief chat with Varda. She emphasized Varda's interest in seeing the drawing.

"I'm still waiting for a report from our psychologist, but I'll get Varda a copy," Leo said.

She nodded. "Harrison Bell showed up at the hospital as I was leaving. Once again, pissed that he couldn't see Lynn. Clearly a man who doesn't easily take no for an answer," she added. "I definitely get the feeling there's something going on between Bell and Lynn. Or, at least, there *was* something going on." As soon as the words were out of her mouth, she realized the same could be said about her and Leo.

There was an awkward silence.

Nat hurried to fill it in by giving Leo a brief rundown of her conversation yesterday with Claire Fisher. Another topic they hadn't discussed in the wee hours of the morning. Words hadn't been on last night's agenda, period.

"I wouldn't be surprised if Claire wasn't secretly in love with Bell herself." Nat hesitated. "I suppose, if that's true, it makes Claire a suspect. She could have seen Lynn as a threat. And Claire wasn't at work on Thursday. She says she was home nursing a migraine." She sighed. "Just what we need. Another suspect."

"Suzanne went to work today?"

"What?" Leo's sudden shift to the inmate caught her off-guard. But not for long. Of course. Leo hadn't come over to see her. The only person at this center who was on his mind right now was the mother of his child.

"Suzanne—"

Nat raised a hand to stop him from repeating the question. "Yes," she said crisply. "Hutch dropped her off and he's picking her up when she's finished for the day." So far, Suzanne had received no threats, but they weren't taking any chances.

Leo nodded. He looked tired. Well, neither of them had exactly had much sleep last night.

But Nat suspected that Leo's weariness had more to do with worrying about Suzanne than it did lack of sleep.

And, she suspected, her own weariness had more to do with worrying about Leo. Wanting him. Hating herself for wanting him. Round and round in a vicious cycle. A cycle that she'd been through before and didn't want to repeat.

Leo cut into her thoughts. "Oates and I are meeting with Bell's wife this afternoon. Thought you might like to tag along."

"Your partner's never been particularly thrilled to have me tagging along."

"Actually, Oates thinks having another woman present might make Carol Bell feel more . . . comfortable."

Nat didn't believe for a second that this was Oates's opinion, but she wasn't going to argue about it. Nor was she about to let it go to her head that Leo wanted her along. It was nothing personal, she told herself. Leo knew damn well she was a good observer. And given the opportunity, she could ask the kind of probing questions that often got positive results.

"What time are you going over there?" she asked, hoping it would be late enough for her to drop in at the charity luncheon first.

"Two o'clock."

"Fine. That's great."

"I'll swing by here, then, at, say, one-thirty?"

"Great."

Leo appeared in no hurry to leave. "Or I could come by earlier. We could have lunch—"

"I can't," she said quickly. "Too much work."

Leo gave her an assessing look. "You aren't giving me the brush-off again—"

Her office door opened before she could respond to Leo's question—not that she had a response—and Jack came waltzing in. Leo was standing off to the side of the door, so Jack didn't spot him immediately.

"How you doing?" he asked Nat. Both the tone of his voice and his smile reflected unmistakable warmth. Jack had wanted to stay over last night. Even though she'd sent him off, he'd seemed more optimistic about a future invite. A little shiver ran down Nat's spine as she thought of what might have happened if Jack had stayed the night and the two men had met up in her apartment. It was tense enough whenever they encountered each other in her office.

Nat's eyes darted over to Leo. Jack's eyes followed.

"Oh," he said, all signs of warmth obliterated.

The charity luncheon for Women Against Domestic Violence was being held in a private ballroom at the glitzy Harborside Hotel. The doors to the room were closed. Nat hesitated, worrying that there'd be someone on the other side checking names off the invitation list. She could always claim there'd been a mistaken omission and show her ID. Who was going to turn away a corrections official?

She breathed a sigh of relief as she opened one of the doors. No one was on duty.

Nat's hope was that if she showed up to the charity function early enough—while the luncheon guests were still in the meet-and-greet phase and hadn't yet sat down at the tables in their assigned seats—she wouldn't have a problem party-crashing.

She was right.

Well-groomed women of all ages were chatting in small groups around the spacious dining hall. No one blinked an eye as Nat wove slowly, casually, around the beautifully set tables as if she were looking for the right little group. Whenever any of the women caught her eye they nodded and smiled as if they knew her. Because they were supposed to know everyone here. Because anyone attending this pricey little charity luncheon was someone worth knowing.

Nat nodded and smiled right back, trying to act as if she had pockets as deep as the rest of them. They'd probably drop dead on the spot if they got a glimpse of her current checkbook balance. Let's just say being a civil servant was not going to make her a wealthy woman. Not that she was complaining. She made a decent salary and she did work she felt was valuable and rewarding. Most of the time.

As it turned out, it wasn't Beth Milburne who caught Nat's eye first. It was the woman with whom Beth was engaged in an earnest one-on-one conversation—a woman Nat had also never met in person but had seen on a number of occasions on television and in the newspaper.

Beth Milburne was standing with the supposedly reclusive philanthropist from Martha's Vineyard, Jennifer Slater.

Well, well, well.

Talk about killing two birds with one stone.

Unfortunately, it probably would be easier to kill them than to get either of the pair to talk to her.

Now what? Nat was acutely aware that she'd spent a lot of time thinking about getting in here and not enough time figuring what she'd accomplish once she'd crashed the party.

Time was running short. The meet-and-greet phase wouldn't last much longer. Nat had to make a move and make it now.

She made a beeline for the pair.

"Jennifer. Jennifer Slater. How nice to see you." Nat gave the woman a big, warm smile, then turned to her companion. "And you, too, Bethany. Hey, didn't I spot you the other day over at the cafeteria in Boston General?"

"It's Beth," the councilman's wife responded snappishly. "Beth Milburne. And I've been out of town for the past few days. You must have me confused with someone else."

Nat went right on smiling. "But your maiden name is Colman, right?"

"So?" Beth challenged.

"And your mom's maiden name is Graham, isn't it? Andrea Graham? From San Jose, California?" Nat had spent some time that morning doing a bit of homework on Bethany Graham's family tree.

Beth Milburne looked like she'd like to take a swing at Nat. Instead, she held her arms rigidly at her side. "My mother's name was Lillian. She died a while ago. And she was from Chicago. You obviously have me confused with someone else."

Nat shrugged. "Oh, well, those things happen." Her focus shifted back to Matthew Slater's widow. "But I know I don't have you confused with someone else. You are Jennifer Slater, right?"

"Yes," the woman said guardedly. "And you are—?"

"I knew your husband, Matt. It was tragic, what happened to him," Nat said, acting oblivious to Jennifer's question. "I'm sure you've heard on the news what happened to his . . . well, the woman who's serving time for his murder. Lynn Ingram."

Jennifer Slater's complexion turned ashen. Beth Milburne glared at Nat as if she had the manners of a heathen. "Who are you?" she demanded.

Nat kept her cool but figured she was fast using up her time. "An acquaintance of Jennifer's brother, Rod. I just stopped by to say hi."

Jennifer's eyes narrowed. "No one calls my brother Rod."

"Really? It's just a nickname. Just like Beth. Beth is short for something, right?"

"Elizabeth," Milburne said acidly. "I still didn't catch—"

But before she finished her sentence, Nat looked past her as if spotting someone else she knew. She waved cheerily.

The woman who caught Nat's eye waved back. Naturally, she thought she should know who Nat was. As Nat hurriedly made her way over to the woman, she was sure both Jennifer and Beth were following her every step.

"Hi," Nat greeted the woman warmly. "Tell me, do you have any idea where the rest room is in this place?"

fifteen

Inmate 43906 (Lynn Ingram) has been treated for facial abrasions which she states resulted from having tripped over a crack and falling in the prison yard. That would make it her fourth accident this week.

JANICE RYAN, R.N., CCI GRAFTON

CAROL BELL REGARDED them warily at the doorway of her brick Georgian colonial on a quiet, upscale, suburban, tree-lined street in Newton, a town fifteen minutes west of Boston. The first thing Nat noticed about Harrison Bell's wife was that she looked even more athletic in person than she had in that family photo on her husband's desk. She was dressed much like she had been in that photo. Black spandex shorts and a red jersey, both of which hugged her muscular frame. Her cheeks were flushed, like she had just returned from biking or a run. Although, upon seeing the three of them at her doorstep, her face was rapidly losing its healthy glow.

Carol looked older in person. Older than in the photo on her husband's desk. Older—at least appearancewise—than her husband. Possibly by several years. Nat also noted that while Carol's hair had been blonde in the picture, it was now a medium shade of brown, worn severely pulled back from her face and fixed with an elastic.

The only accessories the doctor's wife was wearing were a pair of small gold loops in her pierced ears and a diamond-studded wedding band. Nat's gaze was drawn to that band, not because it was particularly eye-catching—the diamonds were modest-size chips—but because Carol Bell was absently twisting it as she scrutinized the two detectives' IDs.

"I don't really understand why you need to come here," she said. Her lips, already thin, almost disappeared as she pressed them together. In direct contradiction to Oates's supposed belief that Nat's presence would make Carol more comfortable, she seemed to regard Nat with even more suspicion than she did the two detectives.

"I thought you'd prefer it to having to make a statement at the station, Mrs. Bell," Leo said pleasantly.

His casual tone immediately put Carol Bell on the defensive, as Nat was sure Leo knew it would. Carol's cold expression instantly gave way to nervousness. "I already . . . made a statement. My husband and I were on the phone—"

"May we please come inside?" Leo interrupted. When she hesitated, he added, "I don't think you want your neighbors seeing us all discussing police matters on the street." He emphasized the word *police*.

Carol Bell's cheeks regained their flush, but this time it was not the result of exercise. Nat wasn't sure if Carol was embarrassed, alarmed, or angry. Probably a combination of all of the above. Whatever emotions she was experiencing, the doctor's wife did begrudgingly step aside and let them in.

"Are you home alone?" Oates asked as they entered a wide foyer painted a soft blue.

"Yes. My boys are at sports practices. My daughter's playing next door. And I dismissed my cleaning lady early." She sounded much aggrieved as she announced the latter, although, as Nat glanced around, she didn't detect so much as a smidgen of dirt on the glistening wood floor. From where she was standing Nat could also see a spotless dining room through an elegant archway on the right and an equally ordered living room through a matching archway on the left. At the front of the living room, sitting just inside the bay window was a mahogany baby grand whose surface had been polished to a high sheen. A fresh bouquet of irises artfully arranged in a gleaming silver vase sat atop the piano.

On its best day, Nat's place didn't look a fraction this clean and tidy. And she didn't live with three active children. Then again, she did have a rambunctious dog who had a particular fondness for gnawing on the wooden legs of her furniture. Still, Nat would take Hannah anytime over a husband who had a fondness for gnawing on her heart.

Carol Bell made no move to escort them into either the living room or dining room. Arms folded firmly against her chest, she planted herself in the foyer near the wide, curved staircase leading to the second floor. "As I've already stated on the phone to that officer there"—she pointed at Oates, who was standing closer to the door, notepad and pen in hand—"Harrison and I were on the phone—"

"Your phone records indicate no outgoing calls this past Thursday between eleven A.M. and one P.M."

Although Leo's tone was mild, with no attempt at provocation, you'd never know it to look at Carol Bell's expression. She looked as though she'd been challenged to a duel and wasn't at all prepared for the challenge. "I . . . I didn't call . . . from home. I was at Josh's school. They'd called me in. You can check with the principal if you don't believe me. I . . . I called from a phone booth across the street from the school."

"Why?" Leo asked.

"Because I was very upset—"

"No." He cut her off. "I mean, why not call from the principal's office?"

Carol looked at him like he was clueless. "Because I didn't want the principal or the office secretaries knowing my business, that's why."

"And you were upset because your boy got suspended from school."

"Men," she muttered under her breath.

Leo gave her a baffled look.

"You, my husband, even the principal—also a man—think it's no big thing if your son gets into a fight and is suspended from school. 'It happens,' you all say. 'Boys will be boys. Especially teenage boys.' Well, I'm sorry, but I do happen to think it's a big deal."

"I agree with you," Nat said. Partly because it was true, and partly because she was hoping to encourage a woman-to-woman connection with Carol Bell.

Nat thought she'd managed the latter to some extent, because as Carol looked her way, her expression softened. "Josh has never gotten into trouble before. He's a good boy. An A student. At least he was, until . . ."

"Until when?" Leo prodded when she hesitated.

Carol began absently twisting her wedding band again. "He's fourteen. Boys at fourteen, they start thinking they know it all. And suddenly it's not cool to be smart. To get good grades. To show up with your homework done."

"So this is pretty recent," Leo said.

"This semester. Not right off. No, Josh started ninth grade on the right foot. But then . . . I don't know . . . he started acting up, not just at school but at home, too. Sassing us. Especially me. Of course, I'm the one who's home all the time, so naturally I get the brunt of it."

Nat picked up a tinge of resentment in her voice. So Harrison isn't home much. But then, what doctor is? Still—

"Does Josh know Lynn Ingram?" Leo asked.

Leo's question clearly threw Carol Bell for a loop. Her face went almost as gray as her blouse. "I don't understand . . . your question. Josh has nothing to do with that . . . with her. What are you trying to do here?"

"I was just thinking, if Josh does know Lynn—and I imagine he would—he's probably quite upset about what happened to her."

"We're . . . We're all . . . quite upset," she stammered.

"Right, there's your younger son, Billy, and your little girl, Daphne, isn't it?"

She glared at Nat. "My children have absolutely nothing to do with . . . with—" She left off abruptly, her expression turning grimmer. "I don't have anything more to say."

She briskly checked her watch. "I have to pick up my boys. Their practices are almost over." She plucked up a ring of keys from a crystal bowl sitting on her oak hall table. "I hope this is settled now. My husband and I were on the phone discussing Josh when . . . when that terrible incident took place. Harrison has told me he's . . . under suspicion—" She was clutching the keys so tightly, Nat wouldn't have been surprised if one of them didn't cut through her skin. "I hope my corroboration—yet again—finally puts an end to such a ridiculous notion. Harrison has nothing but . . . but the highest regard for Lynn Ingram."

"Despite the fact she's a confessed murderer?" Nat asked, putting a touch of incredulity in her voice.

"Harrison says it was self-defense." Her anger gave way to a kind of exhaustion. "My husband is very loyal."

"Do you believe it was self-defense?" Nat asked.

Carol merely regarded her with a tired expression. "I believe that a man is dead, Ms. Price. Dead at the hands of Lynn Ingram."

"Did you ever worry for your husband's safety?"

Carol Bell stared at Nat in silence for several moments. "I was very much against Harrison taking Lynn back," she finally said in a quiet, even voice. "I told him as much. But like I said, my husband is a very loyal man. As well as a stubborn one. When he makes up his mind to do something, or about someone, there is nothing or no one who can change it." Then she added, both pointedly and rather poignantly, "Especially me."

"You did good in there."

Nat gave Leo a sideways glance as she settled into the passenger seat of his car. Oates had taken off in his own vehicle. "Thanks."

"So, what do you think?"

A loaded question if ever there was one.

Leo knew it, too. So he quickly added, "About the Bells."

"Your typical married couple," she said ruefully. "They don't spend much time together; when they do, they make a lot of small talk; she feels misunderstood, he feels beleaguered; he wants less, she wants more—"

"Less and more of what?"

She smiled wryly. "Involvement."

Leo made no response. They were both aware that as she was describing the Bells' relationship, she might as easily be describing her own past marriage.

He pulled out from the curb and began following the route back to the Mass Pike.

"Varda told me Oates picked up his therapy records on Lynn this morning. Anything useful there?" she asked.

"I haven't had a chance to go through them yet. There's a copy for you on the backseat. Read it through and we'll compare notes." He paused briefly before adding, "Come have dinner tonight at my place."

She looked over at him, but Leo's eyes remained fixed on the road.

"I don't think so," she said quietly. Spending more time with Leo's family would only complicate an already-too-complicated situation. "Come by the center tomorrow and we'll talk in my office."

"Tomorrow's Sunday," he reminded her.

"I know. But I'm still buried in work. And I haven't been at the center much in the past few days."

When Leo pulled up in front of Horizon House fifteen silent minutes later, Nat reached behind for Varda's records, then opened her door.

"Jakey asked after you this morning. He wanted to know when he was going to be seeing you again."

She glanced over her shoulder at Leo. "Next time he's here

visiting his mother." Which would be the next day. Jakey and his grandma hadn't missed a Sunday visit yet.

"That may be some time," Leo said.

"Why is that? They always come on Sunday." She didn't add that Leo hadn't missed many Sunday visits himself.

Leo sighed. "You'll have to ask Suzanne. She phoned this morning and told me she doesn't want my mother or Jakey to visit for a while."

"And you?"

Leo didn't respond. Which was response enough for Nat.

"What's up?" Jack sauntered across Nat's office and perched himself on the corner of her desk.

"I've been going over the notes Dr. Varda kept of his therapy sessions with Lynn Ingram."

"Come up with anything interesting?"

"Maybe." She riffled through the pages until she found the one she was looking for. "This is from their sixth session. Goes back to about two months after Lynn was placed in isolation. Listen. I want to read you a few highlights."

Jack nodded.

" 'Lynn is quite depressed today. Says she isn't sleeping well. Reports several nights of bad dreams. Reluctant to talk about them. Does admit to a common thread in all of them—being cut up.' " She heard Jack's sharp intake of breath. A very similar response to the one she'd had when she first read those words.

"Does she say who was cutting her up in her dream?" he asked.

"If she did, it's not in his notes. Varda connected it to her sex-change operation."

"Shrinks," Jack muttered disdainfully

"But there's something else interesting. Here: 'Lynn becomes noticeably agitated when I question her about her visit yesterday with Harrison Bell. I ask if she'd prefer he didn't visit, but that only increases her agitation. Finally, she says, "He needs me." She refuses to elaborate.' "

"Bell is our man. I can feel it," Jack said. "I've been around enough of these psycho creeps to know one when I see one."

"Feelings won't convict him. Besides, we aren't at a loss for suspects in this case. Bell is definitely not alone on the list."

Jack smiled sardonically. "Now you sound like your boyfriend."

She gave her deputy a sharp look. "Leave it, Jack."

Jack held up his hands in mock surrender. "Sorry."

Her phone rang. She was happy for the interruption.

Her happiness was short-lived.

sixteen

Some of the inmates felt sorry for me. My roommate,
certainly. But what could Suzanne do? What could I
do? What could any of us do? We were all afraid. We
all had plenty of reason to be afraid.

L. I.

"OKAY," NAT SAID sharply, "take me through it again. From the
top."

Hutch knew his boss well enough to know that her biting tone
masked extreme agitation bordering on panic. So he merely
shrugged, broad shoulders stretching the fabric of his khaki shirt.
He looked from Nat to Jack, then back to her again. They were
standing in a secluded corner of the small lobby of Mercy Medical Center, a small hospital located on Beacon Street, two blocks
south of Newbury. Nat was starting to spend more time in the
city's hospitals than she did in her own office.

"I get to the boutique maybe ten minutes to five, park outside right at the curb, my eyes on the front door," Hutch said. "When I dropped her off this morning, she asked if I could wait outside for her when I came to pick her up."

"Why's that?" Jack interrupted.

Hutch cocked his head. "I don't exactly look like your typical upscale boutique customer. I figured my presence would make her feel self-conscious." He laughed sharply. "Now I figure it differently."

"Go on," Nat prodded, wanting to focus on the details right now and not her CO's analysis.

"So, anyway, she says she'll be out at five sharp. Five sharp comes, no Suzanne. I wait about five more minutes and—I don't know, I get this uneasy feeling—so I go into the shop.

"It's empty. Door's unlocked, and I mean the place is empty. No customers. No Suzanne. The owner, what's her name, Joan Hayward, she's nowhere to be found, either. I call out. Nothing. I gotta tell you, it spooked me."

Nat opened her mouth, but before she could get so much as a word out, Hutch jumped in. "Yeah, I know. I shoulda called the cops there and then. But I didn't so let's move on."

They eyeballed each other for a couple of moments and then he continued: "I go into the back room. Nobody. Then I see the door to what I figure is the bathroom. I think at first it's locked. But when I give it the old heave-ho it starts to budge. And then I realize why it's so hard to open. Suzanne's sprawled on the floor right behind it."

Hutch shook his head. "When I finally managed to get inside, I thought, at first, she was a goner. Man, was I relieved when I picked up a pulse. Then I spotted the works on the floor. Shit, I really thought that kid had gotten it together. But I guess 'Once a junkie always a junkie.' "

. . .

"It was my damn car," Joan Hayward, the attractive thirty-eight-year-old owner of Viva, said, looking badly shaken. "The lot I park in closes at five on Saturdays and since I stay open until six, I always dash out at around four-thirty to move the car to an on-the-street space. It's usually no problem because a lot of people are leaving by then and I almost always find a spot close by."

"But this time you couldn't find a spot?"

"No, that wasn't the problem. When I got to my car, it wouldn't start. It's a 'ninety-eight Volvo, totally reliable until today. I had to call the auto club to come and see if they could start it. Or otherwise tow it. Then I called the shop to let Suzanne know I'd be late getting back and could she please stay overtime, but no one picked up. I assumed she was busy with a customer. But I called back several more times and still couldn't get her on the phone. I got worried. So I gave the attendant at the parking garage my cell-phone number and a hefty tip to stick around and wait for the auto-club guy to show up and to call me when he got there. It must have been about five-fifteen when I arrived back at the shop, just in time to see an ambulance pulling away from the curb."

Tears spiked Joan Hayward's eyes. "I still can't believe Suzanne would . . ." She paused to rummage in her large leather tote bag until she came up with an unopened cellophane-wrapped package of tissues. She ran a finely manicured nail along the score marks to open it, then pulled out a tissue. But she merely clutched it in her hand. "Why now? At the shop of all places? I mean, Suzanne couldn't know I'd be detained. I'm usually back within ten minutes, fifteen at the most. It doesn't make sense. It just doesn't make any sense at all."

She gave Nat a searching look as if she could explain it. But she couldn't. It didn't make any sense to Nat, either.

"She's a very lucky young woman," the intern said soberly, close to an hour after Suzanne had been rushed into the emergency room. "When they brought her in, I didn't think she had a prayer."

Leo, who was standing beside Nat, didn't say a word, but she could feel the tension and relief emanating from him. She'd called him as soon as they'd gotten to the hospital. It took him close to twenty minutes to make it over there because of the rush-hour traffic. Nat was glad for the delay. It meant less time for the two of them to have to make stilted conversation.

As it turned out, she needn't have worried. After Hutch repeated what had happened yet again for Leo's benefit, Leo had opted to play the torturous waiting game out in the corridor, only returning once the doctor had arrived. Jack and Hutch had hung out with Nat for a brief time, but then she sent them back to the center to keep things in check over there.

"I saw a lot of old tracks," the young doctor continued. "But this was the only fresh one. You'd think she'd be experienced enough with H to know better than to do such a big hit after so much time off the stuff. It's downright suicidal."

Out of the corner of Nat's eye, she saw Leo's lips tighten. Did he think Suzanne was trying to kill herself? Was he browbeating himself—feeling responsible in some way for what she'd done? Or, at least, tried to do?

"Can I see her?" he asked, his words clipped.

The intern stepped away from the closed door. "She's not feeling too great, but then, that should come as no surprise."

Leo headed into Suzanne's room. Nat was right behind him. He gave her a quick glance over his shoulder and, although he didn't say anything, his expression said quite plainly that he wasn't pleased to have her joining him.

Right now, the last thing on Nat's mind was worrying about pleasing Leo Coscarelli.

As soon as Suzanne saw Leo approach her bed, her eyes filled with tears. She started to speak, but her lips were trembling so badly, she pressed them shut without saying a word.

Leo took hold of her hand. "It's okay," he said softly.

Now Nat was feeling on the verge of tears.

"Leo, I didn't . . ." she managed to eke out in a hoarse whisper.

"Not now, Suzanne. We'll talk later."

She weakly turned her head from side to side. "But, I didn't . . ."

"Shhh."

Nat came up behind Leo. When Suzanne saw her, her tear-filled eyes widened in terror. "No. No, please . . ." she whimpered. "Don't . . . Don't send me . . . back."

Even in her drugged state, Suzanne knew full well what the repercussions of her having used again meant. A one-way ticket back to Grafton. It was pretty much a guarantee.

Nat felt angry at Suzanne for screwing up so royally. For putting herself at risk as well as for putting Horizon House at risk. Every time a prerelease inmate flagrantly broke the rules, it invariably raised eyebrows of concern with the powers-that-be. And it was compounded exponentially because they were already high-profile news thanks to the attack on Lynn Ingram.

Nat looked down at Suzanne and she wanted to shake her. But Suzanne looked so frail, so lost. Had she plunged that needleful of dope into her arm hoping to die? If so, why? Why now? Was this some kind of selfless act to keep Leo from getting mixed up with her again? Did she realize she'd never be able to stay clean permanently and that she'd end up causing not only Leo but Jakey terrible heartbreak? Was this why she told Leo she didn't want her little boy or his grandmother to visit? A first step toward a permanent separation?

Now, looking at Suzanne, Nat saw a suffering woman in need of help, even if Suzanne hadn't meant to attempt suicide but simply get high. Nat had long had conflicted feelings about drug addiction being treated as a criminal act instead of as an illness requiring medical and psychological treatment. But the reality was, whether she agreed with it or not, using drugs in this country was a felony. Punishable by incarceration.

"Someone . . . was there," Suzanne rasped.

Nat stepped closer. "Someone was where?" she repeated even as she was thinking, *Sure, someone was there. Your dope dealer.*

Leo cast her an acrimonious look. Papa Bear incarnate protecting his injured cub.

Nat corrected herself. He was Papa Bear protecting Mama Bear.

"In the . . . back. That's why I . . . went . . ."

"Who was there?" Now it was Leo asking the questions.

She shook her head more vigorously than before, flinching from the pain the movement caused. "I didn't see . . . A mask. He . . . wore a mask. And . . . gloves. He was . . . wearing . . . gloves. I saw . . . No, no, I felt something . . . over my mouth . . . Awful smell . . . Couldn't breathe. Couldn't . . . So dizzy . . . Oh, my head . . ."

She flung a hand over her eyes. "So good to . . . just . . . let go. But . . . But I didn't . . . want to . . . I tried . . . to fight it . . . I tried . . . but I . . . couldn't." She was breathing hard and fast. Her body was jerking in agitation.

"Suzanne, listen to me," Leo said, his voice raised. "It's over. It's okay. We'll get it all sorted out. Just take it easy."

She didn't, however, appear to hear him. She was close to hyperventilating.

A nurse walked in. She took one glance at her patient, and now she was looking plenty agitated herself. "Out," she ordered, as if they were nothing more than disruptive children.

"You're sure nothing looks . . . out of place in any way?"

"I already told the other officer, Detective Coscarelli, the storeroom looks the same way it always does." Joan Hayward was beginning to lose her patience. It was almost eight P.M., and she was still suffering the aftereffects of this afternoon's drama. Nat could well imagine the shop owner wanted nothing more than to go home, take a nice hot bath, and pour herself a good, stiff drink.

Or maybe Nat was projecting onto Joan her own desires.

Leo was once again pulling open and studying the locking mechanism on the back door that led out to an alley behind Newbury Street. "And you're sure this door was locked?"

Joan shifted her weight from one foot to the other, her hands folded across her chest. "Again. Yes, Detective. If someone came in here, Suzanne let him in."

She paused, looking over at Nat now. "I can't have her back. I hope you understand—"

"You don't have to worry," Nat said quietly.

"I'm not saying I don't feel sorry for her. I had very high hopes for Suzanne. She had a wonderful sense of style. And she was good with customers. Helpful without being intrusive. It's not a skill everyone has, believe me. Suzanne was a natural."

Hayward kept referring to Suzanne Holden in the past tense. As if she'd actually died of the overdose.

Maybe, in a sense, she had.

"By the way, did the auto club get your car started?" Nat asked as Joan was opening the boutique's front door, clearly eager to show them out so she could lock up and go home.

She scowled. "Yes. As a matter of fact, all it turned out to be was a couple of loose spark plugs. If I'd known anything about cars, I'd have been able to take care of it in a matter of seconds. But I'm hopeless when it comes to anything mechanical." She shrugged. "I don't even know how spark plugs get loose in the first place."

"Look, Leo. I know what you're thinking. But you know, better than I do, that without any proof—"

"Yeah, I know." He had pulled up at the curb in front of Nat's apartment building. "I also know Lynn's psychiatrist was roughed up and warned off. You got that creepy drawing warning you off. And now Suzanne—"

"I need proof, Leo. Without it, no question she'll be shipped back to Grafton. She broke—"

Leo cut her off. "If Suzanne's sent back now, it would destroy her."

It hit Nat then. It didn't really matter to Leo if Suzanne was telling the truth. Whether she shot up of her own volition or not, he wanted to protect her. You have to care deeply for someone to feel that way. An overwhelming sense of loss washed over Nat like a tidal wave.

Without a word, she opened the car door.

"Natalie."

Her back stiffened. "Twenty-four hours, Leo. That's as long as I can keep her in the hospital. Either you produce something to back up her story by then or—"

She didn't bother to finish the sentence. They both knew the rest of it.

seventeen

There are probably few people as adept as transsexuals at keeping secrets. Many have lived their entire lives honing this skill.

DENNIS PORTMAN, PH.D., *Lives of Transsexuals*

IT WAS A little past eight on Sunday morning when Nat arrived at Boston General. Over seventy-two hours since the attack. Although Dr. Madison had said that Lynn was past the most critical phase, she was still a long way from easy sailing.

All Nat needed was one look at the patient to know that.

"How are you feeling, Lynn?"

She gave Nat a blank look, her eyes still glazed over. "My mouth . . . is dry."

Nat eyed the private nurse who was sitting near the door. She nodded. Nat reached over to the nightstand and picked up a glass of water with a straw in it. She held the straw to Lynn's badly

Lynn took a small sip. It seemed to take a great

just to manage that.

better," Nat lied.

r wasn't able to absorb the compliment or simply

e was still on heavy-duty pain medication.

Bell wanted me to be sure to send you his best."

ed.

Is this pure reflex or does it mean something? And if it does, what?

"I almost forgot. I was talking with your mom yesterday about Bethany." Nat was watching Lynn closely, knowing that the nurse sitting a few yards behind her was on alert. Nat had been cautioned not to press the patient for information. All she could do was throw out feelers and see if any of them produced a spark.

Lynn closed her eyes. For a minute Nat thought she was drifting off to a drugged sleep, but then she saw tears slip past Lynn's closed lids and begin rolling down her bandaged face.

Nat laid a hand lightly on hers, her heart aching for the inmate. "Is there anything I can do, Lynn?"

She didn't answer right away. And when she did, Nat's heart nearly broke. "I want my mommy."

"Ruth?"

"Who is—" She stopped abruptly, recognizing Nat's voice. "I have nothing more to say to you, Superintendent. And my husband says if you continue to bother us, he's going to bring you up on charges of harassment."

So she'd told him about her previous phone call. And very

likely got an earful from him in return. Maybe more than an earful.

"I'm calling about Lynn."

"Is something wrong? Has something happened to . . . to her?"

Nat could hear the coldness in Ruth's voice quickly give way to anguish. The anguish of a mother desperately worried about her child's welfare. But Nat could also hear the strain, the awkwardness, the discomfort.

"She's asking for you, Ruth. She wants to see you."

"I . . . can't."

"Of course you can." It was all Nat could do to keep the rage out of her voice. She was particularly sensitive when it came to the issue of parents abandoning their children, be it a physical or an emotional abandonment. Lynn's mother and father had managed both.

"I just left your daughter's bedside, Ruth, so her words are very fresh in my mind. Her exact words were, 'I want my mommy.' " Some of Nat's anger was seeping into her voice. She couldn't help it. It wasn't that she was completely unsympathetic to the emotional turmoil Ruth Ingram had to have gone through in coping with—or *not* coping with—her child's transsexualism. But, shame and embarrassment, and the wrath of her husband, were not good-enough reasons, in Nat's opinion, for her to have cast her daughter from her life, to stay away even as her child lay in a hospital bed, fighting to stay alive, most likely disfigured for life.

There was silence on the other end of the line. For a few moments Nat thought Ruth Ingram had stealthily hung up the phone. But then she heard muted sounds. Stifled sobs.

Nat's voice softened. "Please come see her, Ruth. I know you want to. Your husband doesn't have to know. You don't have to tell him anything you don't want to."

"You . . . don't understand," she managed through her sobs.

"That's not what matters. You *do* understand. You understand completely how much your child needs her mother."

In the background, Nat picked up a man's voice. "Who's on the phone? What is it? What's wrong?"

Ruth Ingram's hand must have clamped over the mouthpiece because her response to the man Nat assumed was Lynn's father, was muffled. "Nothing. Nothing's wrong."

"Ruth, I'm here at my office. You have the number. Call me back when you can talk."

There was a distinct click. This time Ruth Ingram had indeed hung up.

Leaving Nat—and Ruth's daughter—hanging in more ways than one.

"Superintendent?"

Paul LaMotte was standing at Nat's office door. The inmate clerk looked uneasy.

"What is it?"

"There's—"

But before he could finish, her clerk was shoved aside by an imposing, irate middle-aged man dressed in a dark gray business suit.

Nat was up out of her chair, awash with outrage at this intrusion. "Who do you think—?"

"Scram," the intruder ordered her clerk; his gaze, however, fixed solely on Nat.

Paul LaMotte's eyes glinted with a fury Nat had never seen

in them before. For an instant, she worried that her clerk might act out on that wrath. Which was something she dearly wanted to avoid happening. If LaMotte attacked someone, even in self-defense—or in this case, *her* defense—his status as a trustee would have to be revoked and he'd end up back behind the wall.

"It's okay, Paul. I know this man. You can go."

Her clerk remained wary. "You sure you don't want me to get a coupla officers in here and boot this nutcase out?"

"I'm sure Councilman Milburne will behave himself," she said with more confidence than she was actually feeling. Not that she was worried the politician would physically strike out at her. No politician was that stupid. And Milburne might be a lot of things, but he was certainly not ignorant. Nat was less sure about a verbal outburst, so her comment to her clerk was really meant as a directive to the furious councilman.

LaMotte hesitated for few seconds, but then exited, deliberately leaving her door open.

Milburne slammed it shut.

Nat was still on her feet, loath to sit back down while Milburne was standing. She thought it would be best if they remained on equal footing. Best for her, that was.

"You've got one hell of a nerve."

Nat made no response, choosing instead to silently size up the politician. This was the first time she'd met the man, but she'd seen him on television and in the press. Daniel Milburne seemed not only to relish the spotlight, but to make concerted efforts to put himself in it.

Not that Milburne was particularly photogenic. The forty-seven-year-old councilman was not a good-looking man. His complexion was riddled with the pockmark scars of teenage acne. His nose was broad. His hairline had receded, leaving a formidable widow's peak. His eyes were narrow slits, giving the impression that he was always squinting.

But no question Daniel Milburne was imposing. Especially when he pulled himself up to his full six-foot-three-inch height and expanded his broad ex-linebacker's chest so that you could see the strain on the buttons of his suit jacket.

He billed himself as a man of the people. Strong on family values. Strong on drugs. Strong on crime. And a big-time proponent of the death penalty.

All this from a man who was on his third marriage. Who—according to the tabloids—was estranged from his son from his first marriage, and whose daughter from his second marriage had been in and out of drug rehab for several years. Milburne was also a man who had had quite a bit of trouble explaining away a recent candid photo that appeared in the Boston papers showing him having a cozy little dinner in a swanky South End restaurant with Louis Ferrara, a wealthy businessman rumored to be one of the key figures in organized crime in the Boston area.

"I don't know what your game is, but you get one thing straight: Stay away from my wife. Don't write her again, call her, or show up within ten miles of her, or I swear," he said, jabbing a finger in Nat's direction like it was a gun, "I'll press charges against you for harassment and attempted blackmail before you can say—"

"Bethany Graham?"

"What the fuck is your problem?"

"I don't have a problem, Dan," she said blithely. "And I don't know anything about any letters or phone calls."

"Is that right? Next you'll tell me it wasn't you who approached my wife at the charity luncheon yesterday. Don't waste your breath. I've got witnesses who IDed you."

"I was there," Nat admitted, seeing no reason to deny it. "But, again, I never wrote or phoned your wife."

"So you explain how it is that she finds a letter in the mail last week addressed to *Bethany* Milburne. My wife goes by the name Beth, but her full name is Elizabeth, not *Bethany*. Everybody knows that. Everybody but you, that is."

"What did the letter say?"

Milburne sneered.

"Humor me, Dan."

He fiddled with his blue-and-red paisley tie. "Two lines: 'I know who you are. And you tell your husband, so will everyone else if he doesn't own up.' "

"No signature?"

"No, guess you forgot to sign it. And before you bother asking, there was no return address. It was on ordinary white letter-size paper. The warning and the address on the envelope were both typed on a word processor. She didn't know what to make of it."

"Didn't she?"

Milburne ignored her question.

"Then yesterday morning she gets a phone call from a kid. Asking for 'Bethany.' When Beth started to explain that her name was Beth, this girl says to her, 'Your husband is a bad man.' Then she hangs up."

"I'm not a *kid*, Mr. Milburne."

"No, but maybe you have one. Or pretended to be one. All I do know is you're the one who showed up at that luncheon on Saturday. Calling my wife 'Bethany.' Making up some cock-and-bull story about her mother coming from San Diego—"

"San Jose," she quietly corrected him.

Milburne clenched his hands into meaty fists. "I've had about as much of this shit as I'm gonna take. So now, *I'm* warning *you*."

Nat flashed on that vile drawing, wondering if this wasn't his first warning to her. How far would Milburne go to protect his career? To protect his hide?

eighteen

All the women knew I was a favorite target. Derision, revulsion, mind-games, unjust disciplinary action. I was getting it from all sides—figuratively and literally. When it comes down to it, there is no one I can risk trusting.

L. I.

WHEN THE NURSE at Mercy informed Nat that Suzanne Holden had a visitor, she immediately assumed it must be Leo.

She was wrong. It wasn't Leo but Ross Varda sitting in the orange plastic chair beside the inmate's bed.

"You look surprised," he said.

Not that it would take a psychiatrist to discern that.

"Suzanne had one of the nurses call me and ask me to come in to see her," Varda explained. "My prison credentials got me past the officer on duty outside."

"I didn't know the two of you knew each other."

"Suzanne was in one of my therapy groups at Grafton for a short time."

Varda got to his feet, offering her the chair. She turned down the offer which left them both standing.

"Suzanne has been telling me about her terrible ordeal. That someone jumped her—"

"She doesn't believe me," Suzanne said plaintively. "No one believes me."

"Now, now, Suzanne," Dr. Varda soothed.

"No one's discounting your story," Nat said. "The police are doing a very thorough investigation."

A flicker of hope briefly lit her eyes. "Leo will prove I'm telling the truth. I know he will. He has to."

Just hearing his name uttered from her lips caused Nat's stomach to clench.

"You look tired, Suzanne. Why don't you try to sleep?" The psychiatrist glanced at Nat. "She says she hasn't slept in the past two nights."

"The nurse wouldn't even give me a damn Tylenol P.M. It says in big red letters on my chart: NO MEDS. Like what? I'm gonna OD on fucking acetaminophen."

"I'll go have a word with her," Dr. Varda said. He paused for a moment at the door. "Don't stay too long, Superintendent. Suzanne really does need to rest."

As soon as he left, Nat sat down in the chair he'd vacated.

"I got a visit today from Daniel Milburne, Suzanne."

She gave Nat a blank look.

"He was very angry. He told me a woman has been threatening him. She sent a letter to his wife a few days ago. Yesterday, she phoned her. He thinks I'm behind the threats."

Suzanne shrugged.

"This woman called his wife 'Bethany.' Which is interesting because she hasn't used that name in a long time."

Suzanne looked away.

"In fact, hardly anyone knows she used to go by the name Bethany. But you knew, right?"

Suzanne continued avoiding eye contact. "I don't know what you're talking about."

"Lynn never talked to you about Bethany?"

"No." Suzanne snapped out her response a little too quickly.

"Bethany Graham?"

"No."

"This is a real puzzle, Suzanne. Because very few people other than me know about Bethany Graham. And since I wasn't the one who threatened her—"

"It wasn't me. Shit. First you accuse me of using again. Now you're trying to pin some blackmail scheme on me—"

"I didn't call it blackmail." But, of course Nat was thinking, drugs weren't free.

"Whatever. It wasn't me. That's all I know."

"Well, what worries me is that Milburne might think you know more than that. He might think Lynn did talk to you about Bethany. And I'm pretty sure he doesn't want anyone talking about his wife. Lynn. Her folks. You. Anyone."

Suzanne wet her dry lips as she studied Nat closely. "You think he's the one put the jump on me and shot me up? So you believe I'm telling the truth?"

"It's not a matter of what I believe. We need proof."

"Look," she said pleadingly, "I didn't see who did it. I swear."

"And you have no idea who it might have been? Or why someone would do that to you?"

"No," she maintained stubbornly. Or, Nat wondered, was it fear more than stubbornness?

Nat's frustration was mounting. "So when you learned that Lynn was violently assaulted and nearly killed last week, Milburne's name didn't pop into your mind?"

"I told you, I don't know him," she snapped.

"Whose name did pop into your head?" Nat pounced right back.

She shut her eyes. "No one."

"I don't believe you. His name popped into your head again just now when I asked you that question."

"Leave me alone."

"You could have died, Suzanne. Hutch says you were right on the brink when he found you." Nat paused deliberately before adding, "If someone did this to you, it's very likely you were meant to die."

She clamped her hands up to her ears. "Stop. Can't you just stop?"

"I don't want anything to happen to you."

Her eyes flew open and she fixed Nat with a disquieting stare. "Don't you?"

Nat was stunned by her words. "Suzanne—"

"If I'm out of the picture, Leo won't be torn—"

Nat gripped her shoulders hard enough that she winced. But she didn't let go. She was too angry. "Listen to me, Suzanne. If you love someone, the last thing in the world you want to do is cause them grief and suffering. If Leo's torn"—and Nat did believe he was feeling pulled between them—"then he's got to sort it out for himself. If what he and I share isn't strong enough to hold him, then . . . that's how it is. It has nothing—do you hear me?—*nothing* to do with you. It's between me and Leo."

"Fine."

"So let's leave Leo out of this, okay?"

"Okay, okay. I'm sorry."

Nat dropped her hands to her sides. "You know there'll have to be a disciplinary hearing when you're out of the hospital."

"You can't send me back to Grafton. You can't. I've been clean for so long. I'd never do something so stupid. Especially not now. Not now when everything's starting to come together for me."

Everything. Did that include Leo? So much for Nat wanting to leave him out of this.

"Please, you can't send me back," she pleaded. "I'll die if I go back."

"You have a greater risk of dying if you don't help us nail the bastard."

"I can't. I can't. Don't you understand? I can't."

"Yes you can. Tell her, Suzanne. You must."

The voice coming from the doorway startled both women.

Ross Varda strode purposefully across the hospital room and over to the bed. "It's for your own safety, Suzanne."

Nat wondered how long he'd been standing there, listening.

Dr. Varda maintained his focus on his patient. And her eyes were glued to his. "I . . . can't," she said hoarsely.

"Yes you can, Suzanne."

Her hands were trembling as she touched them to her face.

"Back when you and Lynn were at Grafton, something happened, isn't that so, Suzanne?" he coaxed.

Suzanne nodded.

"What happened?"

"Lynn was . . . raped."

"Yes, go on," he said.

"Lynn was scared." Suzanne swallowed hard. "She told me she was scared."

Nat moved in a little closer to Suzanne. "Who was she scared of, Suzanne? Who raped her?"

She compressed her lips.

"Did he rape you, too?" Nat asked gently.

"No, no, it wasn't . . . like that. He didn't . . . want me. Not . . . sexually." She shot Varda a look. As if wanting confirmation.

"Suzanne," he said softly, "you will never fully recover if you keep this all inside. We've chatted about that, haven't we?"

She bit down so hard on her badly chapped bottom lip, it started to bleed. "He's not a bad man. He looked out for me. It would have been so much worse without him."

A cold chill seeped into Nat's bones. This wouldn't be the first time an inmate, especially a female inmate, had been brainwashed into thinking her abuser was really a good guy. There was even a name for it: Stockholm syndrome, coined from a hostage situation in the 1970s at a Stockholm bank where employees, held hostage for days, developed an intense attachment to their captors.

"You may not think he hurt you, but he did. And two days ago, he nearly killed you," Nat said. "It was the same man, wasn't it, Suzanne?"

Suzanne turned her head away. "Stop."

"And what about Lynn?" Nat persisted. "He certainly hurt Lynn. She told you she was scared of him. She had good reason to be scared, Suzanne. It would break your heart to see Lynn now. Her face all cut up, her breasts, her—"

"Stop!" she screamed.

But Nat kept hammering home the reality: "When the bastard

was finished mutilating her, he threw her ravaged body into a Dumpster and left her for dead."

Suzanne looked pleadingly at Dr. Varda. "Make her stop."

"Please, Superintendent. You can see that Suzanne is over-wrought. And very frightened. With good reason."

"That's precisely why she's got to tell me who this bastard is."

Varda took hold of Suzanne's hand. "Tell Ms. Price the man's name, Suzanne. It's okay. Once she knows, you'll be safe. I promise you."

When she finally uttered his name, she said it in such a low whisper, Nat could barely make it out.

"Joe?" Nat repeated.

Suzanne hesitated, then nodded.

"Joe who? What's his last name?"

Suzanne squeezed her eyes shut.

"Please, Suzanne. You have to tell me. Joe who?"

The inmate mumbled a name but Nat didn't catch it.

"Parker." It was Ross Varda who repeated the name.

Nat gave the psychiatrist a studied look, then turned back to Suzanne, who was still crying softly. "You've done the right thing." *And the psychologically healthy thing,* Nat thought. It was a first step in breaking the syndrome.

"I'm not saying he did it. Cut Lynn up and . . . jumped me," Suzanne said anxiously. "Maybe it wasn't him. Maybe, like you said before, it was that guy Milburne. I mean, shit, I wasn't there when Lynn was attacked. And I never saw who came at me. You don't know it wasn't Milburne, right? It could have been him. Just like you said. He had plenty of reason."

Varda gave Nat a puzzled look. She was sure he was wondering who Milburne was and how he fit into the investigation. Nat was beginning to wonder now if he did.

"But you are sure this Joe Parker raped Lynn when she was in Grafton? She told you it was Parker." Nat wanted confirmation from Suzanne.

Tears began falling down her cheeks. "No. She didn't tell me."

"*He* told you? Parker told you he'd done it?"

Suzanne put both hands over her eyes.

Varda looked wearily at Nat. "He didn't have to *tell* her."

It took her a few moments to take in the full measure of the psychiatrist's words: Suzanne *saw* them. Suzanne Holden witnessed Joe Parker rape Lynn Ingram.

"He's not a bad man," Suzanne rasped. "He . . . couldn't help himself. He was . . . sorry afterward. He really was . . . sorry."

Nat's cell phone rang as she was heading out of Mercy Medical Center. It was Leo.

"You still with Suzanne?"

"How did you know . . . ?" But then Nat remembered the cop posted at Suzanne's door. Leo must be having him report in on visitors.

"We got something. I'm at the Precinct House. Can you come over?"

"I'll head there now." Nat almost added that she had something, too. But her shocking news was not something to share on the phone. Nat was more than a little worried about how Leo would feel—and react—when he found out about Suzanne and Joe Parker. There was little question in Nat's mind that Parker'd served as Suzanne's "daddy" when she was in Grafton. He may have protected her, but Nat was sure Suzanne had paid a hefty price for that protection. Did she really think what he'd done to her *wasn't* rape?

This ugly business was getting more personal by the minute.

Nat punched in Jack Dwyer's direct number at Horizon House. "Joe Parker," she said abruptly. "You know him?"

"Who?"

"Joe Parker. He's a CO at Grafton." Only now did Nat realize she hadn't actually confirmed with Suzanne that Parker was a corrections officer. He could be one of the vocational education or shop teachers, a mental health person . . .

"Why are you asking?"

"Suzanne broke down and named him—with a little coaxing from Ross Varda. Suzanne saw this Joe Parker rape Lynn when they were at Grafton. She said Lynn was scared to death of him."

"Joe Parker?" Jack repeated slowly. There was no missing the note of disbelief in his voice.

"That's right," she said impatiently. "Joe Parker."

"You got the wrong guy." Jack's statement was adamant. "Believe me, Nat—"

"Obviously you do know him. Is he an officer?"

Jack didn't answer right away. "Nat, Joe Parker is a good buddy of Hutch's. They go back a long way."

"That makes it awkward, but it doesn't change the fact."

"He's a priest, Nat."

Her mouth fell open. "What?"

"He's a Catholic priest. He and Hutch grew up together in Dorchester. Hutch and his family have been members of his church for years. Kerry, his oldest daughter, was married by Father Joe. I was at the wedding. Like I said, Nat, you got it wrong."

"A priest. Oh, Christ," Nat muttered, wanting to kick herself. Father Joe. The priest Carrie Li told her had called to check on Lynn's condition. Very likely the same priest Leo had spoken to on the phone. And Nat was willing to bet the bank it was also the Father Joe Parker who'd showed up at the hospital on some trumped-up excuse about visiting one of his parishioners so he could find out firsthand from the surgeon about Lynn's condition.

"Nat? You still there."

"Yeah."

"You gotta be wrong about this," Jack said.

Leo's greeting was perfunctory. A man with a lot on his mind. Well, Nat was a woman with plenty on her mind, too. Before she could start to unload some of it, Leo jumped right in, setting a plastic evidence bag on his desk.

"What is it?" she asked.

"A scrap of cloth."

"I can see that."

"A scrap of cloth containing still-detectable remnants of ether, according to our lab boys."

Nat immediately remembered Suzanne's words. *"I felt something . . . over my mouth . . . Awful smell . . . Couldn't breathe. Couldn't . . . So dizzy . . ."*

"Where did you find it?"

"One of my boys plucked it out of a trash can." He paused. "The trash can was in the alley behind the boutique."

Nat picked up a faint note of triumph in his voice. She'd wanted proof; here was proof.

"I've also doubled the watch outside Suzanne's hospital

room," he said brusquely. Nat now remembered seeing a second officer coming down the hospital corridor when she'd left her a short time ago.

"Suzanne's being released tomorrow morning," he continued. "I want her put in protective custody. At Horizon House."

Nat nodded slowly. Even though they both knew this evidence wasn't enough to unconditionally prove Suzanne's story, it was more than enough for Nat to put the inmate's disciplinary hearing on hold. Nat was also in complete agreement with Leo that Suzanne should remain at Horizon House. No way, knowing what she knew now, was she sending Suzanne back to Grafton.

Nat was about to tell Leo about Father Joe when she was distracted by the gruesome drawing Leo placed on the desk. Her warning note.

"This is a photocopy," Leo said. "You can pass it on to Varda. Tell him I'd like his analysis. I'm curious to see if he comes up with the same conclusions our man Carl Miller made. You want to read his report?"

"I'll take a copy home with me. Give me the highlights."

Leo placed a copy of the report beside the drawing, but he didn't have to refer to it. "Interestingly, Miller, like you, observed that there was a childish quality to the drawing. He even went so far as to theorize that a child might well have done the sketch."

Nat gave Leo an incredulous look.

"For all the gory details, Miller says that the way the lines are done and the way it's been colored in are typical of a child's style. Also, what Miller views as key is that he sees no signs of rage or panic in the way it's drawn. He goes into a detailed explanation about how and why he reaches these conclusions."

"This doesn't make any sense, Leo. Lynn wasn't attacked by a child."

"Let's say this was done by a child." Leo tapped the photocopy. "There's nothing to say this creep we're after did the drawing himself."

"He asked a child to do the drawing?" Her tone was openly dubious.

"It's not so far-fetched. He knows we're gonna analyze the shit out of this drawing, and he wants to send us off on a wild-goose chase." There was a pause before Leo went on. "Also, Miller pointed out that the suspect may feel a need to bring someone else into his scheme. A co-conspirator."

"A child?"

"The bastard describes to the kid what he wants drawn, gives the kid a few pointers along the way—"

"You wouldn't ask just any kid. Does Miller think our guy's a pedophile?" Nat's stomach clenched. The news was full of cases being brought against Catholic priests on charges of pedophilia. As if things weren't bad enough, was it possible Father Joe's crimes were not only against female inmates but children as well?

"Same question I asked Miller," Leo said somberly. This was not only a cop speaking, but the father of a little boy.

"And?"

"Miller said not necessarily. And he made another interesting observation. The way the face is drawn leads him to think it's more likely a little girl than a little boy who did it. A kid as young as five." He paused. Waiting for Nat to draw the same conclusion he had drawn.

But Nat's mind was still on Father Joe.

"Harrison Bell has a little girl. Daphne. Four years old. Turns five in November." Clearly, he'd been studying his notes on Bell. "And I've checked into whether Milburne or Rodney Bartlett have any young children. Milburne's youngest is nineteen. He and Beth have no children. Bartlett is discreet about it, but he's gay. No current lover, no kids. Jennifer and Matthew Slater were also childless. And, by the way, no luck confirming Bartlett's absence at the funeral. The witness we were pretty sure of is now saying it wasn't Bartlett who left; it was another guy closer to the aisle."

"A friend of Bartlett's?" Nat asked.

"Nope. A doc who got paged by his nurse and hightailed it to the hospital."

"Bartlett could have paid off the witness."

"It's possible." Leo didn't sound very enthusiastic about this possibility. "Given what we've got at this point, we're definitely moving Bell to the top of our list."

"I don't know, Leo." Granted, Bell had been one of her prime picks as well—until that morning's meeting with Suzanne. Now, like Daniel Milburne and Rodney Bartlett, he was quickly fading into the woodwork. Nat was thinking about Father Joe Parker. True, the priest wouldn't have children of his own—unless he had an illegitimate child that he'd secretly fathered—but he certainly would have ample contacts with plenty of youngsters via the church. Youngsters who would look up to their priest. Who might do whatever Father asked of them . . .

"According to Bell's clerk," Leo went on, "Bell left the clinic at four o'clock on Saturday. More than enough time for him to have zipped over to the boutique on Newbury Street. Not to mention how easy it would have been for him to get his hands on a hypodermic needle and drugs."

"Easy enough for anyone to get their hands on dope and works," she muttered.

"I saved the best for last. I want you to listen to something." He opened the top desk drawer and pulled out a small cassette player and a second evidence bag—this one containing a cassette. "I got this in the mail this morning. I want to play it for you."

He removed a pair of rubber gloves from his jacket pocket and slipped them on before removing the cassette and placing it in the player.

He hit PLAY. A woman's voice came on, husky-sounding, like she had a terrible cold—

I am a patient of Dr. Harrison Bell's. That is . . . I was his patient. I won't give my name because I do not want to become involved in this sordid business. But I feel it's my duty as a citizen to come forward. On what ended up being my final visit to Dr. Bell . . . this was a couple of weeks ago . . . I was waiting in his examining room when I heard an argument going on next door. That would be Dr. Bell's consulting room. I recognized his voice immediately. It took a bit longer to recognize the . . . woman's voice. It was Dr. Ingram. I had seen . . . her a few times for pain management. I have . . . well, that's neither here nor there. The argument they were having was . . . personal. I distinctly heard Dr. Bell yelling at Dr. Ingram. He was shouting— "You can't just end it. You can't just dismiss everything we've had, everything we've been to each other." Dr. Ingram . . . she wasn't really screaming so much as . . . well, I guess she was really pleading with him—first to keep his voice down, but then when he kept shouting, I heard her say, "You leave me no choice. We can't go on this way."

And then she said—now it sounded like she was crying—
"It isn't that I don't love you. I will never stop loving you."
But Dr. Bell, he only got angrier. Shouting even louder—
"I won't let you go. Not now. Not ever." And then Dr.
Ingram was definitely crying. I thought she was just so up-
set, but then I heard her say—"Stop, you're hurting me,
Harrison." I guess he did stop, because seconds later I heard
the door to his office slam shut and next thing you know
he breezed right into the examining room as if . . . as if
nothing had happened. He greeted me with a warm smile
and he looked . . . cool as a cucumber.

Leo hit the OFF button. "True, this wouldn't be admissible in court—"

"And," Nat pointed out, "it could be a fake."

"We're gonna lean on Bell. See if we can't get him to come clean. And there's always the possibility, if the tape is legit, that Lynn Ingram will remember some of this." He waited for a response from Nat. When he didn't get one, he looked at her more closely. "Something's up. What is it?" he asked cautiously.

"I have a new suspect for you, Leo. I'm pretty sure this one will drop Bell down a notch on your suspect list."

Leo got up from the desk and started to pace. Not a hell of a lot of space for it in his small office. He managed maybe ten steps to the wall, then crossed back ten steps. His expression was grim. Frown lines cut across his brow. His eyes were cast to the floor as though he was searching for something he'd dropped.

The tension in the office was palpable.

Leo paused for a moment, shooting Nat a look. He opened

his mouth to say something, but then shut it again without uttering a word.

"I know it's hard to believe," she said softly. No matter what one's denomination, it was difficult to imagine, much less accept, that a priest, a man of God, would be capable of such heinous crimes. Nat was sure it was especially hard for Leo, who was Catholic. While he wasn't a regular churchgoer, she knew from Jakey's grandmother that Jakey had been baptized and that she took the little boy to church once or twice a month. Nat had been invited along with them one time, even though she wasn't Catholic. She hadn't really been raised with any religion. Her mother believed only in her delusions. Her father put all his faith in the bottle. Their gods failed them utterly.

And what did she believe in? It was a question she'd pondered a good deal over the years. There'd been times she'd thought she knew, only to be proven wrong. She'd yet to come up with a lasting answer.

Leo stopped pacing, dropped back into his chair. Still not a word. Was he thinking about what the priest did to Lynn? Or trying to sort out exactly what Suzanne's relationship was to Father Joe? Not that it was hard for him to figure out.

"I'm sorry, Leo," Nat said finally, his continued silence wearing on her heart.

He mimed an indifferent shrug—she didn't believe for an instant that was the way he was feeling—then pulled open the top drawer of his desk and took out an opened pack of Lucky Strikes. He tapped a cigarette out, jabbed the unfiltered tip between his lips, rummaged in the drawer until he unearthed a book of matches, and lit up.

Right behind him on the wall was posted the ubiquitous NO SMOKING sign.

It was no big surprise to Nat that Leo wasn't swayed by that stricture.

What surprised her was the smoking itself. Leo'd quit smoking before she knew him—he told her once that he'd stopped right after Jakey was born—fiercely determined not to endanger his child with secondhand smoke. It would take a lot for Leo to light up again.

Nat was smart enough not to comment on it.

She was smart enough to keep her mouth shut altogether.

nineteen

Lynn sought religious counsel prior to making her de-cision to go ahead with the sexual-reassignment surgery and was told by the pastor that it was a sin against God.

DR. ROSS VARDA
(THERAPY NOTE)

NAT WAS MORE than a bit surprised when Melissa Raymond introduced herself at the front door of the rectory. She looked nothing like Nat's stereotype of a priest's housekeeper. She'd envisioned a late-middle-aged, plain-looking, broad-faced woman with steel-gray hair, wearing a matronly black dress, a large silver or gold cross prominently hanging from a chain around her neck.

Melissa Raymond's cross—if, indeed, she was wearing one—was nowhere in sight. She was a willowy woman who looked to be in her mid-thirties. She was smartly dressed in a pair of finely tailored charcoal-gray slacks and an emerald-green sweater that highlighted her green eyes—not to mention clinging to her shapely bosom. Her chestnut hair hung sleekly down around her shoulders.

Nat wondered facetiously how well she cleaned house.

"Father Joe is working on next Sunday's sermon and he hates to be interrupted," Melissa said in a crisp, proprietary tone.

Leo whipped out his badge. Melissa's eyes widened slightly, but otherwise her features registered no alarm.

"Is this about Tommy Matthews?" she asked, lowering her voice a notch. "Father Joe's been saying for weeks that one of these days that boy is going to—"

"It's not about Tommy Matthews," Leo cut her off brusquely.

This elicited a slight flush on Melissa's fair and flawless skin. "Oh," she muttered. "Well, I suppose I . . . could interrupt Father."

"Do that," Leo said.

Melissa's flush deepened.

Leo and Nat eyed each other as Melissa hurried off, leaving them standing in the gloomy and airless foyer of the large, late-nineteenth-century stone-and-brick rectory beside St. Bartholomew's Church.

It couldn't have been any more than thirty seconds before Father Joe himself was bustling down the hall from his office toward them.

If Nat had been surprised by the housekeeper's appearance, she was doubly surprised by Father Joe's. Not that she'd formulated a vivid image of what a priest/sexual abuser/psychopath would look like, but it certainly wouldn't have been this small, pudgy, fifty-something-year-old man with graying hair and a benign demeanor, dressed in baggy khaki slacks and a navy-blue T-shirt.

It was hard to imagine he'd be big enough or strong enough

to attack the nearly six-foot-tall Lynn Ingram, much less be capable of lifting her limp body and tossing it into a Dumpster.

But then Nat had encountered numerous men—and women—in prison whose size and apparent lack of strength had proved no deterrent to their commission of heinous crimes against seemingly bigger and stronger victims. In the heat of rage or passion or both, with the adrenaline flowing, it was amazing how strong a person could become.

As Father Joe approached them, he was smiling beneficently, but Nat detected a shadow of worry on his face.

"Please," he said, sounding a bit out of breath, "forgive my appearance. I wasn't expecting—" He stopped. "Well, of course I wasn't expecting you." He extended a hand in Nat's direction. She gave the priest's hand a perfunctory shake. When Father Joe extended his hand to Leo, Leo stuck his hands in his jacket pocket.

"Please, come into the parlor." Father Joe Parker was already heading over to the closed heavy mahogany pocket doors to their right. As he slid them open, he glanced back at them. "I've asked Melissa to bring us all some tea. I hope you like tea. Of course, if you prefer coffee—"

"Nothing for me." Leo gestured to the priest to step into the parlor. They followed him inside. Leo slid the doors shut.

The dark-wood–paneled room that Father Joe referred to as the parlor more resembled a library. Bookcases lined two walls from floor to ceiling. Heavy dark-umber drapery covered much of the triple-bay window that faced the street. Narrow openings in the curtains allowed only thin shafts of light to filter into the space. The floor was covered with a muted Persian rug. The furnishings looked to be authentic Victorian antiques—deep-blue velvet sofas, a pair of ornate brocade armchairs, a large, intricately carved mahogany desk. Father Joe approached the desk and turned on a desk lamp. Then, after a pause—possibly reflecting that this amount of lighting did not exactly flood the room with brightness—he moved to a standing lamp by the sofa and turned that on as well. The lighting, while now adequate for their purposes, didn't expel the essential gloominess of the parlor.

The room was meticulously tidy and there was a lingering hint of fine-furniture polish. Melissa might not have looked like a housekeeper, but then, looks, as Nat knew so well, could be deceiving. She had to remember to keep that in mind in connection with the unassuming priest.

Father Joe ushered them to the two respective armchairs, selecting the couch for himself. He settled himself before he spoke.

"Now, please, tell me how I can help you."

"Let's start with Suzanne Holden," Leo said gruffly.

Not even a hint of alarm or wariness in the priest's demeanor in response to this question. "Suzanne Holden?"

"An inmate at Grafton."

"Let me think. I've been volunteering there for a number of years. So many women . . ."

"She has very clear recollections of you."

"Is that right?" He spoke with a tone that indicated nothing more than curiosity, then pondered the name aloud again. A few seconds later, he snapped his fingers. "Of course. Suzanne. Yes. Yes, yes. I'm sorry. I should especially remember Suzanne."

Nat's stomach clenched. *Yeah, I bet you should.*

"Very troubled. She has a little boy, you see. It's all coming back to me. Wasn't she released a few months ago? No, wait, she was transferred. Yes, I remember now. She went to a prerelease center. Something hasn't happened, I hope. She is all right, isn't she?"

Leo ignored the question. "What's 'all coming back' to you?"

Father Joe scowled in thought. "All the times she spoke about her son. What a sweet and clever little boy he was. Suzanne was always bringing me in photos of the child. Oh, yes, and little drawings he made for her when he came to visit."

Nat glanced surreptitiously over at Leo to check out his reaction. His poker face was in place, but she suspected it was taking a concerted effort. Did he know how much Jakey meant to Suzanne? How much pride she took in her child?

Her child. Nat felt an ache in her chest. And she was sure her own attempt to maintain a neutral look was not nearly so successful as Leo's.

"You said she was very troubled," Leo said.

"May I ask what this is about? I know Suzanne had a drug problem. I hope she hasn't . . . slipped. One of the things, in fact, that concerned her deeply was that she had passed the illness on to her little boy and that he'd grow up to be a drug addict. Is she all right?"

"No," Leo said succinctly.

The priest looked genuinely alarmed. "Is she back on drugs?"

Nat grit her teeth. It was all she could do not to leap up from her chair and slam her fist into Father Joe's face.

But Leo continued to appear cool and collected. "Let's move on to Lynn Ingram."

Father Joe nodded, resting his small hands over the paunch of his belly. Nat found herself studying those hands with their short, pudgy fingers—a plain band of gold on the marriage finger of the left hand. Father Joe was married to the church.

Was it really possible that these were the hands of a slasher? Was this man of God capable of wielding a knife and viciously, brutally, cutting up a woman? Leaving her for dead? Were these the hands of a man who would plunge a hypodermic needle full of heroin into the vein of a recovering drug addict?

"I have been praying for Lynn daily." He pressed his palms together as if to demonstrate the gesture of prayer. Or was he saying a silent prayer at that very moment? Praying for another go at her? Another go at Suzanne? Praying that his crimes would go undetected?

Father Joe dropped his hands over his belly again. "I keep listening to the news, reading the daily paper, hoping to get word on her condition, but there's been absolutely nothing—"

"You've done more than follow the news," Nat challenged.

Father Joe gave her a blank look. "I don't—" His expression quickly changed. "Oh, yes, that's true. I did have a brief word with a doctor over at the hospital. I was paying a call on one of my parishioners and—"

"The name?" Leo interrupted.

"Excuse me?"

"The name of the parishioner you were visiting." Leo had his notebook out and was withdrawing a pen from his pocket.

"I can't remember offhand. It was actually the mother of a parishioner. Visiting from out of town—"

"The parishioner's name, then," Leo pressed.

"Alice," the priest said after a short pause. "Alice Morrisey."

"How would you describe your relationships with Suzanne Holden and Lynn Ingram?" Leo asked, deliberately throwing the priest a curve ball.

Father Joe merely gave Leo a puzzled look. But before he could respond—probably only to question the question—there was a firm knock on the door. "Yes, come in, Melissa," Father Joe said in the direction of the closed doors.

The doors slid open. Melissa's eyes darted immediately over

to the priest. He smiled pleasantly. "You may bring in the tea, my dear."

She disappeared for a moment and reappeared with a silver tea set sitting on a silver tray that she must have put down on a nearby table.

Nat spotted the housekeeper catch the priest's eye again as she set the tray down on a coffee table in front of the sofa.

"Is there anything else?" she asked.

"No, Melissa." He checked his watch. "It's nearly noon. You better hurry off and meet the school bus."

Now it was Leo and Nat who exchanged glances.

"You have a child?" Nat asked Melissa as she was starting toward the doorway.

Her back stiffened as she glanced back at me. "Yes. A little girl." There was a hint of defensiveness in her tone. Nat's gaze instinctively fell to her left hand. No wedding band.

But it wasn't Melissa Raymond's marital status that was on Nat's mind. It was the fact that she had a child. A daughter. A daughter who was likely very close to Father Joe. If he'd asked her to draw a picture for him . . .

"Melissa and Emily live here at the rectory," the priest was saying. "Emily's a delightful little girl. Bright, pretty, and very well behaved."

Yeah, I bet she's well behaved, Nat thought.

Melissa made a speedy exit while Father Joe was talking, and firmly shut the doors behind her.

"How long have they lived here with you?" Nat asked the priest.

Father Joe paused to mull this over. "Let me see. It must be close to nine years now. Yes, Melissa just turned thirty-three. She came here when she was twenty-four. Yes, so that would be nine years."

Nat's mind was racing. *Nine years. And Emily is in kindergarten. So Melissa got pregnant while she was living at the rectory. Did she get pregnant* at *the rectory? Was I on the right track when I considered the possibility that the priest had fathered an illegitimate child? Is Emily his?*

"Who's the father?" Nat asked bluntly.

"Excuse me?" Father Joe said, visibly taken aback for the first time.

"She asked you who Emily's father is," Leo repeated.

"Well, I can't really . . . That's not a question I feel I . . . I have the right to answer." Finally, a crack in the veneer.

"I suppose we can wait until your housekeeper gets back and ask her," Leo said offhandedly. "Let's get back to my earlier question."

"What was that?" Father Joe looked plenty flustered now. Maybe they were actually getting somewhere.

"How would you describe your relationships with Suzanne Holden and Lynn Ingram?" There was nothing offhanded in Leo's voice now.

"I'm a spiritual counselor, Detective. I am spiritual counselor to many inmates, Suzanne and Lynn among many." He shifted uneasily on the sofa.

"Is that right?" Leo said, eyeballing Father Joe.

The priest looked away, letting his gaze rest on the tea service. He didn't, however, make any move to pour the tea. Although, Nat bet he could use a drink right about now, probably something stronger than tea, though.

There was a prolonged silence.

Leo broke it big-time. "Suzanne Holden witnessed you raping Lynn Ingram at Grafton."

The priest stared at Leo, looking dazed. "What?"

Leo glared at him. "My bet is you raped Suzanne as well. Maybe you didn't call it rape. Probably not. You probably told yourself—and her—every time you fucked her that you were just tending to her physical as well as spiritual needs."

The priest didn't look half as shaken by these reprehensible charges as Leo looked dishing them out. All signs of being cool and collected had vanished. Nat was starting to worry that Leo might decide to tend to some of his own physical needs any moment now. There was no doubt in her mind: Leo would have liked to punch the living daylights out of Father Joe.

Father Joe rose slowly. It seemed to require some serious effort, as if he'd aged twenty years in the last few minutes.

"I am deeply saddened by the poor girl's utterly unfounded charges, Detective. What grieves me most is that I am certain these lies are causing her to suffer deeply. And Suzanne's already suffered so much. May God forgive her." He paused for a few moments. "Please tell her, next time you see her, that I understand. And that I forgive her."

Without another word, Father Joe crossed the room, shoulders drooping, his step no longer spry.

"Where were you Saturday afternoon at four forty-five?" Leo said sharply, just as Father Joe was about to slide open the doors.

The priest didn't turn around. "I was here at the rectory."

"Can anybody back up your story?"

The priest turned slowly to face Leo. "My 'story'?" He nodded sadly. "I was putting the final touches on my sermon. I believe Melissa was here— No, wait, I'm sorry. All this . . . I'm a bit . . . flustered."

He looked more than flustered to Nat. He looked close to panic.

"Saturday is Melissa's day off. She took Emily to the zoo. Emily was so excited when they got home. She started darting around the room imitating a monkey—"

"What time did they get home?" Leo's voice was as hard-edged as his expression.

Father Joe sighed. "I believe it was sometime after six. As a special treat, Melissa took Emily to McDonald's for supper. Emily adores the Happy Meals, but it's really for the little toy they put inside. And the fries. I think she likes the fries—"

"And last Thursday between the hours of eleven A.M. and one P.M.?" Leo continued in the same iron-fisted tone.

Father Joe fixed a weary gaze on Leo. "An alibi for the time Lynn was attacked?"

Leo said nothing.

"I don't remember exactly—"

Leo folded his arms across his chest. "Think about it. I've got plenty of time."

The priest cast Nat a quick glance. She remained silent and grim.

"I believe I was again here at the rectory during that stretch of time." He nodded slowly. "Yes, I was here until shortly before three o'clock." An anguished look shadowed his face. "I did not harm either of those women, Detective. Not while they were in Grafton. Not since they left the prison. I swear—"

"To God?" Leo finished bitingly.

twenty

The goal is to break you. They thought I'd break easily.
I thought I could prove them wrong. I couldn't.

L. I.

AT THE END of the day, Nat was back in the ICU at Boston General. She felt worn out, and while Father Joe was now a prominent name on the suspect list, Leo had been firm in reminding her that there was still no hard-core evidence tying the priest, Harrison Bell, or anyone else for that matter, to the recent attacks on either Lynn or Suzanne.

As Nat approached Lynn's bed, she noticed the inmate's eyes dart anxiously past her—as if she was checking to see if Nat was alone or not. When she saw there was no one else present, she seemed to relax a bit, leaving Nat to wonder who it was she didn't want to see.

"Good news. The doctor says she might move me out of ICU by the end of the week," Lynn said, clearly pleased by this possibility.

Nat was less pleased. It was easier to protect the inmate in the ICU, where the comings and goings of outsiders—and insiders—were rigidly controlled. If she was moved, Nat was sure Leo would increase the number of cops on watch.

"I look pretty bad, huh?" she said softly.

The truth? Lynn looked awful. What little of her face wasn't bandaged was blotchy and discolored. Her hair was matted. Her eyes were so bloodshot, Nat still couldn't see the whites. Her lips were horribly chapped. Had Lynn seen herself in a mirror yet? Nat knew that the doctor had been gently feeding her patient more details about her condition—but had it all really sunk in yet? What state would she be in when it did?

"You look a lot better than you did last Thursday," Nat said. But then, it was hard to imagine she could look worse than she had that day and still be alive.

"Yes, I guess that's true." She tried to smile but couldn't quite manage it. "Oh, and my mother called this morning after you left. I was . . . so surprised."

Nat was relieved that Ruth Ingram at least had called her daughter. Nat was sure Ruth had phoned while her husband was at work.

"Your mother was here the day you were brought in." Nat hoped that would give Lynn some measure of comfort.

"Yes, Dr. Varda told me. I couldn't believe it. We haven't exactly been, well, close these past few years." The pained look in her eyes spoke volumes. "She's going to try to come in to see me again. I told her it wasn't necessary. My dad—" She let the rest of the sentence fall away.

"Yes, I know."

Lynn nodded, blinking back tears.

"Harrison called, too. But it seems they weren't authorized to put the call through." There was no missing the note of disappointment in Lynn's voice. Surely, if Harrison Bell had been her assailant, it was hard to imagine Lynn would speak his name now with that unmistakable hint of longing. But then Nat was reminded that Lynn's memory of the attack remained deeply buried. Maybe she didn't even remember the argument in which she'd called off their affair—or what Nat was assuming was an actual affair, if that tape was to be believed. The woman on the tape gave no indication of when that argument had taken place. Was it shortly before the attack? Weeks before? Nor was there any way to know why Lynn called it off. Was it the old, familiar story of a young woman falling in love with a married man—a married man who fills her with promises that he's going to divorce his wife and marry her? Was Lynn's relationship with Harrison Bell a replay of her relationship with Matthew Slater? Did she finally come to her senses, realize that Bell, like Slater, wasn't about to leave his wife? More significantly, that he was not about to make his relationship with her public. It was one thing to have a secret affair with a transsexual, quite another to announce it to the world.

And when Lynn did finally break it off, had Bell been unwilling to let her go? Did he—? Nat abruptly stopped her ruminations, realizing that on some level she preferred thinking that Bell, rather than a priest, was behind the attacks. But even if Father Joe wasn't responsible for the assaults, there was no dismissing Suzanne's confession. She'd seen Father Joe rape Lynn at Grafton. The priest had committed a crime, even if it wasn't the crime currently under investigation.

Unless Suzanne had been wrong. Unless she'd been mistaken. Was it possible?

Nat focused back in on Lynn, who also seemed lost in her own ruminations.

"I visited Father Joe today," Nat said quietly, her gaze fixed on the patient.

"Who?"

"Father Joe Parker," Nat repeated, watching Lynn intently for any signs of . . . of what? Nat wasn't sure what she was antici-pating Lynn's reaction would be, but it certainly wasn't this blank look. How far back in time did her memory lapse extend?

"Don't you remember Father Joe? From CCI Grafton?"

A worried expression replaced the blankness. "Oh, yes. Yes, I . . . think so. I'm still a little . . . foggy about . . . everything." Foggy, or afraid?

Nat pulled up a chair close to the bed. "What do you remem-ber about Father Joe?"

Lynn didn't respond right away. Her eyes darted around the room again. She definitely seemed to be growing agitated. Nat experienced a wave of guilt. Was Lynn ready for this? Was Nat pushing too hard too soon? But time was weighing heavily on her. On all of them. A lot of people were in mortal danger here: Lynn, Suzanne, Ross Varda, Nat herself. The longer it took to nail the bastard, the greater the risk to all of them.

"Lynn," Nat said softly, "Suzanne Holden has already talked to me about Father Joe."

"Suzanne?"

"Something's happened, Lynn."

"To Suzanne? Is she all right?" Lynn's agitation was palpable. Well, at least she remembered her roommate.

"She's fine," Nat quickly assured her. "But she nearly ODed the other day."

Lynn looked incredulous, then horrified. "No. No, that's not possible. Not Suzanne. She wouldn't go back . . ."

"She says she didn't. She says she was knocked out by an unknown assailant who then pumped her up with enough heroin to kill her."

A small, strangled cry escaped from Lynn's throat. "No, no, no . . ."

"She told me about Father Joe. Do you understand what I'm saying, Lynn? She told me what he did. To you. I went to see him. I know this is hard, Lynn, but please, please try to remember."

"No, no . . ."

"What's going on here?" Carol Jacobson, the head ICU nurse, came storming into the room, fuming. "Whatever it is, it stops now. Out." She pointed a finger at Nat as if it was a weapon. Like, if Nat didn't leave instantly, she'd gun her down.

Nat got to her feet, but she paused long enough to murmur an apology to Lynn, adding, "It'll be okay. Don't worry." Her words sounded hollow to her own ears.

Nat could feel the head nurse glaring into her back as she made her exit.

Ross Varda was coming through the ICU doors as Nat stepped into the corridor. Just the man she wanted to see.

"I need to talk to you," she said.

"Can't it wait until after—"

"No."

• • •

"I hope you realize you may have caused irreparable damage," Varda said sternly.

"I went through all your notes on your therapy sessions with Lynn. There's no mention of Father Joe. Of any priest. She must have talked about him. A trauma like that—"

"Are you listening to me, Superintendent?"

"Nothing I've done compares to what might happen to Lynn if we don't catch this bastard."

He sighed heavily. "Yes. Of course that's true."

"We got nothing out of the priest."

"No," Varda said. "I don't expect you would have."

She pulled out a copy of the gruesome drawing of the woman. "Do you think a child might have drawn this?"

The psychiatrist was taken aback. Nat wasn't sure if it was her question or the drawing. He took hold of the photocopy. "Is this—?"

"Yes. Pretty awful, isn't it?"

He studied it more closely. "What makes you ask me if I think this is a child's work?"

"It's one professional's opinion. What's yours?"

"I'm not a child psychiatrist, but I did some testing with children years back. During my training. Using their drawings as a way of getting at their underlying feelings. The drawings are often crude, sometimes shockingly graphic."

"Like this one?"

He nodded. "Yes. It could have been drawn by a child. But—"

"Father Joe's housekeeper has a five-year-old daughter. Mother and child live at the rectory."

Ross Varda continued staring at the drawing.

"Father Joe's not handing us a confession on a silver platter, Ross."

"I really don't know what to tell you."

"You believe the priest was Lynn's assailant, don't you?"

He gave her a helpless shrug. "I don't know."

"But you believe Suzanne was telling the truth about having witnessed him rape Lynn at Grafton."

"I see no reason why she would lie about such a thing."

"Maybe it wasn't a lie. Maybe she mistook someone else for him. Another priest. Or someone dressed like a priest. Someone who—"

"Do you really think that's likely?" Varda's tone suggested the psychiatrist was questioning a not-too-lucid patient.

"Obviously you don't," Nat said, somewhat defensively. And then it came to her why Varda wasn't giving any credence to her theory: "She told you as well, didn't she? Lynn told you."

He deliberately averted his gaze.

"There was nothing in your therapy notes," Nat persisted. "But maybe you didn't write everything down."

Varda continued to make no response, which only added to Nat's mounting frustration and anger. "Why didn't you do something? Why didn't you report him? See to it that, if nothing else, he wasn't allowed back in the prison? At least that would have kept him away from the women. Prevented him from continuing—My god, he probably had access to Lynn even when she was in segregation. And you did nothing. *Nothing.*"

Varda held up a hand against the onslaught of her words.

"I know, I know," she said angrily. "You were bound by confidentiality. But you could have talked to the priest. Not mentioned names. You might have gotten him to come clean and then you could have—"

"I did speak to him," Varda said wearily. "Ironically, he sought me out."

"Sought you out? Why?"

Varda looked her square in the eye. "For help. He was my patient."

She stared at him, dumbfounded—a feeling she'd been having far too frequently these days.

Nat spotted her as she was crossing the hospital lobby. Beth Milburne was standing near the exit. Nat fully expected the councilman's wife to bolt as she started toward her. But she didn't.

"Could we . . . talk?" Beth asked when Nat approached her.

Nat nodded, observing that the woman seemed anxious and looked drawn.

"The cafeteria?" Nat suggested.

Beth shook her head, looking furtively around the lobby. "I have my car. Just outside."

Nat hesitated. Surely it would be a lot wiser—not to mention safer—to have their little chat in a public setting. But Beth was already out the door, heading to her car, a shiny silver Mercedes sports coupe.

Nat slid into the passenger seat and Beth drove off quickly down Massachusetts Avenue.

"Well?" Nat asked.

"How is . . . she?"

"You mean your ex?"

Beth's jaw tightened.

"Your present husband paid me a visit—"

Beth promptly cut her off. "He doesn't know. About my . . . past."

They came to a red light and she screeched to a stop. Nat's hands instinctively shot out against the dash to keep her body from propelling forward. In her anxiety, she'd forgotten to put on her seat belt, as had Beth. Nat put hers on now.

Nat saw that the woman's hands were trembling as she lifted them off the wheel and tucked her blonde hair behind her ears.

"There's a café on the other side of the street," Nat said. "Let's get a drink."

The light turned green. The car behind them honked before Beth jerked forward. She maneuvered the Mercedes across the thoroughfare and managed to pull into a spot with a wide berth. As soon as they were parked, Beth began to cry softly.

Nat reached across and killed the engine. Then she rummaged in her bag and extracted a tissue for the distraught woman.

Beth dabbed at her eyes. "Dan doesn't know. No one knows about my first marriage."

"That's not true, Beth. What about the letter you received addressed to 'Bethany'? And the phone call?"

Beth crushed the tissue in her hands. "I have no idea who's behind it. Dan thinks it's a scam. I swear, he doesn't believe for an instant there's any truth to the story. He's just furious because he believes we're being set up. Something like this, if it hit the papers, even if there's no truth to it, would mean political ruin for him."

"But there is truth to it," Nat reminded her.

"Not as far as Dan believes, I promise you," Beth insisted.

"He seemed awfully agitated when he barged into my office." *To put it mildly.*

"He was just trying to protect me," she muttered.

"Protect you from what?"

"He thinks one of his political opponents is behind this—"

"So, it isn't really you he's protecting; it's himself."

Beth flinched. "His career would be destroyed—"

"So you said. And my guess is," Nat added, "so would your marriage."

Beth shut her eyes. "Yes, I suppose it would. Which is why you must believe that I would never tell him—"

"There are other ways he could have found out," Nat said.

Beth looked square into Nat's eyes. "If he had, believe me I would know."

Nat nodded slowly, holding Beth's gaze. "So, maybe the real question here is, how far would *you* go to keep him from finding out?"

Beth blanched but didn't look away. "When . . . When Daniel asked me to marry him, I went to see Larry . . . I mean . . . Lynn. He . . . She . . . It was before . . ." The councilman's wife was having trouble getting the words out.

Nat helped her. "Before the Slater trial?"

Beth nodded. "I went to see . . . Lynn . . . at the pain clinic. We had a long talk. A . . . A good talk. He . . . She promised me she'd never . . . let the truth be known. I really never thought she would, but I had to be sure."

"What about Lynn's parents? How did you keep them quiet?"

Beth bit down on her lower lip. "I paid off Larry's dad."

"Where'd you get the money?" Nat doubted Beth had very deep pockets of her own. On the other hand, her fiancé—

"Larry. Lynn."

"I don't understand," Nat said.

"It was his money. *Her* money. Savings. It wasn't my idea. Larry saw it as a way to give something back to his folks for . . . making their lives so miserable. A way to make it up to them. Of course, I had to promise they would never find out the truth.

Larry was sure his father would throw the money back in his face. I'm sure Mr. Ingram believes the money came from Daniel. Which was just as well. Until . . . now." Beth nervously looked at her watch. "I've got to go. Dan is expecting me. We're having a dinner party." She looked over at Nat. "I kept my promise to Larry. And I know he kept his promise to me. And always will. It's probably hard for you to understand, Ms. Price, but we did love each other. And in our own ways, we probably always will."

Nat could hear her labored breath, smell a mix of stale air and gasoline. She felt the darkness closing in on her. She tried to break free, but something was holding her back. Holding her down. No, not some*thing*. Someone. Icy fingers dug into her flesh. Her skin prickled with revulsion. A cold object was pressed to her lips.

A cross.

Pray for salvation, Natalie.

She tried to cry out, but no sound emerged. And then, with abject horror, she realized why.

Her tongue was gone. It had been severed. She could taste blood. It was slowly filling her mouth. Making her gag.

And the darkness . . . It wasn't that she was locked inside the trunk of a car as she'd first thought. As she once had been. The smell was not gasoline after all. It was ether—

And the darkness was not outside. It did not surround her. It was within her. It was dark because she couldn't see. She was blind. Her eyes—oh, God, her eyes had been gouged out.

She was crying bloody tears.

. . .

"You sound out of breath."

Nat squinted at her bedside clock. It was a few minutes before seven A.M., at which time her alarm clock was due to go off.

"Just a bad dream," she muttered, glad for the call from Leo. Grateful to be yanked free of the nightmare.

"Yeah," he said soberly. "There's a lot of that going around these days."

"What's up?" Leo wouldn't call her at this hour without a good reason.

There was a brief pause. "I'm over at the rectory."

An image of that cold metal cross flashed in Nat's mind.

"Are you arresting Father Joe?"

"No. That won't be necessary."

Because she was still groggy and hadn't entirely put her nightmare to rest, it took her a few seconds to get the full meaning of Leo's remark.

"He's dead?"

"The housekeeper's little girl found him," Leo said grimly.

"Oh, no." She was now fully awake.

"Seems the mom let Emily, as a special privilege, bring the priest his tea each morning. Apparently, he was an early riser—up at the crack of dawn and usually down at his office in the rectory by six A.M."

Nat picked up the pressurized tone in Leo's voice. She was sure he was as disturbed as she was that the little girl had been the one to find the dead priest. Surely it would be an image that would haunt her for the rest of her life.

"How did he die?" she asked, afraid to hear the answer. How gruesome was it?

"He was hanging from the chandelier. The drapery cord from the curtain in the room was used as a noose. Rigor was setting in by the time we got here. He'd been hanging for several hours, anyway."

"Did he leave a note?"

"Yeah, there was a note," Leo said.

"What did it say?"

" 'May God have mercy on our souls.' "

twenty-one

*Recent research studies indicate dissociation can pro-
long PTSD. Many therapists now encourage patients to
recall the trauma and relive it over and over in a controlled setting so that they can work through it.*

DR. HARVEY YOUNG, TRAUMA EXPERT

NAT'S OFFICE DOOR slammed shut with such force, it literally worked
one of the pins loose from its hinge. Her breath caught in her
throat, her alarm instinctual at such a sound in a place like this.
She released the breath as she saw that it was Hutch, and not an
inmate gone berserk, storming into the room. Not that her anxiety abated by any means. Her head CO had a serious temper
that he usually managed to keep in check. It took a lot to tip
him over the edge. At the moment, he looked as far over the edge
as she'd ever seen him.

"Are you out of your mind? Do you have any fucking idea
what you've done? You drove a man to suicide. Not just any

man. One of the finest, most decent, kindhearted men I've ever had the blessed fortune to know. A priest, Nat. A priest." He slammed a fist on her desk. Nat was sure he'd have preferred it make contact with her jaw instead of wood. But he was not that far over the edge. Not yet, anyway.

"Hutch, listen to me—"

"No, damn it. You listen to me. Father Joe told me the whole story and it's bullshit. The father wouldn't hurt a fly. So I don't care what the fuck you think you know. You're wrong." Tears of rage and anguish spiked his eyes. His tone was only slightly less explosive.

"If I'm wrong, Hutch, why did he kill himself?"

He stared at her as if she was severely mentally challenged. "Do you believe in God, Nat?"

"Isn't it a sin for a priest to take his own life?"

"I doubt he was in his right mind when he did it—when you drove him to it," Hutch added accusingly. "His death is on your conscience now, Nat. It's gonna be there for all time. I pity you." But there was not even a hint of pity in his voice.

"People aren't always what they seem, Hutch. Not even priests."

"Not even prison superintendents," he snapped before he turned his back on her and walked out, leaving Nat with the bruising sting of his final words.

Nat wanted to believe it was over. But of course it wasn't. There was still no convincing evidence that Father Joe had attacked Lynn Ingram in that alleyway and viciously cut her up. Or that he'd shot Suzanne up with a near-lethal dose of heroin. While the priest was still alive, Nat could at least hold out hope that he would confess to those assaults. But he hadn't. Nor had his suicide note provided them with anything concrete. Even Suzanne Holden's admission of having seen Father Joe rape Lynn in prison didn't prove he was the one who'd mutilated and tried to kill Lynn last Thursday. The priest was dead, but the case remained open. Would it ever be put to rest? Now their only hope lay with Lynn. If only her memory would return—

Nat was barely pulling herself together from her stressful encounter with Hutch when Leo arrived at the center with Suzanne in tow. He had personally escorted her from the hospital, along with a uniformed officer who would be stationed outside her room. Leo wasn't taking any chances regarding Suzanne's safety—a pointed-enough reminder that the case wasn't closed.

Suzanne looked pale and shaky. Given what she'd been through, it was no surprise. But what did surprise Nat was the way she stiffened when Leo placed his hand lightly on her back as he guided her toward the stairs. Nat imagined that Suzanne's response surprised Leo as well, and troubled him.

Nearly a half hour passed before Leo appeared at Nat's office door. What had he been doing upstairs with Suzanne all this time?

"Does she know about Father Joe's suicide?" Nat asked.

Leo nodded. "I thought it might ease her mind a little. I mean, to know he's no longer a threat."

"It didn't?"

"No."

Nat wasn't surprised. It fit with her belief that Suzanne was suffering from Stockholm syndrome and therefore felt guilty for turning in a man she viewed as her protector—and, most likely, her lover. Leo had no doubt drawn the same conclusion.

"Maybe I should give Dr. Varda a call. Have him come in and talk to her," Nat suggested.

"She says she doesn't want to talk to anyone."

"She's been through a lot, Leo."

"Yeah." He dropped into a chair across from her desk.

"We've all been through a lot," she added pointedly.

He looked at her but didn't respond.

Nat suffered his silence until it got oppressive. "What about the little girl? Emily?"

"Her mother took her to stay with a friend. I need to show the kid that drawing, but it can wait. She's in no condition to be answering questions."

"And Melissa Raymond? Have you questioned her?"

"I questioned her, but I didn't get any answers. She's not exactly in a cooperative mood."

Nat told Leo about Hutch's mood.

"Nobody wants to see their priest as a rapist," Leo said bleakly.

"What happens next?"

"I'm going to attend the autopsy this morning, and sometime this afternoon I'll head out to Grafton to talk with some of the staff and female inmates. This kind of thing doesn't happen in a vacuum. If Father Joe raped Lynn Ingram, then odds are there've been others."

She noticed he omitted Suzanne's name. "It still won't confirm that he assaulted either Lynn or Suzanne outside of the prison," she said.

"No, we're still beating the air on that one. But one step at a time."

And then Nat remembered something. "Leo, we definitely need to get ahold of Ross Varda."

He rolled his eyes. "I told you, Suzanne doesn't—"

"Not for Suzanne. Father Joe saw him."

Leo leaned forward in his chair. "What do you mean?"

Nat hit her intercom. "Paul, track down Ross Varda. Get him on the phone for me. It's urgent."

Leo was putting it together. "You're telling me the priest was a patient of Varda's?"

"And there's no confidentiality stricture now. It doesn't carry past the grave."

Ross Varda apologized when he finally arrived at Nat's office in midafternoon. "My sister took ill and I had to take her to the doctor."

"I hope she's going to be all right," Nat said.

He smiled, but she detected a shadow of worry on his face. Nat wondered how sick Varda's sister was, but she sensed from the psychiatrist's lack of response that he didn't want to discuss it.

"I presume you asked me here to meet with Suzanne. I got word from the hospital that she was released this morning," he said. "I presume she knows about the priest's suicide. It's been on the news all day, although there's been no information as to why—"

"The police are trying to keep things quiet until they gather more facts." She gestured to a chair. He sat down, but grudgingly. "I'd really like to see Suzanne as soon as possible."

"She doesn't want to see anyone right now."

"Then why am I here?" There was a little edge to his voice.

Without responding directly, she pressed her intercom button and asked her clerk to get in touch with Leo and let him know

Ross Varda was here. "You can probably reach him out at CCI Grafton," she added.

She knew she should wait for Leo to get back to her office before questioning Varda, but she had no idea how long it would be until he showed up. She figured she could always fill him in. Besides, Leo and the psychiatrist hadn't exactly hit it off up to now. She might get more out of Varda talking alone to him.

"I presume this is about Father Joe Parker."

"You told me that he was a patient of yours."

Varda lifted one eyebrow but made no response. What psychiatrist ever offered anything without a bit of coaxing, if then?

"Did he confess to raping Lynn in prison?" Nat decided a straightforward question was her best offense.

"Not in so many words," Varda said after a lengthy delay.

"He was aware that Suzanne saw them—"

Varda looked suddenly weary. "He never felt he had anything to fear from Suzanne."

"Because she was afraid of him? Or because she thought she was in love with him?"

"Sometimes the line can blur between fear and love."

"Do you think that line is still blurred? After all, Suzanne did finally admit at least some of what happened." In saying this, Nat was reminded that Suzanne never had actually spelled out what her own relationship had been to the priest.

"I won't really know the answer to that question until I can talk with Suzanne," Varda said. "I must tell you I'm concerned about her mental state. She has to be experiencing a vortex of conflicting feelings now that the priest has committed suicide. I'm sure a part of her is blaming herself for having betrayed him. And then there's the sense of loss, abandonment—"

"Surely another part of her has to feel some relief," Nat interrupted, not certain whether she was angry at Suzanne or Varda at the moment. Probably both: Suzanne for no doubt having these feelings, and Varda for being so damn calm and accepting about it.

"I'm confident that relief will come in time, but first she is going to need to process these other emotions. I hope you'll do everything in your power to encourage Suzanne to let me see her as soon as possible."

"I'll do what I can, but it's got to be her decision," she repeated.

Varda nodded.

"You treat other inmates over at Grafton. Have any of *them* been raped by Father Joe?" Although Leo was probably out at Grafton that very minute trying to find out the answer to that question himself, Nat figured she had nothing to lose by asking Varda directly.

"You know I can't—"

"You don't have to name names," she said impatiently. "Did Father Joe tell you about any other women—"

"I think you have the wrong impression of the priest, Superintendent. It wasn't that Father Joe was your typical sexual predator and used his position within the prison to have sexual relations with every attractive female inmate with whom he had contact."

" 'Sexual relations'? You mean *rape*."

Varda's eyes dropped away, troubled. "We all have a dark side, Superintendent. Even priests."

"Maybe, but most of us manage to keep that 'dark side' in check. Especially priests."

"He was a sick man. I thought I could help him. I failed."

"You not only failed. You sat back and did nothing while he raped two of your patients."

He appeared momentarily puzzled, but then he nodded. "You mean Suzanne."

"Am I wrong?"

He hesitated. "I don't think Suzanne would call it rape. She never felt that he forced her to have sex."

Nat gave a harsh laugh.

"Yes, I know," he said somberly. "It's always rape in that kind of situation. But all I can tell you is that Suzanne did feel he cared for her. And I think she was right."

"Is that what Father Joe told you? That he 'cared for' Suzanne?"

"Yes."

Nat's stomach was churning with anger and disgust. "And what about Lynn? Did he 'care for' her, too?"

Varda sighed. "The priest's feelings about Lynn were complicated, at best. Father Joe only met with me for a few sessions. Far too brief for us to even make a dent in unraveling all his feelings."

"Did he confide in you about having brutally stabbed Lynn? Did he tell you why?"

"Father Joe terminated therapy with me months ago. I've had no contact with him since."

"Did you make any effort to see Father Joe after Lynn's attack?"

Varda shook his head.

"But you did think it could have been him," she pressed.

"I hoped he would get in touch with me, but he didn't."

"You hoped Father Joe would confess to having tried to kill Lynn?"

"If he had, all I could have done was endeavor to convince him to turn himself in."

"Do you think you could have convinced him?"

"No." His expression was forlorn. "I wish I could have done more. People frequently say doctors think of themselves as God. Believe me, I have never felt that way. Being a psychiatrist is, at the least, a humbling experience. At times, it can fill me with utter despair and a terrible sense of failure. Sometimes I wonder why I go on trying."

Varda glanced at his watch. "I'm due at my sister's for an early dinner. I'm afraid there's nothing more I can tell you, Superintendent."

He smoothed down his gray sports jacket, adjusted his paisley tie. "Would you at least let Suzanne know I asked after her? And that I'm here for her whenever she feels ready to see me?"

"Of course." Her phone rang. "Just a sec, Ross. Maybe that's Detective Coscarelli. He may have some other questions—" she said as she picked up.

"Superintendent Price?" It was a woman's voice. Vaguely familiar.

"Yes?"

"It's Claire Fisher. Dr. Bell's nurse." There was a note of urgency in her voice.

"Yes, of course. Is something wrong, Claire?"

"Yes, well . . . I don't know. I found . . . something tucked behind one of Lynn's old files. You see, I was cleaning out—"

"What did you find, Claire?"

"A loose-leaf binder with a thick sheaf of handwritten pages inside."

"Lynn's handwriting?"

"Yes, I believe so."

"Does anyone else know you've found it?"

She hesitated. "I . . . I'm not sure." She sounded clearly anxious now.

"What do you mean?"

"Well . . . Dr. Bell was in the file room with me when . . . I don't know if he saw it."

"You didn't show it to him."

Again, she hesitated. "No. No . . . I . . . There are some things I haven't told you . . ."

Yes, Nat was thinking, she was sure there were. Like the fact that Lynn and Harrison Bell had been having an affair. It suddenly struck Nat that the voice on that tape Leo had played for her at the precinct house might not have been an ex-patient of Bell's at all. It could have been Claire Fisher.

"Look, I don't feel comfortable talking here," Claire said in a lowered voice. "Could you possibly come over to my apartment this evening? I'll bring . . . it . . . home and give it to you there."

"Sure. What time—?"

"I need to run some errands when I leave here. Would seven be okay?"

"Seven is fine. Just give me your address."

Nat scribbled it down as she said it, then she heard a male voice in the background—Harrison Bell's?—and Claire abruptly clicked off.

Varda was watching Nat closely.

"Lynn's journal?" he asked.

"Possibly."

"Good. That's good it turned up."

"Yes. It might help. But, obviously, there won't be anything in it since the attack. Even if she wrote about Father Joe and what he did to her in prison, it won't prove he was the one who tried to kill her. Or Suzanne."

"No," Varda said. "That's true enough."

"Still, she might have written something about the priest contacting her, even confronting her since she's been in prerelease—possibly threatening her not to reveal what took place between them."

"It's possible," Varda said.

"Then again," Nat said thoughtfully, "Lynn might have written about someone else she feared. This is far from an open-and-shut case."

twenty-two

Sometimes I wonder—would it have been easier if I wasn't able to pass? Would I have posed less of a threat?

L. I.

"A COMPLETE WASTE of time," Leo said glumly. It was nearly six P.M. and he'd just come back from CCI Grafton, having spent most of the afternoon there. "If the priest was messing with any other inmates, they're not talking. As for the staff, they all seem genuinely shocked by the suicide. And they had nothing but good things to say about Father Joe," Leo said sourly.

He started for the door.

"Leo—"

"Later. I need to talk to Suzanne again," he said tightly.

Nat went after him, grabbing his jacket sleeve. "Not a good

idea, Leo. Not the way you're feeling right now. Besides, I have something important—"

"Don't tell me how to do my job, Natalie."

"This isn't about your job. It's personal."

"Well, then, don't mess with my personal life, either," he snapped.

His words were like a cold slap in Nat's face. She let go of his sleeve and stepped back.

Leo winced. "I'm sorry, Natalie. That didn't come out . . . That's not what—Shit."

A sharp rap on her door startled them both.

It was Jack. He stepped into her office, looked from her to Leo then back to her again. "You okay?"

So much for her ability to camouflage her feelings. "What is it, Jack?"

Jack slowly shifted his gaze over to Leo again. "Your partner's here. He's looking for you."

Mitchell Oates, who was standing in the anteroom, started for her office as soon as he caught sight of Leo.

"What's up?" Leo was all business now as he zeroed in on his partner.

"We gotta go," Oates said crisply. "Now. We got a call from a doc over at Claire Fisher's apartment—"

Nat's mouth went dry. "Claire Fisher? What happened?"

Claire Fisher's one-bedroom apartment was on the fourth floor of a brick-and-stone Edwardian mansion in South Boston that had been converted into condominium apartments a dozen years ago. It was small but bright thanks to large windows, high ceilings, and linen-white walls. The decor was simple but tasteful.

A taupe-colored cotton couch and lounge chair, a Berber rug on the pale wood floors, an antique trunk serving as a coffee table on top of which was an oversized book of Impressionist paintings and a blown-glass vase filled with a mix of yellow roses and white daisies that appeared to be only a day or two old.

Dr. Julie Morganstein, the woman who'd discovered Claire's body, was the owner of the condo. Claire Fisher had not only been her tenant, but a friend. They'd met while Julie was an intern at the Boston Harbor Community Pain Clinic.

"We weren't all that close," the doctor was saying, her voice a little shaky, her fair complexion ashen. She was a petite woman with straight brown hair pulled back from her face with simple silver barrettes. She was wearing a black light wool pantsuit. Her jacket was open, and Nat noticed several red smudges on her white silk overblouse. Blood. Nat also noticed the doctor's slightly rounded belly. Given her otherwise slender–to–almost-waiflike figure, Nat deduced that the woman must be pregnant. Probably in her fourth or fifth month. Nat was instantly concerned that the trauma the doc had just been through might have some detrimental effect on the pregnancy.

"Let me make you a cup of tea," Nat offered, thinking that what the poor woman really needed was a shot of whiskey. But not for a pregnant woman. Tea would have to suffice. But Julie shook her head.

"I'm fine." She smiled wanly. "Well, no, not fine at all, but . . . really, I couldn't drink anything."

Her eyes strayed toward the closed bedroom door. On the other side of that door, Claire Fisher's body lay in a small puddle of blood on her beige carpet, two bullet wounds in her chest, at least one of which had proved fatal.

"I came over to bring . . ." The doctor's eyes shifted to a large cardboard box sitting near the front door. "It's a new lighting fixture for the dining room." Her lips quivered. "The old one had a short. It could have been fixed but . . . but Claire was . . . nervous."

The doctor squeezed her eyes shut for a moment, then pulled herself together. "I picked it up at the lighting shop and I phoned Claire to tell her I was bringing it over. She wasn't . . . She didn't . . ." Julie bit down so hard on her lower lip the skin broke and a bit of blood seeped out. She was oblivious and hurried on in a rush. "I left a message on her answering machine saying I'd be by with the fixture. I have a key, but of course I knocked first. When Claire didn't answer, I . . . I assumed she wasn't—"

Again Julie squeezed her eyes shut for a few seconds, but this time she lost her battle to hold back her tears. They began to run down her face. She forced herself to continue, ignoring them. "I went to let myself in, but the door wasn't locked. And the door to the bedroom was . . . ajar. I presumed Claire was in the shower." Her nose was running and she began to sniff as she rummaged in her leather purse for a tissue.

Mitchell Oates, who had been sitting in the living room with the two women most of this time, plucked a crisply laundered white linen handkerchief from his breast pocket and handed it to her. Julie took it gratefully, dabbed hopelessly at her face and blew her nose. Without thinking, she went to hand it back to the detective, then flushed. "I'll . . . launder it for you."

He smiled gently, an expression Nat had never personally witnessed before on the handsome but usually grim detective's face. "Keep it," he told Julie warmly. "I've got a whole drawer full."

She managed to return a small smile of gratitude. "Thank you."

Oates rose and went back to the bedroom to join his partner. He closed the door behind him.

"It must have been some dope addict," Julie said, crumpling then smoothing out, then again crumpling the hanky. "Someone who knew Claire was a nurse. What's this about a journal that the other detective was asking me about?"

Nat didn't respond.

"I mean, it must have been a stranger, right? I can't imagine Claire having any enemies."

"There appears to be no sign of forced entry," Nat repeated, an observation she'd heard Oates make earlier.

Julie's hand went up to her mouth. "Oh, God. You think Claire let the killer in? That . . . That she knew him? But . . . who?"

One name sprang immediately to Nat's mind: Dr. Harrison Bell. Bell knew Claire had found Lynn's journal. Nat had told Leo about Fisher's call on the drive over there. Bell's name immediately popped into Leo's mind as well. Neither of them said anything about the possibility—probability?—that they'd been wrong about Father Joe, but it hung in the air between them.

Leo had immediately radioed in for two uniforms to head to the pain clinic and another two were directed to the doctor's house. Harrison Bell was now wanted for questioning regarding the murder of his nurse, Claire Fisher. And now there would also be more questions regarding the attack on Lynn Ingram.

The problem was, as of yet, Bell hadn't been found. He'd left the clinic early but, according to Carol Bell, he hadn't come home. She claimed she had no idea where he was. Asked if she was concerned, she'd said he occasionally came home late because of meetings or symposiums. Sometimes he'd forget to tell her beforehand.

The journal hadn't been found in the apartment. It seemed likely Claire Fisher's killer had taken it. And equally likely that the nurse had been murdered because she'd had the terrible misfortune to have unearthed the journal.

Had Bell panicked that Lynn had written about their affair? About breaking it off? Had Lynn written that he'd threatened her—that she was afraid of him—afraid for her life?

Was Bell afraid that if the police got their hands on that journal, they'd consider him their prime suspect in Lynn's assault—whether or not he was responsible? That he'd be arrested? tried? convicted?

What if Harrison Bell *was* guilty?

But then, where did Father Joe Parker fit in?

God—what if the priest didn't fit in? Nat staved off her incipient guilt about having borne some responsibility for driving Father Joe to suicide by quickly reminding herself that the priest had been far from innocent. Whatever else he may or may not have done, he had, after all, raped Lynn Ingram when she was in prison. He also had adeptly and assiduously managed to brainwash Suzanne Holden into protecting him the whole time she was at Grafton. And if Ross Varda hadn't been able to break through her defenses, they might never have known the truth about the priest.

Still, it did leave Nat feeling exceedingly unsettled.

She looked over at the distraught physician. "You mentioned you did some work at the pain clinic."

Julie nodded. "That was almost five years ago."

"You worked with Dr. Harrison Bell."

"Yes," Julie said cautiously.

"And wasn't Dr. Lynn Ingram working there at that time as well?"

"Yes." She began refolding the linen hanky.

"You know Lynn Ingram's in the ICU at Boston General"— Boston General being the hospital where Julie Morganstein worked.

"Yes." She hesitated. "Is there . . . some connection? Between what happened to Lynn Ingram and what . . . what happened . . . to Claire?"

"What do you think?"

"I didn't really know Lynn. I worked with her at the clinic for three months and we had a few patients in common, but we never socialized. Not that I had anything against her. She seemed perfectly competent. It's just that she stayed pretty much to herself."

"Did you know at the time she was a transsexual?"

"No. I didn't know until her trial."

"Did you think there was something romantic between Lynn and Dr. Bell?"

Morganstein seemed surprised by the question.

"Is that a no?"

"I don't feel right saying this. But I suppose—" She paused, glanced quickly at the closed door to Claire Fisher's bedroom, then just as quickly looked away. "You see, Claire was the one who was involved with Dr. Bell."

Now Nat was surprised. She'd sensed that Claire was carrying a torch for her boss, but she hadn't considered that he'd reciprocated the feelings.

"How do you know?"

"She told me."

"When?"

"When did she tell me, or when were they having an affair?"

"Both."

"She told me about it when I was working at the clinic. That was several years ago. But I know that until about a month or two ago, it was still going on."

Had it ended when Lynn Ingram returned to the clinic? Had Claire ended it? Or had Bell?

"She told you it was over?" Nat pressed.

"Well, she didn't really volunteer the information. But I stopped by, one evening a few weeks ago—we were planning to have some repairs done on the apartment and I wanted to go over the work with Claire—and she seemed kind of down."

"You guessed they'd broken up?"

"Yes. And she confirmed it."

"Did she tell you what happened? Who broke it off? Why?"

"No, she didn't want to talk about it"

"Did you know Carol Bell?"

"Dr. Bell's wife? Yes, I met her a few times when I was interning at the clinic. She occasionally came over to the office to meet her husband for lunch."

"Planned dates?"

"I don't know. I guess." But after a short pause she said, "Not always. Sometimes, she surprised him."

"You think she might have been checking up on him?"

"I really don't know." Julie hesitated. "Claire once mentioned that she worried that Carol suspected something was going on. I know it upset her."

Nat was sure it had upset Carol as well. She was beginning to feel very sorry for the adulterous doctor's wife. Nat didn't know how many lovers Bell had had over the years, but she knew two of them now: Claire Fisher—and Lynn Ingram.

An image of the Bell family photo flashed in Nat's mind. The little four-year-old girl nestled in her father's arms. Daphne.

Daphne, did you draw a picture of a lady for your daddy? Did he tell you it was a silly monster drawing and make you giggle?

"You don't think . . . The police don't think—Dr. Bell shot Claire? I can't believe it. It's too horrible. Unimaginable." Julie placed her palms flat on her belly and closed her eyes.

"How far along are you?" Nat asked.

"I'm in my fifth month." Her lips quivered again. "It's a boy. I just found out." Tears started to flow again.

"I think I'll make you that cup of tea."

This time Julie didn't turn down Nat's offer.

"You sound awful," Rachel said.

Nat, driving back home, had almost let her cell-phone voice-mail take her sister's call but changed her mind at the last minute. Maybe something had happened to one of Rachel's kids. Maybe Gary had walked out again. It would be no big surprise there. Actually, it would be a big relief. At least as far as Nat was concerned. She believed her sister was only delaying a seesaw of heartache by taking Gary back again.

"I'm okay," Nat said offhandedly. She didn't want to discuss Claire's murder. It was still too raw. Too jumbled. "How are you?"

There was a brief hesitation before Rachel answered. "Okay, I guess."

"Gary?" Nat surmised.

"He's really trying, Nat. We both are. We have our good times and our bad times."

"Maybe you should go into couple's therapy?" Nat said.

"I suggested that to Gary, but he said he'd rather we work it out ourselves."

"Meaning he doesn't want to be confronted by a professional about his behavior," Nat said acidly.

"It's not another woman, Nat. He swears—"

"And of course you believe him."

"You're so bitter, Nat. Maybe if you'd been a bit less . . . unyielding, your own marriage might not have—" Rachel stopped abruptly. "Sorry."

Nat bristled. Probably because the same thought had occurred to her on plenty of occasions. And not just regarding her ex. She could already feel herself erecting barriers between herself and Leo, wanting to shield herself from the rejection she was unable to stop anticipating.

"Let's not argue, Nat. I'm fully aware that Gary isn't a saint. But . . . I love him. And if you love someone enough, it's worth hanging in there and trying to make it work."

"Yeah, Rach. You're right," Nat said, not sure whether her sister was more adept at denial than she was, or whether Rachel was, in fact, wiser and more gutsy when it came to intimate relationships.

twenty-three

I have performed dozens of sex-reassignment surgeries and have never had one patient report regretting the decision. Which is not to say there aren't both complex physical and psychological adjustments.

DR. RONALD CHESSMAN

CARRIE LI HEADED Nat off in the corridor of the ICU as she was on her way to Lynn Ingram's room the next morning at a little past nine A.M.

Nat immediately felt a rush of alarm. "Is she okay?"

"Physically, as well as can be expected under the circumstances," the young nurse said. "Emotionally? Not so good. Dr. Varda is with her."

"What happened?"

"The reality of her extensive injuries is starting to hit her. She asked one of the orderlies for a mirror. Stupidly, he gave her one without first checking—" Carrie frowned. "She started ripping off the bandages, screaming. The police guard outside her door rushed into her room, followed by myself and another nurse. It took all three of us to contain the poor woman. I gave her a shot of Valium and she calmed down some. We put fresh bandages on her face, and Dr. Madison spoke to her for a few minutes. Then the doctor told me to get in touch with Dr. Varda and see if he could come in to talk with Lynn. He got here about twenty minutes ago. It's pretty quiet in there now."

"I'll wait in the lounge until he comes out. Will you keep an eye out for him and let him know I'd like to talk with him before he leaves?"

Carrie smiled. "Absolutely."

Nat's cell phone rang as she stepped into the lounge. It was Leo.

"Have you found Bell?" she asked immediately.

"No. But Carol Bell called the precinct at around ten P.M. She said she'd been out shopping at the mall with her kids and found a message on her answering machine from her husband. He said he was somewhere in Rhode Island—"

"Rhode Island?"

"En route from New York.

"What was he doing in New York?"

"Carol says all the message said was that it turned out his mom was okay after all. That it had been some kind of mistake."

"His mom?"

"Carol says her mother-in-law is in a nursing home in Brooklyn."

Nat rolled her eyes. "Come on, Leo. This is Bell's alibi?"

"Well, we need to hear it from the horse's mouth."

"Where is he?"

"Don't know. He supposedly said in the message that he was

tired and would stop at a motel for the night and be back some-time this morning."

"No mention of Claire Fisher's murder?"

"The wife says no. Apparently her husband didn't yet know about it."

"Yeah, right."

"It gets better. I told Mrs. Bell I'd be right down to get the tape with the message on it and she tells me that won't be pos-sible. Her son Billy 'accidentally' erased it."

"You think she made the call up? You think Carol Bell's cov-ering for her husband?"

There was an awkward silence.

"Where are you now?" Nat asked.

"Over at Horizon House."

Her first thought was that he'd gone there looking for her. But her next and more disquieting thought was that he'd gone there to see Suzanne.

"Where are you?" Leo asked.

"Boston General. Varda's talking to Lynn." She gave him a quick update.

"He's probably heard about Claire Fisher. It's been all over the news by now. If he's not in a panic, he should be. You should be, too, Natalie."

"I'm doing okay."

"Until we get our hands on Bell, I don't want you poking around. You hear what I'm saying?"

"The phone connection is fine, Leo."

"You think Lynn knows about Fisher?" Leo asked.

"Not unless Varda told her. And I can't imagine he would."

"How long you gonna be over there?" he asked.

"I'm not sure. Why?"

"I thought I'd bring you home for lunch. My mom made lasagna. She knows how much you love it. And Jakey's dying to show you his new train set."

Nat swallowed hard. She missed Jakey. She missed Anna. She missed the warmth and sense of well-being she always felt at the Coscarelli home. And most of all, she missed being there with Leo.

Her misty gaze fell on the wall clock. "It's nine-fifteen now. I should be back at Horizon House by eleven. Are you going to hang around there?"

"No," he said. "I'm leaving now. Why don't I pick you up there around noon?"

"Yeah, okay," she said, even as she was telling herself this was not a good idea.

"Good," Leo said, sounding genuinely pleased.

"How's she doing?" Nat asked before he had a chance to hang up.

"Suzanne?" He didn't wait for confirmation. "She's pretty uptight."

"She heard about Claire Fisher?"

"Yeah."

"And you told her about the missing journal?"

"Yeah."

"What did she say?"

"Nothing."

"She must have said something, Leo."

"Yeah, she said something," he responded grimly. "She said she never in her life wanted a fix so bad."

. . .

"Help her to remember? I'm afraid it may have just the opposite effect," Dr. Varda told Nat. "Seeing the mutilation done to her face alone has only intensified the trauma. I'd like to get my hands on that damn orderly."

"Did she say anything at all about the attack? Ask you anything?"

He shook his head. "She's withdrawing more and more into herself. It's all too much for her. It's going to take time."

"How much time?" Nat was growing more and more impatient. Surely, as an experienced psychiatrist, Varda should have some way of breaking through Lynn's defenses.

"I don't know."

"What about hypnosis?"

"Down the line, yes, I would consider it."

" 'Down the line'?"

"When Lynn is emotionally and physically stronger. To attempt something like that now is far too risky."

"And what about the risk of getting killed?" she shot back angrily. Nat was sure Varda realized it wasn't only Lynn she was thinking about, but him- and herself as well. He knew about Claire Fisher, and while the psychiatrist tried to maintain a professional demeanor, Nat could see the flicker of fear in his eyes. He was scared. She was scared. Leo was scared. And out there somewhere, Dr. Harrison Bell was probably scared as well. Scared of getting caught, anyway.

And he might get away, at that. Right now all the cops had was a mounting suspicion. But with no hard evidence, even if they found Bell, they were not going to be able to hold him in custody for more than twenty-four hours. And even if evidence turned up and Harrison Bell could be charged with the murder of Claire Fisher, it remained pure supposition that Bell, and not

Father Joe Parker—or someone else for that matter—had been responsible for the attempted murders of Lynn Ingram and Suzanne Holden.

Their only real hope was that Lynn Ingram not only had seen but would recognize her attacker. And that she could somehow be made to remember before someone else got hurt—or worse.

"Sleep in this morning?" Jack asked sardonically when Nat got to Horizon House at a few minutes past eleven A.M., Ross Varda with her. After recounting Suzanne's remark about desperately wanting to do dope, Varda thought it would be a good idea to ride over with Nat to the center and see if she'd agree to have a little talk with him. Nat thought it was a good idea, too.

While one of her officers escorted the psychiatrist upstairs to Suzanne's room, Nat headed for her office. Jack followed her.

"Where were you?"

"Boston General." She shrugged out of her gray blazer, hung it on the coat rack near the door, dropped her tote bag beside her desk, and sank into her chair.

Jack remained standing on the other side of her desk. "You talk to Lynn?"

"She didn't want to talk." Nat told him about Lynn's distressing encounter with the mirror. "I talked to the surgeon. She's thinking of moving Lynn out of ICU in a couple of days. I told her I wish she would keep her there a while longer. I just feel there's more security up in ICU."

"Any sign of her memory returning?" Jack asked.

"None that I can see."

She scanned a pile of phone-message memos on her desk, relieved to see that none of them demanded her immediate attention.

Still, she felt a flurry of anxiety. She hadn't really been around the center enough lately to know how the inmates were coping with the stress of two inmates having been attacked.

"Everything quiet here?" she asked Jack.

"Quiet enough."

She eyeballed him. "What does that mean?"

"Relax, Nat. Everything's okay. A couple of verbal spats. What looked like a no-show during an on-site visit this morning with Manuel Diaz over at Commonwealth Granite. But it turned out his boss had sent him out on a delivery." Jack sat down. "What else? Oh yeah, Sharon had her hands full with some manager of a hair salon where she's placed a lot of our gals over the past two years. The woman blew a gasket when our latest, Nina Simms, got it into her head to bleach her hair bright orange last night. The manager took one look at her when Simms got into work this morning and told her she was through. Simms got a little worked-up herself, locked herself in the salon's bathroom with an electric razor. The manager got ahold of Sharon, who raced over to the salon and finally got Simms to come out of the bathroom. Sharon sashays out with some kind of a wild buzz cut. Meanwhile, clients were coming in, and the manager was beside herself."

"And?"

Jack smiled. "Two clients flipped over the 'do and wanted Simms to duplicate it."

"So Simms's staying? Everything's cool?"

"Everything's cool."

Nat slumped back in her chair.

Jack gave her an assessing study. "You look lousy."

"Not as lousy as I feel. You heard about Claire Fisher, I suppose?"

"Yeah. On the eleven-o'clock news last night. You might have called me."

"I wasn't up to talking about it," she said honestly. "I just wanted to crawl into bed when I got home and pull the covers over my head."

"Coscarelli spend the night?"

She gave Jack a sharp look.

"Yeah, I know. None of my fucking business." He smiled dryly, no doubt taking a perverse enjoyment in his pun. But the smile faded quickly.

"By the way, Hutch told me he went to talk to Father Joe's housekeeper last night."

"After he heard about Claire Fisher?"

Jack nodded.

"So now he's really convinced Father Joe wasn't the one who stabbed Lynn?"

"He was always convinced of that," Jack said. "Let's just say that now he's taken it up as a personal cause to prove the priest innocent of *all* wrongdoing."

"And what did the housekeeper tell him?"

"She insisted that Father Joe was in the rectory on Thursday during the time of Lynn's attack."

"She saw him?"

"No. But she claims someone else did."

"Who?"

"She's not sure. She's checking around."

"Come on, Jack. She told Hutch someone was with the priest, but she wasn't there herself, and she has no idea who that someone is?"

"That's about the size of it."

"Why didn't Father Joe come forward with a name? If he had someone who could confirm his alibi, why would he say he was alone? Why withhold such vital information?"

Jack shrugged. "I don't know."

"I don't buy it. I think his housekeeper's simply concocting some story to protect the priest's reputation. What she doesn't know is that, even if Father Joe's exonerated, he was still a sexual predator. He still raped Lynn at Grafton—"

"Hey, don't jump down my throat, Nat. I'm not the one arguing with you."

"Where is Hutch?"

"Cool off a little first, Nat. Let Hutch cool off a little, too."

Nat started to protest, but she knew Jack was right. All that would happen was that she and Hutch would get into a pointless shouting match.

"I should tell you, Nat, that Hutch is thinking of putting in for a transfer."

This news devastated her. Hutch had been not only a trusted and supportive member of her staff since the beginning of Horizon House, but, more importantly, a friend.

Jack touched her cheek. "He won't go through with it. He loves this place as much as you do. Once this mess gets resolved—"

"If it gets resolved," she said wearily.

"I've upped Suzanne's dosage of antidepressants," Varda told Nat when he returned from his meeting with Suzanne, which had lasted a little over a half hour.

"Did she say anything?"

Varda smiled wryly.

"Right. It's confidential." Nat felt her frustration and irritation rising to the boiling point.

"I'm sorry, Natalie."

"You're sorry? Well, Ross, here's something for you to mull over: Father Joe may have had an alibi for the day Lynn was cut to ribbons. You know what that means? If that turns out to be true?"

The color drained from his face. "It means we're all still in danger."

"Brilliant analysis," she said sardonically. "And I'm sure you can expand on that. You see, if it wasn't Father Joe who attacked Lynn, chances are he was also not the one who pumped Suzanne full of H. Or assaulted you and ransacked your apartment and left that warning note on your medicine cabinet. Or, for that matter, left that vile drawing for me." Nat paused to let that sink in. "It's looking more and more like the person who murdered Claire Fisher very likely committed all of the crimes."

"Harrison Bell," Varda said weakly.

"He's certainly right up there on the list of possibilities," Nat said. "Bell was having an affair with Lynn. But I'm sure you already know that. What might come as news to you is that Bell was also having an affair with his nurse, Claire Fisher—now deceased."

Varda made no response. His expression was oddly blank.

"Am I getting through to you here?" she shouted, as if to a deaf man.

"Of course you are," he said tightly.

"Well, here's something else for you to think about: Right now, even if the cops track Bell down, they have no solid evidence to charge him with. Unless he confesses, chances are they're going to have to cut him loose. But if you can give us something concrete, or even lead us in the right direction—"

Dr. Varda's complexion reddened. "You think I'm not afraid? You think I want this monster roaming the streets, maiming, killing? Coming after me? I'm constantly checking my back. Every time the phone rings, my heart stops. I'd like to get in my car and just drive cross-country. Run away. Flee. But I can't do that. I have two patients whose lives I hold in my hands. Be-cause—make no mistake about it—Lynn Ingram and Suzanne Holden are both at an emotional precipice, and they're barely able to hold themselves back from jumping off and putting an end to their misery."

"You're saying they're both suicidal."

"If you were in their shoes, wouldn't you be?"

twenty-four

He swears that who I am, what I've done, none of it makes a difference. He says—'I love you.' I clutch those words to my heart.

L. I.

"IT'S BEEN AWHILE. We've missed you, Natalie. Haven't we, Jakey?" Anna Coscarelli tousled her grandson's dark curly hair as the four-year-old hovered close to her leg. His brown eyes were fixed on Nat, but there was no smile. No greeting. No confirmation that she'd been missed. She felt a wrenching of her heart. She'd definitely been gone too long.

"You didn't see my play," Jakey said petulantly. "I was a superhero. 'Superkid.' The strongest, toughest superhero in the world. Even stronger than Superman. 'Cause I'm littler than him but just as strong, so, like my dad says, that means I'm really *more* strong."

No more lisp when Jakey said *s*-words. He was growing up. And Nat was missing it. But then, what right did she have to be part of this child's life? She tried to swallow down the lump in her throat. "Wow," was about all she could manage.

"It was at nursery school," Anna quickly elaborated. "And you know very well, Jakey, that only family members were invited to the performance."

Her explanation only saddened Nat more, reminded her how much of an outsider she was. Had Leo asked Suzanne to attend the play? Nat glanced over at him, but he busied himself at the kitchen counter, dishing out heaping servings of his mother's fabulous lasagna.

Nat knelt down to Jakey's level. "I have an idea. How about if, after lunch, you introduce me to Superkid?"

It took a few seconds for Jakey to grasp what she was saying, but then his eyes lit up. "I have the whole costume. I can go put it on right now—"

He was already dashing across the kitchen as Anna called out, "How about we eat first, Jakey?"

"Superkid needs the lasagna, Gramma. That's how he stays so strong," Jakey shouted back.

Anna beamed. "He's something, isn't he?"

"Yes," Nat said, the lump still lodged in her throat. Again her gaze slid over to Leo. This time their eyes met, but Leo looked distinctly uncomfortable and only held her gaze for a couple of seconds. Nat was wishing now she hadn't agreed to this family get-together. It only brought the writing on the wall into sharper focus.

. . .

Good thing Jakey slipped into his Superkid persona at the start of lunch, because they didn't get to finish their meal. A few bites in, Leo got a call that Harrison Bell had been picked up at the pain clinic.

Nat wanted to be in on the interrogation but only managed to get the okay from Leo to observe the interview through a one-way mirror.

She'd been watching for close to a half hour. Bell had gone from looking irate and dismissive, to haggard and frightened as time wore on. He was sitting next to his lawyer at one side of a long wooden table. Bell's legal counsel was a young woman by the name of Helen Katz. Nat didn't know her personally, but she knew that Katz worked for one of the top criminal-defense firms in the city. In contrast to her client, Ms. Katz had the polished, calm appearance of a woman in control of the situation. Nat wasn't sure whether Bell found his lawyer's demeanor all that comforting, because he was smart enough to realize the potential for things to slip out of control in the blink of an eye.

"Let's go through it one more time," Leo said. He and Oates were sitting directly across from Bell and Katz. A video camera affixed to the wall and angled down at them was taping this session.

Bell looked plaintively over at his attorney, but she merely nodded.

He sighed wearily. "Yesterday afternoon, Claire . . ." He winced, as he had done each time he'd had to say her name. "She told me she'd gotten a call from someone who identified himself as Mark Berman, a nurse at Westwood Manor in Brooklyn. He said that my mother, who's a patient there, had taken a turn for the worse—sadly, my mother has had several strokes over the past couple of years.

"Anyway, as I've already told you, I left the clinic as soon as I was finished with the patient I was treating and drove straight to New York. I got tied up in rush-hour traffic on my way into the city so I called the nursing home for an update on my mother's condition, only to discover that she was fine . . . Well, as fine as she had been the day before. They said they had no one by the name of Mark Berman in their employ, nurse or otherwise. I was befuddled, irritated, and yet, obviously, relieved that my mother was actually okay."

"But Claire Fisher wasn't okay," Oates said.

Bell rubbed his face with the palms of his hands. "I didn't know what had happened to Claire."

Leo took a swallow of tepid coffee. "It was reported on the radio by eight P.M."

Bell's cup of coffee remained untouched. "I didn't have the radio on. Besides, I doubt it would have been on the news in New York. I had no idea. I still can't believe it. Why would anyone—?"

"And again, you used a pay phone to place that call to the nursing home," Leo interrupted.

"Yes. I'd forgotten to charge my cell phone. So I pulled off the road and made the call from a pay phone, then continued up the road a bit and got myself something to eat—"

"This was somewhere in Rye, New York? Just off of I–Ninety-five?" Oates interrupted this time.

"Look, if I'd thought I'd need an alibi, I'd have paid closer attention. It was a diner. Well, not exactly a diner. Just one of those crummy luncheonette-type places in a strip mall. I got a burger and fries, a Coke."

"And you paid cash?" Leo queried.

"It came to seven dollars and change. I plunked down a ten-dollar bill and left. I started driving back home but I began finding myself nodding off. I'd been through an emotional roller-coaster ride. I'd thought my mother was on her deathbed, for chrissakes."

"You can confirm the phone call he placed to the Westwood Manor at approximately five forty-five P.M.," Ms. Katz said with just a hint of irritability.

Leo leaned back in his chair. "Yes, that's true, Ms. Katz. The problem is, the call could have been placed from anywhere." He focused back on Bell. "So you called your wife at—what time was it again?"

"I don't know precisely. Around nine P.M."

"And you waited that long because—?"

"I thought she already knew what had happened. I'd asked Claire to phone Carol and let her know about my mother. I don't for the life of me know why Claire didn't make that call. Maybe she forgot. Or maybe she called and Carol was out." Bell wiped his damp brow with the back of his hand.

"Wouldn't she have left a message on your answering machine, then?" Oates asked offhandedly. "Or maybe that one got 'accidentally' erased as well."

"I don't know. I just don't know."

Helen Katz put her hand on Bell's shoulder. "Take it easy. The detective's just on a fishing expedition." She looked over at Oates as she added, "But he has no bait, so he's not going to catch anything."

Oates appeared unperturbed. As did Leo.

"Let's go over the message you say you left for your wife last night. It was around what time again?"

"Around nine-thirty, nine forty-five."

"And you were in Providence, Rhode Island, at this point?"

"Approaching Providence."

"And you made this call from—?"

"A gas station. Where I filled up my tank. You've got the receipt, for chrissakes."

"And why exactly didn't you drive straight back home?"

"I was beat. I figured I'd better call and let Carol know I'd probably crash at a motel for the night and drive back in the morning."

"And when you stopped for the night, at this Holiday Inn, you didn't think to give your wife another call, let her know where you were?"

"I told you," Bell snapped, slamming his hands down on the table. "When I got into my room, I was exhausted. I lay down on the bed, fully clothed, meaning to just rest for a minute and then call home. The next thing I knew, it was almost eleven o'clock in the morning."

"You always sleep that late?"

"My God, I was exhausted. I haven't slept well in a week."

Guilty conscience, Nat was thinking.

"Okay, so you got up at eleven."

"I missed my first two appointments. I was late for my third—"

"You didn't call your office to let them know?"

"I called several times, but the line was busy. So I ran into the shower, dressed back in yesterday's clothes, and drove straight over to the clinic. I was planning to phone Carol from my office as soon as I got upstairs. I never got upstairs. Two cops strong-armed me, dragging me from my car before I'd even switched off the fucking ignition."

"Let's get back to the journal," Leo said.

"Dr. Bell has already told you," Katz interceded. "He knows

nothing about a journal. You can ask him until kingdom come, and his answer will be the same as it's been for the past hour. Let's face it, Detective, you have absolutely nothing upon which to base a murder charge against Dr. Bell. So, if there's nothing else, I'd like to take my client home."

Leo leaned forward. "I just have two more questions for you, Dr. Bell. Exactly when did your affair with Claire Fisher end? And who ended it?"

Bell flinched. As if he'd been sucker punched. "What? Who told you—? It's a lie. We were never— I don't know who told you that, but they were lying. I swear—"

Carol Bell was in the hallway outside the interrogation room, waiting for her husband to be released. She was pacing back and forth nervously, checking her watch intermittently. She came to an abrupt halt when she spotted Nat approaching.

"Have you seen my husband? What's happening? I'm going out of my mind here." Her eyes were bloodshot, and as Nat watched her anxiously smooth her hair away from her face, she saw that Carol's nails were ragged. They'd been perfectly manicured the last time Nat had seen her.

"Why don't we go get a cup of coffee?" Nat suggested.

Again Carol checked her watch. "I need to pick Josh up at school in twenty minutes. He's got a dentist appointment. He didn't even want to go to school today. Neither did Billy. Fortunately, Daphne's too young to realize what's happening. But it's been all over the news: their father wanted for questioning in the murder of his nurse. It's a nightmare. A total nightmare."

"Why don't I drive you to Josh's school? You don't look like you've had much sleep, and driving back to Newton—"

"Boston."

"What?"

"Josh is in private school. Brigham Academy. Still," she paused to check the time yet again, "there could be traffic. I should get going."

A little explosion went off in Nat's head. *Wait, Brigham Academy.* Brigham Academy was no more than a couple of blocks from the pain clinic. In the statement Carol Bell made to confirm her husband's alibi that they were on the phone together when Lynn was attacked, she'd told the police she'd called from a pay phone across the street from her son's school.

At the time she made that statement, they'd been concerned only with verifying Harrison Bell's alibi.

But what about Bell's wife?

Carol Bell's statement put her within two blocks of the crime scene.

Suddenly Nat was looking at Carol Bell in a whole new, and altogether alarming, light. Now she was seeing her as a betrayed wife. A protective mother appalled by her husband's cheating ways. A humiliated woman fast losing her husband, not even to another woman, but to a transsexual.

And now Claire Fisher was dead. Another of Harrison Bell's lovers.

"What is it?" Carol asked Nat. "You look like something's wrong."

"No, nothing's wrong," Nat said quickly, not about to give away her hand.

Carol looked less than satisfied with Nat's empty response. Her eyes narrowed.

Nat flashed on that vile drawing she'd received and felt a shudder of fear. What if she was right about Carol Bell and Carol suspected she was on to her? Nat had more than giving away her poker hand to worry about.

"Slow down, Natalie."

They were sitting in Leo's car outside Horizon House.

"Granted, it's all guesswork at this point, Leo. But you have to admit, theoretically—"

"Theories are all the fuck I do have. Fine for you to go latching on to one suspect after another, but I've got to mount some kind of a case—"

"I'm not latching on to suspects," Nat said defensively. "Is it my fault that there've been several very viable candidates here?"

"And now you've dug up yet another," Leo said wearily, but he managed a faint smile. "Sorry. I didn't mean to jump down your throat. You did good. Maybe I'm just jealous. If it does turn out to be Carol Bell, you'll deserve a medal."

"I don't want a medal, Leo. I just want to get to the bottom of this mess. Have it over with."

He took her hand. "Me too." He hesitated. "Look, Natalie, I know we've got some loose strands that need to be tied up—"

"Father Joe's suicide being one of them?" The priest's death was still weighing heavily on Nat's mind.

"Yeah," Leo said, fixing his eyes on her. "But I was mostly thinking about Suzanne."

Yeah, that's a problem all right. Thinking too much about Suzanne, that is.

Nat kept the disturbing thought to herself, but she eased her hand from Leo's. "Some strands don't tie up so easily," she muttered.

Leo sighed. "Well, right now I guess we should focus on

where Carol Bell was between five and six-fifteen last night. See if she has an alibi for the time of Claire Fisher's murder. But right now, my money's still on the husband. Remember, he's the one who knew about the journal, not his wife."

"Maybe he told Carol it was found."

Leo gave Nat a dubious look. "Why the hell would he?"

Nat sat quietly for a few minutes, trying to sort it all out. The pieces started to fit together. She looked over at Leo. "What if Harrison Bell knew?"

"Knew what?"

"That his wife attacked Lynn. Think about it a minute, Leo. Take that phone call Harrison and Carol both swear they were having about their son while Lynn was being attacked down in that alley. What if it not only never took place, but what if Carol and Harrison concocted the phone call between them? Creating what they believed would provide an alibi for *both* of them?"

"You're losing me, Natalie."

"Let's say it was Carol out there in that alleyway lying in wait for Lynn. Bell told me Lynn ate in the same restaurant most days. Carol would have known where, and approximately when, Lynn ate lunch. Remember, it was raining that day, so Carol could pretty much count on Lynn's taking the shortcut through the alleyway."

Nat could see by the way Leo was looking at her that he was beginning to see the picture she was drawing. Whether or not he was buying it, was another question.

"Harrison could have headed out of the building and started through the alleyway to go meet Lynn at the restaurant, only to catch his wife in the act of stabbing Lynn. His *wife*. The mother of his children. Is he really going to turn his own wife in? See his family destroyed? Not to mention have his infidelity exposed?

On the front page of every tabloid: 'Pain Doctor in Sex Scandal with a Transsexual.' Besides," Nat added, excited by how much sense her new theory made, "on some level, he's got to feel responsible."

"Yeah," Leo said dryly, "he was the one who couldn't keep his dick in his pants."

"And then—"

"Problem." Leo cut her off. "The clerk who was coming back to the office from lunch? The one who saw Bell and Lynn in the alleyway? She didn't see Bell's wife."

"Carol could have ducked behind the Dumpster before the clerk saw her," Nat was quick to say. "And then Claire unearths the journal. Harrison must have shit a brick. Probably because he was panicked that he'd really be on the hot seat now. One thing to cover up for his wife, another to take the rap for her."

"So you think he called Carol, told her she better do something about the journal?"

"Yes, Leo, that's precisely what I'm thinking."

"I like it. Now all we need to do is prove it," Leo said glumly.

twenty-five

No comment.

Dr. Harrison Bell
(statement to press after Lynn Ingram assault)

FOR THE SECOND time in one day, Natalie Price found herself sitting in an airless room in front of a one-way mirror. On the other side of this mirror, in the adjoining windowless interrogation room, sat Leo Coscarelli and Mitchell Oates across from two men. The older of the two men, heavyset and gray-haired, was wearing a priest's collar. He identified himself as Bishop Edward Michaelson of the Boston Diocese. The younger man, sallow-skinned, rail-thin, tugging nervously at the cuffs of a navy cardigan, identified himself as Alan Forest.

"I'd like you to repeat the statement you made to me a short while ago, Mr. Forest," Oates said.

Forest anxiously glanced over at the bishop, then stared down at the scarred wood table. "I was with Father Joe Parker on Thursday, September twenty-seventh," he mumbled.

"A little louder, Mr. Forest," Oates said.

Forest repeated the statement, this time adding that he'd arrived at the rectory that day at a little before noon and left shortly after two o'clock.

Nat caught a quick glance between Oates and Leo. Leo sat up a bit straighter in his chair.

The bishop leaned forward, clasping his hands together, fingers intertwined. "Alan arrived at my office at approximately two-thirty that same afternoon, telling me that he had come directly from a meeting with Father Joe."

Leo scowled. "Why didn't Father Joe tell me about that meeting when I questioned him as to his whereabouts on the twenty-seventh?"

"He couldn't tell you," Alan Forest said grimly. "I went there for him to hear my confession."

"A two-hour confession? Man, you must have had a hell of a lot to get off your chest," Leo said sardonically.

Forest flushed scarlet, his head dropping so that his chin was practically resting on his chest. "Until September twenty-seventh, Detective, I was a priest. I confessed to Father Joe that day that I had committed a mortal sin. I confessed that I had been having an affair with one of my parishioners." His head, somehow, managed to drop even lower.

Bishop Michaelson remained remarkably poised. "Alan came to me that day and told me that, after a lengthy and soul-searching conversation with Father Joe, he had decided to leave the church."

Nat caught another shared glance between Leo and Oates.

"Why come forward now?" Leo asked.

"I would have come forward sooner had I known the Father was in need of an alibi for that time." Forest had lifted his head and was looking directly at Leo. "When I read in the paper that Father Joe had committed suicide, there was nothing in the article about him being a suspect in a criminal investigation. I merely thought he was depressed. I even worried that I'd contributed to that depression. I had no idea until today, when the bishop came to see me in Waltham, where I've been staying with my mother—"

The bishop interrupted: "I arrived back from a weeklong conference in Washington last night. As is invariably the case, there was a pile of messages on my desk waiting for me upon my return. As it turned out, half a dozen of them were from Melissa Raymond."

Leo scowled. "Father Joe's housekeeper?"

"I phoned her first thing this morning. I've known Melissa since she was a child. She was extremely distraught. She told me this fantastic story about Father Joe having been accused of brutally stabbing a woman nearly to death—I couldn't believe it."

Leo cocked his head. "You knew he'd hanged himself."

The bishop nodded. "Priests are not immune to severe depression, Detective Coscarelli. I wish to God I had known what was troubling him."

Nat felt herself stiffen with anger. She could certainly give the bishop an earful. Despite this affirmation of Father Joe's innocence regarding the September 27 attack on Lynn, raping her when she was in prison gave the priest plenty-enough reason to feel troubled. Or maybe the only thing that really had troubled Father Joe was that, thanks to Suzanne, they were on to him.

The bishop continued after a brief pause. "I checked the date in my daily diary and saw Alan's name penciled in for the twenty-seventh. I remembered that exceedingly emotional meeting we'd had and phoned Alan. He agreed to give a statement to the police and asked if I would accompany him. So here we are."

"It's not that I don't want to remember," Lynn said earnestly. "But it's still a total blank."

Carrie Li came into the room, greeted Nat warmly, nodded at Leo, then stepped over to her patient's bed.

"How are you feeling?" Carrie asked, tapping two capsules from a tiny paper cup into Lynn's palm.

"Still a little dizzy." Lynn popped the pills into her mouth while Carrie picked up the plastic glass of water, deposited a fresh straw into it, and brought the straw to Lynn's chapped lips.

"What are those pills for?" Nat asked.

"One is for pain, the other's for anxiety," Carrie said.

"Maybe the drugs are making her dizzy," Leo suggested.

And, Nat was sure he was thinking, keeping her memory cloudy.

"It's possible. Dr. Madison did cut back on the pain meds yesterday. And I have a call in to Dr. Varda who prescribed the Zoloft to see if he wants to reevaluate the dosage."

Lynn shut her eyes. "Dr. Varda's been trying to prepare me for how I'll look when . . . when the bandages finally come off. I keep telling myself I can handle it. I have to keep reminding myself I'm lucky even to be alive. Dr. Madison says it's a miracle I pulled through. So . . . I won't be . . ." She stopped, her lips trembling as she fought back tears. ". . . Pretty . . . anymore. Big deal."

She managed a faint smile, her eyes opening, coming to rest on Nat. "Women. We're so vain."

Carrie Li rested a hand lightly on Lynn's shoulder. "It'll take time, Lynn, but you do remember that Dr. Madison told you a lot can be done with plastic surgery. Of course, you'll have to go through a long series of ordeals—"

"I've already been through the worst ordeal," Lynn said hoarsely. "And I don't mean what's just happened to me."

Nat stepped a little closer to the hospital bed. "Are you talking about your time at Grafton, Lynn?" she asked softly.

"I'm talking about before that. Before prison. Even before Matthew. The worst ordeal was having to live most of my life in the wrong body. Nothing can be worse than that. I'd rather live the rest of my life as a hideously disfigured woman than be imprisoned in a handsome man's body."

Carrie Li smoothed a damp strand of Lynn's hair from her forehead. "You won't be hideously disfigured," she said with a professional assurance. "I'll stop by later."

"Carrie?" Nat called out as the nurse started to exit the room. "I was wondering if Harrison Bell has phoned or dropped by again."

"No," the nurse said. "He hasn't."

Nat looked over at Lynn, saw the flash of disappointment on her face. Or was the feeling deeper than disappointment?

"Leo, why don't you see if you can track down Dr. Madison?" Nat said. "Find out when she plans to move Lynn out of ICU?"

Nat was prepared for an argument, but she didn't get one. Maybe Leo realized she stood a better chance talking alone with Lynn.

When the two women were alone, Nat pulled up a chair beside the bed. She noticed that Lynn's eyes were beginning to take on a glassy look. The medication was taking hold of her. Pretty soon she'd be out like a light.

"I saw Harrison today, Lynn. Maybe he hasn't called, but I know he's very concerned about how you're doing."

"Is he?" she asked weakly. "Tell him . . . Tell him I'll be fine."

"Do you want to see him?"

She shook her head. "No. Not like this. Not the way I look now."

"Are you afraid he won't want you now that you've been injured?"

Lynn didn't respond.

"You're in love with him."

"No."

"Did you break it off with him because his wife found out?"

"I'm sleepy."

"Lynn, you do remember ending the affair. In Harrison's office. The two of you were overheard. He was very upset, Lynn. You do remember that."

"I didn't want to hurt him. But it wasn't right. It wasn't right."

"His wife knew, didn't she, Lynn? Did she threaten you? Was it Carol Bell that day in the alleyway? You need to remember, Lynn. Try. Please try."

Lynn closed her eyes. She was silent for several minutes. Nat thought she must have fallen asleep.

"He asked me to marry him. He . . . begged me. But I said no. I said, 'No, I can't.' I told him I didn't love him. He wouldn't believe me. I kept trying to make him understand. But he wouldn't listen. He got so angry. I know I hurt him. I'm sorry. Please tell him I'm sorry."

"Lynn—"

"No. No more. Please go away. Please. I need to sleep. Please."

Suzanne stood at Nat's office door, nervously clutching her arms, her gaze skidding back and forth between Nat and Leo. She looked like hell. Dark circles under her eyes, hair not only unwashed but uncombed, her beige blouse wrinkled. She had on a pair of slippers, not even having bothered to put on shoes.

"What did you want to see me for?" Her voice had the husky sound of someone who's just been awakened, yet it was six-fifteen at night. Nat had already had reports by a couple of her officers that Suzanne had been spending much of her time sleeping since she'd been confined to the house. A typical symptom of depression. Nat wondered when the antidepressants Varda had started Suzanne on would kick in.

Leo walked over to her. "We need to talk, Suzanne." He took firm hold of her shoulder—nothing tender in his touch now— and steered her into the room, shutting the door with the heel of his shoe.

Suzanne looked taken aback by his gruffness. And even more nervous.

"Please sit down, Suzanne," Nat said, her tone deliberately softer in an effort to quell the inmate's anxiety. Leo might think he could browbeat her into talking, but Nat didn't agree. Suzanne was scared. Coming down hard on her would only make her retreat more.

Leo didn't give Suzanne the opportunity to comply on her own with Nat's request. He practically pushed her into one of the chairs facing Nat's desk, then remained standing over her.

Nat wanted to tell him to sit down as well, but she thought he'd bite her head off.

"Okay," he said, his eyes boring into Suzanne. "Let's start with Harrison Bell. You knew he and Lynn were having an affair. Lynn told you." He deliberately made these points as statements, not questions.

Susanne stared down at the floor, hands clenched tightly on her lap.

"He asked her to marry him. She told you about that, too."

"Is that right, Suzanne?" Nat asked, annoyed with Leo's drill-sergeant tactics. "Did Lynn tell you Harrison wanted to marry her?"

"He's already married," Suzanne mumbled, eyes remaining downcast.

"You got that right, Suzanne. He's already married," Leo repeated harshly. "So I guess he'd have had to dump his wife if he was going to marry Lynn. Now, how do you think Carol would feel about that? Getting dumped for someone who wasn't even *really* a woman?"

Suzanne's head popped up. She cast Leo an angry look. "Lynn *is* a woman. She's every bit a woman."

"Yeah, you roomed with her so you know," Leo came right back at her. "You know plenty about Lynn. Because you were friends, right? I mean, granted, you looked the other way when Father Joe raped her in the joint. But then, you and the priest had a special relationship."

Suzanne flinched, her already-ashen complexion going whiter.

"Leo, take it easy," Nat said.

He ignored her, Suzanne's silence only fueling his anger and frustration.

"I suppose you know we had the priest pegged for carving up

your roommate. But guess what, Suzanne? Father Joe had himself an alibi. Not that it's doing him much good now that he's ten feet underground. Or should I say, now that he's in hell? Because taking your own life, according to Catholic doctrine, is a mortal sin. You know that, Suzanne. A priest who commits suicide doesn't go to heaven. But then, he wouldn't have gone anyway, since I'd say rape is pretty high up there on the mortal-sins list."

Tears were gushing down Suzanne's face. "Stop," she shouted as she started to spring out of her chair, looking desperate to get away. But Leo shoved her back down.

"I know, Suzanne. Right now, you'd like a nice big shot of H to chase all your troubles away. Then you could just float, huh?"

Suzanne had tears running down her face but she stared defiantly up at him. "You're fucking right, Leo. That's just what I want."

"And what I want is some answers."

"I don't have any," she screamed at him.

Nat got up, walked around her desk, moved a chair next to Suzanne, and sat down beside her.

"Suzanne, we think we know who's responsible for what happened to Lynn. And for what happened to you."

She looked searchingly at Nat.

"Did Lynn talk to you about Carol Bell?"

Suzanne continued eyeing Nat, but didn't respond.

"Was she scared of Carol Bell?" Nat persisted.

Still no response.

Leo angrily slammed his hand down on the desk, causing both women to jump. "Damn it, Suzanne. She can't hurt you in here. No one can hurt you in here. Just tell me and I'll protect you. I won't let anything else happen to you. I swear—"

"You don't get it. You just don't get it."

"Then help us understand, Suzanne," Nat said softly.

Suzanne put her hands up to her face as wrenching sobs erupted. "I can't. I can't."

Leo knelt in front of her, his fury dissipated. "Okay, Suz. Okay, take it easy. I'm sorry I came down so hard on you." He gently stroked her hair. "Shhhh," he soothed, pressing her against his chest.

Now it was all Nat could do not to spring out of her chair and run from the room. But she knew there was no running away from this. No escape from the truth of Leo's feelings for Suzanne.

Not that either of them would have noticed if she had left. They both seemed oblivious to her presence.

twenty-six

I ask him, "Why does it have to be so difficult?" And he answers, "Let me help you."

L. I.

"ARE YOU GAME for a gallery opening tonight?" Sharon Johnson asked.

Nat looked up from the overflowing case file of an inmate from Norton who'd been okayed for transfer and was due at Horizon House in two days. "Is it Ray's work?"

"Well, she's got a couple of paintings in it. It's a group show. All women of color. It's in Cambridge. Lots of free champagne. Maybe you'd like to ask Leo to join us."

Nat's expression must have been answer enough, because Sharon quickly said, "Forget Leo, then." *I wish.*

"Come on," Sharon coaxed. "It'll be a girls' night out."

Nat looked back down at the backlog of reports and files on her desk that she still needed to review—monthly employer evaluations and program updates on current residents, several files on inmates who had been recommended for prerelease, and two more files on already-approved transfers.

"I know," Sharon said. "But you need to put a little fun in your life, girl. Besides, Raylene misses you. She thinks they've got you hermetically sealed in here."

"The problem is I haven't been here enough. I'm so far behind it isn't funny."

"No, life hasn't been a barrel of laughs for you lately, has it? Any progress on the Ingram attack?"

Nat told her employment counselor her theory about the Bells.

"And, honey, a woman scorned is a dangerous woman," Sharon mused. "We've both seen enough of them serving time. Usually they do in the cheating husband. But plenty of them throw in the home wrecker for good measure."

Nat was staring at Sharon, her mind racing.

"What is it?" she asked.

"I wonder if that's what Carol's planning."

"What? To finish off her husband? I don't know," Sharon said. "Without him to cast suspicion on, she'd have to worry the focus of the investigation would shift to her."

"Yes, but that's just it. If Harrison Bell gets backed into a corner and thinks that he's going to end up taking the heat for his wife's crimes, he might very well come clean. And Carol can't risk that. She'd counted on the alibis she'd concocted for him, but now that the police have shot holes in those alibis—"

"You'd think she'd have been a bit more clever," Sharon said. "Come up with alibis for him that couldn't be so easily disputed."

"Yeah, that does bother me a bit," Nat admitted.

Sharon shrugged. "I bet Ross Varda would say in typical shrink fashion that on some level Carol wanted Harrison's alibis to be challenged. Wanted him to be suspected. To suffer. After all, if he hadn't cheated on her, she wouldn't have been driven to take such violent action."

Nat nodded, but something still wasn't sitting right. She just couldn't put her finger on what it was.

"So," Sharon said, "will you come?"

"What?"

"To the show?"

"I'd like to, but really, I've got to catch up on all this." Nat reached for her briefcase and started stuffing in reports. "I should just camp here for the night and get through the whole lot, but I've got to go home and feed Hannah and give my starved-for-attention pup some quality time. I'm sure she's feeling abandoned."

And Nat knew just how she felt.

"Hannah? Here, girl."

A disquieting sensation of déjà vu hit Nat when her dog didn't make an appearance. Had Rachel had another falling-out with Gary? Had she shown up here again and decided to take Hannah out for a walk?

It seemed highly unlikely, but Nat wanted to believe in this scenario. Because any other scenario was too upsetting to contemplate.

Nat pulled open the drawer of the entry table where she kept Hannah's retractable leash. The leash was gone. She didn't exactly feel relieved, but the missing leash supported her hypothesis.

She walked down the hall to the kitchen, went straight to the phone, and dialed Rachel's number.

It was picked up on the third ring. Nat was heartsick when she heard Rachel's voice on the other end of the line.

"Rachel, it's Nat. You haven't by any chance got Hannah over there?" Nat could hear the edge of panic in her voice.

"Of course not. Why would I—?"

"She's gone." Nat's panic was starting to bubble over.

"Where would she go?"

"I don't know."

"What about Leo? Maybe Leo came by—"

"Right," Nat cut her sister off, feeling a surge of optimism. "Leo. Thanks, Rach. I'll talk to you later." She was already seeing it in her mind's eye: Leo coming over to her place because he knew how upset she must be after once again witnessing him embrace Suzanne. Not finding her home yet, he took Hannah out. It not only made complete sense, it buoyed her spirits about their faltering relationship. Maybe there was some hope for it yet.

She dialed Leo's cell-phone number, picturing him reaching for it while he was holding on to Hannah's leash with his other hand.

When he picked up, she heard mostly static. Where the hell was he walking Hannah?

"Leo, where are you?"

"This moment? Going through an overpass on the Mass Pike. In about ten minutes I'll be in Newton."

She made out every other word or so through the static. "You're in your car?"

"What's the matter?"

"You don't have Hannah with you, do you?" Her optimism was fading fast.

"What?"

"Hannah," she practically screamed into the mouthpiece.

"No. What—?"

His voice broke up completely. Nat hung up, feeling close to having an emotional breakdown.

She rushed back to the front door, inspecting both the door-jamb and the lock. Only Rachel and Leo had keys to the apartment. Anyone else would have had to break in. But there was no sign of any forced entry. She ran around the house, checking the windows. All locked. She'd been extra vigilant since getting that drawing. How had the *dog*napper gotten in here?

The phone rang. She snatched it up on the first ring.

It was Leo calling back. The line now was, thankfully, static-free.

"What's happened to Hannah?" he asked immediately.

"She took him. Or he did. I don't know how the fuck either of them got in here but it's got to be one of them. If they harm so much as a hair on Hannah's head, I swear I'll fucking kill them."

"Calm down. You're talking about the Bells, right?"

"They must realize I'm on to them. I was warned, and now they're letting me know I'm going to pay the price."

"Look, Oats and I are going to be at the Bells in a few minutes. If they've got Hannah over there—"

"What do you expect? That Hannah'll come loping down the stairs and greet you at the door?"

"Hannah sheds like nobody's business, Natalie. If the dog's been in that compulsively spotless house, we'll see hairs. Sit tight. I'll call you back as soon as I know something."

"Leo?"

"Yeah?"

"I love—"

"I know, Natalie. Me too."

Were they both talking about Hannah?

As the minutes passed, Nat became jittery with apprehension. She started pacing the apartment. Every time she passed a phone she willed it to ring. The silence was intolerable. A piercing reminder of Hannah's absence. She tried to tell herself it was out-of-hand, this intense attachment she'd formed to a dog. It was one thing if it had been a child—her child. God knew, she'd ached for a child for a long time. She would have happily become pregnant soon after she was married. But Ethan kept saying he wasn't ready for the responsibility of parenthood. Even when he begrudgingly gave in, he seemed relieved each time she got her period. Nat still found it ironic that he'd left her for another woman whom he'd gotten pregnant.

It couldn't have been more than ten minutes when her phone did ring.

"Leo?"

"You'll find your dog in the trunk of your car." The voice was a husky whisper. Nat couldn't even distinguish if it was male or female. It was certainly in no way familiar. "She's still alive. But you'd better hurry."

Before Nat could respond, the line went dead.

She didn't wait for the elevator. Too slow. She bolted down the stairs, flight after flight, her heart pounding. Breathless and frantic, she threw open the door to the underground garage. The parking space she owned was at the far end of the garage, close to the entrance from the street. She was racing toward her car—she couldn't have been more than thirty yards from it—when she pulled herself up short.

What the hell was she doing?

Suddenly, her addled mind started to function again. She'd driven into this garage not twenty minutes ago. Whoever had managed to get into her apartment and take Hannah, had to have stuck the dog in the trunk sometime after Nat had parked her car and gone upstairs. Sometime within the last twenty minutes.

Whoever it was, he, or she, could very well still be lurking down there this very minute. Lying in wait for her.

And Nat, like a complete idiot, had blithely obliged.

The shrill sound of a car alarm abruptly going off had her practically jumping out of her skin. A short distance ahead of her, a car's headlights began flashing on and off, on and off, as the nerve-shattering *beep, beep, beep* of the car alarm echoed through the garage.

One beep sounded sharply louder. Nat wasn't sure if she realized the alarm blare was synchronized with a gunshot before or after the windshield of the car she was standing closest to shattered upon the bullet's impact.

Even as she instinctively lurched in the opposite direction, looking for cover, she was thinking that the shooter was clever. Car alarms were heard going off all the time. If the owner of the car wasn't nearby to shut it off, people ignored the blare, knowing that it would automatically click off within a few minutes. No one would come to investigate. Not that anyone would come running if they heard gunshots, but at least then someone might call the police.

Too far from the exit back into the building, Nat dodged for cover behind a black Jeep. Right now she was damning the enormous number of lights down there that all the condo owners, herself included, had insisted upon having installed in the garage. For safety!

Another shot rang out, again synchronized with another beep of the alarm. The bullet *ping*ed into the metal inches from where Nat was squatting. She dove under the car. Curling herself into a fetal position, she was stricken with panic and dread. There was no escape.

Even as she was literally preparing to die, to be shot in cold blood, a car came roaring into the garage and pulled up short in front of the car whose alarm was continuing to blare.

Seconds later, silence. Merciful silence.

And then, after a few more moments, a man's voice. "Russo calling in. Everything's A-OK with the Mercedes. No sign of tampering."

A security patrol. There couldn't have been more than one car in a hundred that actually had an alarm system hooked up to a security company. Exhaling her first breath in probably a minute, Nat was overcome with relief. She crawled on her belly toward the front of the Jeep.

"Please," she called out hoarsely, "help me."

"Here," Mitchell Oates said gruffly, handing Nat a plate on which were a couple of slices of toast heavily sprinkled with sugar.

"I never figured you for the domestic type."

Leo's partner didn't crack a smile, but Leo grinned. "His wife would second that," Leo said.

"Eat it," Oates said gruffly. "You'll feel better."

Despite the detective's surly demeanor Nat detected an actual hint of concern for her. She found this so remarkable—Oates had never impressed her as feeling anything but irritation toward her—that she obediently bit into the sickly sweet concoction. To her surprise, after a few bites, she did start to feel less jittery.

"A stiff shot of bourbon would go good with that. Got any around?" Tony Russo asked.

Leo glanced over at the guard from Commonwealth Security whose timely arrival in the parking garage had thankfully scared off the shooter. Although he'd given his statement to the police over twenty minutes ago, the burly thirty-something guard was still hanging around, being very solicitous to Nat.

"In the buffet." Leo pointed across the room. "Left-side cupboard. Make it scotch."

Russo arched a brow. "I see you know your way around this place, Detective."

"Don't you need to get back on duty?" Leo asked pointedly.

Russo merely grinned. And, to Nat's amazement, Oates actually cracked a smile. He dropped it when Leo caught his eye.

Russo brought Nat a double shot of scotch, watched her take a sip. "How's that?" he asked.

"It's fine," Leo answered for her.

Oates walked over to Russo, dropped a hand on his shoulder. "You can take off, man. We'll be in touch if we have any more questions."

Russo nodded reluctantly. He slipped on his blue windbreaker with his company's emblem. Oates accompanied him to the front door. Pausing before he exited, Russo looked back at her.

"You be careful, Nat. And don't you worry too much about your dog. I just got a gut feeling she's okay. And that she'll turn up."

"I hope so," she said, fighting to keep the quiver from her

voice. To no one's surprise, least of all Nat's, Hannah hadn't been in the trunk of her car. The dog was still missing. And as much as Nat desperately wanted to believe Russo, she was starting to hold out little hope.

Oates opened the front door and started to steer the security officer over the threshold.

"Tony," Nat called out.

He looked back over his shoulder.

"Thanks. I mean that from the bottom of my heart. You saved my life."

The far-from-unattractive security guard beamed. "Anytime. I mean that now, Nat. You got my card. Home number's on the back. You need anything, you call. Day or night. I live alone so you don't have to worry about waking anyone else up." He winked to make sure she'd got the message.

Oates bit back another smile as Russo exited. Oates followed him out, leaving Leo and Nat alone.

She set her drink on the coffee table. "So, what do you think, Leo?"

"About the shooter? All we know for sure is the two bullets we recovered in the garage are the same caliber as the bullet that was lodged in Claire Fisher's chest."

Shivering, she quickly retrieved her drink and took a long swallow.

"And neither Carol nor Harrison Bell were at home when you got there." She repeated what Leo'd told her earlier.

"Josh said his parents went out for dinner."

"But he didn't know what restaurant they went to. Bullshit," she said. "Parents don't leave their kids at home without letting them know where they can be reached in an emergency."

"I made that same point to the kid. He said he could always call his dad on his cell phone."

"But when you rang his cell-phone number—"

"Yeah, I know. Bell didn't pick up."

"He was too busy firing shots at me. Or too anxious waiting outside in his car while his wife was doing the dirty work."

"Natalie—"

"I know what you're going to say, Leo. It's all supposition. Just like it's 'supposition' that they took—" Her voice cracked. "Do you think they killed Hannah?"

"Honestly?" Leo said. "No. There's nothing to be gained by doing away with Hannah. It's not like whoever it was wanted you to suffer the loss of your beloved dog. You were meant to die down there in that garage, Natalie." He winced as he made that statement.

"So where is she, Leo?"

"Maybe Hannah was turned loose on the street. We'll check with the pound, see if she was brought in. We'll find her, Natalie."

But his promise lacked assurance. And brought little comfort. Nat felt she'd lost Hannah forever. Just like she always seemed to lose everyone she loved.

"I can stay—" he started, but Nat shook her head.

"Don't push me away, Natalie. If nothing else, you need a shoulder to cry on," he said softly.

"Your shoulder's already occupied."

Leo heaved a sigh of frustration. "Jealousy doesn't become you, Natalie."

"Neither does feeling like a third wheel."

He looked at her long and hard for several moments. "This

is no time to get into this. You're upset over Hannah. I know how much you love that dog."

Tears spiked Nat's eyes.

"I'm gonna find her, Natalie. Just . . . hold on."

She nodded tremulously, letting Leo fold her in his arms. Letting herself cry on his crowded shoulder after all.

But she didn't stop him when he left a few minutes later. Even though she wanted to.

twenty-seven

When I get out, when I am finally free, hopefully I'll be able to reclaim my life, my soul.

L. I.

THE NEXT DAY, Nat was in her office at nine A.M., feeling exhausted. The media had quickly gotten wind of the shoot-out in her parking garage last night. Although she'd unplugged her phone after word got out, she didn't sleep a wink. This morning, she'd needed the help of a couple of uniforms to dodge reporters gathered both outside her building and in front of Horizon House. Her knight in shining armor, Tony Russo, on the other hand, had been only too happy to share the story of his daring rescue of the superintendent of Horizon House with anyone who would listen.

Jack had heard about the attack on the eleven o'clock news

the night before and got hold of her by calling her carefully guarded private cell-phone number. He wanted to come over immediately and bring her back to his place. She'd told him that it wasn't necessary. That she wasn't alone. She was sure Jack assumed Leo was with her. But it was only the two officers Leo had assigned to watch over her.

Nat had spent a tortured night praying her dog was still alive and that she'd get her back. Nat didn't pray very often. And when she did, she didn't honestly know who she was praying to. But she hadn't known what else to do. She still didn't.

Her clerk, Paul LaMotte, had been spending the morning fielding calls since seven that morning. The only two Nat had returned so far were to her worried sister and Warren Miller, the commissioner of corrections. She'd assured both of them that the risk to her life had been greatly exaggerated, knowing that only a lie would keep her sister from panicking and the commissioner from ordering a forced "vacation" for her.

Not ten minutes after she hung up with the commissioner, her door burst open. Hutch rushed in. "We have a situation."

Nat was already out of her chair and heading for the door. "What?"

"Suzanne. She's barricaded herself in her room. Says if we break in she's gonna jump out the window. We could call the fire department—"

"No, let me try to talk to her first," Nat said, rushing out of the office. Jack was just coming into the center. She called out to him, "Get Varda over here. Now."

Hutch and Nat continued up to Suzanne's room. It was the first time Nat had been alone with her head CO since their confrontation over Father Joe. It was not only that Hutch had been deliberately avoiding her; she hadn't exactly made herself available lately. Was he still planning on asking for a transfer? Nat kept expecting—and dreading—the request to come across her desk. She didn't want to lose Hutch. Great officers were hard to come by. Good friends even harder.

"How long?" she asked when they got to her floor.

"Burton and Flynn just came on their watch fifteen minutes ago. Got the thumbs-up from the night shift that Suzanne was still sleeping. Then they heard noise coming from her room, went to check, and couldn't get the door to budge. They think she's got a chair wedged under the doorknob. When they started to use muscle to get the door open, she threatened to jump."

Flynn, the older and burlier of the two uniforms on watch, was standing by Suzanne's door, nervously eyeing Nat and Hutch approach.

"Burton's gone outside. Planted himself under her window. I've been trying to talk to her, but she's not responding," Flynn told her. "I don't get why those windows aren't barred," he groused.

"Honor system," Hutch snapped. Not that he hadn't had plenty of misgivings about the openness of the center. But the truth was, except for the Walsh escape the previous year—and he'd taken off from the hospital, not the center—there'd been no incidents of escape from Horizon House. And it wasn't as if there was no security. While the windows weren't barred, the place was locked down tight at night, and there was a very effective alarm system if someone decided to try a getaway via a window.

Suzanne, however, was not planning a conventional escape. She wouldn't care if every alarm in the place went off.

Nat rapped lightly on the door. "Suzanne, it's Natalie Price. I'd like to talk to you."

Silence.

"I know you're very upset, Suzanne. You have every reason to be. Leo came down hard on you yesterday. But he did apologize, Suzanne. I think you know how sorry he was. I think you also know *why* he acted the way he did." Nat was aware of Hutch's eyes on her. She tried not to meet his gaze, afraid she'd embarrass herself by getting teary. "He cares deeply about you, Suzanne. He doesn't want anything to happen to you. That's why he wants you to help him nail this monster. So you'll be safe. So you'll have a second chance. The . . . The two of you."

Her gaze strayed to Hutch despite herself. She was almost done in by the look of sympathy in his eyes. She looked away quickly.

"Suzanne, please open the door. Let me come in."

Still no response.

"We could get it open in three seconds flat," Flynn whispered.

Nat shook her head. She didn't know how close Suzanne was to the window. And she was afraid the frantic young woman inmate would carry out her threat to jump if they used strong-arm tactics.

"By the way, I saw Jakey yesterday. Did you know he was in a nursery-school play the other day? He played 'Superkid.' He was sad that you weren't able to be there. He misses you, Suzanne." Nat swallowed hard, thinking how sad Suzanne would be if she knew that Jakey had never mentioned her name at all. Of course, if he knew she was his mother, it might be different. It might be different for all of them. And for Nat.

She heard a faint sound filtering through the door. She pressed her ear against the wood. The sound of crying. Suzanne was crying.

Nat pressed on. "Jakey wants to wear his Superkid outfit next time he comes to visit you. I know you haven't wanted visitors recently, but I know you must miss your little boy, Suzanne. Maybe I could call Anna and have her bring him over sometime today."

"No," she screamed. "Keep him away from here. Do you hear me? Keep him away."

"Okay, Suzanne. When you're ready."

"Leave me alone. I just want to be alone."

"I'm not going to do that. I'm going to stay right here and wait for you to let me in."

Hutch pulled up a chair for her. "Take a load off, Nat. I think it's gonna be a while."

She nodded, grateful for his kindness. Maybe they would be able to work things out between them.

Jack came hurrying down the hall a minute after she'd sat down. "I got a hold of Varda. One piece of good luck. He was already on his way over to see Suzanne. He'll be here any minute."

"Suzanne, it's me, Dr. Varda. Please open the door."

Hutch, Jack, Flynn, and Nat waited with bated breath beside him.

"Suzanne? I'm waiting." Although the psychiatrist looked strained and exhausted, his tone was not only firm but stern. He might have been a no-nonsense father addressing his misbehaving daughter.

There was no response, however, from the "daughter." Then, just when Nat was certain Varda would have no better luck than she'd had, she detected a scraping sound from the other side of the door. Like a chair being dragged across the floor.

Varda put his hand on the doorknob, turned it, and the door opened easily.

"Give us a few minutes," he said to Nat.

"After I make sure she's okay," she insisted.

He nodded and she followed him into the room. Suzanne was standing by the window. She was still in her pajamas, her hair even more snarled than yesterday, her eyes bloodshot, her face tear-streaked. She was staring out into the street.

Nat felt a flash of panic. Could Suzanne get that window open and jump out before either Nat or Varda could stop her?

But Suzanne stepped away and walked over to the bed closest to the window. Lynn's bed. It was unmade. Had Suzanne begun to sleep in her hospitalized roommate's bed? Surely there must be some psychological significance to such an act.

Varda walked over and sat down beside Suzanne. "Bad night?" he asked gently.

She clutched herself, nodding.

"Did you take your Zoloft before you went to bed?"

"No," she muttered. "It makes me have bad dreams."

"Did you have bad dreams anyway?"

"Yes."

"What did you dream about?" Nat asked.

Varda gave her an angry look. She was stepping on his toes here.

"Father Joe. I . . . I dreamt about Father Joe." Suzanne folded over at the waist and began rocking. "We were in hell . . . together. It was so awful. But then I woke up and . . . and I'm still in hell. I can't stand it anymore. I can't. I can't. I just want it all to stop. Please, please . . . just make it stop."

Her rocking had accelerated and her head was practically touching her knees.

"Getting all worked up like this isn't helping you, Suzanne."

Nat was taken aback by the sharpness in Varda's tone, but Suzanne did abruptly stop rocking and straightened up, so what did she know?

"Good," Varda said, more gently now. "Have you eaten any breakfast?"

Suzanne shook her head. "I'm not hungry. I can't eat."

"Yes, you can." He looked over at Nat. "Do you think you might have one of the officers bring in something for Suzanne to eat? Maybe some orange juice, coffee, a muffin."

Nat's eyes strayed to the open window. Varda followed her gaze, rose from the bed, walked over to the window, and shut it firmly.

"You don't look like you've been sleeping well, either," Nat said when Dr. Varda joined her in her office a short while later.

"I can say the same for you. Is it true that someone tried to gun you down last night?"

"Yes, it's true."

"And your dog was kidnapped?"

Nat didn't trust herself to speak. Just thinking about Hannah might reduce her to tears again.

"Detective Coscarelli phoned me last night," Varda said. "He told me he was stationing an unmarked police car outside my building, and that if I heard or saw anything that was alarming I should turn on my bedroom light and the officers would make a beeline up to my apartment. He didn't tell me what had happened to you—I didn't hear until this morning on the radio— but I suspected something must have occurred for the police to step up security." He stared off into space, looking more bewildered than afraid. "Where will it end?"

"How's Suzanne?"

"She's a bit calmer now that we've talked."

"What did you make of her dream?"

"About the priest?" He sighed. "Maybe I shouldn't have pressed her so hard to tell you about him. Her guilt is weighing heavily on her. Especially since she learned about that nurse's murder."

"Someone has come forward with an alibi for Father Joe during the time of Lynn's attack. It seems pretty airtight."

Varda looked deeply troubled by this information.

"I don't even know if it was a man, Ross."

He frowned. "A woman?"

"Come on, Ross. Lynn had to have talked to you about Carol Bell," she said impatiently. "I think she told you Carol found out about her affair with Harrison. I think she told you she was afraid of Carol. I think she also told Suzanne. And that Suzanne probably told you as well."

Varda's face reddened.

"You think the Bells are all that confident that you won't break your vow of confidentiality?"

"You think they're both involved?"

Nat told him precisely what she thought.

He didn't look particularly shocked. And Nat was not at all surprised about that. If anything, it confirmed her theory about the doctor and his wife.

"And if I broke confidentiality and confirmed that what you say is true . . . ?" Varda countered defensively. "I'm not a police officer or a lawyer, but I do know that my corroboration would prove absolutely nothing. So Lynn was afraid of Carol Bell. So what? Does that prove the woman lay in wait for Lynn in that alleyway? viciously cut her up? Does it prove her husband witnessed the attack and is abetting his wife? Does it connect Carol Bell with any of the crimes that followed Lynn's assault? No," he said angrily. "The only thing it does is put me in even more danger. And frankly, Superintendent, I'm already at my limit."

Nat had only to look at the haggard psychiatrist to believe him on that point.

"That leaves us Suzanne and Lynn," she said. "We need one or both of them to provide an eyewitness account."

"Suzanne says she was grabbed from behind. That she never saw him. Or her."

"What if she's lying? What if Suzanne did see the person who overtook her in the storeroom of the boutique?"

"What makes you think that?"

"It's the only explanation for why she's so afraid."

"If that's true, she would have told me," Varda said.

Which was precisely what Nat had hoped. So much for that wish.

"Maybe not," Nat said, having to rethink her theory. "Maybe Suzanne didn't want to put you at risk. Maybe she was warned that you'd be harmed if she told you."

A line of sweat broke out across Varda's brow. "Harmed? You mean . . . killed."

A heavy silence hung in the air.

"I think you should encourage Suzanne to come forward, Ross. And I also think you should reconsider hypnotizing Lynn," Nat said finally.

"Let's say I do hypnotize Lynn and she does name her assailant. How can you be sure the police will be able to move quickly enough? Have you calculated the risks—to all of us?"

twenty-eight

I think, in the end, I'll destroy this journal. I started it because I thought it would help to put it all down, but it's too painful. Too much like reliving it. If only I could block it all out.

L. I.

DR. VARDA WAS late. After his initial reluctance yesterday, a reluctance understandably born of fear for his own well-being, he'd agreed to meet with Lynn that morning and explore the idea of hypnosis with her. He'd explained he would need her full compliance; otherwise there was no hope of putting her under. And he was not sure if she was ready for this emotionally charged step.

Leo was there as well. If Lynn agreed to be hypnotized, the psychiatrist would proceed without delay. They were all feeling the pressure of time slipping by. Not to mention that everyone's nerves were frayed, especially Suzanne's. Although she'd settled down somewhat after her session with Dr. Varda the previous morning, she'd spent much of the rest of the day pacing in her room or smoking out on the front porch. Of course, every time she stepped out of the building, the two officers assigned to her also stood outside on guard. Talk about frayed nerves—theirs were plenty ragged.

So were Nat's. And they were getting more ragged with each passing minute.

Leo poured himself a refill of coffee as they waited in the doctors' lounge up in ICU. "You sure Varda said nine A.M.?"

Nat checked her watch. It was nine thirty-five. Varda told her he planned to come there straight from home and then go on to Grafton for an eleven A.M. therapy group he was running.

Where the hell was he? Of all people, you'd expect psychiatrists to be punctual.

Shortly after nine, Leo got in touch with the two officers posted in an unmarked car outside Varda's building. They had not yet seen Varda exit. Okay, so he was running a bit late. But now Nat was starting to feel increasingly uneasy.

"Maybe he had some kind of emergency," she said. "He mentioned something about his sister being sick. I don't know how serious it is, but she could have been rushed to the hospital."

"Let's see if he left." Leo phoned the officers on duty again.

"Phil. Do me a favor. Take Lenny and run up to Varda's apartment. Check if he's there." He hesitated briefly before adding, "And if he is, that he's in one piece."

The first thing Nat saw when she followed Leo into Dr. Varda's apartment was the red stain on the psychiatrist's beige carpet. There were a few splatters of red, as well, on the khaki sofa just above the carpet. Bile rose up in her throat, burning its way back down as she swallowed hard.

Mitchell Oates and another plainclothes detective stepped out from the bedroom. Behind Nat and Leo, two Boston crime-scene investigators entered the front door.

"What have we got?" Leo addressed the question to Oates, who was walking over to the crime-scene pair.

"It's what we don't got that's the problem," Oates answered dryly. "We don't got the shrink."

"Isn't that a good thing?" Nat said. "It means Dr. Varda might very well still be alive."

Oates shrugged. "Maybe."

Leo pointed toward the bedroom. "Anything in there?"

"Bed's unmade. Looks like the shrink slept there last night. Alone," Oates added. "No sign of any struggle." He looked over at the red stain on the carpet. "No blood's turned up anywhere else in the apartment from what I've seen."

"Front door was unlocked?"

Oates nodded. "No sign of any tampering. I'd say the doctor let whoever it was in. There's half a pot of coffee in the kitchen. Still warm. Timer was set for seven A.M. Two mugs in the drain board. I got them bagged and tagged, but I don't think we'll get much from them. Unfortunately, our shrink is very tidy. Washed the mugs rather than stuck 'em in the dishwasher."

"So," Leo said, "somebody shows up sometime this morning. Varda lets him or her in, they have coffee, sit around, shoot the breeze, then something happens. Now we've got bloodstains and a missing shrink."

"What about the two officers posted outside?" Nat asked. "They never saw Varda exit."

"There's a service entrance. Locked from the outside so my

men didn't worry about someone getting into the building that way."

A uniform came into the apartment and made a beeline for Oates.

"The neighbor across the hall says she saw a woman ringing Dr. Varda's doorbell sometime around eight-thirty this morning. Neighbor's name is Gloria Weber."

"Mrs. Weber, I wonder if we could nail down the description of this woman at the doctor's door," Leo said.

Mrs. Weber looked very put-out by the intrusion. "I've already done the best I could. Her back was to me. And I only glanced out my peephole. It couldn't have been more than a second or two. I had no idea I was looking at a . . . a criminal."

"We don't know that it was a criminal, Mrs. Weber," Leo cautioned.

"Really, this is very upsetting."

"I wonder if you'd like a cup of tea, Mrs. Weber?" Nat asked.

The woman smiled at her. "Now, how did you know I was a tea drinker and not a coffee drinker?"

Nat pointed to the collection of teapots in her china cabinet.

"Very observant, my dear. And thank you for your offer, but I only have one cup in the morning."

"You impress me as being very observant as well, Mrs. Weber. Could you please try to describe the woman again?"

"Well, let me see. She was a blonde. I did say that, didn't I? And I believe her hair was long. A rather tall woman. Not fat. No, I wouldn't say fat. Big."

"What was she wearing?"

"A coat. A plain black coat. Oh, yes, and sneakers. They were black, too. But I'm pretty sure they were sneakers. I don't know what else I can tell you."

"Please," she pleaded. "Keep your voices down. My little girl is home sick."

"Is she upstairs in her room coloring?"

Carol Bell gave Nat an edgy look.

"We have an eyewitness that places you at Dr. Ross Varda's apartment this morning at approximately eight-thirty," Leo said.

"No, that can't be. I . . . I wasn't there."

"But you know who Dr. Varda is."

She blanched. "Harrison's mentioned him. I . . . I know he's Lynn's psychiatrist."

"You'd better call a baby-sitter to come over, Mrs. Bell," Leo said grimly. "I'm bringing you to the precinct to participate in a lineup."

Carol Bell swayed. Nat grabbed hold of her as she tried to steady herself. "Oh, God, I never should have gone there. It's true. But . . . But he phoned me at seven o'clock this morning. He . . . He told me he had important information that would clear me and Harrison. He asked me to meet him at his apartment. I was supposed to be there by eight, but I explained I had to get the children off to school, and he said I should get there as soon as I could."

She looked wanly from Nat to Leo. "But I was too late. He was already gone."

"How do you know that?" Leo asked.

"He never came to the door."

"Curious, that you haven't even asked us why we are questioning you about this visit," Leo said.

"I, I . . . assumed something must have . . . happened to him," she answered starkly. "Is he . . . dead?"

"I think you know the answer to that better than I do."

"No. I swear, I have no idea."

"What about my dog?"

She gave Nat a blank look, but then her expression darkened. "I want to call my lawyer. I'm not saying another word until she gets here."

"Don't bother. We're leaving. But you can tell her that chances are damn good you'll be needing her services real soon."

Leo and Nat stopped for lunch in Brookline, and they were just about to give their order to the waitress when his cell phone rang.

Even from across the booth Nat could hear a woman crying hysterically on the other end of the line.

"Mom, Mom," Leo pleaded. "Calm down. I can't understand what you're saying."

Nat couldn't make out Anna Coscarelli's words, but she had only to look at Leo's expression to know something terrible had happened.

twenty-nine

I keep praying Jakey just wandered off ... that he wasn't taken. But I guess when your daddy's a homicide detective there's always a risk.

CINDY SHAEFFER,
PLAYDAYS SCHOOL TEACHER, IN A TV INTERVIEW

LEO WAS TEARING ass down Beacon Street, his foot flat on the accelerator.

Nat blinked rapidly, trying to take this in. "Someone at the school must have seen where he went. Who ... Who he went with. They don't just let children wander off. Or turn them over to perfect strangers. They don't—"

Leo wasn't listening. Nat stopped talking. As upset as she was, she could only imagine what must be going through Leo's head. His child was missing.

First her dog, then Varda, now Jakey. It was crazy. Insane.

But then, whoever was behind all this madness very likely was insane.

There were three Boston blue-and-whites parked in front of PlayDays Nursery School when Leo screeched to a shuddering stop. He bolted out the driver's-side door, not even bothering to shut off the engine. Nat turned the key, pocketed it, then hesitated as she reached for her door handle.

She was worried that she'd only be in the way. She worried more that Leo would rather she wasn't there. She was no relation to him, to Jakey. She was an outsider.

If anyone should be there, it was Suzanne. Jakey's mother.

Nat's chest constricted. *Suzanne.* How would she take the news of her son's disappearance? If she was already feeling burdened with guilt, finding out about Jakey could prove her breaking point.

No sooner did Nat think that Suzanne mustn't find out, than two more-potent thoughts hit her like a sledgehammer: Suzanne had to know who'd taken Jakey. And Leo knew that Suzanne knew.

Anna Coscarelli was inconsolable. The physician used by the nursery school and called to the scene shortly after Anna's arrival obtained Leo's permission and gave Leo's mother a shot of Valium. One of the teachers offered to drive her home and stay with her for as long as necessary. The teacher looked like she could use a tranquilizer herself. Everyone at the school did. Leo most of all.

He was laying into the teary-eyed and badly shaken young

teacher who'd been on duty outside with the children when Jakey had disappeared.

Leo was right in her face: " 'Vanished out of thin air'? Nobody vanishes out of thin air. Some fuck came and took my kid. And you were—what, daydreaming about your fucking boyfriend or what the fuck you were gonna cook for dinner?—"

Cindy Shaeffer put her hands up to her face and broke down in sobs. "One minute . . . he was . . . right there . . . and the next . . . minute he was . . . gone. I was just . . . having a word . . . with one of . . . the parents. And then . . . your mother . . . came and I . . . looked around . . . I'm sorry. I'm so, so sorry." Her words, stilted and muffled, were etched in despair.

A plainclothes cop walked over to Leo. Put a hand lightly on his shoulder. Leo jerked away, glared at him.

"Detective Coscarelli, please. You're upset—"

"You bet the fuck I'm *upset*. My kid is gone. And somebody at this fucking school is going to come up with some answers, or I swear I'm going to fucking—" He stopped abruptly, a wrenching moan escaping from his lips, as if the impotence of his fury had finally taken hold of him.

He turned away, caught Nat's eye for the briefest of moments as she stood by the classroom door, then strode briskly across the room, going right by her and heading out of the building. A man on a mission. And Nat was pretty sure she knew exactly what that mission was.

"Leo," she called out, rushing to catch up with him.

"This isn't some dumb-assed dog now. This is my kid," he snarled.

Nat had never seen Leo this ugly. But then, how ugly would she be if it were her child who'd disappeared?

. . .

Before anyone—Nat, Jack, Hutch, even the two cops in the hall—could stop him, Leo stormed into Suzanne's room and slammed the door behind him. Nat tried to open it, but the door wouldn't budge. She was guessing Leo probably wedged the same chair under the knob as Suzanne had yesterday.

The four men beside Nat all offered to break the door down. Any one of them, no doubt, could have managed the task on his own. But she rejected their offer. It was too late now to stop Leo, and it would only cause a futile confrontation. At this point Nat could only hope that Suzanne would quickly tell Leo what he wanted to know. Then all Nat could do was pray that the cops could get to the bastard before Jakey was harmed. If he hadn't been harmed already. Or worse.

Nat didn't have to be in the room to hear Leo and Suzanne. Their voices, especially Leo's, could be heard clearly out in the hall. There were only a couple of other female inmates on the floor at that hour—a recent transfer who'd not yet started her work assignment and one resident home with the flu. They'd both come out of their rooms during the commotion, and Nat disbanded Jack and Hutch to escort the pair down to the visiting room. She told the two cops to go have a smoke. They reluctantly shuffled off.

Nat stayed put, listening—

"No, no. It can't be true." Suzanne was crying.

"Do I look like I'm fucking lying," Leo roared.

"It's all my fault. But they won't hurt him, Leo. They won't."

" 'They'? Who are we talking about? The Bells? Is that who—?"

"Don't. Oh, God, I've been terrified of this happening the

whole time. Don't you see, Leo? That's why they took him. To stop me from talking. If I talk they'll kill him, Leo. Don't you get it? I hold our son's life in my hands. If you ever hope to see him alive again, you'll stop trying to make me tell you."

"So what do we do, Suzanne?" Leo's voice had gone from fury to anguish. "They—whoever the fuck 'they' are—are black-mailing you into keeping silent by holding our son. So how do I get him back?"

"Damn you, Leo," Suzanne screamed. "You should have let me get that abortion! You shouldn't have ever let Jakey be born. I knew it would only lead to heartache. I knew even then—"

"Where is he?" Oates asked as Nat slid into a booth across from him in a coffee shop near the precinct house. It was nearly three o'clock in the afternoon.

"Leo stormed out of the center after his fruitless confrontation with Suzanne, got into his car, and drove off like a bat out of hell."

"He didn't go to the Bells' house. I have an unmarked car over there. No sign of him."

"As wildly upset as he is, he's not going to risk Jakey getting hurt by barreling in there. I think he went back to the nursery school."

"Romero's not gonna be happy to see him," Oates said.

"Romero?"

"The detective assigned to the kidnapping."

"He can't blame Leo for wanting to be in on the investigation."

"We don't even know that the boy's still alive, Natalie."

Nat winced at the thought, then attacked it. "No, they know

that as long as Suzanne can be assured Jakey's alive, she'll keep her mouth shut. It's their only hold over her. She was meant to die from that OD. When that failed, it was too hard to get at her. So they used Jakey as a threat, somehow got a message to her that they'd harm him if she talked. But they must have worried she was close to the breaking point, and so they took it to the next step." She looked wanly across at Leo's partner. "I've got to believe Jakey's okay."

Oates leaned forward, reached a hand across the table, and rested it over hers. Nat was taken aback by his solicitous touch and the even more solicitous expression on his face.

Nat was just pulling out from the curb in front of the coffee shop when she heard a loud thump on her trunk. She slammed down on her brakes and the next thing she knew, Oates was yanking open her passenger-side door.

"The Bells' house in Newton. Let's go."

A flood of possibilities rushed through her mind, but they were all so potentially awful, Nat couldn't bring herself to voice them aloud.

When they got to the Bells' house, they saw Leo's car. It was half on the Bells' manicured lawn, his car door open. So was the door to the house.

Nat's heart was in her throat. Had they found Jakey? Was he alive?

Oates and Nat were just dashing out of her car when two uniforms emerged from the house with a raging man, arms pinned behind his back, wrists cuffed. They were heading for the cruiser.

Nat froze in place. The man being dragged from the house was Leo.

Oates yanked out his ID, waving at the cops as he rushed over to his partner. Leo was acting like a madman. The cops were doing their best not to roughhouse him as they tried to get him into the back of the cruiser. They must have known they were dealing with a police officer because one of them called him "Detective."

"Jakey's jacket," Leo gasped hoarsely. "It was in her car. They've got him, man. They've got my boy. I'll kill them. I'll fucking kill them—"

"I'm on it, Leo. I'll find him," Oates said fiercely.

An unmarked car pulled up to a screeching stop just as the uniforms managed to get Leo into the cruiser.

The plainclothes detective Nat recognized from Jakey's nursery school, and whom she presumed was Detective Romero, got out of the car. He held up a hand to stop the cruiser from taking off. Oates and the detective had a brief powwow, then the detective opened the back door of the cruiser and slipped in beside Leo. He was in there for a couple of minutes. When he got out, the cruiser took off.

Nat rushed over to Oates. "They're not going to arrest Leo, Mitch. They can't."

"Take it easy, Nat," Oates said. "Leo needs a little cool-down time."

The detective, Eric Romero, approached them. "Leo was at the school when one of the parents who was picking up her kid told us she saw a red Subaru Outback racing past the school. She noticed it because she was upset the driver was speeding in a school zone. The instant Leo heard the make of the car, he was off and running."

"Who could blame him?" she said hotly.

"Not me, believe me. But he shoulda let me go. He was in no condition—and I'm still not saying I blame him, because I don't—but still, he should have left it to cooler minds. Instead he went on a raving rampage, tore up half the house, roughed up Carol Bell—"

"She's lucky he didn't kill her," Nat said fiercely.

"No, Nat," Oates said pointedly. "*Leo's* lucky."

Helen Katz entered the interrogation room where Carol Bell sat near the point of emotional collapse. Across from her was Mitchell Oates and Eric Romero.

Nat found herself once again sitting in a room next door, watching through a one-way mirror.

Katz rushed over to Carol, gasped audibly when she saw her bruised cheek. She glared across at Oates, but he raised his hands in a gesture that said, *Not my doing.*

Once Katz found out it was Leo, Nat was sure she was going to push for Carol Bell to press charges against him. Right now, though, the criminal lawyer had other, more pressing concerns to attend to. Her two clients—Harrison Bell was in an interrogation room across the hall—were about to be charged with the kidnapping of four-year-old Jacob Coscarelli.

Carol grasped the lawyer's sleeve like it was her lifeline. And it might well have been. "I keep telling them, I don't know how that jacket got in the car. I never saw it before in my life. Anyone could have put it there. I'm always forgetting to lock the car. Harrison's forever scolding me—"

"You shouldn't have said anything until I got here."

"What about Harrison? Can he explain—?" Carol asked.

"My partner Craig Paulson is with Harrison. Let's focus on you now," Katz said, sliding into a chair beside her client.

Oates leaned forward. "Give us a blow-by-blow accounting of your day so far, Mrs. Bell."

Carol glanced anxiously at Katz. Katz nodded.

"I already told Detective Coscarelli about going to Dr. Varda's apartment at eight-thirty. And that he wasn't home. Or, at least, didn't answer my ring or knock. Then I went home."

"Did you tell your husband you were going to see Varda?"

She hesitated. "No. I thought he might not want me to go."

"Why?"

"I don't know. I got the feeling he didn't like the psychiatrist."

Yeah, Nat thought, *I bet he didn't.*

"I drove back home and caught up on some chores. My housekeeper was there. She can tell you," Carol said.

"She was there the whole morning?" Oates asked.

"Not . . . every moment. She did a few errands. Picked up Harrison's suits at the cleaners, stopped at the bakery, and got a cake for . . . for dinner tonight." She looked anxiously at the lawyer. "The children are going to be so frantic. My sister went over there to be with them, but what is she going to say to them?"

Katz put a calming hand on her client's shoulder.

"Let's talk about where you were from eleven forty-five to twelve-thirty," Oates said, without a scintilla of sympathy in his voice. Nat was actually amazed he was able to hold on to his temper. He was, after all, sitting across from a woman who very likely had kidnapped his partner's son. His partner who was, at that moment, being forced to cool his jets in an unused interrogation room down the hall, with two officers there to make sure he stayed put. Anyone else would have done their cooling off in a jail cell.

"Didn't you go pick up Daphne?" Katz coached.

Carol Bell blanched. "No. I picked her up early from nursery school because she had a tummy-ache. But she felt better later in the morning, so I let her play with her friend next door. I was just about to go over to get her when . . . when that detective nearly broke my door down and threw me to the floor and started storming through all the rooms of my house, knocking things over, pulling clothes out of closets . . . I thought he was crazy. I was never so frightened in my life. He kept screaming— 'Jakey, Jakey!' And he had that . . . that jacket clutched to his chest. I didn't know it was in my car. I don't know how it got there. I would never hurt a child. I'm a mother. I'm a mother." She broke into wrenching sobs.

"You fucking *what*?"

Whatever cooling off Leo might have managed since they'd arrived at the precinct house was gone the instant he heard that Oates had had to let the Bells go.

The two officers in the room with them were about to grab Leo before he started using his fists as well as his vocal cords, but Oates vetoed the move with a shake of the head.

He tried to encourage Leo to get a grip, but Leo was way past that.

Nat, who'd gotten to the precinct house shortly after Leo'd been brought in, was nearly as beside herself as Leo was. She didn't give a damn that the district attorney said there was no case yet, that there was not enough evidence even to charge them.

What about Jakey's jacket? What was that if not evidence?

Nat didn't want to hear that "anyone" could have dropped

that jacket into Carol Bell's red Subaru Outback. Tell her who that "anyone" could be. Tell her that.

Leo shoved his partner roughly aside and stormed across the room, yanking open the door.

"Hold on, Leo. You're not going anywhere. Not the way you're feeling right now," Romero said.

"Try and stop me," Leo snarled.

"Leave it, man," Oates said to Romero. "I'll keep him under wraps."

"Sorry. I don't think anyone's gonna manage that," Romero said. Heaving a sigh, Romero reluctantly gave the nod to the two officers who rushed after Leo. They literally had to battle him to the floor in the hallway. It took a third officer pitching in before they managed to subdue him, Leo kicking and cursing a blue streak the whole time.

Oates, looking grim but resigned, and Nat, her expression pure anguish, watched silently from the doorway.

"I don't know, Nat," Oates said, sounding less than enthusiastic about Nat's proposal.

"You have a better idea?" she challenged.

"Give me a little time and maybe—"

"We don't have time, Mitch," Nat said.

He knew that as well as she did. "What makes you think it'll work?"

"She's the last link. The most crucial one, at that."

"She has been this whole time."

"But no one could get to her. And the pressure to figure out some way to manage it wasn't a priority as long as she couldn't remember."

"What if we bring the Bells in? Maybe if Lynn looks them square in the face—"

"Too big a maybe," she argued. "More time wasted."

"And Suzanne Holden?"

"You think she's going to talk knowing they mean to kill Jakey if she does? Come on, Mitch. And she knows they're not bluffing. Look at what happened to Lynn. To Claire Fisher. To Suzanne herself. This pair is deadly. And damn lucky so far. There's never enough evidence—"

"I'm still worried. A lot of things could go wrong. You could get hurt, Nat. I think about Leo and everything he's going through. If, on top of all that, something happens to you, Leo's never gonna get over it. And he's gonna blame me. With good reason."

"I'm thinking about Leo, too, Mitch. That's why I have to do this."

"Is this Bill Walker?"

"Yes. What can I do for you?"

"It's what I can do for you, Mr. Walker."

"Do I know you?"

"We never met. But I listen to your news show on WBBS all the time. I'm a big fan."

"Yeah, never can have too many of those. Mind telling me who I'm talking to?"

"It's not important. Here's the scoop, Bill. Lynn Ingram, the woman who was attacked—"

"The transsexual. Yeah, what about her?"

"She just got moved out of ICU."

"That's nice to hear. But not exactly breaking news."

"That's because I haven't told you the best part yet: Her memory's coming back, Bill. Lynn's beginning to remember the attack. Some of it's still a little cloudy. A specialist in hypnosis has been consulted. He's confident that under hypnosis she'll be able to identify her attacker. He's being brought in first thing tomorrow."

"Well, that's more like it. Just one question for you: Why are you leaking the story?"

"Sinners have to pay for their sins, Bill."

"Are we talking about the attacker or the transsexual here?"

Sharon Johnson dropped the phone into the cradle. "Okay?"

Nat gave a thumbs-up sign. "Perfect."

"Well, I'm still not one bit happy about this plan." Sharon shot a dark-eyed look over at Mitchell Oates, who was standing by the closed office door.

"Do I look happy?" he groused.

When Oates walked into the private room assigned to Lynn Ingram on the eleventh floor of Boston General, Carrie Li slipped quietly out. The nurse had willingly put her job on the line for them. She said it wasn't solely because she felt she owed Nat her life, but because she wanted Lynn's attacker caught as much as they did. So she got Nat into this vacant room on a floor where she was close friends with the head nurse, and bandaged her up. Oates was putting his job on the line, too, by informing the nurses on the floor that that this was a police-sanctioned maneuver. On his unsanctioned orders, Lynn Ingram had been listed on the hospital roster as being in room 1143.

"Well, it made the six o'clock news," he said, after giving Nat a rueful once-over.

"Great."

"Yeah," Oates said glumly. "What wasn't great was watching photos of Jakey Coscarelli being flashed on the screen. Or a clip of Leo's mom sobbing hysterically as she was led into her building."

"Poor Anna. She must be going out of her mind. I hope she's not all alone."

"That's one piece of good news. We moved Leo out of jail and put him under house arrest. He's home with his mom, along with two uniforms to make sure he stays put."

Nat sat up in the hospital bed. Not an easy effort, considering she was mummy-wrapped in bandages. Which would be uncomfortable enough, but Oates had insisted on her wearing a Kevlar vest beneath the bandages. He wasn't taking any chances. Not that Nat wanted to take any chances herself. Which was why she'd also been wired.

"It's going to work, Mitch. Lynn's got to be silenced at all costs now, because her identification will be the nail in the Bells' coffins. And once they know it's over, they'll tell us where they've got Jakey." Not to mention Ross Varda and her beloved Hannah.

"We still don't know for certain it is the Bells," Oates said. "You know, Nat, someone could be setting them up. The real kidnapper could easily have tossed Jakey's jacket into Carol Bell's Subaru. We've got to consider that."

"You're thinking of Beth and Daniel Milburne?"

"That's one possibility."

Nat reflected on her earlier emotional exchange with the councilman's wife. She'd found herself believing Beth about Daniel Milburne not knowing the truth. And that threatening letter, the intimidating phone call.

"What are you thinking?" Oates asked her.

"I think our real perp was trying to set the Milburnes up. He wanted us to think the councilman knew about his wife's first marriage because that made him a perfect suspect. With Beth as an accessory."

"There's always Jennifer Slater's brother, Rodney Bartlett," Oates mused. "Getting revenge for his sister. With her blessing."

"Well, I guess he had motive, but I don't know," Nat paused, "he doesn't seem the type." Something was niggling at her, but she couldn't put her finger on it. She rubbed her eyes, practically the only part of her from her chest up that was exposed. "I wish I could sort it all out. So much has happened so fast. Three disappearances in twenty-four hours. My dog, Varda, then Jakey."

"That's because our perp, or perps, whoever they are, are getting increasingly more panicked. The closer we get to nailing them, the more desperate they're becoming. So now they're racing around trying to cover their tracks. They took your dog to lure you down to the garage and use you for target practice. Varda was a liability right from the start. And Suzanne was reaching her breaking point. They couldn't get to her so they got to her kid."

Nat nodded. Everything Oates was saying made sense. All the pieces of the puzzle fit, and yet the picture as a whole somehow didn't look quite right.

"Nat, you sure you want to go through with this? We can put an undercover cop—"

"You can't use one of your people. This isn't even sanctioned, Mitch."

"So, we lay the plan out to my chief and have him—"

"And if your chief says no? If he vetoes the plan altogether?"

Oates sighed. He knew she was right, even if he was still very uneasy.

He eyeballed her. "You scared?"

"No."

"Liar. I'll be ten feet away, girl. Right behind that bathroom door. You're gonna do fine."

"You too, Mitch."

thirty

There is nowhere to turn, no one to turn to. My ability to trust, never my strongest suit, has now deserted me completely. In an odd way, this is a relief.

L. I.

NAT HAD ALMOST forgotten about her cell phone until its jarring ring reminded her it was still on in her tote bag, which she'd stashed in the drawer of the bedside table. She quickly jerked open the drawer and nervously retrieved the phone. Oates had the bathroom door open, anxiously watching to see who it was. Nat was hoping it wasn't Leo. She wasn't the world's best liar.

"Nat. It's Hutch. Where are you?"

"I'm . . . having dinner. With a friend. Is something wrong? Something happen at the center?"

"No. Listen, I need to get hold of Coscarelli. I keep calling his precinct and they keep telling me he's unavailable."

"Why do you need to reach him?"

"I just got back from seeing Melissa Raymond, Father Joe's housekeeper."

"If it's about someone being with Father Joe the day of Lynn's—"

"It's not."

"What, then?"

"It's Melissa's daughter. Emily."

"What about her?"

"Melissa says Emily saw someone leaving the rectory in the middle of the night a few hours before Father Joe was found . . . dead."

"What? Who? In the middle of the night? A five-year-old?"

"Look, I don't know all the details, Nat. That's why I wanted to get ahold of Coscarelli. I have a feeling you'll have an easier time than me getting through to him. Maybe it's nothing, a kid's bad dream, the shadow of a tree mistaken for a person, I don't know what, but maybe Coscarelli can get somebody, a shrink or something, to talk to the kid, get to the bottom of it."

It didn't sink in at first, the implication of Hutch's words. Maybe because Nat was still grappling with her sense of guilt about having helped drive a man—a priest—to suicide. She'd tried to rationalize her guilt by reminding herself that Father Joe was a rapist if nothing else. But she'd never fully been able to accept this as absolute fact, despite Suzanne's confession. Nat couldn't let go of the possibility that Suzanne had been mistaken. And now a new, more distressing possibility intruded. What if Suzanne had lied? What if she'd intentionally misled them?

But why would she lie? And if it had been a lie, why would Father Joe commit suicide?

And that was when Hutch's words sank in. What if Father

Joe hadn't killed himself? What if someone had set it up to make it look like a suicide? What if the housekeeper's little girl had seen the killer?

Nat gave Hutch Leo's cell-phone number. "Call him right away."

It was nearly midnight, and a distressing feeling of claustrophobia was settling in. The bandages were only part of it. The narrow hospital bed, the dark room, the silence marred only by the occasional footfalls in the hall. Doctors walking past, Nat imagined, since the nurses and orderlies all wore rubber-soled shoes that made no sound as they scurried about, taking care of their patients. Well, not so much scurrying now. Most of the patients were asleep.

Nat wondered if Lynn Ingram was asleep. She actually had been moved out of the ICU. She was now in a private room on the sixth floor. Listed under the name Maureen Riley. Lynn didn't know this. There was no reason for her to know.

Nat wanted to believe that once the perpetrators were caught, their capture would help Lynn regain her memory of the assault. She knew from articles she'd read on PTSD and memory loss, that remembering was a vital part of healing the trauma. It would be a long time before Lynn was physically healed. Maybe her emotional healing could proceed at a faster pace.

Nat closed her eyes. No fear that she might fall asleep. Far too much adrenaline raced through her veins, not to mention a serious overdose of caffeine. No, she closed her eyes in hopes of seeing things more clearly. Because, try as she might, she couldn't shake the feeling that her vision had been hazy up to now. She pictured all the disparate pieces of all the events that had taken place, starting with the violent attack of Lynn Ingram in the alleyway. She thought about Father Joe, Suzanne, Claire Fisher. She thought about Carol and Harrison Bell, Rodney Bartlett and Jennifer Slater, Beth and Daniel Milburne. She cast one pair, then the next, then the next in each of the scenes.

But mostly she thought about Jakey. She loved Leo's little boy. She desperately wanted him to be unharmed.

Oh, Jakey, where are you?

Suddenly, her breath caught in her throat. Jakey. Oh, God, the missing piece of the puzzle. The key to the solution. How could she have been so blind? Now that she saw the whole picture, it all made absolute sense. Every piece fit. Every piece could be explained. Well . . . almost everything.

Nat shot up in the hospital bed. She had to tell Oates—

It was at that precise moment that the hospital room door opened. Nat dropped back down on the bed, her breath held, as a figure in a white lab coat slipped in. Nat lay there, silently berating herself for not having figured it all out sooner. She might have prevented so much of it. The attack on Suzanne, Claire Fisher's murder, and what she now felt certain was the faked suicide of Father Joe Parker. So now, instead of feeling guilty for driving him to kill himself, Nat would have to live with the knowledge that she might have prevented his murder.

She closed her eyes, her pulse pounding in her ears. Footsteps approached, audible enough to know they were not rubber-soled.

She moaned softly to let her intruder know she wasn't fully asleep.

"Lynn?"

"Mmmm."

"Are you in a great deal of pain?"

She emitted a weak groan.

"It didn't have to be this way, you know."

She tensed as she picked up the scent of stale breath. The intruder was looking down on her.

"I still love you. I've only loved two women in my entire life, Lynn. And do you know what hurts the most? No one else, no one, sees you wholly as a woman. No one else but me. That alone should have made you realize I was the right one, the only one."

She moaned again.

"It's all right, my love. I've come to put you out of your pain. It's my final act of love. You'll just feel a little prick and then peace. Eternal peace."

"And what about you, Ross? Will you ever feel peace after all you've done?"

Ross Varda's shock was so complete, the hypodermic needle dropped from his hand. As the glaring light from the opening bathroom door fell on the psychiatrist, he thrust his white-sleeved arm across his eyes.

"It's over, Varda," Oates said harshly, the barrel of his gun lined up with the psychiatrist's head. At this range, there was no question Oates could easily blow Varda's head off. But Oates wouldn't do that. They needed Varda alive. Badly. Because they needed him to tell them where he had put Jakey.

"You were the one who asked Lynn to marry you," Nat said quietly. "When she told me about a proposal, I assumed she was talking about Harrison Bell. But it was you. And she turned you down. She didn't love you. She was in love with Bell. You couldn't bear it. You wanted to make her ugly, so he wouldn't want her. I don't think you intended to kill her at first. It's only that she saw you. You must have come up behind her and she had the terrible misfortune to hear you approach and turn around to face you."

"That beautiful face." Varda's anguished voice was muffled by his sleeve, his arm still across his eyes. Then he slowly dropped his arm to his side, meeting Nat's gaze. "You weren't surprised."

"It was Jakey," Nat said. "You were the only one who knew that Jakey was Suzanne's child. The only one who knew that if her child was taken, she'd keep quiet about the truth. And once I realized it wasn't the Bells, I remembered that you were in the office with me when Claire Fisher called about the journal. I stupidly told you—" Nat's voice caught. She fought for control. "And you were the one who forced Suzanne to lie about the priest. We have an eyewitness, Ross, who saw you in the rectory the night Father Joe supposedly hanged himself."

There was absolutely no sign of remorse or shame on the psychiatrist's face. If anything, he seemed mildly impressed by Nat's analysis.

"Where's the boy, Varda? Where's Jacob Coscarelli?" Oates barked impatiently.

Varda's gaze remained fixed on Nat. "I love her. You have to understand, I love her. Even now. No matter how she looks. That's the difference. I love her inner beauty."

Nat shivered. He was mad—Dr. Ross Varda was truly mad. *Physician, heal thyself.* But, of course, he was long past that option.

Oates glared at the psychiatrist in utter disgust. "You're going down, man. At least do one decent thing: Tell us where the boy is."

Varda looked uncomprehending. His unfocused eyes gazed past Nat an instant before he whirled away from her. But in that instant Nat read something in his look. And she knew. Too late.

Too late even to form the cry of *No, don't!* into audible words.

When the warning cry did let loose from her lips, it was accompanied by the hideous sound of splintering glass. The psychiatrist had crashed through the window, and before Nat managed to scramble out of bed, before Oates was able to race to the shattered window, Dr. Ross Varda's body was careening down eleven stories—

No question Malcolm Davis, chief of Boston Homicide, was in a quandary. He was mad as hell at Oates for, as he put it on the phone, pulling this "crazy, not to mention illegal, not to mention dangerous" sting. On the other hand, if they hadn't staged the sting, the man who'd maimed Lynn, who'd very likely administered a near-fatal dose of heroin to Suzanne, not to mention murdered Claire Fisher and kidnapped Jakey Coscarelli, might well never have been discovered.

Then again, maybe Nat would have sorted it all out in time, realized that if she eliminated all of their possible suspects, there was really only one other person who had the means, motive, and opportunity to commit each heinous act. And that one person was Ross Varda. He had constant access to Lynn and Suzanne. He'd been with Nat when she got that call from Claire Fisher. Nat had told him herself that Claire had found the journal. As for getting into her apartment, he'd had any number of opportunities to swipe her house key, make a clay imprint, and have a key made for himself.

Varda had obviously pressured Suzanne into lying to give the police a perfect suspect—Father Joe. Which was another element Nat had frustratingly overlooked. Who knew that Jakey Coscarelli was Suzanne's child? It wasn't likely either of the Bells knew;

wholly unlikely when it came to the Milburnes, or Bartlett and his sister.

So now what? It was two o'clock in the morning. Varda's smashed body had been removed to the morgue. Oates and Nat were sitting in her car out front, feeling infuriatingly impotent.

And what did they tell Leo? *"We've found your son's kidnapper. The good news: The kidnapper's dead. The bad news: We still don't have a goddamn clue as to where he's hidden Jakey."*

"Wait." Nat sprang forward in her seat. "Suzanne kept saying 'they.' She couldn't talk because 'they'd' harm Jakey. 'They.' More than one. We had all these couples as suspects—the Bells, Jennifer Slater and her brother, the Milburnes—"

"Yeah, but Varda didn't have a wife. Or a brother."

Nat's heart had started racing. "But he does have a sister. He mentioned her to me several times."

The extent to which Varda ransacked his own apartment was nothing compared to the job Oates, Nat, and four uniforms performed. They were all looking for a clue, something, anything, that would point them to where Varda's sister lived. But they found absolutely nothing with any information on her whereabouts. Not on scraps of paper, letters, envelopes, address book. . . . Oates had already checked the Boston area phone book. No Vardas. Ross Varda's home number must have been unlisted, and so, apparently, must his sister's. Oates had called into the precinct and put a man on the task of checking for any unlisted numbers under the name Varda.

After pitching in for a while, Nat got another idea of how they might track down Varda's sister, and quickly left the apartment. A short time after Nat made her exit, Oates and his men ran out of places to look. It was nearly four in the morning. Oates, exhausted and despairing, dismissed the uniforms, then leaned against the living room wall, surveying the chaos.

He hoped Natalie Price was having better luck.

"Wait here," Nat ordered the two uniforms posted outside Suzanne's door. It was four in the morning. She'd be frightened enough, having Nat come into her room alone and wake her. She'd really freak if she opened her eyes to a sea of cops as well.

Suzanne was in her own bed, the covers pulled up to her neck. Nat left the door cracked open, allowing a thin ray of light from the hallway to slice into the room.

"Suzanne?" She gave the inmate's shoulder a little shake. "Suzanne, it's Natalie Price. Please wake up. I need to talk to you. It's very important."

She got no response from her. More alarming, no movement. Nat's heart seized. She flung back the covers and gasped as she saw even in the faint light a pool of blood soaking into the sheets.

"The cuts are jagged and deep. She's lost a lot of blood. She meant to kill herself, no question about it. She would have bled to death by six or seven this morning." The ER doc smiled at Nat. "You saved her life, Superintendent."

"Can I speak to her?"

"She's been given a shot of Demerol for the pain. Between the medication and the blood loss, she's not going to be up to talking for at least a few hours."

Oates stepped in. "It's very important."

"I'm sure it is, Detective," the young doctor said. "But she's truly out. It's going to have to wait. I'm sorry."

Oates and Nat walked over to Jack Dwyer. Chances were Nat was not going to make it back to the center by the time the news of Suzanne's suicide attempt spread, so she wanted Jack to be prepared. There'd been a riptide of tension among the inmates since the attack on Lynn Ingram. It was not going to get any better when they heard about Suzanne.

"Well?" Jack asked, rising from a waiting-room chair.

"We're on standby," Oates muttered. "At least a couple of hours."

"And the sister?" Jack asked despairingly. "Still heard nothing on her? She's gotta have a phone, right?"

"Hey, come on. We don't even know if her last name *is* Varda. She could be married for all the fuck we know," Oates said. "Or using an alias."

And then it came to Nat: life insurance. Varda worked for the Commonwealth. As part of the package, they got life-insurance policies—and had to list beneficiaries. Odds were Varda had made his sister his beneficiary. Her name would be on the policy.

She looked over at Oates. "You going to wait here?"

He nodded, eyeing her warily. "Why? What are you going to do?"

"I have an idea. I want Leo in on it, Mitch. I want you to get him released from house arrest."

Oates scowled.

"The Bells haven't pressed charges," she reminded him, although she was still worried they would. "And you don't have to worry about him going off after anyone now that Varda's dead."

Oates was frowning now. "He might go after me, and I

wouldn't blame him, when he hears how I drove Varda out that window before I got the bastard to tell us where he stashed Jakey."

Nat put a hand on Oates's arm. "There's nothing to be gained from him knowing that."

Oates made no response. Nat guessed he'd tell his partner what had happened. But he might wait for a bit.

"I'll drive you over," Jack offered.

"No, that's okay."

Her deputy didn't hide his disappointment, but he didn't argue.

thirty-one

Lynn is terrified to let herself love again, but she is slowly making strides in this area.

DR. ROSS VARDA
(THERAPY NOTES)

IT WAS SIX in the morning. Nat was back in Varda's apartment, this time with Leo. Despite looking haggard, at least the haunted expression was gone from his face. He had a sense of purpose. There was something he could do. And at least now they knew what they were looking for: a term policy for Ross Varda issued by Federated Life Insurance Company. Leo took the bedroom. Nat tackled the living room. Given that it was a three-room apartment, the only room after these two was the kitchen, since Nat seriously doubted Varda kept important papers in the bathroom. What worried her was that he probably kept them in a safe-deposit box at a bank.

It was over an hour before she accepted that there was no insurance policy in that room. But she did find something. A small address book tucked away in a cupboard. Maybe Varda had put down his sister's address or her phone number.

No such luck. But Nat did come upon one interesting address: that of Beth and Daniel Milburne. Of course, she realized in hindsight, Varda must have written that letter to Beth. He knew all about Bethany from his therapy sessions with Lynn. And the phone call from the girl? Nat figured it must have been Varda's sister, disguising her voice to sound like a child's.

Nat tucked the address book into her pocket and walked into the bedroom to check on Leo's progress.

He was sitting on Varda's bed, head in his hands.

Nat walked over and sat down beside him. She wanted to say something. Something to ease his pain, his panic, his despair. She wanted to say something that would ignite his sense of hope. But anything she might say would sound hollow not only to Leo's ears but to her own.

"What if they concocted a signal between them, Natalie? What if he told his sister that if she didn't hear from him by a certain time, she should—"

"Don't, Leo. Don't do this to yourself. Come on. Get up. Help me take apart the kitchen. My mother used to keep a manila envelope stuffed with receipts, insurance policies, birth certificates, in a kitchen drawer."

Nat got up and dragged Leo to his feet. Then she literally led him by the hand into the kitchen.

Unfortunately, every drawer in the kitchen had already been taken apart, much of the contents now scattered on the green-and-white-tiled kitchen floor. Leo looked around glumly at the mess. Then he slumped into a chair at the kitchen table that was covered with a plain white vinyl tablecloth.

Nat sat down across from him, pulling her chair in closer so that she could reach over for his hand. Her knee hit something knobby. For a second or two she don't make anything of it.

And then—

Leo looked at her like she'd gone mad as she yanked off the tablecloth.

"There's a drawer, Leo. The table has a drawer. We didn't realize. We didn't see it when we were all here before." Her heart was racing. But she tried not to get her hopes up. Maybe the drawer was empty. Maybe it was filled with utensils or junk mail.

She was afraid to open it. Afraid to come up empty-handed again.

Leo came around to her side of the table and jerked the drawer open.

Inside was only one item. A manila envelope. Just like the one Nat's mother used to have.

Her breath held as Leo uncoiled the string closure. Nat could see the tremor in his hand. She doubted he was breathing, either.

There it was. Right under Varda's car-insurance policy. A Federated Life Insurance Company term policy. Policy holder: Ross Radway Varda. Beneficiary: Patricia Radway.

Nat snatched a Boston-area phone book off the counter.

There was one listing for a P. Radway.

The address listed for P. Radway was 432 St. Botolph Street, Boston.

Until he'd leapt to his death in the wee hours of that morning, Ross Varda had resided at 432 St. Botolph Street.

. . .

Ross Varda's apartment was number 3C.

Leo and Nat checked the tenants' roster outside the building's front door. P. Radway's name was neatly printed: P. Radway lived in apartment 5B.

No wonder no one had seen Ross Varda disappear from the building yesterday morning or the night before. He'd never left the building. He'd set the stage for his own supposed abduction, walked out of his apartment, and merely climbed up two flights of stairs to his sister Patricia's apartment.

Leo started up the stairs, taking them two at a time. He reached reflexively for his gun, forgetting he'd given it up after the mayhem he'd caused at the Bells'.

Nat raced up the stairs after him, grabbed hold of his arm as they hit the third-floor landing. "Leo, we can't just burst in there. What if she's got a gun? Don't forget, Claire was killed with a gun. I was shot at. Varda wasn't carrying when he showed up at the hospital. Nothing on him or on the street where he crashed. And we didn't find the gun in his apartment."

He pulled his arm away. "My boy's in there, Natalie."

"And the last thing you want is for Patricia Radway to panic, grab up her gun, and shoot Jakey in the head." Her choice of words was purposefully brutal, in an effort to penetrate his rage and urgency. Otherwise she doubted she'd get through to him.

As it was, it didn't seem to work. He whipped around and tore up the stairs, Nat trailing breathlessly behind.

Gasping for air, Nat cleared the fifth-floor landing and saw that Leo had come to a halt. But he looked prepared for his final charge as Nat ran up to him.

"Please, Leo," she pleaded breathlessly. "Let me go to her door. A woman is less likely to alarm her than a man. I'll say

I'm a new neighbor. I'll make sure there isn't a gun in sight. If the coast is clear, I'll cough. And then you can—"

"And if she opens the door with a gun in her hand?"

"I'll think of something," she said, already heading for the door.

The instant she rang P. Radway's doorbell, a dog started barking wildly. Nat would recognize that bark anywhere. A wave of exquisite relief washed over her.

A couple of seconds later the door flung open.

"Ross—" Patricia Radway gasped when she saw it was not her brother at the door. "Where's Rossy? Where's my brother? I want my brother. Oh, hush up, doggy. Rossy bought me a new dog. And I have a new best friend, only he's fast asleep. And Rossy says I can keep them both for a long, long time." She had to shout because the barking didn't stop.

It's okay, Hannah, I've come to get you. You and Jakey. Nothing's going to stop me. That goes double for Leo.

Nat's whole body was trembling as she looked at this short, overweight, disheveled woman wearing a fuzzy pink robe and a pair of bunny-rabbit slippers. She appeared to be in her late thirties, early forties, but her mental age couldn't be more than eight years old. Possibly younger. Nat was certain she had finally come face-to-face with the "little girl" who'd drawn that vile face and made that phone call to "Bethany" Milburne.

"Do you live here all alone, Patricia?" Nat asked, looking carefully around the living room just beyond the door. Nat's tone was artificially bright, but she was quite certain Ross's mentally retarded sister wouldn't detect her deception. Especially as Hannah was barking so loud that Patricia could hardly hear her.

"I have my doggy and my friend. Sometimes Rossy stays with me. Sometimes my friend Cindy visits. She's a nurse. She wears a white uniform. She promised she'd buy me one, too, so I can be a nurse. Are you a nurse?"

"I'm a friend of . . . Rossy's. Can I come in and visit?"

Patricia pursed her lips. "Rossy says I can't play with strangers."

"I'm not a stranger, Patricia," Nat said with false warmth. "In fact, I know your doggy and your best friend."

Patricia's mood altered in a flash. Her pupils dilated; her neck turned bright red. Nat berated herself for provoking her.

Patricia was glaring at Nat. "They're mine. And I look after them real good. You can't take them away. Rossy promised."

"Oh, I won't. He told me they were yours, Patricia. I saw him just a little while ago."

Patricia's mouth instantly burst into a sunny smile. Nat tried to swallow back the lump of pity welling up in her throat. What would become of Patricia with her brother gone?

"Do you want me to draw you a picture? I can draw good pictures. Rossy says I draw the best pictures."

Nat swallowed hard, remembering that horrible drawing she'd received as a warning.

"Do you know how to play checkers?" Patricia asked.

"A little. But you'll probably beat me."

Patricia eagerly tugged Nat into the living room and shut the door. Nat was relieved Patricia didn't throw the lock. If there was trouble, Leo'd be able to get inside without a problem. Nat just hoped he wouldn't jump the gun.

Seconds after Nat entered the living room, a door opened from across the way. A little boy clad in Spider-Man pajamas padded into the room, yawning and rubbing his eyes. "Hannah's barking. She woke me."

"Hi, Jakey," Nat said softly, her voice flooded with relief.

Jakey's hands dropped away from his eyes and they widened like saucers as soon as he heard Nat's greeting. "Natalie! Natalie!" he shrieked, running to her.

Unfortunately, Jakey had to run right by Patricia. Despite her bulk, Varda's sister moved very quickly, grabbing the boy up in her arms just as Leo came bursting into the apartment.

Hannah was now barking at a fever pitch, thrusting herself against the closed door in an effort to get to Nat.

"Daddy! Daddy!" Jakey cried.

Leo ran to him, but stopped dead in his tracks when he saw Patricia yank a gun from the pocket of her fuzzy robe.

"I can shoot," she announced proudly. "Rossy showed me."

Jakey began to cry uncontrollably. Nat was desperately close to tears herself. She could just imagine what Leo's state of mind was at that point.

"Patricia, you're making your new best friend cry." It was hard for Nat to keep her tone sounding soft and unthreatening while at the same time having to shout to be heard over Hannah's barks.

"She is such a naughty dog," Patricia said.

"Daddy . . . I want my daddy!" Jakey was wracked with sobs and trying, to no avail, to wriggle free of Patricia's strong hold.

"He's not your daddy," Patricia snapped angrily. She was becoming seriously frazzled. Not a good thing. And Hannah's frenzied barking wasn't helping matters.

Nat took a cautious step toward the door behind which Hannah was now yelping. "I'm really good with dogs, Patricia. I bet I could get her to stop making so much noise."

Leo's eyes were glued to the gun. "Why don't you put Jakey down, Patricia?"

"Why don't you go away?"

Nat took several more steps toward the door.

"Jakey, if you stop crying I'll let you play with Rossy's gun," Patricia said brightly. "But you have to stop crying."

Nat's chest constricted.

Leo cried out in desperation, "No. Please."

Nat bolted for the door, threw it open. Lunging from her prison, barking frantically, Hannah bounded for her.

Startled by the dog's arrival, Patricia let out a cry of alarm and confusion. Nat saw her start to point the gun at Hannah. Leo made a dive for Patricia's legs. She dropped to the floor, still holding the gun, still clutching Jakey. Nat rushed over to help Leo. Hannah rushed over to protect Nat. The large dog went straight for Patricia, leaping on top of her, barking and snarling. Patricia burst into tears. Nat wrested the gun from the crying woman's hand. Leo wrenched Jakey from her arms, clutching his son to his chest.

Patricia's tears disappeared and she shouted angrily, "Bad doggy. Bad doggy. You are not nice. I don't like you anymore. I don't like any of you. I want my Rossy. I want my Rossy."

epilogue

Being in prison has changed me. In what ways—only time will tell.

L. I.

"IS IT AWFUL?" And then, before Nat could respond, she said, "No—please don't say anything."

"You're still a beautiful woman, Lynn."

Tears spiked Lynn's eyes. Her fingers delicately traced the jagged line slashing down the right side of her face. It was still raw, not yet a scar. The plastic surgeon who'd performed this first in what was to be a long series of operations, considered it a success. The bandages had been removed today, nearly three weeks after Ross Varda's death. Three weeks since Lynn had begun to remember.

"How's Patricia doing?" she asked.

"She seems quite happy at the group home. There's even a dog there, Noodles. She adores him."

Lynn hesitated. "Does she still ask about her brother?"

"Not very much, I'm told."

"I don't hate him. Even now. My new therapist says I won't really be over the trauma until I can feel angry. But right now, I feel too sad to be angry. He did love me. Me and Patricia. No one else mattered to him."

"Lynn, he raped you when you were in Grafton." Lynn might not feel angry, but Nat was filled with rage. "No matter who'd done that to you, it would have been abominable—but a doctor, your own psychiatrist, I can't think of anything more reprehensible."

"It's true. Everything you say. But I honestly believed at the time he . . . cared about me. And he seemed in so much pain—"

"You were the one who suffered, Lynn," Nat was quick to interrupt.

Lynn nodded slowly as tears slipped down her marred cheeks. "Yes. Yes, I know." She hesitated. "I'm not sorry he's dead. Is that terrible?"

"No," Nat assured her. "I'm not sorry, either."

Lynn's eyes met Nat's. "Thank you."

"For what?" Nat asked.

"For everything. I won't forget what you've done for me. I'll be eternally grateful."

"I was doing my job," Nat said, feeling awkward. Taking compliments had never been her strong suit.

Lynn smiled. "And you do it exceedingly well."

Nat smiled back. "Thanks. That means a lot to me."

Now both women felt a bit awkward. Lynn reached for a tissue and carefully dabbed at her eyes.

"Have you heard from Harrison Bell?" Nat asked.

Lynn's hand dropped from her face. "That's over." She looked down at her hands. "I got a short note from him. He's agreed to go into marital counseling with Carol. I'm glad. It's the right thing. They have three kids, a home, a history. I don't know if they can save their marriage but I believe Harrison very much wants to."

"Sharon Johnson is working on a new placement for you. Dr. Madison says you'll be released from the hospital in a few days. She advises a week home—"

"Home," Lynn echoed wistfully.

"I know Horizon House is a far cry from—"

"No, no that's not it. I . . . I had a visit from my mother yesterday." She paused for a moment. "But you know that already."

Nat nodded. Lynn was still an inmate. All visitors had to be cleared and recorded. There was a corrections officer posted around the clock outside the door of Lynn's private room.

"It's very hard for her," Lynn said. "She's hoping my father will eventually relent and at least make some sort of contact with me, even if it's only a get-well card. She wishes I could visit them in Westfield, but—" She sighed. "Seeing my mom is already more than I ever hoped for."

"I understand you had another visitor yesterday."

Lynn lifted an eyebrow, newly plucked, a sign of her feeling better. "You more than understand. You had to okay the visit."

"True."

"It was strange seeing her again. Like seeing a ghost. I mean, I thought she was dead." Lynn grinned. "Talk about being beautiful. My god, I wouldn't have recognized her. I really wouldn't."

"Yes, she is a looker," Nat said with a laugh.

"I'll never say anything. I was the one wholly at fault. I should never have married her in the first place. Bethany's a good woman. I'm not thrilled with her husband's politics—"

"That makes two of us."

"But she deserves to be happy." Lynn paused. "I told my mother about the visit. I thought she'd be stunned to learn Bethany was alive. But she wasn't. My father told her. He also admitted that he took money from Daniel Milburne to ensure their silence about his wife's previous marriage to their transsexual son. She's ashamed about that, but then, shame is nothing new for my mother. I didn't tell her it was my money, not Milburne's."

Nat put her hand over Lynn's. "I'm sorry."

"Hey, I feel some of that buried anger bubbling up. That's a good thing. See, I am getting better."

"Yes, you are," Nat said, meaning it.

"Did you know the police found my journal?" she asked after a while.

"Yes. It has to be held in evidence, but then it will be returned to you."

"I'm thinking of trying to publish it. I don't know if reading about my experiences will help anyone to understand me any better, understand what I've been through, but I hope it might. And, who knows, maybe it will help other women in my predicament."

"I brought Hannah a doggy bone. Can she have it?"

The instant Hannah heard Jakey's voice she was out from her favorite spot under Nat's desk and bounding for the boy.

Jakey waited for Nat's nod of okay, then gave the eager Hannah the bone. To be polite, Hannah stuck around long enough for Jakey to give her a pat on the head. Then, bone in mouth, she hurried back under the desk to savor the treat in peace.

"How are you doing, Jakey?"

"Guess what?" he said brightly.

"What?"

"Dad says I can come with him when he comes to pick up Mom."

Nat planted a bright and artificial smile on her face. "Hey, that's super."

He held up two fingers. "Just two more weeks. And she's never coming back here. That's what Suz . . . Mom told me. I hope you won't be too sad. You could still be her friend."

"Yes, of course I can." Nat struggled to keep her smile in place. She knew it was a good thing that Suzanne had finally told Jakey the truth. Suzanne had made the decision when she was in the hospital after her suicide attempt and told Jakey about being his mom as soon as she got back to Horizon House. Jakey took the news with amazing aplomb. He'd always wanted a mommy and now he had one. Simple as that. Since then, Jakey had come to visit her each week. Being a mom had transformed Suzanne. Nat actually did think she had a real chance to make it this time. Of course, she'd been proven wrong in the past, but without optimism, Nat knew she could not survive in her job.

"Hey, guess what, Natalie?" Jakey intruded into her thoughts. "Gramma's gonna make lasagna."

Nat gave up even the pretense of a smile. "I bet your mom will love it."

"Sure she will," he said confidently. "You do. Daddy says it's your favorite. You're gonna come, too, right?"

"Well . . . I don't think I can, Jakey." *I'll be too busy nursing my broken heart.*

"Sure you can, Natalie." Nat looked over to see Leo standing at the door.

It was all she could do not to break down and cry.

"I'm gonna go back and play checkers with Mom," Jakey said. He scurried over to the door, then looked back at Nat. "You know, Patricia wasn't mean to me when I stayed with her that time. She taught me how to play checkers. And she let me eat two candy bars for breakfast."

Leo closed the door after Jakey ran off to be with his mother. "I expected nightmares, all kinds of emotional problems, but the kid is amazing."

"Yes. Yes, he is." She looked away.

"Natalie—"

She held up a hand. "Leo, it's all right. Really. Now, I need to get back to work—"

"She's his mother—"

"I know that," she snapped, then immediately was ashamed of her outburst.

"I want Jakey to have a relationship with her," he went on in the same even tone. "It will be good for Jakey and it will be good for Suzanne."

She nodded, not trusting her voice.

"I'm not going to tell you things will be exactly the same with us—you and me—as they were before. But I still want there to be a 'you and me,' Natalie. What about you? What do you want?"

She smiled crookedly. "Talk about a loaded question."

He smiled back. "Yeah." And then his smile faded. "So?"

Their eyes met and held. "Why don't we see how it goes?"

Leo didn't respond.

"It's an answer, Leo. It's the best I can do."

"I guess I can't ask for more than that, Natalie."